POSEIDON'S FURY

A SEAN WYATT ADVENTURE

ERNEST DEMPSEY

138 PUBLISHING

Copyright © 2023 by Ernest Dempsey

All rights reserved, 138 Publishing.

No part of this book may be reproduced in any form or by any electronic or mechanical means, including information storage and retrieval systems, without written permission from the author, except for the use of brief quotations in a book review.

All names, places, people, and events are fictional or used in a fictional way. Any resemblance to such is coincidence or a figment of the author's imagination.

For my friend Eric Johnson. Rest easy, brother.

PROLOGUE
CONSTANTINOPLE | 1547 AD

"You're certain this is the place?" Francisco peered at his comrade with eyes that were darker than the night. His black hair rustled over his ears as a warm breeze washed through the quiet street.

He and his partner watched from the shadows of a vacant market stall, crouching behind a stack of baskets and unused tables.

Flickering lights danced in the windows of the apartments along the street. Many had already extinguished their lamps for the night. No sounds of children's laughter filled the air. Only the occasional adult speaking rattled through the canyon of buildings on the streets.

"Of course I'm certain," Luis answered. "You asked me that ten times on the way here. Why would it be different now?"

His dark blond ponytail shook as he emphasized his words by bobbing and twisting his head.

Francisco only breathed steadily in response as he glanced over to the three-story home. Palm trees swayed in the wind thirty feet beyond the nearest corner.

Even though the two Spaniards had already accounted for the trees, the movement still startled them.

Luis, twenty years old, had served the Spanish Navy for two years.

Francisco, twenty-two, had done so for four. Both men had distinguished themselves from most of their peers with valor in battle, and courage when it came to volunteering.

The two were easily among the best swordsmen in their ranks, their reputations already spreading in the military. Only some of the higher-ranking officers could best them while sparring.

Even considering their prowess—something the two young men were surely aware of—Luis and Francisco were surprised when given the honor of this mission. After all, it had come directly from the Holy Roman Emperor himself.

They'd been called in from duty in Southern Italy, and told that they were being given a mission of the highest importance. At the time, the two young men didn't know they were going to meet the emperor from the rising Hapsburg Dynasty. But when they were taken to the palace and given audience with the emperor of the entire Holy Roman Empire, they realized the gravity of the situation.

The meeting had taken place in a lavish sitting room in the east wing of the palace. "Completing this mission," the emperor had said, "will bring peace to the entire world. No more suffering brought by the evil hands of the Ottomans. And now that our greatest enemy is dead, nothing will stop us from accomplishing this holy task."

Holy task, Francisco thought, just as he had the evening the emperor said the words. *What does that mean?*

He still didn't know. The emperor had given no other details regarding how this quest would bring such peace, such lasting prosperity for the world.

Neither Francisco, nor Luis, understood how finding a book could accomplish something so big.

Being more pragmatic than Luis, Francisco couldn't help but think the emperor had embellished his view of the mission as something holy. He'd tagged it as such, but deep down, Francisco believed the man's reasons were nothing more than ego driven. Like all the other pawns serving under various banners, Francisco knew his role, and while he loathed it to a degree, he played the game knowing it was better than becoming a slave. His standing in society was better than average, and once he and Luis pulled off the mission, he had no doubt they would receive titles, land, and all the trappings that the emperor afforded his heroes.

If the man wants a book, we'll get him the book.

"Strange, no?" Luis asked out of the blue.

Francisco wasn't sure what he was talking about. "What?"

"All this for a book," he clarified. "The emperor sending two of his best deep into enemy territory, just for a book? Seems a bit much, no?"

"You read my mind, Luis," Francisco confessed. "I was just thinking the same thing. But we have no choice. And it shouldn't be too difficult. I saw no guards below."

Luis snorted. "Why would there be? He's a scribe, a historian. Who would be guarding him? And for what? It isn't as though the man is wealthy."

Francisco looked around the street and again at the three-story villa. "He isn't poor either," he observed.

The building looked like all the others in the city, but instead of it being divided into apartments on every level, this one was a single-family home, owned by a man with more to him than met the eye.

Most scribes wouldn't have been able to afford such accommodations, often living in much humbler abodes. The two Spaniards knew the man who owned this home was much more than a mere scribe.

Muradi Sinan Reis was a pirate, a corsair who had sailed under the banner of the Holy Roman Empire's greatest nemesis of the seas —Admiral Hayreddin Barbarossa. At the end of Barbarossa's life, he'd dictated his memoirs to Reis—both a friend and a comrade in arms.

That much was all Francisco and Luis had been given regarding the book they were to find. That, and where it was hidden.

A spy for the emperor had gained entry into the Reis home by way of servitude. This servant worked diligently for his master, earning the former buccaneer's trust in a short amount of time. According to their spy, Reis had been gone for several weeks—probably on a mission to plunder and pillage one of the emperor's holdings.

Now, months into his employment, the servant's work had paid dividends, and he'd passed along the message to the emperor's men as to where the book could be found. None of the people who managed the household—loose relatives and friends—would notice if the journal was gone.

"What do you think is in the book?" Luis asked, his voice impatient.

"Our deaths if you don't quit talking."

Luis sighed. "No one can hear us up here. No one saw us."

"And I would prefer to keep it that way."

"You aren't the least bit curious?"

Francisco stared out into the night. "Of course I am," he said. "Maybe it isn't memoirs we're trying to steal. What if it's a map to a treasure? There's no way we can know what's in that book."

That seemed to shut Luis up for a minute as the younger man considered the words.

While they hadn't seen any guards during their reconnaissance of the home, that didn't mean there was no danger. The man known as Sinan Reis had been one of the most dangerous people in the world as far as Charles V was concerned. The pirate had killed untold hundreds, or even thousands, and that didn't include what his ships had done on the seas. Reis was a scourge against the Holy Roman Empire, and with him gone on some mission, the emperor knew it was time to seize the opportunity.

"Do you think it's some sort of book of magic?" Luis whispered.

Francisco rolled his eyes at the insinuation, though he'd considered the notion himself at one point. "No. I don't think it's magic. Now, shut up. It's nearly time."

"What is he waiting for?" Luis complained. "He should have signaled us by now."

Every window in the villa was dark, which would have seemed ordinary to any passersby, and there'd been few of those since the two Spaniards arrived in the stall.

"Patience, Luis. You really must learn patience. It will come."

Luis sighed and continued watching.

He didn't have to wait long. A window on the third floor at the right end of the building suddenly lit up with lamplight. Then a figure appeared in the opening, looked out at the stars as if simply taking a deep breath of fresh air, and then disappeared.

"That's it," Francisco said. "Come on."

The two men left their hiding place, checking down both sides of the street to make sure no one was watching.

It wouldn't have been so dead quiet on the streets of Barcelona. That much the two knew for certain.

They scurried across the thoroughfare and stopped at the front door. Francisco checked the door while Luis continued to watch the streets.

Francisco twisted the latch and found it unlocked, as the servant had promised. Even though the two Spaniards had been told it would be, Francisco felt a measure of relief as the door gave way to his subtle force.

He led the way in and held the door open for Luis, closing it behind him once he was inside.

With the door locked, the thieves took in their surroundings. The downstairs featured a small kitchen to the right and a wooden table with four chairs close by. A hearth fit into the back-left corner, where a couple of chairs with lavishly designed cushions angled toward it.

"Third floor," Francisco said. "I don't want to be here longer than necessary."

He hurried over to the steps that disappeared up into the second floor. Taking them two at a time, Francisco bounded upward until he reached the next landing. He ignored the second floor's design and the things that occupied it. He wasn't there to take a tour of the pirate scribe's home. He was there to rob it.

They continued up the next flight of stairs until they reached the top floor, slowing only at the final step just in case this entire ruse had been one elaborate setup.

Francisco drew his sword and held it at his side as he rounded the wall that blocked the view of the steps from the rest of the room.

He saw the servant standing near the window where he'd been a few minutes before. The lamp flickered on a wooden desk next to it.

Several papers festooned the surface, along with multiple writing utensils, maps, and navigational tools.

The young man—no more than sixteen years of age from what Francisco could tell—watched the two interlopers with both curiosity and fear.

"Where is it?" Francisco asked. He kept his tone direct and firm.

The boy trembled for a few seconds then raised a skinny arm and pointed his bony finger at the opposite wall.

"It's in there," he said in forced Spanish.

Francisco and Luis followed the servant's finger across the room to a table where a small wooden chest sat on the surface.

The Spaniards hurried across the room and hovered over it for only a moment. The chest, made of sturdy timber, was bound with iron brackets and closed with an iron clasp—a lock dangled from it.

"Do you have the key?" Luis demanded of the boy.

"No," the servant replied. "He did not leave it with me."

Luis felt a twinge of irritation. "Perhaps you could have told us that before we got here. No?"

The boy lowered his head, as Luis figured he'd done much of his young life so far. He was nothing more than a servant, and servants were often put in their place—no matter what culture or nation they lived in.

"It is no problem," Francisco said. He set his sword down on the table and drew a thin blade from a sheath on his belt. He stuck the knife tip into the keyhole and began to work it around.

The sounds of metal scraping on metal filled the room, and while subtle, the three occupants felt it might have been as loud as a thunderstorm.

After finagling with the lock for nearly two minutes, the clasp suddenly let go, and the piece of iron hung loose on the clasp.

Luis looked surprised, despite being aware of his partner's skills to some degree.

Francisco returned the knife to its sheath and flipped up the clasp. He held his breath for a second and then lifted the lid.

For a second, he merely stood there staring into the chest, his eyes blinking every few seconds. Then he turned to the servant by the window.

"What is this? Some kind of joke?"

Confusion, quickly turning to concern, the boy shook his head rapidly. "No, sir. That is the chest. I'm sure of it. I saw him put the book in there many times."

"Are you sure it was the right book?" Luis pressed.

The boy nodded, never showing a doubt in his eyes. "Yes. I'm sure of it."

"And you didn't see him take it?" Francisco asked. He took a menacing step across the room, picking up his sword once more. He brandished it at the servant. "Do not lie to me, boy. Did he take it? Or did you sell it to someone else?"

The young man shook his head vehemently. "No. Of course not." Tears welled in his eyes. "I did not sell it."

Francisco searched the boy's face, angling his chin down to see if he could meet the servant's eyes and find a lie within them. All he found was a harsh truth.

"So, the book is not here," Francisco realized. "The emperor will not be pleased."

"It was there the other day. I swear it. I saw it with my own eyes. He put it in there."

Luis let his anger get the better of him. "And were you watching him every minute of the day?"

"What? Of course not." The servant sounded baffled. "How could I?"

"This is information that could have saved us a lot of time," Luis sneered. He felt the handle of his sword at his hip, and with it the temptation to cut down this whelp where he stood.

"Easy, Luis," Francisco urged. "Killing him won't bring us the book. Master Reis must have taken it with him." He reached out the sword and touched the flat end of it to the boy's chin, lifting it carefully in a show of sympathy, and threat. "Where did your master go?"

The boy shook his head. "I... I don't know, sir," he said, his Spanish faltering. "I overheard him say he had business in Italy. But that was all."

Francisco lowered his weapon and turned around. He paced back over to the chest and looked into it again, as if doing so might somehow manifest the book. He shook his head in disappointment, and closed the lid.

"Italy," he muttered. "That doesn't narrow it down much."

Luis glowered at the servant for a few more seconds before he tore his gaze from the young man. He looked to his partner. "What should we do?"

"What can we do?" Francisco answered. "He's gone. And I suspect we won't find him now. A man like Reis is cunning. He won't make any mistakes."

He reached out and touched the edge of the wooden chest, running his finger along the side of it.

"It would appear we have failed our mission, Luis. The emperor will not be pleased."

"No. He won't," Luis agreed with a snarl back over his shoulder at the servant.

"Pay him."

"What?"

"I said pay him. He held up his end of the deal," Francisco stated. "Give him his money."

"But he didn't—"

"Do it." Francisco fired a warning look at his partner. "Reis left. And he took the book with him. There's nothing we can do about that now."

Luis grumbled something unintelligible as he reached into a pocket and withdrew a small leather pouch. It jingled as he handled it. Then he tossed it to the servant, who caught it reluctantly.

"Enjoy it, urchin," Luis spat.

Francisco kept his eyes locked on the bottom of the chest. The emptiness of the container signaled the end of any dreams he may have had of titles, land, and riches that would provide him a life of ease for the rest of his days.

As he watched those visions slip from his grasp, he could only stare at the symbol of a trident engraved on the chest's bottom, and wonder what could have been so important about that book.

1

KILWA KISIWANI, TANZANIA

Sean Wyatt didn't even think about moving. He wanted to. His pistol hung in the leather shoulder holster, dangling near his ribs. He felt it there—so painfully close, yet so abysmally far away.

"What's going on in there?" Tommy asked. The voice came through a radio earpiece concealed in Sean's right ear. "Do you see it?"

Sean felt beads of sweat rolling down both sides of his face. The Braves baseball cap he wore backward helped with some of the perspiration, but not all of it.

"Sean? Do you copy?"

He swallowed as he tried to decide what to do, and based on the breed of snake staring back at him, he knew time wasn't necessarily on his side.

Black mambas were known to be some of the most aggressive snakes in the world, and highly venomous. Sean felt somewhat fortunate he hadn't been bitten already.

The huge, skinny gray snake sat with two-thirds of its body coiled in front of an opening in the ancient stonework. The other third of the serpent sat erect, dancing back and forth as it flicked its tongue at the warm body that had entered its abode.

"Sean?"

"Tommy," Sean finally replied in a muted, desperate tone. "Please. Shut. Up."

"What's the problem? You need me to come in there?"

"Shut. Up."

The serpent continued to waver back and forth as if trying to decide when, not if, to attack.

Sean knew a little about snakes from his childhood. He hadn't been allowed to watch regular television on Saturdays due to his parents' strict religious guidelines, but he was permitted to watch nature shows.

In the colder months of Tennessee's winter, a boy didn't have many options. So, nature videos it was.

He'd viewed several about snakes, learning as much as he could about the reptiles. It wasn't because he liked snakes. Quite the opposite. In fact, the only thing Sean seemed to fear more than snakes was heights—and given the current circumstances, the former was easily winning.

"Okay," Tommy said. "I'll hang back."

What part of shut up don't you understand, Schultzie?

The mamba continued flicking its tongue, tasting the heat radiating from Sean's body. From what he recalled, black mambas could, and often did, strike more than once. He'd heard stories of them attacking groups of men, killing more than one in the process.

For the moment, Sean felt lucky the thing hadn't come after him already.

There was nothing else in the chamber that could help him besides the gun dangling from his shoulder, and making a move for that might scare the snake into an attack.

"Easy, snake," Sean soothed, hoping the calm tone of his voice might send the serpent retreating through the three-foot-high hole in the wall behind it. Not that that would make things better. Sean needed to get through that opening. Beyond it lay the Eye of Akulu—or so he hoped.

The eye was supposedly an extremely large ruby, about the size of a fist, and had been hidden in this ancient temple for over a thousand years—which predated most colonial settlements in this region.

Sean and Tommy had spent months preparing for this expedition, but nothing could have prepared him for the deadly mamba he faced now.

Keeping the flashlight on the snake, Sean remained perfectly still. He wondered if the snake thought the black rope dangling behind him was another serpent—perhaps a friend, or more likely a rival.

Sean knew that was ridiculous. The rope gave off no body heat, and so posed no threat to the mamba.

Getting down to this level in the tunnel—where no one had been in centuries—required descending a forty-foot drop into the heart of a hillside. Why the snake was down here where the temperature was cooler, Sean didn't know, but the fact was the thing was here, and he had to deal with it.

If he drew his pistol, the mamba might strike. The creature only being ten feet away didn't give Sean any comfort about that option. But he was running out of time, and ideas.

The snake abruptly snapped its head forward. Sean took a step backward to the sheer rock wall behind him while at the same time pulling the pistol from its holster. He reacted on instinct alone, and twitched his trigger finger without even trying to aim.

The tiny box on the end of the pistol muted the report to the sound of a loud click. The snake's head instantly exploded in a splash of blood, dropping the creature to the floor.

A shiver shot through Sean's body as he watched the lifeless serpent continue to writhe and flop on the stone at his feet. He kept the pistol trained on the thing, even though it no longer presented a threat.

For nearly two minutes, Sean merely stood there watching the headless creature until it stopped moving. And then for another minute, he couldn't make himself move. Paralyzed by the encounter, he breathed slowly to calm himself down.

He'd faced enemies in the field when he was a covert operator for the Axis agency, but he'd never felt this kind of fear from facing an assassin or a terrorist. Then again, they didn't have fangs. Not usually.

"What was that sound? Did you just fire your weapon?"

Sean stuffed the pistol back in its holster and dusted his hands off on his khakis. "You heard that?"

"Of course I heard."

"Let's just say I wasn't alone down here," Sean said. He looked around the circular space in the pit, making sure there weren't any other creatures hanging around.

"What?"

"Black mamba," Sean said. "Nasty suckers. Don't want to get bitten by one of them."

"Is it dead? Are you okay? It didn't get you, did it?"

Sean chuckled as he shook his head. "If it did, I'd have about one hour before I went into a paralytic coma. Dead in three."

"Okay, just be careful."

"Thanks for the warning, Mom." Sean shuffled past the dead snake and then kicked the rest of the body out of the way with his boots.

He got down on all fours, casting a last glance back over his shoulders at the serpent—as if blowing its head off hadn't made certain it was dead. Then he pointed his flashlight through the opening.

At the top of it, a symbol of an eye stared back at him—carved into the stone.

"There's a room down here," Sean announced. "I'm gonna go through and see what's in there."

"Okay. Be—" Tommy cut himself off. "I mean, let me know what you see."

Sean lowered himself a little more so he could belly-crawl through the hole in the rock. He slithered forward, not missing the irony of his movement in comparison to the snake he had just killed.

He only had to crawl ten feet before emerging on the other side in a square room with four pillars, each a grotesque-looking animal wearing distorted, angry faces.

The mouths of the stone totems pointed inward, toward an altar in the center. As Sean turned his flashlight around toward the middle of the room, a red glow danced along the far wall.

"I'm in the other room," Sean said, his voice full of awe. He ran the flashlight beam around the ceiling where it met the four sides, examining a sequence of ancient runes and hieroglyphs. "I gotta tell you, Schultzie. You and I have seen a lot of weird stuff. But this is a new one."

"I hope you're taking pictures."

Sean slid his phone out of its pocket and started doing just that. He turned on the phone's light, and combined with the flashlight in his hand and the one on his headlamp, was able to get incredible images from the chamber.

"When I get a signal, I'll send these to you," Sean quipped as he noticed the lack of bars on the phone.

"Shoulda brought your SAT phone."

"Thanks for that."

"Anytime."

"Well, if I did have a signal, and I was able to send you the pics right now, you'd see something pretty amazing."

Sean walked unconsciously toward the middle of the room. He approached the stone altar, staring straight at a four-pronged golden claw sitting on top of it. The claw clutched the largest ruby—or precious gem, for that matter—Sean had ever seen in his life. The thing was bigger than his fist, and from what he could tell, the ruby was immaculately cut.

"Do you see it? The eye? It's there?"

Sean nodded absently. "Oh, it's here, all right, buddy. We did it. We found the Eye of Akulu."

A loud "woo-hoo!" pierced Sean's ear, and he grimaced, squeezing both eyes shut tight. "Thanks for blowing out my eardrum."

"Oh, sorry, man. My bad. But this is so incredible. I wish I could have come down there with you."

"Yeah, well, I don't think you would have liked the snake."

"You seemed to handle it just fine."

"I guess. Then again, if I missed, the ricochet could have killed me. In hindsight, not my smartest moment. Probably shoulda just jumped for the rope and climbed back up, sent you down to handle it."

"Okay, okay. What does it look like?"

Sean tilted his neck to the side, inspecting the piece. "Uh, it looks like a huge ruby. What did you think?"

Tommy sighed through the radio.

"There's some kind of a golden claw holding it."

"Claw?"

"Yeah," Sean confirmed as he cautiously climbed the first step up to the altar. He aimed both lights onto the glimmering gem and its unusual pedestal. "The thing comes up out of the stone altar like a zombie coming out of a grave."

"That's an interesting description."

"Well, I'm happy to hear suggestions."

"Is it a bird claw?"

"No. Looks more like a dragon claw. Weird. The talons are longer. Really interesting they did it this way."

"Cool. Hey, listen, maybe you should go ahead and grab it and get the heck out of there."

Sean chuckled at his friend's suggestion. "What's the hurry, man? We have permits to be here."

Silence.

"Schultzie?"

Still nothing.

"I said we have the permits to be here, right?"

"Sorry, you were breaking up there, buddy. Yeah, we got the permits."

Sean sighed. He and his partner had done a few things without the required paperwork in the past; not that they advertised that.

The International Archaeological Agency was a world-renowned artifact recovery operation. Their exploits, and their reputation, had spread to every corner of the globe—for better or worse. While most of the time they operated by the book, certain missions required a less "official" way of doing things. When working in areas where the governments were more corrupt than others, the agents of the IAA often had to bend the rules.

Sometimes those rules were shattered into a thousand brittle pieces.

Sean took the second step up to the top tier of the altar. He leaned closer to the object in the center, studying it carefully.

"Hey," he said, inching his nose closer to the gem, "do you ever wonder why people so long ago would go to such ridiculous lengths to hide their valuables?"

The square altar's surface stretched seven feet from one side to the other. Half-inch grooves were cut into the stone and ran to the center from each corner, meeting at the arm of the golden claw.

"What?" Tommy asked.

"Treasures like this. People always hid them. They did it throughout history. I just think it's weird."

"What is? That they'd hide treasure?"

"Yeah, I mean, I understand them hiding it."

"Then what is your point?"

"If you'll let me finish."

"By all means."

Sean rolled his eyes, exasperated. "As I was saying, they hid their stuff. Which doesn't surprise me." He craned his head to the right, tilting it in such a way that the ruby cast bizarre, melting refractions onto the wall. "But all the clues and booby traps. Those are the things I don't understand."

"Oh, you mean why all the traps?" Tommy clarified.

"Yeah."

"To keep other people from finding their treasure, obviously."

Sean stood up straight again and shook his head. "I know that, genius. But think about it. They left all those clues for someone to eventually find their loot."

"Yes. Ideally, themselves."

"Yeah, but if it was them, why did they need the clues? The treasure maps? The ciphers? All that stuff."

Silence came through the earpiece, then: "I guess I never really thought about it like that before."

"Exactly!" Sean exclaimed, extending both hands out to no one.

"I mean maybe the point was that if they couldn't return to it, someone should have it if they could prove themselves worthy."

Sean rolled his head to the other side in a dubious expression. "Even the pirates? Lifelong criminals? Those guys were worried about someone being worthy of their treasure?"

"It's just a theory," Tommy said. "You're the one asking the crazy question. And could you hurry up? I don't want to hang out here longer than we need to."

Sean caught something in his friend's voice that caused a spear of doubt to stab through his gut. "Schultzie? Is there something you're not telling me? You got the permits, right?"

"Permits, yes," Tommy answered.

"Okay, why did you say it like that?"

No response.

"Tommy? What did you do?"

"Nothing. But I don't think poachers care too much about permits."

"Poachers? Did you say poachers?"

"Yeah."

"As in guys that hunt animals illegally for profit? Those poachers?"

"Yeah."

"Schultzie, I need you to be real honest with me. Are we in an area known to have a lot of poachers?"

Tommy hesitated. "No. I mean. Yes, but there haven't been any incidents or sightings in this area for the last two months."

"Two months? We should have brought a whole team. I knew we should have."

"Relax," Tommy said. "But please hurry. I hear something."

Sean felt a surge of concern pulse through him. "What do you hear?"

"Sounds like truck motors."

"Motors? Plural?"

"I know. Not good."

"No, Schultzie. Definitely not good. You could have mentioned the poachers."

"I didn't think they'd be around right now."

Sean mustered every ounce of patience he could so he didn't lay into his lifelong friend. "Okay. Stay on the rope. I'll be right up. We'll figure it out."

"If it's poachers," Tommy guessed, "and they see the gem—"

"I know. I know. You don't have to spell it out for me. Just keep a lookout."

Sean leaned across the altar, stretching out his arm at full length until his torso lay on the surface and his legs left the floor. It was still out of reach, so he pulled himself up onto the altar and squatted down next to the priceless relic.

He inspected the artifact more closely, noting how the claws seemed to clutch the gem in such a way that simply lifting the ruby from its grasp wasn't an option.

"You got it?" Tommy pressed, urgency trembling in his voice.

"Almost."

"Almost? What's taking so—"

"This claw, it's gripping the gem."

"Then pull up the claw with it, and let's get out of here."

Sean had considered that, but something in his gut told him that was a bad idea. He looked around the chamber for any signs this could be a trap, but noticed nothing out of the ordinary—other than ancient architecture that no eyes had seen for centuries.

"Okay," he said, reluctance still coursing through him. "Here goes."

He cradled the base of the claw with one hand and the stem with the other. Sean took one deep breath, sighed, and pulled.

The entire piece came up from the stone with such ease he nearly lost his balance and tumbled over backward.

"Wow," he exclaimed. "That was easy."

"You got it?"

A loud click echoed through the chamber, reverberating deep inside the altar. Sean's eyes flicked left and right, from one side of the surface to the other.

"Um. Yeah. I got it." Sean sounded uneasy as he stuffed the artifact into the drab green satchel strapped across his shoulder.

A sense of dread filled his gut as more clicks and thumps continued from somewhere underneath him.

"Great. Now get the heck out of there. We need to go."

"Schultzie?"

"What?"

"I think there was a booby trap."

"What?"

"Yeah. And I think I tripped it."

More clicks. Then suddenly, a deafening scrape of metal like a sword sliding from a scabbard.

2

Sean rolled to the left and off the altar just as two spinning blades flashed across the room and smashed into the wall on the other side.

His shoulder crunched into the hard step next to the plinth, and he tumbled down to the floor. Two seconds after he stopped, pain radiated from the shoulder. Sean grimaced but managed to get to his feet.

More sounds filled the room now. Louder thumps and clicks, and something grinding from below.

"Schultzie?"

"I hope you're on your way up, man. They're getting close."

"I got my own problems down here." Sean aimed the flashlight over to the wall where the two circular blades lay on the floor. He pointed the light to the opposite wall and noticed the two slits where the blades had exited the sprung trap. Based on the height and the trajectory, they would have cut him in half.

Something overhead snapped, and Sean dove to his right just before a heavy cube dropped onto the floor a few feet away from where he'd been standing. Another snap released a second massive stone, this time safely on the opposite side of the first. He didn't hope to be that lucky again.

Sean pumped his legs and sprinted toward the round opening, but another snap from above sent a warning to him, and he cut to the right just as another stone fell to the floor, shaking the earth under his feet.

"Crap," he muttered.

"What? What's that sound?"

"Yeah, you should probably get out of here."

"What? I can't—"

"The exit out of here is blocked, Tommy. I'll have to find another way out."

"What?"

"Just go. I'll find a way out."

Sean darted back toward the center of the room as another giant block dropped behind him.

His mind worked fast, noting the size of the blocks—height and width, but most importantly the height.

He ran to the altar once more and skipped up the steps as another cube crashed to the floor behind him. Sean rolled to a stop on the top of the altar, clutching the satchel with its cargo in one hand and his flashlight in the other.

A look around showed him that the stones were only a few feet higher than the altar. And above, he noted a shaft leading up into an area where daylight snuck through.

"Schultzie?"

"You okay, man?"

"Shut up and listen. I need you to work your way back toward the entrance of the temple."

"Okay."

"I'm seeing an opening here in the ceiling. It must lead up into one of the other parts of the ruins."

"I didn't notice anything like that when we came in," Tommy countered.

"Yeah, I know. But it's there now. Maybe in an offshoot passage or something. Just go. I'll need you to lower the rope down to me through that shaft when you find it."

Another cube fell with a crash. Then, everything went silent.

Sean pulled the bandana around his neck up over his face to filter out the dust that hung in the air.

"I think it's over," he said into the radio. He aimed the beam through the dust and twisted around, shining it into every corner. The dust fog cut visibility down to less than 30 percent, but Sean could still make out the lines of the walls around him.

"Okay. I'm on the move. How far from where you went in do you think this shaft is?"

Sean considered his friend's question and looked back at the wall where he'd entered. Numbers ran through his head. He visualized how many steps it would take to reach the now-blocked hole he'd crawled through, plus a few more from where he'd climbed down the rope.

"Like thirty yards. Give or take."

Sean heard his friend breathing hard through the earpiece. He imagined Tommy picking his way back through the passage they'd used to find the first shaft. There'd been a few alcoves along the way. Three of them contained pillars with strange idols perched atop them, each displaying a creature that was something between mythical and real—much like those from famed mythologies of ancient Egypt, Greece, or Rome.

There'd been one empty one, though. Sean remembered because he'd thought it was odd that there would be one missing. He and Tommy had even mentioned it.

"Remember the little alcoves with the weird idols?"

"How could I forget? Two of those things are gonna give me nightmares."

"Look for the empty one."

Then Sean had a thought. "Hey, you're in the temple. How in the world are you able to hear those engines outside?"

"Acoustics here are weird," Tommy offered. "I don't know. Some kind of sound channel or something."

"Strange," Sean muttered to himself. He shelved the thought and focused on the shaft above, hoping that any second he'd see Tommy's shadow drift over it.

A sound ripped his focus from the hole above, and he looked around, snapping the flashlight in every direction.

"What was that?" he breathed.

"What?"

Sean didn't answer his friend. He'd heard something, something moving in the darkness. It was subtle, almost imperceptible. It grew louder, and after holding his breath for five seconds, he realized what it was.

Hissing. A lot of hissing.

"Oh, come on."

"What?"

Sean aimed his light down to the floor around the altar. "You gotta be kidding me."

The floor writhed and seethed around the steps to the altar. Only it wasn't the floor that moved. The beady eyes, flicking tongues, and scaly gray bodies of a colony of black mambas stared back angrily at Sean.

"Tommy? You mind hurrying up a little? I kind of have a problem down here."

"I'm moving as fast as I can. You think I'm trying to take my time?"

The snakes wriggled their way to the first step at the base of the altar and continued upward toward the second. Sean knew what they were doing. The aggressive serpents gravitated toward his body heat. And it would be mere seconds before they reached him. Whether they could consume him or not wasn't a concern to a mamba. They attacked anything they perceived as a threat.

Sean considered his pistol for a half second but knew he could only take out a handful of the creatures with the limited number of rounds, and time, he had left.

The slithering mass reached the second step.

Waiting for Tommy was no longer an option. The snakes began

climbing the altar on all sides. A shiver shot through Sean's spine at the living nightmare surrounding him.

Out of time, he looked to his only possible chance at escape. The nearest stone cube stood eight feet away. *I hope it's only eight.*

To Sean, it may as well have been twenty.

He took a last look around the edge of the altar and saw the first serpent's head appear to his right. *No time to think about it.*

Sean clipped the flashlight onto a belt loop, took one step back and then charged forward. He planted his left foot on the lip of the altar and leaped, but his foot slipped on the smooth surface, and he didn't get as much distance as he could have.

He flew over the surging sea of snakes and hit the top of the rough-hewn cube with his hands and arms. His chest smacked against the edge of it, and his boots kicked the side.

He desperately clawed at the top, pushing his toes against the stone, praying they would find purchase.

The hard rubber gave him enough upward momentum combined with his fingers pulling that he managed to drag himself up over the pillar's lip and onto the top.

He swallowed hard, gasping for breath both from the exertion and from the sheer terror surrounding him that he'd nearly fallen into.

Sean pointed his headlamp at the altar and watched as the snakes swarmed over the spot where he'd just stood.

His relief was short-lived.

Once the mambas' target moved, the snakes followed the heat signature and rerouted.

Sean watched as the serpents mobbed the altar, then immediately began descending it to make for the cube where he stood.

"I could really use that rope right now, Schultzie?"

"Isn't that ironic," Tommy answered, breathing hard into the radio. "Always giving me crap about my rope."

"Yeah. It's not lost on me. But can we skip past the gloating and get to the part where you drop the bloody rope down the hole so I can get out of here?"

"Hold on."

The mambas swirled around the base of the pedestal where Sean stood. He didn't want to look over the edge, but the need to know how much time he had was too great, and he stole a peek.

He immediately wished he hadn't. The seething mass of serpents were already climbing the side of the cube. Sean knew he had only a handful of seconds before they reached the top.

He quickly looked over to the nearest cube. It stood only four feet away, but snakes were climbing the sides of it as well.

Sean was out of options.

"It's now or never, Schultzie!" he exclaimed.

"Okay. I'm here."

Sean looked up into the hole above and saw a shadow move across it. Then a new kind of snake dropped down through the shaft and dangled over the center of the altar.

"I hope you have it secured," Sean said in a loud tone. "I'm going to jump for it."

"Hold on. One second."

"I don't have a second, Tommy."

A gray head appeared over the top of the stone cube to Sean's right. "It's gotta be now."

"I'm tying it—"

Sean yelled a desperate battle cry as he took two running steps and leaped, pushing as hard as he could with every muscle in his left leg.

This time, his foot didn't slip. The stone pillar being taller than the altar helped make covering the distance a little easier.

He hit the rope with both hands and his torso, his boots just three feet above the writhing surface. But the rope gave way, and he felt himself drop immediately as his momentum swung him forward.

His boots slapped into several leathery bodies on the altar, sending serpentine bodies flying over the edge and back to the floor.

Sean's heart sank into his gut as he realized Tommy hadn't secured the rope yet, but he'd had no choice.

As soon as it was won, gravity's temporary victory turned. Sean felt the rope go taut with a jerk, and his arc continued upward like a pendulum.

"Okay, it's secure," Tommy announced with pride.

Sean's instincts between a wisecrack and survival kept him silent as he swung toward the ceiling. He at least had the awareness to wrap the rope around his right wrist as he tried to position the left hand higher.

But like any pendulum, his inertia began to slow. He spun around and around, twisting as gravity fought against him once more. Now, though, he was lower than the top of the altar, and when he swayed back to it, he'd smack right into a wall of black mambas.

He reached up with his left hand and clasped the rope, wrapping it around his wrist as he'd done the first. Then he let go with the right and kicked his legs up as the rope oscillated back the way it had come.

Holding on to the rope with his left hand, Sean drew the pistol from its holster as he neared the altar, and aimed. He twitched his finger over and over, as fast as he could. Snake bodies exploded as rounds crashed into the mass. Sean grouped the shots along the top of the plinth, trying to clear a semblance of a path along the surface.

The weapon clicked when the magazine ran dry, a second before he reached the altar. He dropped the gun and reached above his left hand with his right, and pulled, kicking his legs up above his hips.

Like a teenager on a rope swing about to do a gainer into a lake, Sean swung through the scattering path of serpents on the altar. Two of them snapped at him, narrowly missing his rear as he passed.

"Tommy?" he shouted. "Would you mind giving me a lift?"

"A lift?"

The rope swayed out away from the altar but again started to slow.

"Pull the rope, man! For the love of all that's good! Pull me up!"

"Can't you climb?" Tommy joked.

"Do it!"

"Fine."

Sean felt his weight shift back downward toward the altar. He looked to it, the headlamp illuminating a wide circle of slithering terror awaiting him.

"Tommy?" Sean yelled.

A mere seven feet from the altar, he felt a sudden jerk on the rope. His feet whipped over the altar as he flew by again. A particularly long snake snapped at him but missed his heels by a foot, a foot that felt like a millimeter.

His momentum carried him away again. This time, Sean had no intention of allowing such a close call. He reached up higher on the rope with one hand, then the other, pulling with all his strength to get him clear of the mass of deadly serpents below.

His momentum stemmed with every pass, but he was clear of trouble now, and still climbing.

Ten feet above the altar. Twelve. Sixteen.

He reached the ceiling, where the square hole opened into the shaft.

"You okay, buddy?" Tommy grunted, exerting tremendous effort to pull the rope—Sean imagined hand over hand.

"Just keep it steady now. I'm almost there."

"Easy for you to say."

"Trust me. It isn't."

Sean didn't dare look back down to the floor. The last thing he needed was to frost the terrifying sight of the snakes below with his renowned fear of heights.

Once in the shaft, he used his feet to brace himself on both sides, relieving some of the tension on his forearms and back. He shimmied up the shaft, now using the rope as support, until he reached the glorious light in the room above.

He tugged himself over the lip of the shaft and let his torso fall to the dusty floor. He gasped for air, and muscles burned through every part of his arms. He looked straight ahead and saw Tommy holding the rope with his feet braced against the inside corners of the opposite alcove. His tanned face burned red, and sweat dripped down both sides from his thick brown hair. Veins rippled his forearms.

He dropped the rope and breathed hard.

Sean gulped in the air too.

After a few gasps, he dragged his legs out of the shaft and stood up.

"What had you so spooked down there, man?" Tommy asked, clenching his fingers several times to ease the muscles in his forearms.

"Oh, nothing. Just a few hundred venomous snakes."

"What?"

"Don't look. We still have the poachers to deal with."

"Right. Let's get out of here."

Tommy started to reel in his rope.

"Really? Leave it. I'll buy you a new one."

"But."

"I know. It saved my life. We can get a new one. We need to move."

"Okay," Tommy sighed. He knew his friend was right.

The two rushed down the tunnel, Sean clutching the satchel on his right hip. They stopped at an intersection, where the corridor cut left and right.

"Hold on," Sean insisted, grabbing Tommy's dense shoulder. "I don't have a gun."

"What?" Tommy asked, looking at his friend as if he'd lost his mind. "What happened to it?"

"I'll explain later."

Tommy let out a long breath, flapping his lips as the air passed through. "Fine. Just stay close. I'd prefer not to get into a shootout with a bunch of poachers anyway."

The two continued to the right, moving quickly while walking on the edges of their feet to keep the sounds of footsteps to a minimum. The daylight at the end of the tunnel brightened with every step.

As the two neared the exit, they slowed down and listened, stopping at the last corner. They heard voices, but it was difficult to understand what was being said.

"How many you figure?" Tommy asked, leaning around the curved stone corner to take a peek outside. "I can't see them."

"How do you think I can guess how many there are?"

"I don't know. I thought you had some kind of super special agent abilities or something."

Sean rolled his eyes. "Special agents aren't superheroes. We don't have X-ray vision."

Tommy looked back at his friend. "Shame. Because that would make everything way easier."

"Yeah. Well, we've never done things the easy way."

A laugh echoed into the temple. A female laugh.

Sean and Tommy peered at each other, puzzled.

"Was that a woman?" Tommy asked.

"Sure sounded like one. I've never met a female poacher."

Tommy huffed. "How many male poachers have you met?"

Sean pressed his lips together and nodded. "Point taken."

"What should we do?"

A man's voice shouted something, but he wasn't barking orders as a military person or a guerrilla might. Instead, it almost sounded as if he were giving a long description of something—like a tour guide.

"Wait a minute," Sean said. He stepped around his friend and into the opening. Bright rays of the afternoon sun warmed his face. He narrowed his eyelids against the light, and pressed the bridge of his hand against his forehead. "You gotta be kidding me."

He stepped out of the opening and skipped up a set of stone steps leading to ground level.

"Dude. What are you doing?" Tommy stepped out from his hiding place and shielded his eyes against the sun.

Sean slumped his shoulders and glanced back at his friend. He motioned with his right hand. "Come take a look at this."

"What is it? How many? Did they see you?"

Sean laughed as his friend cautiously ascended the steps with his pistol in hand.

"You should probably put the gun away," Sean advised. "Might scare the tourists."

"Tourists?" Tommy's eyes adjusted, and then he saw them. Forty yards away, five safari trucks sat parked along the trail, packed with people toting cameras and cell phones, taking pictures of the ancient temple.

Tommy clumsily stuffed the pistol in his rucksack and slung the bag back over his shoulder.

Sean waved to the people. A few of them waved back. They wore confused expressions, befuddled by the two men who'd emerged from the ancient site.

"Poachers, huh?" Sean stabbed as he continued to wave like a deranged parade queen.

"Yeah," Tommy mumbled, embarrassed. "My bad."

The truck engines revved to life again as the drivers readied to continue the expedition. The two Americans watched them drive away before Tommy asked. "What was the deal down there, anyway? You sounded like you saw a ghost."

Sean nodded, keeping his eyes locked on the last truck until it disappeared into the woods. "Remember that scene in Raiders of the Lost Ark where he was in a pit full of snakes?"

"How could I forget?"

"Well, it was like that, but ten times worse."

3

BEŞIKTAŞ, ISTANBUL TURKEY

Jack Madsen stood outside the Felingra Auction House in Beşitkaş, a warm breeze brushing through his short blond hair. Looking around, he understood why the wealthy elites of Istanbul lived and played here.

Luxury supercars rolled up to the sidewalk in front of the auction house, where red carpet padded the way to the entrance. Three long, silky banners with golden borders hung from the top of the six-story building, draping all the way down to the second floor—each pronouncing the extraordinary event taking place on this warm evening.

The darkening sky overhead had already revealed its first stars as the light of the sun waned and the moon climbed high above the horizon to the east.

Jack watched a red Ferrari pull up to the entrance and stop. A valet in a red uniform hurried around to the driver's door and waited for it to open. An Italian man in a shimmering silver suit stepped out and handed him a bill. Jack knew it was probably more than a normal valet would make in a week. On the other side, his exquisite date—a slender woman with brunette hair down beyond her tanned, bare shoulder blades stepped out onto the sidewalk and waited. Her black dress fluttered just above her knees, the top cut in a V that nearly reached down to her navel. Jack wondered how the garment stayed on. He doubted the teardrop necklace that featured no less than thirty diamonds did much to help.

The bearded Italian man tightened his suit jacket and walked casually around the front of the sports car, then allowed his date to loop her arm through his before strolling through the gauntlet of photographers on either side of the red carpet. The two entered the building through open glass doors, which were part of an entire glass façade that made up the corner of the building.

The Ferrari pulled away, and a black Aston Martin rolled up in its place.

Jack wasn't here to people watch. He'd already memorized the list of buyers showing up for tonight's event. Except one would be absent, though not officially.

Men like Jack didn't receive invitations to high-end auctions such as this, or to any other events held for the uber wealthy. That wasn't to say he was poor. His livelihood paid him well enough, as evidenced by the expensive black suit he donned. But he was a far cry from the kind of money on display here tonight.

He raised the cream-colored invitation and inspected it for the hundredth time. The name on the card read Dr. Robert Banner.

Banner had made a fortune in the field of plastic surgery with one of his inventions. Fortunately for Jack, Dr. Banner had no interest in ancient artifacts. So, Jack forged a few documents, an identification, and requested an invitation to the private auction.

He'd received his invitation within a week.

He stared at the holographic square in the bottom right corner— a security measure to make sure no riffraff tried to forge one, and sneak into the event.

Jack had to give the auction house credit; security was as tight as anything he'd ever seen short of a presidential inauguration.

He checked his Bulgari watch and noted the time. *Never be on time to something like this. And not too late either.*

Showing up first, or last, always drew more attention than he cared to fetch. And as a master thief, Jack had no desire to be noticed.

He waited another five minutes, watching the parade of supercars drive up to the entrance and drop off their wealthy owners. He found it surprising more of the locals hadn't gathered around the street corner to ogle the lavish cars and the people getting out of them. It wasn't like the event was a big secret. The building was lit up with huge lamps that illuminated the façades all the way up to the top. If anything, the auction house was screaming for attention. Yet only a few dozen people hung out on the street corners to watch.

As Jack considered it, he remembered where he was standing. Beşitkaş was known for its affluent population. So for the locals in this part of town, this kind of event was just a typical Tuesday evening.

He decided he'd waited long enough, and when the crosswalk signal changed, he strolled across the street to the auction house. Jack walked the part. His stride was casual yet confident, the way a CEO with vacation homes in four countries would move. He turned his head side to side, noting the vehicles on either side of the intersection. A Lamborghini Diablo sat to his left as the valet helped a beautiful blonde woman in a sparkling red dress out of the passenger's side.

Jack barely regarded her, or the car.

He wasn't about to give undue attention to people who already gave more than enough to themselves.

He kept his brown eyes straight ahead, focusing on the doorman in a burgundy suit who stood by the door checking invitations and identification.

Jack reached into his jacket pocket and pulled out the fake passport for Dr. Banner. He pinched the invitation card and the ID in his right hand as he approached, offering a pleasing but not friendly smile to the doorman.

The black-haired man grinned cordially back at him, his thick mustache twisting on the corners with the gesture.

"Good evening," he paused and looked at the invitation, "Dr. Banner. A pleasure to have you here tonight."

This guy doesn't have a clue who Banner is. I bet he says that to everyone.

"Thank you," Jack replied. "Looking forward to it."

The doorman opened the passport, gave it a quick once-over, and then handed the two items back to Jack. "Enjoy the auction, Dr. Banner."

"I'm sure I will." Jack offered a single, unmemorable nod to the man and walked by.

He entered the lobby through the glass doors and stopped at a gray metal detector where a security guard stood behind a table just to his left. Another guard waited just beyond the detector's arch.

Jack took his keys and phone out of his pocket and deposited them into a plastic bowl.

"Thank you," the guard behind the table said and slid the bowl to the other end beyond the archway.

Jack stepped through. Unsurprisingly, the machine didn't make a sound.

He retrieved his keys and phone from the bowl, gave a nod to the second security guard as he passed, and continued into the heart of the enormous lobby.

He looked around as if it was his first time in the building, but Jack had already reconnoitered the place twice before this evening. Having a good idea of where all the exits were was of utmost importance for a job like this. He'd done no less than one hundred hours of research on the place, the staff, and their protocols for this kind of auction.

With the plan in place, all that was left was the execution.

He stopped in the center of the room near a tower of champagne glasses stacked in the shape of a pyramid on a glass table. A pretty young woman stood behind it in a peacock costume with brilliant feathers fanned out behind her back. Jack wasn't sure about the significance of the bird in regards to the auction, but he figured it was just a garish show for those with opulence to spare. A few people even took pictures of her, which boggled his mind even more.

He continued sweeping his gaze across the room, noting the long purple tapestries draped from the walls, the expensive chandeliers hanging from the ceiling, and the millionaires and billionaires milling about. Some of them chatted—no doubt about the new superyachts they had just purchased. Others waited in line at the bar off to the left where three bartenders poured drinks. Some filled plates with food from a table with a white cloth draped over it. An ice sculpture of the Greek god Poseidon stood in the center, towering over the patrons with his familiar trident in one hand.

Two security guards at each of the three doors, he noted to himself, looking to the entrance of the grand hall, where the auction would take place.

The guards stood on either side with hands folded in front of them. They wore stern looks on their faces. With the black suits, they might as well have been Secret Service.

Jack turned his attention to the hallway off to the right. He'd been through there each of his previous visits and knew exactly where to go.

He strode away from the mob of elites and into the corridor. A sign on the wall pointed to the restrooms straight ahead. Jack didn't need the facilities. His destination was farther down the hall, where two more security guards stood next to a pair of metal doors.

He already knew about the cameras in the corners that watched over the secure entrance, and had taken measures to account for them.

Taking out his phone, he looked at the screen as he might have when reading a text message. Except the device didn't display messages. It was a jamming and rerouting app he'd created, and with the receiver he'd put in place three days before, he could alter the images of every camera in the building.

On the screen, he tapped the feeds of the cameras directly ahead of him. Within seconds, a green checkmark appeared in each box. Now the surveillance system was displaying a ten-second loop, and any security people in the video room wouldn't notice the difference. He left the cameras in the lobby and auction room alone.

As Jack neared the security guards, he minimized the app but kept looking at the device, pretending to read something until he saw the feet of the guard nearest him.

"Excuse me, sir," the burly man said under a thick beard. "This area is restricted."

Jack took two more steps and then feigned surprise. He looked up and around the corridor as if lost.

"I am so sorry," he slurred. "I was looking for the bathroom. Someone told me it was down this hall."

"It's back that way. Next door on your left. You just passed it."

Jack turned around and slid his right foot backward, pretending to be drunk. "Oh. I guess I did. That champagne is good. I guess they don't let you guys drink on the job, though, huh."

"No, sir."

He slid the phone into his left pocket and retrieved a tiny black plastic box no longer than his thumb. He wavered, then stumbled into the guard, who immediately stuck out his arms to catch Jack.

"Take it easy, sir," the guard warned. "Perhaps you should have a seat in the lobby."

As Jack fell into the man's arms, he threw up his hands as if trying to catch himself. In a quick, subtle movement, he jabbed the plastic box against the man's neck, and felt the top of it depress with a nearly undetectable click.

The man's eyes widened in an instant at the prick in his skin. He turned to Jack with confusion washing over his face. Within two seconds, the man's arms weakened, and then went limp as he fell to his side on the floor.

"Hey," the other guard shouted. "Amir? Are you okay?"

"I don't know what happened," Jack said. "He tried to catch me."

The second guard rushed to the first's side and knelt down to check him. Jack retrieved a second plastic box from his other pocket and pressed it into the conscious guard's neck on the right side.

"Hey," he protested, but it was all the man could muster. The tranquilizer worked so quickly, he was down on the floor next to his partner before he knew what happened.

Jack stuffed both the boxes back in their respective pockets, the ceramic needles within having delivered the paralyzing toxin into the men's bloodstreams.

They'd be fine when they woke up in an hour or two.

He looked back down the hall where he'd come from, glad no one was heading to the restroom. He retrieved the security card from a lanyard on one of the guard's necks, slid it through a panel, and opened the metal door. He flung it wide enough that it would give him time to drag the first guard into the back room. Then he tugged the second out of sight and let the door close behind him.

After catching his breath for a second, Jack looked down the corridor that led to the rear of the auction house. Stairs to his right went up to the next floor, but he knew those didn't lead anywhere except to the roof.

What he was after waited at the other end of the hall.

Jack adjusted the cuffs on his shirt sleeves as he walked swiftly ahead. His polished black shoes clicked in steady rhythm on the hard floor.

The auction prep room loomed ahead.

"Ladies and gentlemen, please take your seats. The auction will begin in five minutes."

He heard the announcer's voice echo down the hallway.

"Right on time," Jack mumbled.

The prep room was nothing special—a thousand-square-foot area surrounded by plain white walls and lights that hung from metal rods below a twenty-foot-high ceiling. The minimalism of the design highlighted the spectacular array of artifacts that waited on pedestals dotted around the floor. Two men wearing white gloves and matching suits stood by a deep red curtain at the front of the room, waiting for the call to bring out the first of the items up for auction.

The one on the left noticed Jack as he entered and immediately held up his hand.

"I am sorry, sir. This is a restricted area."

Jack looked around, again pretending to be lost. "I am so sorry," he said, still approaching the man. "I had no idea I was—" He punched the guy in the nose, then in the jaw, knocking him out cold.

The second prep man—an older gentleman with white hair and gaunt features, held up both hands. "Please. Don't hurt me."

"Then please don't try to stop me," Jack ordered.

"Whatever it is you're trying to do, you won't get away with it."

Jack wasn't about to hit this guy, but if he raised the alarm, there'd be no choice. "Why don't you leave that up to me?"

He turned and spotted the item he'd come for—a small wooden chest about the size of a mailbox. The iron clasps and hoops on it, while weathered, still resembled what they might have looked like when it was created over five hundred years before.

"There it is," Jack said. He turned and hurried over to the chest, picked it up, and tucked it under his right armpit. Then he looked back at the older man. "I know you're going to raise the alarm the second I'm out of this room. I won't hold that against you. A man's gotta do his job, after all."

The worker looked at Jack, beleaguered by the statement. Then Jack reached into his pocket and retrieved a small metal disc. He tossed it at the man's feet and started for the exit.

The curator looked down at the disc, curious. Then the object fizzed, and within ten seconds, the noxious chemical inside reached his nostrils.

Jack didn't look back when he heard the man's body hit the floor, unconscious from the gas. Just like the other two guards, he'd be fine soon enough. And Jack would be long gone.

4

Konstantin Morovski marched through the lobby until he and his entourage reached the center of the room. There, the major stopped and surveyed the area along with the many guests talking, drinking, and eating.

In Russia, at such an occasion, he would wear his Russian army uniform, along with all the commensurate medals and ribbons and other trappings that went with it.

But they were not in Russia, and for this endeavor it was of vital importance that no one suspected he, or his crew, was with the Russian military. His captain, Boris Semenov, accompanied him by his side, with two more soldiers—Oleg and Yuri staying close behind them.

The four men were dressed like businessmen, in expensive suits to blend in with the rest of the crowd.

Russian oligarchs often attended events such as these, a fact of which Konstantin was well aware. He'd ordered Boris to check the roster and make certain none of them were showing up. If he or his men were recognized, their motives could be revealed by loose lips.

Fortunately, none were in attendance, and no one at the auction house, or the crowd, knew their true identities.

With documents forged by the best Moscow could offer, the four men purported to be multimillionaires from Bulgaria, there to peruse the items up for sale. Konstantin knew the security detail wouldn't be able to discern their accents, nor would any of the guests were they to be unexpectedly engaged in conversation.

Just in case, he and his men wore gruff, unapproachable expressions as they entered the building.

Konstantin looked over at the doors leading into the auction room and noted the guards surrounding each one.

He and his men had been forced to leave their firearms in the trunk of their car, and he felt naked without it, though he doubted any threat would arise in such a place. Most of the auction patrons looked soft and weak, made so by lifetimes of luxury and a lack of self-control.

Still, it paid to be vigilant.

"Sweep the room," he ordered the other three. "Make sure we're not going to have a problem."

Each man nodded without saying a word, as they'd discussed prior to arrival. No "yes, sir" here. He'd made that abundantly clear to them. Speaking in such a manner could blow their cover to any eavesdropper standing nearby.

The men split up and melted into the crowd.

Konstantin knew that if any kind of threat loomed in the lobby, his men would root it out. The metal detector at the door made sure no one else carried any weapons, but there were other kinds of trouble to be found, often signaled by the way a person carried themselves, or the fire in their eyes.

The other reason he'd sent the men around the room was to check for a tail. So far, he didn't think they'd been followed. And no one in this country had a clue who they really were, much less in the building, but prudence always paid, and now was no time to slip up —not when they were so close.

Konstantin sauntered over to the table where an offering of finger foods adorned glass plates set atop white pedestals. Falafel, lamb chops, garbanzo beans.

He put on the best, official-looking smile he could muster, and leaned against a marble pillar as he crossed his arms. Konstantin watched the crowd, sweeping his gaze across the room from left to right and back again. He missed nothing, including the out-of-place American who walked into the building in an expensive suit.

The threads might have fooled the rest of the crowd, but not the Russian. The American thief might as well have been a goat in a herd of sheep. He watched as the man played his way through the crowd of wealthy elites and then disappeared down the corridor on the far side of the lobby. Konstantin knew where the man was headed, and what his plans were.

"Always have a backup," he muttered to himself.

A few minutes passed before his men returned. "The room is clean, sir," the one with a shaved head reported.

Konstantin knew their limitations with the security check, and accepted them along with the declaration.

"Very good. Let's make our way into the auction room. I'm certain they'll begin soon."

The major spun away from the table in a fluid motion and strolled toward the entrance to the inner sanctum of the auction house. Each set of doors was surrounded by guards, the likes of which Konstantin held no concern for. He was there to buy a priceless artifact that, ironically, he would acquire for a price.

They walked through the nearest set of doors, between the guards who wore menacing expressions of warning on their faces, and into the auction room.

The grand space boasted opulence in every way. Silken red curtains hung from the walls along the side of the sloped auditorium, adorning the edges of the aisle all the way to the stage at the front.

Seats were already filling quickly with eager elites ready to spend their money on baubles from history they thought looked cool or would make them look cultured to their friends. Konstantin sneered at the thought. *All fools.*

He didn't care what they spent their money on. Aside from one item.

The chest was all he cared about. More importantly, what was inside it.

He made his way down along the center-left aisle and stopped in the middle of the room. There, he turned into a row and moved in until there were enough seats for him and his men.

Konstantin sat down and crossed his leg over his knee and his hands over his lap, holding the number that had been placed upon the seat's edge.

He panned the room as his men sat down next to him, observing the modern-day lords and ladies entering the spacious chamber where the bidding would soon begin.

A shiny black pedestal stood in the center of a stage that curved outward toward the crowd. The curtain fifteen feet behind it matched the drapes along the wall.

A man in a sharp black suit emerged from behind the curtain and announced that the bidding would begin shortly, and for everyone to begin taking their seats.

Within a minute of his announcement, the throngs of people loitering in the lobby began entering the auditorium en masse.

"When do you think they will offer the box?" Boris asked, leaning in from Konstantin's right.

"I don't know," the major replied. "Hopefully near the beginning. There are several prettier pieces that I think these people will be more interested in buying. What would any of them want with an old, wooden box that belonged to a dead pirate? It's of no use to anyone else except for a person who is a rabid fan of Barbarossa."

"Unless someone else knows what it really is," Boris hedged.

"How could they?" Konstantin countered. "The chest was only recently discovered and connected to the famed admiral. No one would think it to be anything else. We should be able to purchase it easily, unless there is someone here who happens to be particularly interested in that part of history."

"We *are* in the right country for that."

"True. Which is why we have backup plans in place."

Boris nodded, understanding the conversation was over and his concern had been noted.

The men sat in silence as the wealthy audience poured into the room, taking their seats amid a murmur of conversation. One middle-aged brunette woman in a black dress with sparkly golden scales around the neckline, sat in the row directly in front of Konstantin. She leaned toward her date and pointed to the brochure, her finger resting on the image of a vase that had been procured recently by a team of archaeologists in eastern Turkey.

Konstantin rolled his eyes. She fit the description of many of the women in this room, wanting pretty and rare things as if they were nothing more than expensive broaches to pin to their gowns, or necklaces decorating their necklines.

The men would pay, too. Though Konstantin noted several females in the audience without dates—women from industry who controlled their own wealth. Konstantin admired these, and knew the struggles they'd gone through to attain their standing in society.

Not that he cared about that struggle or any of the people in this room, the few that had been through such a life path. He knew most had not. Born into opulence and entitlement, the vast majority of the people in this room—while empire builders in their own right—had used family funds to make those kingdoms a reality.

The master of ceremonies stood behind the podium and waited as the crowd settled into their seats. Only a few stragglers entered intermittently, carrying drinks in both hands as the proof of their tardiness.

The bar lines had been considerably long.

"Welcome, everyone. Please, take your seats. We are about to begin the first auction of the evening."

He spoke in English, which most of the people in attendance could understand, and if they couldn't, they usually had translators with them.

A frown abruptly stretched across the man's face, and he turned his head to the left, looking at the curtain behind him.

Morovski leaned forward, peering at a gap between the bottom of the curtain and the stage floor. A dark shadow occupied the space. He recognized the outline immediately.

It was a body.

The MC called for one of the stewards to come forth, but for a few seconds no one emerged.

He called again and then finally stepped over to the curtain and pulled it back.

The two stewards lay on the floor at his feet, unconscious.

The MC searched the display room, but saw no one else.

Konstantin's eyes widened, and he turned to Boris. "We need to leave."

"What? Before the auction?"

"The item we're here for has been taken."

"What?"

"Don't question me, Captain. Move."

Boris did as told, and stood with the others.

Konstantin spoke into the radio again. "The chest has been taken. Control the exits."

"Yes, sir," was the only reply that crackled through the earpiece.

He'd taken precautions for this. "Don't let him escape."

As the Russian contingent stalked up the aisle toward the exits, they heard the MC's voice echo throughout the auditorium again. "Is there a doctor in the room? We need a doctor."

Konstantin snorted. It wasn't a doctor they needed. He guessed the thief merely knocked the men out to get what he was after. What the auctioneer needed was a competent security team to lock down the building.

But by the time he'd discovered the two stewards, the major knew it was already too late to implement such a plan.

Which is why he'd stationed some of his men around the building.

Just in case.

5

Jack knew the Russian soldiers posing as bodyguards would be guarding the exits. Konstantin Morovski hadn't risen to the rank of major, and gained favor with the Russian president, by being an incompetent idiot.

It paid to know one's enemy.

And Jack knew everything an American citizen could know about the guy, including his overcompensation for caution when it came to procuring sensitive or important things.

He'd run into Konstantin once before, hunting for an amulet of power in the Greek Islands.

The major had offered him a deal, but the amulet wasn't to be found—either it didn't exist, or they were in the wrong place.

Jack had no love for the Russians, especially their leader, but money was money, and if the men wanted to work out a deal, their cash could be converted to something more suited to his needs.

That was the last he'd seen of them until two weeks ago.

Jack had been tracking the chest of Hayreddin Barbarossa since the minute he noticed the article come across the newsfeed on his phone.

He'd waited for this moment, hoping it wasn't a false flag like so many others of his treasure hunts had been.

Jack longed to cut out of his career as a thief and settle down, maybe on a nice beach in the summer and on the slopes of Switzerland in the winter.

He loved snowboarding and traveling, but the constant pressure of being chased by the authorities, and always having to watch his back, wore on him. And the cops were the least of his troubles.

Underground criminals were far more dangerous than any police force. All the cops could do was put him in jail for a while. Criminals wouldn't hesitate to kill him.

He carried the chest under his right arm like a heavy wooden football, cradling it with his hand to keep it from shifting as he moved quickly through the underbelly of the auction house.

Jack had discovered the system of maintenance tunnels during his investigation of the blueprints, and had walked them once just to make sure he wouldn't get lost on his way out of the building.

As he pushed ahead into the dimly lit concrete tunnel, he wondered if one visit had been enough.

The walls started to look the same, and the corridors ran together like an intricate maze. Except he'd already gotten the cheese at the end, and was now trying to find his way out.

He passed an electrical box with pipes and cords leading out of it, running up to the ceiling, and then along the wall in both directions.

"I remember you," he said, and pressed faster ahead.

Jack didn't know why the tunnels existed under the auction house other than they might have been designed as part of a safety feature in case of a robbery, or perhaps in case of war. He'd heard of museums and places like this one that contained escape corridors or massive underground vaults.

One of the more famous such locations he knew of was the Library of Congress, and its fantastic security measures to protect the Declaration of Independence.

He remembered watching Hollywood's rendering of it in the first

National Treasure movie, and figured they got pretty close to the mark.

But Jack wasn't sure that was what these tunnels were for, especially considering how lax security had been in the auction hall.

The two inept stewards might as well have been wearing red shirts from the old Star Trek movies.

Easy targets. Easy takedowns.

He wasn't out of the woods yet, though, and he was well aware of the more dangerous predators out to find him.

Konstantin had approached him about this heist, which was how Jack found out about the chest in the first place.

The Russian major wouldn't tell him anything else about Barbarossa's box, though, which caused Jack's curiosity to spike all the more.

He remembered the meeting from a month before. Although calling it a meeting was generous. It was more like an abduction.

Konstantin and his men had tracked Jack down to a bar in Amsterdam. When Jack left, after more than a couple of pints, they cornered him in an alley, threw him in their car, and drove to a park where they dumped him on the sidewalk. From there, Konstantin offered a stroll and a conversation.

Jack had been partially relieved that the men hadn't drowned him in one of the many canals.

Of course, he didn't know who the men were when they captured him. At first, he wondered if the Russians were hired goons working for someone Jack may have robbed—or wronged in some other way. There was that wealthy man's twenty-year-younger wife in Monaco, after all.

But it turned out Konstantin had an offer for Jack.

After a twenty-minute walk through the park, Jack offered to look at the schematics for the building, and the security detail.

While he agreed that the guards would be simple enough to avoid, and the stewards obviously nothing to worry about, it was the system of alarms that would follow, and the inevitable lockdown from the Turkish police that were probably circling the building for an event such as this.

The Russians, however, were insistent.

And that potential of being drowned in one of Amsterdam's waterways looked like it might not be off the table.

So, Jack had agreed to the job. But he wanted to know more about this chest he now held tight in his arm.

He found surprisingly little information on the internet about the box, and pressed the Russian officer for more details, particularly the part about how he came to find out about this chest, and what was so important about it.

Konstantin told Jack that he'd come across a collection of letters from the Holy Roman Emperor to some of his men—assassins, from what Konstantin could gather. The letters were orders to procure the box from Barbarossa after the admiral's death. The instructions told these elite soldiers where they could find the chest. But after that, there were no more letters.

"The assassin-thieves," Konstantin had said, "found the box to be empty."

"Then why do you want it?" Jack wondered.

"You might say I am a collector of all things having to do with Admiral Barbarossa" was all he would offer. Along with one million American dollars for the job.

The sum was enough to make any thief say yes without a second thought. Any thief except Jack.

The generous offer sent a stream of questions through Jack's mind—the biggest of which being, what was so special about a five-hundred-year-old empty chest.

The finding part didn't really baffle Jack. Those military types—especially the spec ops ones—had their ways of tracking people; at least that's what he assumed.

There was one other big question that loomed in his mind. Maybe it was just the fact that he was a thief, and by nature somewhat greedy. But if this guy was willing to pay him a cool million without batting an eye for a wooden box, Jack had to wonder how much it was really worth.

He'd told the Russian he'd think about it, but the man demanded an answer right away.

That's when Jack noticed the two guards that had been following them in the shadows close in around him.

"Sounds good," he'd said, trying to shake off the tremor of fear that shot through him. "When do we start?"

Now Jack found himself winding through tunnels under Beşitkaş with who knew how many security guards and cops after him. He had a head start, but it wasn't much.

He knew he needed to get back to the apartment and figure out his next steps.

The tunnels forked in two directions, and his memory jogged back to the last time he'd been in this spot.

"Okay, Jack. Now you know where you are."

The one to the left cut off into a concrete wall with several gray electrical panels hanging from the blocks.

The short passage to the right continued beyond a single gray metal door on the right-hand side and stopped at a chain-link fence at the end. Beyond the fence, the tunnel continued—without lighting.

A faint stench wafted into his nostrils as he hurried toward the fence. The corridor past the barrier was fed by storm drains on the street above. It was better than escaping through the sewers, though just barely. And he hadn't ruled that out as an option should the necessity arise.

He hoped the dummy lock he'd left on the gate remained intact from his previous visit—because if someone had come along and checked it, then replaced it with a new one, he'd be screwed.

Jack exhaled as he stopped next to the fence. He set the chest down on the hard floor and pinched the lock, pulling the hook out of the receiver. It slid out easily, and he felt relief pour into his gut like someone had dumped a pitcher of the stuff down his gullet.

He pushed open the gate, switched on his phone light, and gathered the chest in his right arm once more.

The dark tunnel filled with musty odors that hung in the dense, moist air. He did his best to ignore it, as before, though he felt slower this time now that he had the prize in his possession.

When he'd timed his earlier run from the gate to the ladder leading up to the street where he'd make his getaway, it took ten minutes. That distance would put him outside the perimeter he knew the police would set up around the auction house, and he'd be well on his way to the apartment.

This time, it took him an extra seventy seconds with the bulky wooden box in his arm. As he moved, he changed it from left to right to give his muscles a break, but the exchanges slowed him down.

Jack tried not to worry about it, knowing that doing so wouldn't help.

Once he reached the ladder—a series of steel rungs fixed to the concrete—he clutched the chest tight against his side and began climbing.

This part proved more difficult than he'd considered, since going up a ladder usually required both hands.

He managed, though, and after another minute, arrived at the top and the manhole cover he'd pried loose prior to making his way to the auction.

This, like the ascent of the ladder, proved extremely difficult with the box under his arm, and as he pushed up on the cover, he nearly lost his balance and fell.

As he teetered backward, he snapped his left hand forward to the top rung, and gripped it to steady himself. Then he used his shoulder to barge the lid free, and climbed out onto the asphalt in an alley.

The sound of sirens screamed through the city. Jack paused, letting the chest rest on the blacktop as he listened. The sounds echoed from around the corner in the direction of the auction house.

Certain the cops were no threat, Jack pulled himself the rest of the way out of the hole, pushed the lid back over it, and sprinted down the alley into the shadows.

6

ISTANBUL

Jack burst through the front door of the apartment building. He looked back out the window set in the upper center of the door, checking the sidewalk and street beyond.

He'd watched the rearview mirror nearly the entire drive from where he'd parked his car, constantly checking for tails. As far as he could tell, no one had followed him, but Istanbul was a busy city, and followers could easily duck in and out of traffic, blending with the mobs of other vehicles.

More than once he thought he'd seen the same motorcycle lingering just far enough back to keep up with him but never lose sight. That bike pulled off onto a side street two minutes before Jack arrived here, and so he let it go. Still, paranoia gripped him.

He glanced down at the chest before continuing to the stairwell. No way he was going to chance the elevator. Not tonight. The sooner he got back to his apartment, the sooner he could figure out what was so special about this chest.

Jack climbed four flights then stopped and opened the metal door onto the fourth floor. He poked his head through and looked both directions. An empty hallway greeted him.

He quickly slipped into the corridor and hurried to his door forty feet to the right. There, he checked both ends of the hall again as he fished the key out of his pocket. For a second, he fumbled with it, and nearly dropped it.

"Calm down," Jack told himself.

He blinked slowly to help steady his nerves, and then inserted the key into the lock.

Jack pushed the door open and entered the studio apartment. Inside, he walked to the island in the kitchen and set the chest down on the surface. For several seconds, Jack merely stared at the box. Something clicked inside him, and he snapped out of the daze.

He unhooked the clasp and pried the lid up. The chest was empty.

"Why would this empty chest be worth anything?" he wondered out loud. He reflected back on what Konstantin had said to him about being a collector, but Jack remained unconvinced.

There's something more to this chest, he thought.

He eased onto a black wooden stool and craned his neck, leaning in close to the chest. The smell of the old wood and iron filled his nostrils.

Jack inspected the outer edge of the box first, looking for a clue, but the only thing he found was a trident engraved into the side. He looked inside the box again, thinking there could be a false bottom, but he didn't notice any seams.

He leaned back and stared at the chest, trying to gauge the bottom as compared to the interior.

"That doesn't add up," he said and turned to the utensil drawer on his left. He slid the drawer out and selected a sharp knife, then closed the drawer and returned his attention to the chest.

Jack slid the edge of the knife against the floor's edge and the inner wall, applying a steady amount of pressure to make sure if there really was a crease, the knife would push through.

After working the blade back and forth several times, it broke through and slid deeper into the chest.

"Well, well, well," he said. His fingers worked the knife back and forth a little faster, encouraged by the empty space. "What do we have here?"

He managed to separate the bottom from the side wall and lifted it. The chest's floor protested with a creak from the wood that had been fixed in place for five centuries. It squeaked for a second, but finally broke loose with an abrupt snap.

Jack felt a shudder of concern whip through him at the thought of breaking such a valuable artifact. A quick once over of the piece revealed no splinters or cracks, and the guilt immediately melted.

He pulled the bottom the rest of the way out, tilting it up like a door. As he raised the piece of wood, Jack's eyes widened. His lips creased into a thin smile, and for a few seconds, he stood there staring into the bottom of the chest, still gripping the piece of wood in his fingers.

"What have we here?" he said.

Inside the chest lay a leather-bound book, closed with a matching strap around the cover. No words told of what filled the pages within. Only a symbol occupied the dark brown surface, burned into it like a brand.

"A trident," Jack whispered. "Why is there a trident on this?"

He heard a door close in the hallway outside his apartment and froze for a second, listening intently for another sound. He waited, and when nothing else signaled him, he pulled the piece of wood out of the chest and carefully lifted the little book.

Jack blinked rapidly as he cradled the book in his fingers, unable to make himself open it for nearly a minute. Then, he gently laid the book down on the table next to the chest.

He untied the leather strap that bound the cover and carefully opened the journal.

The words on the first page were written in Turkish, but something about the language was different than what Jack had seen around the city. He knew virtually nothing about the language except enough to order food, drink, and how to ask for directions.

He'd only acquired the apartment as a base of operations for the job, and would ditch the place as soon as his mission was done.

That mission had been to steal the chest and find out what was really in it.

The auction house had claimed there was nothing inside the box. They'd actually gone to great lengths to make sure no one purchased it on the misguided assumption that there might be some kind of treasure inside.

Still, the chest was expected to command a significant amount of money at auction, which Jack still didn't understand. Now that he gazed upon the secret contents of the chest, he wondered how many people truly knew about this little book.

There was no doubt in his mind that it was this book the Russians were really after, and why they'd wanted him to get it for them. The other certainty Jack remained fully aware of was that the Russians would now be looking for him.

He took out his phone and looked up a translator for the two lines penned in old ink on the page. Then turned to the counter behind him where he'd left a pen earlier that day, and pinched it in his right hand along with a day planner he'd left next to it.

Then he rounded on the journal and began entering the letters, one at a time, into the translator.

Not all of the words made sense, and the translator only revealed a garbled and confusing message.

Jack frowned as he stared at the screen in his palm. "Strange," he said. "Maybe I entered a letter incorrectly."

He erased everything he'd entered and tried a second time, but the same result blinked onto the screen.

Jack's frustration escalated.

"Key. Power. Guide. Those make sense," he said out loud. "But these other words don't seem to go with them."

He set the pen down and paced over to the door leading onto the balcony. He crossed his arms and stared out at the city around him. "What am I doing wrong?" he wondered.

Then an idea popped into his head. "Hmm. It's been a long time. But if anyone can help me with this, it's him."

He took the phone and looked up the number of an old friend in his contacts, then typed out a quick message. He hesitated for a second before he sent it, then hit the arrow button.

The text sent in an instant.

Jack walked back over to the island and sat down on the stool, staring at the screen to wait for his friend to respond.

A minute passed. Then another. Nothing.

Probably busy off saving the world or hunting some ancient artifact, Jack thought.

Then the three dots in an oval seemingly everyone on Earth recognized appeared on the screen.

"There you are."

The reply appeared thirty seconds later.

"What's up, man? Long time," the message read.

Jack typed rapidly. "I have a question. What do these words mean?" He added the ones that were throwing off the translation. "I tried looking them up, but none of the Turkish translators seemed to get them correct."

He waited another two minutes before the next message appeared.

"Those come from Old Turkish, if I'm not mistaken. I could double-check. But I know there are a few subtle differences between the Turkish spoken now and Ottoman Turkish from that era. What are you reading?"

Jack grinned at the question and replied, "You're not the only one who can dabble with artifacts."

He waited for a minute before his friend responded again, and this time he chuckled as he read the response silently. "The IAA doesn't dabble."

Jack heard a door close out in the hall again, and snapped his head around. That one sounded like the door from the stairwell. He turned his attention back to the phone and started to type another message when his phone started vibrating.

The name on the screen filled him with dread unlike any he'd ever felt in his life.

He knew he couldn't ignore the call. With the VPN he used, he knew the call wouldn't be trackable.

He pressed the green button and put the device to his ear. "Konstantin? Is that you?"

"You know it is, Jack. Don't play games with me, boy."

"Boy? I'm a grown man, same as you." Jack hoped semantics might distract the Russian, but that plan didn't work.

"You disappeared from the auction house in a hurry," Konstantin continued. "I have to wonder, why?"

Jack swallowed hard. He hadn't seen the Russian at the auction.

"Well, you know. I wanted to get back to the safe house and inspect the item."

"Good. Then tell me where you are, and me and my men will be there momentarily to collect it."

"Where I am? Oh, sure. No problem. I'm at the corner of get a map and get bent."

"Is that supposed to be a joke?"

"It's not supposed to be anything. It's just funny."

"And yet I am not laughing. Not to worry. My men will be there shortly to collect the chest. I hope you haven't damaged it."

Jack's eyes widened, this time in fear. "Your men? They don't—"

"We followed you, Jack. My men were stationed around every possible exit in and out of the building. Including the one you took through the tunnel that led up to the alley. Did you really think I wouldn't be smart enough to cover every potential escape route?"

"No. I mean. I just—"

"I sincerely hope you weren't thinking of keeping the chest for yourself, Jack. That would be... unfortunate."

"For myself? Of course not. What would I want that old thing for? It's just an old wooden box, and there's nothing in it."

"You opened it?" Concern laced Konstantin's voice.

"Of course I opened it. I had to see what the big deal about this chest was."

Jack moved away from the island and over to the bed, where his backpack sat on the floor next to the nightstand. He unplugged the phone and laptop cords from the wall and stuffed them into the bag. Then shoved his laptop in after them.

He shouldered the bag and rushed back over to the table.

"You know, Konstantin, if I didn't know better, I'd say you don't trust me."

"I don't. You're a thief."

"Okay, now that's harsh. Stereotype much?"

Jack walked over to the glass door leading onto the balcony and slid it open. He stepped out into the warm night. The sounds of cars and motorcycles echoed up to his floor, filling his ears. The scent of various foods tingled in his nose.

He looked over the edge down to the street and spotted four men getting out of a black sedan. He recognized two of them right away.

"It sounds like you're outside now, Jack. Did you go for a walk? Or did you step out onto your balcony to see if my men had arrived yet?"

"Yes. I mean, no. I did step out onto the balcony. But if your men are here, that's great. Means I don't have to come out and meet you somewhere. Tell them to come on up. I'll be here waiting with your box." He ended the call and stuffed the phone in his pocket.

Jack turned and reentered the apartment, but he left the door open behind him.

He rushed back to the island and closed the book. He took the piece of wood that had been in the bottom of the chest and carefully placed it back where it had been, pressing it down hard to make sure it aligned perfectly.

Jack shut the lid and closed the clasp, though now he knew that was superfluous. He'd already admitted to Konstantin that he looked inside it.

Details, he thought.

He set the backpack down on the island next to the chest and scooped up the journal, then stepped over to the door. He flung it open and looked down the corridor in both directions, expecting to see one of Konstantin's goons. Thankfully, the hall remained empty.

He fished a key out of his pocket and shuffled over to the door across from his, fit the key into the door, and pushed it open.

This apartment was barren, free of any decor or furniture. Jack had rented it just in case something like this happened, and while the plan was far from perfect, it was the best he could do.

He stalked over to the kitchen counter and set the journal down on the surface. With one last look at the leather-bound tome, he turned and retreated out into the hall, closing and locking the door behind him before going back into his own apartment.

Just as he closed that door behind him, he heard the elevator ding at the center of the hallway.

He let out a sigh and retrieved his phone once more.

His thumbs flew across the keys as he sent one last message to his friend.

A heavy knock pounded the door.

"Jack? Open up. We know you're in there."

"Hey, guys," he said cheerfully, hoping his nerves didn't flitter through his tone. "One second."

"Not one second. Open now," the Russian demanded.

"Jeez. Relax, it's not like I'm going anywhere."

He kept typing the text message.

More knocking, this time so hard Jack thought the door might burst open from the force.

He hit the Send button and waited until it went through, then scanned it one last time to make sure he'd said what he needed to.

"I'm in trouble. Don't reply to this text. I left you something in my spare apartment." The address and apartment number followed. Then it read, "I don't know what this is, Sean. But if anyone can figure it out, you can."

Satisfied with the message, Jack deleted the thread, then stuffed the device back into his pocket as he made his way over to the door.

"Would you take it easy? Good grief, guys. I'm coming."

He reached out and opened the door.

Two big men stood outside wearing angry faces and black suits. Jack recognized them immediately. He also knew the other two were probably covering the exits, and there were likely more just like them around the back of the building.

"Hey, guys. Good to see you again—"

The one closest to him shoved Jack backward into the apartment. He stumbled but caught his balance before tripping and falling.

"Take it easy, Mikhail," Jack said, using a generic name. "I've got your precious box. It's right there. See?"

He stuck out his hand and pointed at the chest.

The goon looked over at it and motioned toward Jack. "Watch him," he ordered.

The second henchman nodded as he stepped into the apartment and crossed his arms to block the way.

Jack wished he had a gun right about then.

The first thug ambled over to the chest, unfastened the clasp, and pried open the lid.

He looked inside for a second, then over at Jack. "Where is it?"

"Where is what?" Jack answered with a question of his own. "I already told your boss it was empty when I looked inside. He knows it was empty for crying out loud. The auction brochure even made sure to state there was nothing inside the chest. Don't you guys read?"

The goon closed the lid and looked over at the other. "Search the apartment. Leave nothing unturned."

Again, the other man replied with a curt nod and began pulling out drawers, opening cabinets, and rifling through everything.

Jack's eyes flashed toward the door, and for a split second, he considered making a break for it. He went back and forth in his mind, arguing he could make it before one of Konstantin's men drew a weapon and fired.

But that would make him look guilty, and there was no telling if he even had a way to get out of the building that didn't involve a long fall with a sudden stop.

So, instead of running, Jack simply rolled his eyes as the second guy continued scouring the apartment. Soon, Jack heard the elevator ding again, signaling another arrival on the fourth floor. He knew it had to be more of Konstantin's men, if not the man himself, because there was never this much activity on Jack's floor at this time of night.

He waited with as much patience as he could muster, but inside his chest his heart pounded like a jackhammer as the sounds of footsteps in the corridor reached his ears.

When the clicking shoes on the floor could draw no closer, Konstantin appeared in the doorway.

"Hello, Jack," the Russian drawled.

"Hey, Konstantin. You know, it would be so much easier if you had a nickname. Like Konsta. Or Tinny. Your real name has so many syllables."

"Thought you might take off with the chest on your own?"

"Seriously?" Jack answered. "What would I do with an empty box? Seems like a pretty niche collector's item to me. And believe me, I know niche stuff. I have a friend who sells movie props for a living."

Konstantin ignored Jack and trundled over to the island where the chest sat on the surface. His henchman stepped aside to give the boss some room. The Russian major peered inside the chest, then looked up at Jack with suspicion written in his eyes. Then he looked back down and ran his finger along the inner wall of the box.

"See?" Jack asked. "Empty. Just as advertised. What did you expect, Konsta... or Tinny? Which one do you like? I'm kind of partial to Tinny."

"Give me a knife," Konstantin ordered, speaking to the soldier to his left.

The man immediately produced a small blade from a hidden sheath within his pocket and handed it to his commander.

"What are you doing?" Jack asked.

Konstantin didn't answer, instead slipping the knife into the box between the bottom and the floor—just as Jack had done earlier.

The Russian leveraged the bottom up. If the man was disappointed, he didn't show it. His face remained stoic in light of the lack of discovery.

"A false bottom?" Jack said, acting surprised as he inched forward to get a better look of what he already knew was there. "But it's empty."

Konstantin let the bottom fall back into the chest and passed the knife back to his soldier. Then, the major reached into his jacket and drew a pistol. He pointed it at Jack, who stumbled back against the wall with both hands raised.

"Whoa, man. What are you doing?"

"Where is it, Jack?" Konstantin demanded.

"Where is what?"

"You know exactly what."

"Konstantin, I have no idea what you're talking about. Okay? What was supposed to be in that thing?"

The major's jaw tightened. "I will give you three seconds to tell me where it is. If you do not, I will splatter your skull on that wall. Do you understand?"

"Pretty hard not to."

"One."

"Look, man. I did what you asked. I got the box."

"And you tried to get away with it. I suppose you were going to call me when you got here?"

"Actually, I was," Jack confirmed.

"Two."

"Konstantin. I have no idea what you want here. What was supposed to be in that chest? If you tell me, maybe I can help you find it."

For a second, the Russian seemed to consider the option.

Jack took that moment to add one more bit of convincing. "You got here right after I did, man. Your guy over there has wrecked my apartment. I had no idea there was a false bottom in that box. And if I did, where would I have put whatever was in there?"

From the look in the major's eyes, Jack felt like he'd finally convinced the man he was being unreasonable.

"Think about it," Jack pushed. "If there was something in that chest, whoever discovered it probably already took it. And if they didn't, maybe someone at the auction house got nosy and figured it out. It's the only thing that makes sense."

Konstantin nodded, and for a second, Jack felt relief fill his gut.

"You're right, Jack. That does make sense." Then he shrugged. "Three."

7

ATLANTA

Sean blinked as he stared at his phone's screen, reading the message over and over again.

Tongues of orange, yellow, and white flames lapped at the chimney in his fireplace. The last rays of sunlight pierced the tall windows to the right, sneaking by the black curtains to spill onto the walnut floor.

"What is it?" Adriana asked.

Sean's wife sat on the brown leather couch next to him, holding a novel in one hand. She peered at him with her dark chocolate eyes. Her nearly black hair splashed over her right shoulder.

"I'm not sure," Sean confessed. "A friend of mine from a long time ago sent me a message a few minutes ago. He was asking about an Old Turkish translation. Ottoman Turkish, actually."

"Oh?" She lowered the book to her lap. "That sounds interesting."

"Yeah, but then I get this message from him." He handed her the phone to let her read it.

"I'm in trouble. Don't reply to this text. I left you something in my spare apartment." She looked over at Sean. "Do you know this address?"

"No. I haven't seen Jack in ages. It's probably been seven years or more. Last time we hung out was when he was in town and wanted to watch a Falcons game. After that, he left for Europe, and I haven't heard anything out of him since."

"So, no 'How are you, Sean? What have you been up to?' Just a question about a Turkish translation?"

Sean chuckled. "Yeah. That's Jack. Always direct, and usually always about himself. He was my friend when we were in high school. Tommy never trusted him. But I gave him a chance. Then he got kicked out of school for stealing things out of other kid's lockers."

"So he's a thief?" Adriana's interest piqued even more.

"Yeah, but not like you. There was no nobility in what he did."

She offered a flirty smile at his response. "Aww. I didn't realize you considered what I do as noble."

She handed the phone back to him, and he leaned close as if he might kiss her, then pulled away. "Of course I do. You're a very noble woman. Between you and Tommy, I'd say the most noble of anyone I've ever met."

"Always have to bring him into it, don't you?" She shook her head, pretending to be disappointed.

"I can't help myself."

His playful expression turned sour again as he returned his gaze to the phone. "I don't know what to make of this thing with Jack, though."

"It sounds like he doesn't either. The part where he says he doesn't know what this is... That's a little vague. What is the *this* he's talking about?"

"I don't know, but apparently, he thinks I can figure it out."

"Without telling you what *it* is."

Sean sighed. "I'm just as baffled as you."

"Istanbul isn't a short jog from here. Sending you the address, and the apartment number, insinuates he wants you to go there to find something. Or meet him. But I doubt it's the latter."

"Agreed." Sean scanned the message one more time and then set the phone down on the couch between them. "It sounds like he didn't have much time. I guess he tried to steal from the wrong people."

"What are you going to do?"

Sean rolled his shoulders and crossed his arms over his chest. "I'm not sure. I don't have any projects pressing right now. So, I could take a trip across the pond. Haven't been to Turkey in a while."

"I'll come with you."

"I figured."

A wry grin stretched across her face. Her dark red lips teased him. "You aren't getting rid of me any time soon, Sean Wyatt."

He smiled back at her and leaned in again, this time fully intent on delivering the kiss he had taunted her with a moment before. "Getting rid of you is the last thing I want to do."

He paused an inch from her lips and inhaled the sweet scent of her perfume, then brushed his lips against hers for a second before pressing firmly against them. Sean withdrew, running his fingers across the side of her head and through her thick hair.

An epiphany snaked through his mind. "Jack said I wasn't the only one who could dabble with ancient artifacts."

"Does that mean he found something?"

Sean nodded. "Yeah. Could be. He was asking me a question about some words that came from Ottoman Turkish."

"Like I said, that's interesting. You mean the old language, right?"

Sean nodded. "Yeah. He said he was entering something into a Turkish translator, but it was giving him some weird results."

"Like the nuances between British English and American English."

"Right. Sort of like that."

Sean thought for a moment, the gears turning in his eyes. Adriana could see his mind racing through the windows of his wolf-like eyes. "If he's in Istanbul, then I wonder if the artifact is from the Ottoman Empire."

Adriana hummed a thoughtful sound. "Probably. That would make sense since he's asking you about the language from that period in history."

Sean shook his head. His brow furrowed. "I just don't see Jack as the kind of guy taking part in an archaeological dig or study."

"Because he's a thief?"

"Yeah. I mean. Partly that. History was never really his thing. Okay, school wasn't his thing. But it seems strange he'd be working on something in our field. Which brings me back to the likelihood that he stole something from the wrong person."

Adriana reached across the gap between the sofa and the black wooden coffee table and retrieved her tablet. She pressed her finger to the Home button, and the screen bloomed to life with an image of her and Sean standing next to a wall at the Acropolis in Athens. The city sprawled across the barren hills behind them, dotted intermittently with patches of olive trees.

She opened the search app and entered a few words, then waited. "A-ha," she mumbled upon seeing the first result.

"What?" Sean shifted closer to get a better look.

Adriana tapped the first link and waited for a second as the screen blinked and changed images.

The article headline sprayed across the top in bold, black letters. *PRICELESS TREASURE CHEST OF BARBAROSSA STOLEN.*

"Barbarossa?" Sean blurted, inching closer.

"The Ottoman pirate who became an admiral?"

"Unless you know of another one," Sean shrugged. "Treasure chest. That's strange."

The two read through the first few paragraphs.

"Stolen from an auction house in Beşitkaş," Sean summarized. He noted the writer's declaration that the chest was empty and its only value was historical. "Why would someone steal an empty chest?"

"I think you mean, why would your friend steal it?"

"Exactly." Sean pored over the lines again. "It says they don't have any leads."

"So, whatever trouble he's in, it isn't with the police."

Sean couldn't connect the dots. He stood up and paced over to the fireplace and stopped there, staring into the flames with his hands on his hips. "The only thing I can figure is he was either supposed to steal it from someone, or a dangerous person that wanted to buy it figured out where he was. Either way, I'm afraid if he pissed off the wrong people. Jack may already be dead."

"All over an empty chest."

"You know as well as anyone there are fanatical collectors around the world. Some of them would do just about anything to bolster their personal galleries."

She hummed her agreement.

"There must be more to it," Sean decided. He turned and faced her. "If Jack was sending me a message about Ottoman Turkish, he must have found something written in that language inside the chest."

"But this says the chest was empty."

"Maybe it was. But what if there was a secret message written in it somewhere?"

"Like in invisible ink?"

"Sure. Maybe. Or a code. It could be anything. Whatever it is, Jack gave us that address so we could find it and figure it out. I'm sure of that, at least."

"But if that was his apartment, whoever was after him would have torn it apart to find whatever it was he was hiding."

"True," Sean considered. He raised his right hand to his face and rubbed the stubble on his chin. "Which means the apartment number he gave us was unknown to whoever was after him."

"That's a possibility. But even if that were the case, you'd need a key to get in there."

Sean's lips creased into a mischievous, suggestive grin.

She looked at him for a few breaths, trying to understand the goofy look on his face. Then it hit her. "Oh, come on. Really?"

"You're the best thief I know. An apartment lock shouldn't take someone like you more than a few seconds."

Adriana could only shake her head. "You have no shame."

"None."

She rolled her eyes as he stepped closer to her and bent down as if to kiss her again. "You know I love you."

She allowed a muted laugh. "I know." Then she leaned up, traced her lips across his, then slid away, stood up, and walked into the kitchen.

"Call your boss," she said over her shoulder, swinging her hips teasingly as she disappeared out of the room through an archway. "See if we can borrow the plane."

Sean remained bent over for a second before he straightened up, pressing his lips together. He bobbed his head. "He's not my boss," he muttered. "And it's not borrowing if he comes along."

"Yes, he is your boss!" she shouted from the next room.

It was Sean's turn to roll his eyes. "Does she have superhuman hearing or something?" he whispered to himself. He waited for a second to see if she'd heard the question, then let out a relieved sigh.

Sean picked up his phone, glanced at the message from Jack one more time, then looked up Tommy's number in his contacts, and pressed the call button.

8

ISTANBUL

"Do you ever feel weird about carrying guns in countries where they aren't allowed?" Tommy asked.

He, Sean, and Adriana stuffed their bags in the back of a black sedan outside the airport. Sean closed the trunk, then turned to his friend.

"Not really. That would be like all but two countries."

"Good point."

The midmorning sun beat down on the three, warming their skin before they climbed into the car—a rental their driver had arranged at Tommy's request.

"Is that everything?" the young Greek man asked with a smile.

"We travel light, Niki. You know that," Tommy replied cheerfully.

"Just making sure, Mr. Schultz."

Tommy shook his head at the title. "Please. For the hundredth time, Niki, call me Tommy.

"Yes, sir, Mr.... I mean, Tommy."

Sean slapped the young man on the shoulder. "Good to see you again, bud. How have things been on this side of the world?"

"Going well, Mr.... uh, Sean." He caught himself. "IAA Euro Division is doing some amazing things."

"So I've heard. It was you that headed up the recovery of that artifact from Norway, right?"

Niki acknowledged with a humble nod. "Yes, sir. But our teams did most of the work. My part was minimal."

"That's not what I heard," Sean hedged as he held the door open for his wife on the passenger side of the car.

She eased into the back seat while Tommy slid into the front.

"Don't believe everything you hear. I simply oversaw the operation."

"And solved the riddle behind the entire thing. Humility is a good thing, Niki. But don't undervalue yourself. You do good work for this organization. Tommy was smart to bring you on board."

Niki grinned bashfully and gave a curt nod. He turned and climbed into the driver seat while Sean joined his wife in the back.

"Do you three want to go straight to the apartment or get something to eat first?"

"I'm famished," Tommy blurted without hesitation. "Could we grab a bite first?"

Sean felt a tug of anxiety in his gut. He wanted to get to the apartment and figure out what Jack had left there, but he also knew they couldn't work on an empty stomach. On top of that, Jack was long gone by now.

If he wasn't dead, he probably wasn't in Istanbul anymore.

Sean found himself hoping that his friend had somehow escaped whoever was after him, but he felt that was probably a long shot. Based on the urgency in the text message, if Jack hadn't been killed, he'd been taken.

That last thought gave Sean a sliver of hope. If Jack was abducted, he could still be saved. But focusing on that could be a distraction.

"You don't happen to know a good baklava place around here, do you, Niki?" Sean asked, deciding to go all in on the eating idea.

Niki grinned in the rearview mirror. "I like your style, Sean. And I know just the place. It's about twenty minutes from here, probably ten from the apartment complex where we're headed." He shifted his eyes to Adriana. "Adriana, is the temperature okay in the car?"

"Perfect, Niki. Thank you."

The driver shifted the car into gear and merged out onto the street.

Sean watched the city pass by. Its many colorful homes along one side of the street contrasted with much of the rest of the buildings' drab façades. Istanbul had always been a place of wonders to Sean, offering incredible food, music, nightlife, and mystery.

It seemed everywhere he looked he saw something ancient, whether from Ottoman times or beyond, all the way back to the Byzantine era. The city had been a crossroads for most of the world's civilizations since the dawn of time, and it showed.

"What is it that brings you to Istanbul?" Niki asked, striking up friendly conversation as he guided the vehicle through the busy city traffic.

"I received a message from an old friend yesterday," Sean explained. "He said he wanted us to come here to find something he left in an apartment. It sounded urgent. Said he was in trouble."

"Trouble?" Niki laughed. "Seems like you guys find that a lot."

"You're not wrong," Tommy admitted. "Of all the knacks to have, that's a tough one to deal with on a regular basis."

"Finding trouble? Yeah, I would definitely trade it for something easier like... finding the best spots for trout fishing."

"You know they have guides for that," Sean said.

"Always an answer with this one," Tommy complained and jerked his thumb back toward Sean.

Niki just laughed and continued the drive.

They arrived at the café fifteen minutes later. Niki found a spot to park the car in front of the shop just a few cars down from the entrance.

"You're going to love this place," he said as they climbed out of the vehicle and stepped onto the sidewalk. "Great coffee, excellent baklava."

"Yeah, but who has the better baklava?" Sean pressed as his young friend opened the front door to the café. He leaned in so only Niki could hear. "Greece or Turkey?"

The young Greek man pulled back his head and scowled at Sean. "Greece, obviously."

Sean merely grinned as he allowed Adriana to enter the building first, then followed her in with the other two in tow.

They sat in a corner table near the back of the café, as was Sean's custom—always facing the door.

The delicacies they'd purchased did not disappoint. The baklava was so good, sweetened with a drizzle of honey over the top, that Sean thought maybe his young Greek friend might have overplayed his hand with his assessment of which country had the better version.

As expected, the coffee was strong—the way the Turks traditionally liked it.

"So, you say the apartment is near here?" Tommy clarified.

"Yes. Not far. We could walk if you prefer, but I think driving is a better idea. Ten minutes by car."

"Driving is fine," Sean said.

"This friend who was in trouble, did they give you a reason? Or were they able to let you know any details, such as what they left for you in the apartment?"

"Nothing. Don't know who was after him. Don't know what he left."

"The only clue we were able to discover," Adriana jumped in, "was the item that was stolen from last night's auction in the Beşitkaş neighborhood."

"Stolen?"

"You didn't hear about it?"

Niki forked a piece of baklava into his mouth and chewed for a moment before answering with a shrug. "I just got into town a few hours ago from Greece. So, I'm not up on the latest local news. What was taken?"

Adriana continued. "An empty treasure chest that belonged to the great admiral Hayreddin Barbarossa."

"Who?" Niki took his tiny cup of coffee and sipped it.

"You don't know who Hayreddin Barbarossa was?" Tommy

blurted, drawing the attention of a few people around them. He lowered his head and kept talking in a quieter tone. "The famous pirate who turned admiral?"

Niki shook his head.

"He was one of the greatest naval commanders in history," Sean said, seeing that Tommy was about to take this conversation on a way-too-long journey down history lane. "Originally, he and his brother were pirates. They learned to navigate the seas and became expert strategists. Both men of modest upbringings, they had an unusual amount of ambition. Hayreddin believed that he could forge his own kingdoms through hard work, and by making a name for himself on the high seas. And that's exactly what he did. Eventually, the Ottoman emperor asked him to become the grand admiral of the entire Ottoman fleet in their war against the Holy Roman Empire. The man was unbeatable in sea battles."

"Wow. That sounds interesting."

"Yes," Adriana said, cutting Tommy off before he could rejoin the conversation. A move that caused Sean to snort. "It was rumored that he used sorcery or witchcraft to achieve such incredible feats. On more than one occasion, he was outnumbered and outgunned by significant odds, and still managed to obliterate the enemy."

Niki flicked his eyebrows up, looked down at the last piece of baklava on his plate, then stuck the fork into it. "Sounds like he was just a better commander than anyone else."

"There were other rumors, though," Tommy said, finally able to get back in. "The magic was only one of them. Others suggested that he had a powerful weapon, something on board his ship that made him and all his allies invincible."

"A weapon? What kind of weapon?"

"No one knows. They were just rumors, after all."

Sean sipped the strong coffee. He set his cup down and cleared his throat. "Francis Drake was similar for the English Navy. Rumors about him using witchcraft and magic snaked its way through the Spanish ranks like wildfire. He, too, was a great commander, but leadership and skills have limitations that the results of his battles couldn't seem to explain."

Niki chewed on the last piece of his baklava and nodded. "So, what do you think it is?"

"The weapon?" Tommy asked.

"Yeah. Or whatever Sean's friend left here."

"There's no telling if there ever really was a weapon," Sean answered. "And as to what Jack left for me to find in his apartment... no clue. Maybe it was the treasure chest he stole."

"So, he's the one that stole it from the auction house?"

"Probably," Sean humored. "Jack is... well, he's a thief." Sean couldn't think of a better way to say it, so he just called it what it was.

"Oh. You keep interesting company, Sean."

"You're part of that interesting company, Niki," he said with mischief in his tone.

The younger man merely bobbed his head dramatically. "Fair."

The group finished their brunch and returned to the car.

As promised, the drive to Jack's apartment took around ten minutes and could have been less if traffic had cooperated.

When they arrived, the four exited the car, leaving it parked along the curb a half block away. The gray building gleamed in the bright sun.

"Nice place," Sean commented as they ambled down the sidewalk toward the entrance. "Modern."

"Looks like one of the newer buildings in town," Tommy observed.

"Nothing but the best for Jack." There was a hint of derision in Sean's voice.

He opened the front door and let the others in, then checked the street around the building one last time before going in after them.

The lobby was clean, minimalist, with white walls and a gray faux hardwood floor. Black mailboxes fit into the wall to the left, and straight ahead the elevators waited in a little alcove.

Sean checked the apartment numbers on a board outside the elevators, then pressed the up arrow.

The one on the right dinged, and the door opened. "Up we go," Sean said.

Once inside, he pressed the button for the fourth floor, and the doors closed a moment later. They opened again when they reached their destination, and Sean led the way out into the empty corridor.

He peered down the hall in one direction, then the other, then continued toward the apartment number given him by his friend.

He stopped in front of the one with a 457 hanging next to the door. "This is it," he announced. "Honey, you mind opening it for us?"

Adriana rolled her eyes, not at being called honey but at the assumption she could pick any lock. It was a combination of flattering and annoying.

Sean's nonsense notwithstanding, she stepped up to the door and withdrew a tool from her pocket. She knelt down in front of the doorknob and flipped a hinged pin out of the little tool. She then stuck the pin into the lock and left it there while she drew a flat piece of metal out of the tool's other end.

She used the thin, flat piece in conjunction with the tiny rod and pressed it into the keyhole. Adriana manipulated the lock for a few seconds before it clicked. She turned the doorknob, and to Niki's astonishment, the door opened.

A door down the hall to their left also opened. Adriana quickly stood, brushed off her black leggings, and pushed the door open to step inside.

The other three hurried after her, none of them in a mood to deal with questions from curious tenants.

Tommy closed the door silently behind him and moved deeper into the unfurnished apartment.

Sean immediately saw the leather book sitting on the counter. The others saw it, too, and gathered around, ignoring the bare room that surrounded them.

Sean gently lifted the book and inspected the cover. "Is it me, or is that a trident on the cover of this thing?"

The others gathered around and looked down at the book.

"That's what it looks like to me," Tommy said.

"Yes, definitely,' Adriana commented.

Sean frowned as he carefully turned the book over and looked at the back. There were no inscriptions on that side, so he turned it back over again and peeled open the cover—carefully using his fingernails so as not to damage the centuries old pages.

He noted the signature inside, then turned to the first page. "That must be the message Jack was talking about. It's written in Ottoman Turkish."

Tommy nodded. "Yeah. Definitely the old version."

"You wouldn't happen to have something that can translate that, do you?"

"I could do an online search, but I'm not sure if those have this version of the language."

"Call the kids?" Adriana asked.

"You read my mind," Tommy said. He took a picture of the words on the page, then sent a text message to Alex and Tara back in the IAA lab in Atlanta. Then he tapped on one of the numbers and hit the Call button.

Within two rings, Alex answered. "Hey, boss. Just saw your message."

"That was quick," Tommy noted.

"Technology is a wonderful thing. Well, until it isn't. What's up?"

"That message I sent you is in old Ottoman Turkish. I was wondering if you could feed it to the computer for me and see what it spits out."

"They don't have a translator on one of the search engines?"

Tommy chuffed. "Maybe. But I would prefer the accuracy of our machines in this instance."

"I got ya. One second. Tara, Tommy wants us to translate that text message for him. You mind running it through the system?"

"Already on it," she said, her voice distant from somewhere else in the lab.

"Should only take a minute. So, you guys went to Istanbul, huh? How's the weather there right now?"

"Warm. Pretty sure it's always warm here. Every time I've been here it's that way. I guess I've never come in January, so maybe then it's colder."

"So, you guys are there doing what again?"

Tommy looked around at the others standing around him. "Oh, you know, doing a little investigating. Someone stole a chest from an auction house last night. The chest was empty. But apparently, it's worth some money. It belonged to Hayreddin Barbarossa."

"The famous pirate?"

Tommy snorted a laugh. "Yeah. I guess most people have heard of him."

He glanced over at Niki, who offered a questioning shrug as if to say, "What?"

"Got it," Tara said in the background. "Tell Tommy I'm sending him the results now."

"She said she—"

"I heard her," Tommy said in a humored tone. "Thanks, you two. I really appreciate it."

"No problem. Let us know if you need anything else while you're over there."

"Will do. And I'm sure that'll happen."

He ended the call and checked his text messages. Within two seconds, the phone vibrated, and he had a new text from Tara.

"Never ceases to amaze me how fast those two are," Sean observed.

"What does it say?" Sean pressed, staying on task.

"Right." Tommy held up his screen and read the message out loud to everyone. "The key to ultimate power rests with the great one. I alone can guide you."

For several seconds, everyone in the room stood still, and remained totally silent except for the breath escaping their lungs.

"What does it mean?" Niki asked first.

"Who would be the great one?" Adriana followed up.

"We're putting the cart ahead of the horse here," Sean answered them both. "We came here expecting to find an empty treasure chest and instead found this journal." He flipped through the rest of the pages but found no other entries. "So, where is this chest?"

"Good question," Tommy asserted. "I would guess whoever was after Jack must have taken it when they—" He stopped talking abruptly, not wanting to scratch any wounds.

"It's fine, Schultzie. We weren't that close. But your point is correct. Whoever Jack was afraid of must have the chest."

"But is there anything of value to it?" Adriana wondered.

"There's no way for us to know. If Jack felt like the book was enough, then the chest must be what contained it. Perhaps it was hidden inside it somehow."

"I've seen such things," she affirmed. "Drawers with false bottoms, things of that nature. It's possible Barbarossa had one last trick up his sleeve before he died."

"Right," Tommy half agreed, "except that the lines in this book say the key to power rests with the great one. So, who is this great one if not Barbarossa?"

Sean flipped the pages back to the beginning and inspected the name written in a flourished script. "This book didn't belong to Barbarossa," Sean realized.

"Then, who did it belong to?" Niki asked.

Sean met his questioning gaze. "It belonged to his scribe."

9

"Scribe?" Niki asked.

Sean nodded slowly, then lowered his eyes to the page and pointed at the name.

"This isn't Hayreddin Barbarossa. It's another name, but I can't read it clearly."

Tommy held his phone in his hand, already conducting the search. He gambled that Tara and Alex back in Atlanta weren't necessary on this one. While the two twentysomethings were an invaluable team to have on board with IAA, there were some tasks Tommy and Sean could handle on their own.

"This says Sinan Reis wrote Barbarossa's memoirs," Tommy announced.

Sean huffed. "I take it this book is not the memoirs."

"It would appear not," Tommy said, taking the journal from his friend's hands. He studied the cover carefully, then turned the pages within, looking intently at each one as if there might be a hidden message contained on the paper.

"What are you looking for?" Niki asked.

"Invisible ink," Adriana answered first. "Pretty common way to hide secret or encoded messages."

"Was that popular during the Ottoman period?"

"It's always been popular," Tommy answered without looking up from the book. "But I don't think there's any of that going on here. But we can find out."

He moved toward the stove, and as he did so Niki stepped out of his way to clear a path.

Tommy stopped and turned on the front-left stove burner and waited until the dark ceramic surface burned with a red circle.

He held the paper close to the heat source, cautious not to get too near that it might ignite.

The other thing about this journal was that with the pages being so old and brittle, any drastic change in temperature could damage them. Tommy would have preferred to have gloves for a task such as this, but there was no time. And he hadn't brought any with him.

After a few seconds, he tried another page, then another, until he'd seen enough.

"I don't think there was any other clue left in this journal," he stated.

"Do we really need it?" Sean asked. "It's pretty clear at the beginning when it talks about the great one."

"Because it's talking about Barbarossa?" Niki asked.

"Exactly. This book belonged to Sinan Reis. He sailed under Barbarossa. The two were good friends, probably the only people the other trusted in this world."

"It is a tough life being a pirate," Adriana said. "Always watching your back, unable to trust anyone. And perpetually on the run."

Sean turned to her with both eyebrows raised. "You just described our lives since we met."

"Indeed."

"You almost make it sound like you want to slow down?"

"Speak for yourself." She offered a wry grin with the dry comment.

He loved it when she talked to him like that.

"At any rate," Tommy cut off the moment, "I agree. This suggests that there is a key resting with Barbarossa. I guess that means his tomb?"

"Would make sense," Sean said. "But what about the other part, the piece where it says that only he can guide us? He being Reis."

"I'm not sure," Tommy said. "Look, you're just as good at these things as me. Better sometimes."

"That's why we make such a good team, Schultzie. Why don't we focus on what we know? If we think that this supposed key is with Barbarossa, then the first thing we need to do is find his tomb."

Adriana faced Niki. "You wouldn't happen to know where that is, would you?"

"I didn't even know who Barbarossa was before today. But we can find it. That's what the internet is for." He took a phone out of his pocket and began searching.

The others waited until Niki found what he was looking for. "It will take us about twenty minutes to get there from here. Simple enough."

Sean blurted a laugh. "Twenty minutes? Is everything in this town twenty minutes? It's a geographical oddity."

"Good one," Tommy said, catching the film reference.

Niki obviously didn't get it, and Adriana seemed equally uncertain.

"Forget it," Sean said. "But your next assignment when we get done with all this is to watch *Oh, Brother, Where Art Thou*."

"Is that a movie?"

Sean sighed. "Yes, Niki. It's a movie. What do you do for fun, anyway?"

The younger man shrugged. "I read a lot."

"Give him a break, Sean. He's like fifteen years younger than us."

"Or twenty," Sean corrected.

"Lead the way, Niki," Adriana ordered, trying to get the group back on track. "We're wasting daylight."

Tommy held out the journal toward Sean. "You want to hold this?"

"Sure." Sean accepted the book and tucked it into the satchel he'd brought along.

Adriana walked back to the door and opened it, holding it long enough for Niki to exit. Then she followed with the two other men in tow.

A few minutes later, they were back down on the sidewalk, heading to their car.

Sean surveyed their surroundings as they reached the sedan. Whenever he was on a job like this, he felt like he was being watched. Without exception, that pervasive feeling crowded his thoughts every single time.

It didn't matter how or why.

For the most part, those kinds of things didn't enter his mind when he was back home in Atlanta or Chattanooga, or when he was on vacation. And for that he was grateful.

He finished scanning the area and decided there was nothing to worry about. Not that that kept him from letting concern flitter through his mind. It was a busy street in a huge international city. There could be threats all around disguised as ordinary people, and Sean would have a tough time telling one from another. And he was an expert at that sort of thing.

Years in the field with the Axis agency had honed his skills to a level most would never know. But even Sean Wyatt was human.

He opened the door and held it for Adriana, allowing her to climb in first before he stepped around to the other side. After one last look around, Sean got in the back seat, and Niki pulled the sedan away from the curb.

Boris watched the four people leave the apartment complex from inside the lobby.

He'd been sitting in Jack's apartment for hours, and had finally had a chance to get a bite to eat and some coffee while he waited.

The stout Russian hadn't known what he was waiting for, or

rather whom. He knew better than to question his commander, but if they'd already taken the chest and found nothing accompanying it, why station anyone here?

Fortunately, Konstantin had given his captain the explanation, telling him that Jack might have friends who could show up looking for him. And possibly a buyer. Bringing a new player into the mix could also bring new information regarding the whereabouts of the chest's contents.

Boris still wasn't sold that there really had been anything in the box, but this was their assignment, and he would do his duty until instructed otherwise.

So, he sat in the apartment, nibbling on his breakfast pastries and sipping his coffee until he heard a door in the hallway open and close.

He'd stood and walked over to the entryway of Jack's apartment, and watched through the peep hole, keeping an eye on the opposite door.

Boris had been there all night, and not once had anyone come or gone. For a second, he considered returning to the counter to finish his food, assuming whoever lived across from Jack simply worked odd hours and had returned from their shift.

But something told him to wait, and so he did, standing there at the door with his eye pressed against the tiny, circular window.

Five minutes passed. Six. Seven. He was about to give up and go back to eating when he heard the sound of the door opening. Then it had swung wide, and a woman with blackish-brown hair appeared in the doorway. She held it open for a young man with tousled black hair—probably in his early or mid-twenties. Then she stepped out, followed by two other men Boris figured were in their late thirties. The blond one looked athletic and lean, strong, but not as strong as the muscular brown-haired one that walked behind him.

Boris frowned as he watched them leave his limited field of view. He waited until he heard the elevator signal its arrival, then hurried back to the kitchen island, grabbed his keys, and rushed to the door.

Now he stood in the lobby after having taken the stairs to reach street level. When their car drove off from its parking spot, he barreled out the door, nearly running over a young woman with two bags of groceries in her hands, and charged to the black Mercedes four-door he'd kept out in front of the building.

He started the car and shifted into gear quickly, merging into traffic almost without looking. He almost cut off another vehicle, whose driver honked angrily at him.

Boris didn't care.

He kept the car in view, but just barely. There were so many vehicles on the street, it was going to be a task just to keep them in sight.

As he sped around a series of other cars and delivery trucks, a few motorcycles and mopeds, he took out his phone and found the only number he'd needed for the last few weeks, then pressed the green Call button.

After three rings, Konstantin answered. "Go ahead, Captain."

"I left the apartment. I'm pursuing four people who went into the unit across from Jack's."

"Why would you do that, Captain? Your orders were to stay there in case someone came around."

"Yes, sir. I'm aware. But the four people who went into the other apartment aroused my suspicion."

"And why is that?"

"All night, no one came or went from that unit. I thought maybe it was empty."

"Perhaps they work odd hours," Konstantin offered.

"I thought of that, sir. But there is something you should know about these four."

"And what is that?"

"One of them carried a satchel."

"So?"

"The satchel had the letters IAA on it."

Silence followed the statement for several seconds. Boris swerved around a white compact car, then back into the right-hand lane. He'd closed the gap significantly between himself and the car.

"If the IAA is involved, then Jack must have left something in that other apartment. Clever." He paused. "You're in pursuit now?"

"Yes, sir."

"Good. Set your phone to share location. We'll join you shortly."

10

BEŞIKTAŞ

"This is going to prove problematic," Sean said as he stared out across the square.

The sprawling area stretched a few hundred yards from the street all the way to the water's edge. People walked aimlessly along the stone tiles covering the entire space. High spires towered from the four corners of a mosque behind the street. A ten-foot wall wrapped around the religious sanctuary, a spiritual and literal barrier from the hustle and bustle going on in the world outside.

"Yeah," Tommy agreed. "Lot of people here."

"Too many eyeballs," Adriana added.

"I'm sorry," Niki said. "Too many eyeballs for what? And what is going to prove problematic?"

Sean smirked at the younger man. "Breaking into the tomb," he replied.

"Oh." For a second, the Greek seemed to accept the answer. Until he realized what Sean said. "Wait. Break into the tomb?"

"Only way to find whatever Reis left there. The clue says it rests with the great one, so there must be something in that mausoleum the clue refers to as the key."

"Unless someone already found it," Tommy offered.

Sean's head turned back and forth. "Seriously, you need to work on your positivity, man."

"I'm just being real." Tommy threw up his hands as if he couldn't help himself.

"There doesn't appear to be any security guarding the place," Adriana noticed. "Not that there usually is in a cemetery."

The mausoleum containing the remains of Hayreddin Barbarossa stood within a three-foot-high wall topped with an iron fence. Beyond the barrier, trees grew next to the domed two-story structure. Sean had read just a little about the place, but he'd gleaned several details about it.

The tomb had been designed and built by the Ottoman architect Mimar Sinan in 1541. Most of the original features were still intact.

The square, located near this ferry port of Beşitkaş district on the European side of Istanbul, overlooked the very spot where Barbarossa's fleet had assembled so many centuries ago.

In years past, the Ottoman Navy would visit the mausoleum and conduct ceremonies and present offerings before expeditions. The Turkish Navy, Sean learned, still kept up that tradition to this day.

He also learned the tomb was open to the public only on special occasions, such as July 1 for the Cabotage Festival, and on April 4 for Memorial Day of Naval Martyrs.

The windows near the top were screened with an Ottoman-style grid to let in natural sunlight. A portico stretched out from the entrance, propped up by stone columns. Several other graves filled the lawn on the sides and in front of the tomb, as well as on either side of the walkway leading to the only door in and out.

The graves were different than in most places in the States, with stone boxes resting above the ground and grasses and small plants growing out of them.

Multiple ship cannons dotted the square, propped up in various locations, seemingly all pointing at the sea. Sean wondered if the ancient guns were relics from Barbarossa's ships, and how many times those cannons had been fired throughout the pirate admiral's life.

Across the plaza from the tomb stood a thirty-foot-high monument. The sharp angles of the white stone pointed forward toward three bronze statues standing on a platform at the head.

Two pirates stood at the ready behind their leader, a man in a bulging corsair hat, complete with a feather.

"So that's what he looked like," Tommy said, noting the monument at the same time as Sean. "Let's have a look."

Sean passed over the throng as he always did, assessing as many faces as he could while strolling across the square.

No one seemed to pay any attention to them. People were busy playing with their children, or laughing with friends. Some were sitting against the wall reading quietly in the warm sunshine.

The group stopped at the base of the monument and noted the name on the bronze plaque attached to the side. Sean stood next to a black stone plinth just in front of the monument, staring up at the figures who likewise stared back, out toward the sea. The three figures looked ready to answer the call to arms, to defend their beloved nation at all costs.

Two Turkish flags flew on poles on either side of the monument, flapping in the breeze. The sounds of the fabric snapping with each ripple mingled with the chatter and laughter of the people in the plaza.

Sean turned back toward the tomb and inclined his chin. "We'll have to come back tonight, I guess," he said.

"Agreed," Adriana chimed. "No way I'm doing this in the middle of the day."

"There could be people here this evening, too," Niki cautioned.

"Fewer of them, though," Tommy said. "We'll come back late, when most people are in bed."

"Might seem suspicious if we're the only ones here."

Tommy grinned at him. "'I'm glad you're being wary, Niki. Recklessness causes disasters."

"I just don't want to go to prison. Especially a Turkish prison."

"Yeah, none of us do, kid. And I've used up all my get-out-of-jail-free cards with Emily."

"You have a finite number of those?" Tommy asked with a glint in his eye.

"Let's just say I don't want to push my luck too far."

"The area is pretty open," Adriana pointed out. "And the tomb is close to where we parked the car. So that's an advantage in case we need to hurry."

"I'd suggest we do that anyway."

Sean indicated the mausoleum with a nod. "Let's mosey on over there and take a look around. See what we're dealing with."

He led the way across the square, observing children playing with a soccer ball, running around in a circle. When he arrived at the wall that wrapped around the tomb, he stopped and looked inside, then back behind them, as if concerned they might have been followed on the crossing.

He didn't detect anything or notice anyone suspicious, but he'd been wrong before. Not often. But it did happen on occasion. Especially when there were so many faces to search.

"What do you see?" Sean asked his wife, returning his attention to inside the cemetery confines.

He continued staring out into the plaza while she assessed the door to the tomb. "Not much," she said, indicating the mausoleum's wooden door with a nod. "Just a simple lock. Shouldn't take me long to pick that one."

"How long?" Tommy pressed.

"Two, three minutes at the most. One minute if I'm lucky."

"That fast, huh?"

She looked over at Tommy with a scathing glare. "You've seen my skills time and time again, and still you doubt me." She cracked a smile at the end.

"You know I'm messing with you."

"I know."

"Once we're inside," Sean interrupted, "we'll have to close the door behind us. Don't want anyone coming by thinking there's someone in there. And we'll have to work in the dark."

"I have night-vision goggles," Adriana confessed.

The three men looked at her with surprise written all over their faces.

"What?" She raised her hands. "You guys didn't bring any?"

Sean shrugged. "I was good to remember to bring clean underwear." He looked over his shoulder at Tommy. "I'm sure he's got plenty of rope if you need it."

"Ha-ha," Tommy countered. "Very funny. That's the last time I save your life with my rope you always make fun of. If it weren't for my rope, your carcass would be in a pile of mambas right now."

"Mambas?" Niki asked after having been silent for three minutes.

"I'll tell you about it later," Sean said. "If you're interested in having nightmares for the rest of your life."

Niki shook his head. "No. I'm not interested in that at all."

"Don't take everything so literally, kid. You'll drive yourself crazy."

Sean turned around and looked through the iron fence into the tiny cemetery. "So, we come back around midnight, break into the tomb, find the key, and then figure out what to do next."

"I've been thinking about that," Tommy said. "It sounds simple enough, which we all know won't be the case, but what about the last part of the riddle—the part where it says I alone can guide you? I know we mentioned leaving it be until we figure out where or what this key is, but the two go hand in hand."

"If it's meant to be literal," Adriana suggested, "then we should assume Reis is the only one who can guide us. Since he's dead, perhaps we're meant to search his tomb next."

"And I thought you said not to take everything so literally," Niki joked. Then his grin washed away as he realized they were talking about not just breaking into one tomb, but two. "So, we're grave robbers now?"

"We're preserving history," Tommy rationalized. "Not doing it for profit."

"It's a sound theory," Sean said, pulling the conversation back.

"For now, we need to focus on this tomb and finding the key of Barbarossa. I guess we're coming back this evening." Sean peered across the square, then mumbled under his breath, "I just hope that this plaza clears out after dark."

He took a step away from the fence. "Come on. We need to recon the rest of the area. We'll split up and meet back at the car. Take note of every possible way out of the plaza, and any place where someone could lay an ambush."

Tommy scowled. "That could be anywhere out here, Sean. The whole place is wide open. And who else knows we're here?"

"I don't know. But I'd rather be ready. Where would the best point be to catch us with our guard down?"

"The getaway car," Niki answered.

"Right," Sean agreed. "So, we need to have multiple vehicles in case our primary gets cut off."

"Nowhere to go over there," Adriana said. "Just the waterfront." She rolled her head to the side with a shrug. "Unless you want to try a boat getaway."

Sean's right eyebrow raised, and she read his mind.

"Fine," she said. "I'll see about getting a charter boat."

"Something fast," Sean added.

She leaned close and kissed him on the cheek. "It's cute you think I need to be told that." She stepped away and started toward the far corner of the square to her right. "I'll check this direction and loop around."

Niki decided to go with her, while Tommy stuck with Sean.

"You did sort of deserve that one," Tommy said.

Sean couldn't help himself butt watch as she sauntered away from him. That walk had done him in a million times. And it was working now, too.

He simply nodded his head. "Yep. Come on, Schultzie. Let's check the other direction.

11

Boris wandered into the plaza with a white bag he'd picked up at a bakery earlier that morning while watching Jack's apartment. Inside were a couple of pastries to sate his hunger, but now the sack doubled as a prop—something an ordinary citizen might carry to the square to have their morning breakfast or an early lunch.

As he walked, the Russian kept his eyes casually locked on the four visitors he'd followed from the apartment, only deterring his focus now and then to make sure they didn't think they were being watched.

He noted the blond one looking around several times, perpetually checking to find the wolf amid the flock of sheep.

Boris found an empty bench midway across the plaza against the wall that lined that portion of the square.

He sat down and fished out one of the breads he'd bought. Noting the birds flocking around atop the wall and skittering along the ground, he decided it was the perfect cover.

He tore a crumb off the bread and tossed it onto the ground eight feet away, then watched as the birds descended onto the offering. Boris watched the creatures consume the bread, tearing it into smaller and smaller pieces as they vied for the meal—unaware there was plenty more where that came from.

Boris looked up from his new pets and watched his targets cross the square and walk over to the mausoleum, stopping at the wall just outside it.

He wished he could hear them talking, but from his vantage point he gleaned enough information. It was hard to miss how much attention they were giving to the tomb of Hayreddin Barbarossa.

"What is so interesting about the tomb?" Boris asked himself.

The only fact he had was that the chest stolen from the auction house had belonged to the famed admiral, but without knowing what was inside it, he could only go by what his eyes and ears told him.

The blond man in the group looked over in his general direction, but Boris was ready with another collection of crumbs he'd separated into his palm. He tossed them out to the birds as the blond American's gaze swept past him.

After a few minutes, the group dispersed, splitting up into groups of two. The female and the younger of the three males walked toward the corner to Boris's left, while the other two men went in the opposite direction.

He wondered why they were dividing in such a way but decided to sit and wait to find out. Boris didn't have to linger long. When the groups of two reached the corners of the plaza, they circled around, inspecting the area—though they tried to pass as casual tourists having a look around.

Boris knew immediately what they were doing. He'd have done the same were he in their position.

They were scouting the scene, making sure they weren't missing anything—more than likely, so they could plan their getaway.

Boris had already sized up the area and tentatively planned where Konstantin might choose to position men to prevent their quarry's escape.

The first spot was obvious, over by where the majority of cars parked along the street between the square and the mosque.

After that, there were only two legitimate points of escape—on an adjacent street and a parallel one. The choppy sea beyond the boundary of the plaza presented no threat in the Russian's mind.

He continued offering crumbs to the birds even as the female and her partner skirted by in front of him.

They said nothing as they passed and offered him little regard—as would be expected of a random person feeding birds in the park.

Boris maintained his ruse until the two reached a corner to his right. Then he took out his phone and made a call.

Konstantin answered on the first ring.

"Tell me some good news, my friend."

Boris grinned, flashing his crooked teeth. "Whatever they found led them to Barbarossa's tomb in the Beşitkaş neighborhood."

"The same place where the auction house is located?"

"Correct. It's not far from here. The tomb is on the waterfront. Several people here right now just hanging about."

"What are the marks doing?" Konstantin asked.

"Looks like they're planning something. My guess is their escape."

"Escape from what? Were you spotted?"

"No, sir. Not a chance. I think they're just being exceedingly cautious, covering all their bases."

"Yes," Konstantin agreed. "That's how these types operate. I've heard of the International Archaeological Agency, but after a little research, it seems these people may be more trouble than we first suspected."

"Sir?"

"They specialize in discovering and recovering artifacts. Their track record is splattered with blood, though. Whoever their friends are, they are high up."

"American government?" Boris guessed.

"Probably. I've seen pictures of their founder and lead agent with the current and former president. So, they're connected. We'll need to proceed with caution with this group."

"There are three ways out of the plaza," Boris said, shifting the focus of the conversation. "Not including the sea."

"Include the water."

"Sir?"

"Rule nothing out. If they're making plans for an escape, they'll consider we could block the streets. Get one of our men to procure a boat. Just in case."

"Yes, sir."

"Any idea what they're looking for?" Konstantin ventured.

Boris peered across the square as the four came together again. "No, not yet. Just that they're very interested in the tomb. Whatever they're after, it's in there with Barbarossa."

"Hmm." Konstantin sounded perplexed. "If we knew what they were trying to find, we could beat them to it. But we don't. So, we wait. The rest of our team will be there shortly."

"I don't think they'll try anything during daylight hours," Boris offered. "Too many people loitering around here. If they're going to try to break into the tomb, it will be tonight."

"Very well. We'll be ready when they come back. Good work, Boris. Stay there until we arrive."

12

"Why are there so many people still here?" Sean asked from the passenger side of the sedan.

The waxing moon hung over the square in a cloudless sky, rivaled only by a star twinkling brightly nearby.

Fewer people occupied the square than what Sean had observed earlier in the day—far fewer, in fact. But there were still a few dozen hanging out in the plaza.

The population, however, had changed.

Instead of families with young children milling about or playing with soccer balls on the stone tiles, teenagers sat around on the ground smoking cigarettes and from the smell of it, a few other things. No elderly people remained in the area either, replaced by homeless vagrants who occupied the benches or corners where the encircling wall met the ground.

"It's not as many as before," Tommy said with a glass-half-full attitude. "And from the looks of most of these folks, I don't think they're really going to care if we simply walk straight into the tomb."

"If only," Adriana said.

Sean peered through the windshield toward the waterfront. He'd already made certain Niki was in position on the boat they'd procured, but double-checking never hurt.

"Well, it's not going to get any better," Sean finally realized. "We could wait here until two in the morning, and these people would still be here."

He pulled on the door latch and opened the car door, setting his boot down on the pavement.

No cars drove by behind them, and only two others filled parking spots along the quiet street.

Tommy and Adriana joined him and quietly closed the doors to the sedan. Then they walked around behind the vehicle and opened the trunk. Sean slung a lightweight black rucksack over his shoulders. Adriana looped her messenger bag-style daypack through her right arm and pulled it around so the pack part was on the center of her chest. Tommy slipped on a pack similar to Sean's.

"Should we take the guns on this one?" Tommy asked, staring down at three black cases in the trunk.

"Don't we always?" Sean asked, looking back at the plaza over his shoulder.

"Good point."

Sean already had a shoulder holster on under his button-up shirt, and stuffed a Springfield XD .40 into the leather sheath.

Adriana slid her compact 9mm into a hip holster concealed beneath her black leggings and matching leather jacket.

Tommy tucked his weapon into his shoulder holster, then buttoned up the plaid shirt over a white T-shirt.

"How are you going to draw that thing if you button up all those buttons?" Sean asked.

"Right. Sorry. Not sure why I did that. Autopilot."

"Been a minute since you've done one of these, huh, buddy."

Tommy sighed. "Yeah. Too much paperwork behind a desk over the last six months."

"You mean the last year."

"Ugh. Yeah. It *has* been a year. Wow, how time flies when you're requesting permits and filling out government forms."

Sean smirked at his friend as Tommy unbuttoned his shirt. "All good, Schultzie. Let's go break into a tomb."

Tommy winced at the statement. Most of what he did with the IAA was on the up-and-up, ethical, and certainly not of a criminal nature.

But there were times such as this, when securing a piece of history required a touch of criminality. The irony didn't skip by Tommy.

"Let's just get in, find the key, and get out before anyone notices."

The smell of burning cannabis littered the air and reached their nostrils. Sean chuckled.

"Based on the smell of that weed, I don't think any of these people are going to care what we do. So long as we keep it quiet."

"Considering how highly illegal that is here," Adriana noted, eyeing a particularly large group of youths near the Barbarossa monument, "I'm surprised they're just out here in the open doing it. The Turkish government doesn't take that offense lightly."

"Let's just hope they don't attract police attention," Tommy added, then closed the trunk.

The three left the sedan and entered the plaza, walking straight toward the entrance to the tiny cemetery that housed the mausoleum.

Despite it being night, things were far from dark. Multiple streetlights illuminated the corners of the square and cast their glow across the space. While not as brightly lit as daytime, the night offered only sparse relief from curious eyes.

Sean swept his gaze across the plaza, double-checking the few cars that occupied parking spots near their ride. So far, he hadn't seen anything unusual. But that could change in a heartbeat.

The three arrived at the gate to the cemetery, where Sean waited as the other two passed through. He raised one hand over his head as if to stretch. It was a signal to Niki to let the young Greek know they were going in. Then Sean passed his gaze over the groups of people in the square. None seemed to even realize he and his team were there.

A few chatted—about what he had no idea, but from their tones it sounded like something philosophical.

The more engaged they were, the less chance they'd notice anyone breaking into the mausoleum.

As Sean entered the cemetery, another consideration popped into his mind. The tomb and the surrounding graves were well maintained and free of graffiti or other vandalism.

He found it surprising that young people so willing to disobey one strict law were so unwilling to take another step in the direction of unlawful expression.

Then again, maybe they simply revered Barbarossa, as it seemed everyone else in this city did.

Adriana led the way along the path between several graves, then veered right toward the tomb's entrance.

Tommy followed close behind with Sean bringing up the rear. Both men's heads swiveled back and forth as they watched for danger on all fronts, but so far it seemed no one had even seen them.

Adriana stopped at the wooden door and reached into her pack. She produced a lockpicking tool and set to work.

Sean and Tommy took a knee on either side of her, both facing away from the mausoleum in case anyone decided to see what they were up to. As of yet, no teenagers or cops interrupted them.

Just short of a minute, a click escaped the lock, followed by "Done!" from Adriana.

The two men looked back at her as she inspected the door seals to make certain there were no alarms attached. She leaned in close, carefully eyeing every inch of the frame.

"Doesn't look like they have any sort of alarm system," she announced in a whisper.

"Let's hope not," Sean said as he leaned his shoulder into the door. The hinges only protested with a slight creak, then the door swung open.

The smell of old incense and dust filled the room. Moonlight streamed through one of the upper windows in eerie beams that settled on the wall to the left.

The three interlopers hurried inside and closed the door behind them, locking it in place in case anyone else decided to have a look.

"At least I don't need the goggles," Adriana said, noting the moonlight pouring into the mausoleum.

"No, but a little extra light wouldn't hurt," Sean said.

The three stood at the foot of a sarcophagus draped in fabric. Even in the dimly lit tomb, they easily saw the markings on the coffin's covering.

"The war flag of Barbarossa," Tommy realized. "The double sword. The Seal of Solomon, plus a Christian and an Islamic symbol."

"Weird to see the Star of David on a pirate admiral's war flag," Sean quipped.

"That's not what they called it back then," Tommy corrected.

"I know. Seal of Solomon. I still think it's weird in current context."

"Are you two going to help me find this key, or are you just going to let the woman do all the work?" Adriana asked. She'd already walked to the other end of the sarcophagus and was looking around the edges of it for any clue as to where the supposed key might be.

Sean crouched low and lifted the flag to get a better view underneath. "Hey, guys? I think I found something."

"What is it?" Tommy pressed.

"A symbol, carved into the underside of the sarcophagus. It looks like a horse."

"A horse?"

Adriana knelt down at the head of the coffin and ran her finger along the stone until she felt an anomaly. She lifted the flag and spied a second symbol. "I have a trident here."

"A trident," Sean muttered, noting the correlation between the strange journal of Sinan Reis and this location.

Tommy bent down and found a third emblem. "I have a strange-looking fish with huge scales over here. It kind of looks like a button."

"I was thinking the same thing," Sean agreed.

"But a button for what?" Adriana asked.

"I don't know, but—"

"Don't say it."

"There's only one way to find out."

Sean pushed in against the horse emblem with his thumb. The object sank into the stone with a click.

"What was that?" Tommy asked, concern filling his voice.

"I pressed it." He looked to Adriana. "Do yours and see what happens?"

She applied pressure to the symbol and felt it budge, sliding into the stone with a loud click.

"Last one," Sean said to Tommy.

"Are you sure that's a—" Tommy protested.

"Just do it. We don't have all night here. Besides, Niki is still hanging out in the harbor."

"Fine, but if a bunch of poisoned arrows shoot out from this thing, I'm going to be really mad at you."

Sean rolled his eyes as his friend hesitantly pressed the symbol. Nothing happened.

Sean noticed Adriana's eyes fixed on one of the windows near the door. He followed her concerned gaze and immediately saw the problem.

A few flashlights wobbled back and forth, drawing closer to the mausoleum.

"Are you pressing it?" Sean asked his friend, trying not to sound hurried.

"Yeah, I got it. One sec."

Sean pinched his lips together, frustration seeping from his pores. One second felt like an hour. "Any time, Schultzie," he insisted.

"I'm trying, but it feels stuck."

Sean glanced back toward the window. The flashlights drew ever nearer, bouncing up and down, left to right, carried by dark-shadowed hands.

The lights did nothing to illuminate the faces of the people who held them, but Sean's imagination filled in those gaps. He figured, at first, that somehow the local cops had either been alerted or had seen him and the others enter the cemetery.

Even as careful as Sean had been, and always was, he couldn't cover every square inch of the area outside, no matter how hard he tried. There were trees, cannons, the monument, and other places where a person could hide.

There was something about the lights, however, that caused Sean to think whoever approached weren't with the police.

The bright bulbs were tiny—phone lights. Cops would more likely have used actual flashlights, which meant the intruders were probably teenagers from the plaza, or had just arrived at a really inconvenient time to pull a prank.

Either way, Sean preferred not to be caught by anyone in the tomb of a revered national hero.

Adriana shifted around the head of the sarcophagus to where Tommy knelt, pushing hard on the symbol.

"See? It's stuck."

"Shh," Adriana cautioned. Then she indicated toward the window to the right of the door.

The whites of Tommy's eyes swelled in the moonlight. He immediately returned his focus to the emblem and pressed harder. Still, the thing didn't budge.

"Let me," Adriana whispered.

"Fine," Tommy hissed. "But I'm telling you, that thing is not going to move."

She produced a knife from her left hip and worked the tip into a thin seam surrounding the stone button. She wiggled the blade, and then drew it back before pressing her thumb against the emblem.

It sank into the sarcophagus wall, and a split second later, a click echoed from beneath it.

"You were saying?" Adriana jabbed.

Sean scooted around to the head of the sarcophagus and looked down at the bottom, noting the seam between it and the floor.

"That click," he said, "what do you think that was?"

"It sounded like it came from beneath the sarcophagus," Adriana answered.

Sean agreed silently with a nod. His initial instinct had been to pry open the lid, but the sound had come from within the floor, as if an ancient lock had been unclasped. He looked around to the front of the tomb and noted the distance between the front of the stone coffin and the door. There was more space than where he now sat with his legs bent and his back against the wall.

Then the idea bloomed in his mind.

"Hold on," he said. "I'm going to try something."

"Uh, buddy?" Tommy wondered.

Sean pressed his shoulder blades against the wall and pushed his boots into the sarcophagus. He grimaced as the muscles in his legs strained, but he felt the heavy container shift slightly toward the entrance.

"It moved," Tommy realized.

"Yeah," Sean grunted. "And it would move a lot faster if you got back here and helped."

"Right."

Tommy slid next to his friend while Sean narrowed the gap between his feet to accommodate.

The two then leaned into the wall and pushed on the sarcophagus. The heavy stone box shifted forward until the men's legs were fully extended.

Sean rolled forward and looked at the floor; a square hole now occupied the spot where the sarcophagus had been a moment before.

He looked up at Tommy then Adriana. "It's a staircase," he whispered, then checked the entrance again.

The flashlights were gone, but the corona of their glow remained. Whoever was out there was at the door, and would likely soon be inside.

"We don't have a choice," Adriana said, taking her phone from a pocket. She tapped the screen so its dull light shone into the cavity in the floor. "Only one way out now."

She descended into the darkness below, leaving Tommy and Sean waiting.

"After you," Sean insisted.

"Do you ever get tired of being the less decisive one in your relationship?" Tommy asked.

"Occasionally."

The two men switched on their phones and disappeared into the dark, narrow staircase.

13

Boris felt a twinge of irritation ripple through him as he watched the teenagers enter the cemetery and make their way to the entrance of the mausoleum.

He clenched his jaw and looked over at his commander. Always stoic, Konstantin appeared unaffected by the unplanned interruption.

As if reading his mind, Konstantin turned his head only slightly toward Boris. "Patience, Captain," he urged in a voice as calm as a still river. "They have nowhere to go."

"Yes, sir," Boris answered against every instinct in his body.

He'd always been reactive, and in the field of battle, that instinct had served him extremely well. But being a hunter was far different than being a warrior. In this scenario, the most important skill was the ability to wait even in the face of potential catastrophe.

Konstantin, Boris, and two others watched the group of unruly teenagers carelessly traipse through the cemetery from a position across the square, behind a dumpster. There, in the alley behind a convenience store and a café, they remained concealed in shadow where the eyes of their quarry would not find them.

The rest of Konstantin's men were covering two other escape

points out of the plaza—one just out of sight around the corner on the street and the other positioned near the waterfront, where a path led in both directions along the shore.

The men watched from their vantage point as the teenagers laughed and chattered. Konstantin didn't understand what they were saying, but he figured it didn't matter. They were just a bunch of kids partying too much and up past their bedtime.

He considered the possibility that one or more of the youths had noticed the Americans go into the cemetery, and maybe even saw them enter the mausoleum. Even if that were the case, it changed nothing.

"Teams Two and Three, move into second position," Konstantin said into the radio.

His order was confirmed with a dual reply of "Yes, sir."

He observed the two groups move in closer toward the cemetery. The team down by the waterfront was divided into two in order to cover both directions of escape. The other team closed in from the street, the four men moving purposefully as though they were cops there to break up a drug deal.

"So soon?" Boris asked.

Konstantin understood the question not as a knock on his decision but from a desire to learn. Boris had been an excellent student of strategy ever since he'd been put under Konstantin's command—one of the many qualities the major appreciated about him.

"Three primary exit points," Konstantin said. "We had them blocked off. Now we can squeeze like a python."

"But the teenagers."

"Will be frightened when they see our men moving in. They'll think them to be police. Or worse."

Boris allowed a chuckle. "What's worse than that?"

Konstantin grinned at his second, but said nothing. He knew of monsters in the world that made the authority and threat of cops seem like a walk through a field of daisies. After all, he was one such monster.

"Should we move in as well, sir?"

"Not yet," the major replied. "Let the rest of our men flush out the kids. Then we will make our move and cut off every possible way out of the cemetery. If Wyatt and his companions found anything in there, we will take it from them. One way or another."

Boris nodded and continued to observe.

The other eight Russians moved closer to the cemetery wall from their respective points but didn't do anything to draw attention to themselves.

Several people hanging around in the plaza noticed the men walking toward the mausoleum and immediately took off at a dead sprint in multiple directions.

"See?" Konstantin asked. "They think we're the police."

Some of the young people were too drunk or stoned to react to the perceived threat, or they simply didn't care and were willing to go peaceably to jail.

Between the shrubs, trees, and graves in the cemetery, the teenagers were difficult to see, but their lights gave away their presence. They were hovering around the tomb, a few near the entrance —probably trying to figure out a way to pick the lock.

Another one looked through one of the windows on the ground floor, shining his light into the tomb.

Meanwhile, Konstantin's men moved ever closer.

The four men from the waterfront arrived first, each converging on a corresponding corner, cutting off that exit.

To go that way, anyone inside the cemetery would have to scale the short wall and vault over the fence, and by the time their feet struck the plaza floor, Konstantin's men would be on them.

The team from the street took thirty seconds longer, but they arrived at the northwestern corner of the cemetery wall and waited for further orders.

"Team Two, split up. Two of you stay there. The other two cover the northeastern corner."

In an instant, two of the men broke away and stalked to the prescribed corner—the nearest to where Konstantin and his team waited in the alley shadows.

"Now, Captain," Konstantin said, "we spring the trap."

Boris nodded and motioned to the other two, who immediately popped up from where they crouched and took the point, making their way around a fence that blocked off the square from the back of the businesses. Konstantin and Boris followed, with the latter taking up the rear.

The men marched out into the open and around the fence. The first teenager inside the cemetery to spot them was a boy probably around the age of seventeen. He wore a black hoodie with white drawstrings dangling over his chest, and torn blue jeans.

Upon seeing the supposed authorities, he shouted at the others and took off at a sprint toward the exit.

Konstantin merely responded with a devilish grin.

He had no intention of engaging with the youths, only to send them fleeing the scene.

Soon, more phone lights danced and jittered as the other members of the group of young people heeded the warning and started running.

Within twenty seconds, the kids spilled out of the cemetery and into the plaza, splitting up and sprinting in different directions.

"Let them go," Konstantin ordered the other two teams. "We're not here for them."

He and his team continued toward the cemetery entrance at a steady pace, just as they would had they been actual cops there to break up a party.

Fear and intimidation were rarely employed by rushing.

The four stalked to the opening in the wall and passed through, veering right to make their way toward the mausoleum.

"Teams Two and Three, cover us. And if any of those kids decide to come back, handle it."

"Yes, sir," both team leaders echoed.

Now in the relative safety of the cemetery confines, the four men drew their pistols. The two running point extended their weapons out and swept both directions as they moved to make sure no threat lingered behind a grave or shrub.

When they reached the tomb, each of the point men took up positions on either side of the door and waited for their next order.

Konstantin stopped on the doorstep and reached out his right hand. He pulled on the handle, but the door didn't budge.

"Interesting," he mused to himself. "Trespassers, we know you're in there," he said louder. "Come out with your hands up."

There was no way Konstantin sounded like a Turkish cop. At least not to his own ears, but perhaps the authoritative way he spoke would be enough to coax the three on the inside to do as instructed.

He waited for nearly a minute before issuing another warning. "You will have to the count of three to come out. If you do not, then we will be forced to come in. And I promise you, you do not want that."

He left no doubt in the threat, but still nothing stirred within the tomb.

"One."

Still nothing.

Boris stood next to him with his pistol extended toward the door. If anyone inside tried to get out, he would cut them down before their feet touched outside ground.

"Two."

The men on either side of the doorway tensed their trigger fingers in anticipation. But no one heard anything from inside the mausoleum.

"Three."

Konstantin narrowed his eyes and nodded at the point man to the right. "Open it."

The man stuffed his pistol into a holster and knelt down in front of the door. He spent thirty seconds analyzing the lock, then turned to his commander. "I don't have anything to pick it, sir. I'll have to blow it."

"Do it," the major ordered without hesitation.

"Sir," the man confirmed.

He unbuttoned a pouch on his belt and retrieved a sealed dark green plastic pack from it. Then he tore the packaging and pulled out a few inches of gray putty before closing up the pack and stuffing the remains back in his pouch.

He took a tiny detonator out of another holster and attached it to the putty before pressing it against the lock.

When he was satisfied with the explosive, he gave a nod to the major, who twirled his finger to signal the men to fall back.

They retreated behind the nearest gravestone and ducked down. The man with the ordnance took a small black device with a switch and a red button on it out of his belt, and flipped the switch. He gave one more look to the commander.

"Do it," Konstantin said.

The man pressed the button, and a loud pop erupted from the tomb's entrance.

The blast was nothing more than a quick burst of orange-white light, followed by a plume of smoke. Anyone left in the square who was half paying attention would have noticed both the sound and the quick blast, but it was hardly enough to draw attention from anywhere else.

As the acrid smoke cleared, wafting beyond where Konstantin and his men crouched, the leader stood and stepped out onto the path again—ahead of his team.

Boris quickly hurried ahead of him, and with his pistol extended, crept toward the tomb.

The damaged door hung slightly open, pieces of mangled wood still smoldering from the explosion. When he reached the threshold, Boris swung the door open and jabbed his weapon into the mausoleum.

The other two men stayed close to the major until Konstantin ordered the one on his right to go in with Boris.

The soldier obeyed and covered the other angle inside the tomb before stepping inside.

Konstantin and the last of his men followed into the mausoleum. Bitter smoke still lingered like a deathly fog in the crypt. Fragments of the door and the lock littered the floor. But the most striking observation was that the tomb was empty.

"Impossible," Boris blurted. "We all saw them come in here."

One thing the major noticed immediately was how close the sarcophagus was in proximity to the door. *A tight fit,* he thought. But that notion was quickly dispelled as he moved around the stone container to the back of the room.

Boris continued around to the head of the sarcophagus. He stopped there, eyes fixed on the floor for a breath, then looked up. "Sir, look at this."

Konstantin strode over to the spot where Boris stood. He pointed his light down into an opening in the floor and the narrow staircase that led down into the earth.

"Fascinating," the major said.

Boris and the other two were surprised at the lack of anger or frustration in the man's reaction.

"Team Two, stay in place. Team Three, get in here. We have tunnel rats to root out."

14

Wide beams of light danced along smooth block walls as Sean and the others carefully navigated their way down the spiral staircase. It seemed like they'd been descending for hours, though only a few minutes had passed.

That fact pressed Sean to hurry a little faster, knowing that someone above might well have broken into the tomb and discovered the hole in the floor.

He listened intently while keeping his footfalls silent but heard no sign of trouble above. The absence of sound did little to calm his pace, and he continued with Adriana and Tommy close behind him.

Just as Sean began to wonder how deep this shaft actually went, he reached the bottom, where the stairs met a stone-tiled floor in a narrow, arched passage.

"This is incredible," Tommy whispered from behind.

Sean winced instinctively at the sound, but at this point he realized worrying about someone following them was moot. If anyone had entered the mausoleum after them, they'd have surely entered the stairwell—whether they heard anything or not.

"Yeah," Sean breathed as he pushed forward.

"The amount of resources to construct this must have been

immense," Adriana observed. "The stonework alone would have taken forever to construct."

"Which means whatever's down here must be extremely important. Or valuable."

"Or both," Tommy added.

The three continued single file through the passage, but their progress dragged due to numerous cobwebs stretching across the path. Sean swiped at the ancient, silken strings to clear the way, moved forward, then repeated the process.

"You don't think the spiders that built those are still here, do you?" Tommy asked, his voice rippling with a tremor.

"Nah," Sean said. "Nothing for them to eat down here."

"Right. Right. Good point."

Sean shook his head. He was no fan of spiders, but was far less afraid of them than heights. And given recent events, he could throw snakes onto the pile of things he feared more.

He cleared another section of webs and pointed his light forward into the tunnel.

"Looks like there aren't any more ahead," he stated. "Better pick up the pace. You two go ahead."

Sean slipped his rucksack down one arm and set it on the ground.

"What?" Tommy asked even as Adriana passed Sean and took the lead. "What are you doing?"

"Just setting a little alert for us in case we're being followed."

Sean unzipped a pouch and removed a pair of four-inch-long black metal rods. He unfolded three small prongs from the base of each, which clicked on a tiny red light in a window near the top of one. He placed the first mini tripod against the wall to his right, and then the other on the left until the laser lined up with the opposing window.

Tommy lingered, watching Sean set up the devices.

"What are those?"

Sean grinned up at his friend as he slid the backpack back onto his shoulders. "I thought I told you to go ahead."

Down the passage, Adriana was already thirty feet away—her light scanning every crevice as she pushed forward.

Sean turned his friend around and urged him to follow her. "Little gift from my buddy at DARPA," he said, moving in his wife's direction. "Laser tripwire."

"Wait," Tommy hesitated. "That thing isn't going to cause a cave-in, is it?"

"No. Just a loud bang and a flash of bright light."

"Oh, so it's a flash-bang."

"Figure that out all by yourself?"

Tommy sighed. "For an idiot, you have some good ideas now and then."

Sean slapped his friend on the shoulder. "Thanks, Schultzie."

The two men saw Adriana disappear from view as the passage veered to the right at a corner. They hurried to catch up and found her again, this time only a dozen feet ahead.

She crept forward a few more steps, then stopped and pointed her light at something on the wall.

"What is it?" Tommy asked as he and Sean caught up to her.

She didn't have to say anything. The answer was written on the wall.

Her light illuminated a one-foot-wide circle with the image of a fish carved into it.

Sean turned his light to the left and found the symbol of a horse likewise engraved into the wall.

"There's one on the ceiling, too," Tommy said, looking up at the image of a trident overhead.

"The same symbols from the sarcophagus," Adriana realized.

"But why here?" Sean asked. His eyes fell to the floor and found another clue.

"Look," he uttered.

The other two gazed down at the floor, where the symbol of the double sword of Barbarossa was cut into one of the stone tiles.

"Wonder what that means," Tommy said.

"Guess we have to keep moving if we want to find out," Sean answered.

Adriana took the cue and stepped forward.

The three moved as one for another fifty feet until they reached an archway that opened into a room.

As the group spilled into the chamber, they shined their lights around the circular space. The wide glow of the beams brought to life murals of sixteenth-century sea vessels—some with Ottoman flags flying from the masts and some with the flag of Hayreddin Barbarossa.

The images depicted battles against the Spanish and against the Holy Roman Empire, each of which portrayed the enemy ships being torn apart by cannon fire, or pillaged by the men who boarded them.

In the center of the room, a stone cylinder stood atop a short platform. Beyond that, on the far wall opposite the entrance, an image of the great pirate admiral Barbarossa adorned the stonework.

"Look at that," Tommy said as he tiptoed near the fading artwork. "Do you guys see this?"

"Hard not to, buddy," Sean quipped as he too neared the fresco.

"Why is he holding that?" Adriana wondered.

Their three lights converged on the picture, and on the trident the man held in his hands, resting it over his left shoulder.

The prongs of the trident, as well as Barbarossa's gaze, pointed to their right, where another archway stood—blocked by a massive stone.

"A trident," Tommy gasped. "But why would Barbarossa be holding a trident?"

"Why have we seen a few of those now?" Sean asked. "The journal, the buttons in the tomb, the passage, and now this one."

Tommy nodded as he traced his light upward from the image of Barbarossa toward the domed ceiling overhead. "Guys?" he managed, his mouth agape. "Look at this."

Sean and Adriana looked up, their lights joining Tommy's.

"It's like a Michelangelo," Sean muttered.

On the ceiling, a fresco spanned the ceiling. This one featured

Barbarossa on the left, standing on a ship with a hand extended toward the middle of the dome. Across from him, the image of a muscular, shirtless man with flowing white hair stood in ocean waves. He wore a golden crown and faced the grand admiral with an arm extended, the hand grasping a trident.

"Is... that Poseidon?" Adriana asked no one in particular.

"It has to be," Tommy stated. "But what does this all mean?"

"Looks to me like the fabled god of the seas is giving his trident to Barbarossa."

"Wait. You don't think...."

Sean turned his attention to the pillar in the center of the room. He stepped over to it with the other two immediately behind him. They hovered over the cylinder.

"What is that?" Sean asked.

Adriana was the first to lean closer. In the middle of the surface, five rings expanded out from the center where the emblem of Barbarossa's double sword was carved into the stone.

The ring nearest the sword contained three symbols—one, the trident, was the same Sean and company had seen before. Every successive ring contained more emblems. These carvings featured different animals, shapes, and faces. The latter looked much like Greek gods or famous leaders of the ancient nation.

"It's a four-hundred-year-old combination lock," Adriana realized.

"Amazing," Sean said.

"But how does it work?" Tommy thought out loud. "I guess we have to line up the symbols?"

Sean shifted his stance so he stood between the cylinder and the doorway. He bent his knees and crouched lower toward the surface, then placed his fingers on the innermost ring and turned it until the symbol of the trident was aligned with the sword handle.

A thump reverberated up from the floor, and a loud clap echoed from the blocked archway to the right. The stone blocking the exit dropped several inches, revealing a dark passage on the other side.

"It's working," Tommy said with excitement. "Now move that fish into position."

Sean looked up from his task, meeting his friend's eyes with a sarcastic glower. "Thanks, Captain Obvious."

"Sorry."

Sean merely chuckled and twisted the ring to the right. Suddenly, a loud pop burst from the tunnel accompanied by a dimly reflected flash of light. Sean froze for a second with the image of a bear aligned with the trident. As he turned his head back toward the chamber entrance, another loud bump shook the floor. A door-size stone dropped into the upper part of the portal's archway, stopping about a third of the way down.

"Honey, I don't think that bear is supposed to go there," Adriana cautioned.

"Crap," Sean blurted, and twisted the ring until the fish aligned with the trident.

The door to the right lowered again.

"I'll cover the door," Sean said, drawing his pistol and pointing it at the door. "Finish the combination."

Adriana joined him by his side and raised her weapon with her right hand, and the phone with the other. The lights on their phones did little to illuminate the passage beyond the doorway, the glow barely stretching more than a meter beyond the threshold.

"Put it down," Sean said. "No reason to give them the edge."

She nodded and lowered the device, then gripped her weapon with both hands.

Beyond the corner turn in the corridor, flashlights bounced wildly off the wall. Whoever approached was in a hurry, and probably pissed about the flash-bang.

"Any time, Schultzie," Sean said, recalling a similar urgent command he'd issued his friend recently.

"I got it," Tommy said as he turned the third ring to align the image of the horse with the other two.

The door to the right of Barbarossa's image dropped again. It was halfway down now, and low enough for them to climb through and make their escape.

"We can get out now," Tommy announced. "The door is low enough."

"But what about the key?" Sean reminded.

"Right," Tommy sighed. "Um, guys. The last two symbols. What are they?"

The flashlights drew closer to the corner. Any second, the pursuers would appear.

Adriana glanced over her shoulder at the rings. "The three symbols we've been seeing are all associated with Poseidon," she said. "So the other two must be as well."

"You don't happen to remember what those might be, do you?"

Adriana spoke fluent Greek and was a student of the language's ancient form as well. With that education had come a deep understanding of Greek history. But even she couldn't recall that piece of trivia.

Sean's nearly eidetic memory kicked in. He'd always had a keen interest in ancient history, particularly Egyptian, Greek, and Roman, but there were others mixed into that bag.

"Is there a bull on there?" Sean asked.

The lights on the wall in the passage tightened as the people chasing them drew nearer.

Tommy ran his finger along the fourth ring. He didn't see a bull on it. "No."

"Is there one on the fifth ring?" Adriana asked.

Tommy searched it and found the symbol. "Yes."

"Okay, good."

"Should I move it?"

"No!" The couple nearly shouted at him in tandem.

"Don't do it out of order," Adriana commanded.

"Fine, but what's the fourth symbol?"

"Look for a dolphin," Sean snapped.

"A dolphin?" Tommy scanned the ring and found the symbol. "Found it."

The first pursuer emerged around the corner. The lights behind him outlined his body, and the pistol in his hand. A flashlight attached to the bottom of it shone brightly through the corridor and into Sean's eyes just as he made the instant assessment that this guy was no cop, and definitely not one of the teenagers from the plaza.

He reacted and squeezed the trigger. The muted pop echoed around the room as the bullet discharged from the box-suppressed muzzle.

A spark splashed off the wall near the target, and the man ducked to his left, which didn't help him. Adriana lined up the figure silhouetted by the lights behind him, and fired twice.

The man twisted around and fell just as another was stepping around the corner. The sight of the other getting dropped sent him retreating to use the wall as cover.

"Hurry up, Schultzie," Sean urged.

"Spinning it now."

The second gunman poked his gun and light around the corner and fired a shot through the passage.

It cracked the air near Sean's head and sailed by Tommy, narrowly missing him by a foot. The round struck the painting on the wall and ricocheted off the stone, causing Tommy to wince and stop the ring before he'd lined up the dolphin image.

A loud clack sounded through the chamber and the stone at the entrance dropped lower.

"Sorry," Tommy offered.

Now the shooting window was much tighter, which actually helped Sean and Adriana since they didn't have cover. The two could have moved to the entrance and taken either side, but that would have left Tommy exposed.

With trembling fingers, Tommy revolved the ring until the dolphin lined up with the rest of the symbols.

Another loud thud rumbled through the room, and the stone at the exit dropped down until it was flush with the floor.

The gunman around the corner emerged again to fire, but the stone at the entrance also dropped, and blocked the way in.

Sean glanced over at Adriana with surprise dripping from his eyes. She returned the same expression. Then they rounded on Tommy.

"I got it," he said proudly with a tense smile on his face.

Another click reverberated through the room from the base of the pedestal. This one was a quieter sound and drew everyone's eyes down to the side of the platform, where a tile had slid away. As they shined their lights down into the cavity, the beams were reflected by a glittering yellowish light.

"The key," Tommy mouthed in a barely audible tone.

The three moved as one down the step to the open tile. Inside the hole, a golden double sword rested, propped up by three prongs.

Sean reached into the opening and started to lift the ten-inch-long artifact, but Tommy grabbed his shoulder and stopped him.

"What if there's another trap?"

Sean nodded and lowered his phone down into the hole to inspect the prongs and make sure they weren't weight sensitive.

"I don't think a giant stone ball is going to come out to chase us with this one, Schultzie," Sean said, and lifted the key.

He held it aloft, waiting for a second to make sure no traps were sprung, and silence sent a sliver of relief through him.

They pointed their lights onto the shimmering yellow artifact, noting several unusual notches along the two blades.

"Someone went to a lot of trouble to hide this," Adriana said. "It must be part of something extraordinary. But what?"

Sean turned his head upward and stared at the depiction of Poseidon and Barbarossa on the ceiling.

Tommy noticed his friend's stare. "You don't think...."

"I've seen too many crazy things to say it's impossible," Sean said, halfway finishing his friend's thought.

Adriana gazed at the ceiling too. "The trident of Poseidon." She looked at Sean and Tommy. "Could it be that Barbarossa found it, and this fresco is a depiction of that?"

Muted shouts from the other side of the blocked door trickled into the room. Sean and the other two whipped their heads around and listened for a second.

"Russians," Sean realized. He looked toward the newly opened archway. "We need to keep moving. And we have no idea where this passage comes out."

15

Konstantin clenched his jaw. His nostrils flared, inhaling the bitter scent of burned powder.

Boris shouted at the other four remaining men, ordering them to do something—anything—while pointing at the huge stone blocking their way into the chamber.

He looked back down at the fallen member of their team. The man's dead gray eyes stared at the opposite wall. Konstantin didn't need to check his vitals. The young man was gone. One round to the chest and one to the gut had made certain of that.

Konstantin inclined his head. "Quiet," he barked. Boris immediately snapped to attention and closed his mouth.

"Team Two, do you copy?"

"Yes, sir."

"Stay alert. We've lost the targets in the tunnels down here."

"Yes, sir," the man repeated.

Boris looked at the stone and then back to his commander. "They could be trapped inside, sir."

"No. I doubt it. There must be another way out of here." He rounded on one of the men behind him. "Blow it. Use whatever you need. I want this passage cleared. We cannot let them get away."

"Sir," the man blurted with a single nod and set his gear bag down on the floor.

"The rest of you," Konstantin said, "clear out. If there's a cave-in, I don't want any more casualties."

He ignored the temptation of regret tugging at his heart due to the death of one of his men. It wasn't the first time he'd lost a soldier. Not by a long shot. And it might not be his last.

The men moved back around the corner and waited for further orders while Konstantin remained next to his demolition expert.

He watched as the young man took out the rest of the ordnance he carried. The blond soldier's pasty skin virtually glowed in the darkness, illuminated by the lights around him.

He carried the three bricks of C-4 over to the door while Konstantin aided him by pointing the flashlight at the heavy stone.

The soldier worked carefully, attaching one of the bricks near the archway on the barrier before placing the other two near the bottom. Once the detonators were connected, he returned to the corner and picked up his rucksack.

Konstantin gave an approving nod, then waved the men back. "Move," he commanded.

The group retreated down the corridor until they'd put twenty meters between themselves and the corner.

"This is far enough," the major said. The men stopped. He waited for his explosives guy to give the signal.

The man plugged his ears, then removed the little black box from his bag as he'd done at the door of the tomb, flipped the switch, and looked to his commander. "Ready."

Konstantin checked with his other men. "You know the drill."

Every man in the group covered their ears and opened their mouths.

The major narrowed his eyelids as the soldier with the radio box pressed the button.

A loud blast rocked the tunnel, shaking the floor under their feet. The concussion blew through the passage and hit the men. Muted slightly by the distance and hitting the first wall, they were well braced for the impact of air pressure that struck them.

The second the wave passed, Konstantin looked up at the ceiling, well aware that his order could have doomed them all to a crushing death under tons of rubble.

The corridor held firm.

A thick cloud of dust rolled out from around the corner ahead. He knew they'd need to give it a moment to settle, otherwise they'd simply be plunging forward into a zero-visibility situation.

Despite that, he took a step forward ahead of the rest of his men and peered into the dust with his light beam churning in the thick air.

Konstantin gave it a minute and then motioned to his men. "Cover your mouths. We don't have time to wait for the dust to settle completely. If they did get away, they have a head start."

The two men behind the demolition expert moved forward, followed by Boris and another. Konstantin followed, all of them pulling their shirts up above their mouths as they plunged into the dusty portion of the tunnel.

The first two reached the archway—or what was left of it. A pile of rubble lay on the threshold, but more of it sprayed out into the chamber. The men spilled into the room with their weapons drawn, flashlights pointing into every crevice of the space as they checked to make sure there was no threat.

"Clear," one said.

"Clear," announced another.

The men wrapped around the room amid a dying cloud of dust. Konstantin was the next-to-last one in. He stepped over the rubble, kicking a few chunks out of the way. His eyes scanned the room, taking in the surroundings.

The first thing that drew his attention was the stone pillar in the center of the chamber, set in the middle of a six-inch-high platform.

Konstantin walked over to it and tilted his head to the right, examining the top of the cylinder. He traced his finger over the rings, considering for a few breaths what it could be. It didn't take him long.

He looked to the floor where he'd noticed a hole in the tile, and retraced his steps back over to it. There, Konstantin knelt and inspected the cavity where three empty prongs stuck up from the ground.

"They've gone, sir," Boris announced.

"Yes, I can see that, Captain. Thank you for the counsel." He could tell the man was eager to pursue into the new passage, but the major waited, shining his light around the room. He looked up at the mural overhead, and for the briefest of moments admired the artistry of the image. Then he turned to the fresco of Barbarossa holding the trident of Poseidon on the far wall, head turned toward the open archway to the right.

Konstantin smiled grimly. "So, the legends are true after all," he mused to himself.

He'd climbed the ranks of the Russian military through years of hard work and perseverance. All the while, though, Konstantin studied the more unusual sides of history, growing into an unlikely expert in the field.

When he'd sat in on a meeting with the Russian president and other advisers regarding the war in Ukraine, it was Konstantin who offered an unconventional solution.

Part of it had been hopeful. There'd been little evidence to support that the trident was a real thing. Yet he'd pushed the idea anyway, sensing how desperate his president had become.

With allies all around the world rallying to the Ukrainian cause—mostly by way of military supplies—the war had drawn on far longer than the president had foreseen.

While certain options were off the table due to international conventions and laws, others were still available—unassailed by the ludicrous treatises signed by man.

Now, all those years of study, and risking his reputation on a wild possibility, were proving fruitful.

The paintings on the ceiling and wall proved it.

Hayreddin Barbarossa had discovered the trident of Poseidon. The grand admiral had hidden it somewhere. This chamber was the first step in finding it, and the only thing in Konstantin Morovski's way were a few American archaeologists.

He smiled to himself, almost relishing the feeble challenge. "Find them," he said. "We'll take what they discovered from their dead bodies."

16

The explosion echoed through the corridor, startling Sean and his companions. The three spun around and looked back through the tunnel.

"What was that?" Tommy wondered out loud.

"Sounds like they blew the door," Sean answered. "We'd better keep moving."

He checked his watch and noted the time, just as he'd done before they left the key chamber.

They had a five-minute head start. Give or take. He figured he could add a minute for the Russians to get through the rubble and dust, check the room, and eventually push through into the next passage.

That was a decent amount of time, but Sean knew it could evaporate rapidly if they dallied around.

The corridor widened as they moved. And the ceiling grew taller. The sound of water trickling and dripping reached their ears about the same time the scent of must, garbage, and rot hit their noses.

"Ugh," Tommy complained. "Are we in a sewer?"

"Smells like it," Adriana answered, seeming unaffected by the stench.

"Could be worse," Sean said, despite wincing at the odor. "Likely a storm sewer. So, we're getting the smells of garbage and runoff. Be glad it's not an actual sewer."

Sean pressed the button on the radio in his right ear and waited for it to beep. "Niki? Do you copy?"

He listened as he and the other two picked up the pace to a jog.

"I hear you, Sean," Niki answered. "Is everything okay?"

"That depends on your definition of okay, but we're underground. Not sure where we are at the moment."

"We're four blocks from the tomb," Adriana said.

Sean looked over his shoulder at her, surprised by the quick and precise answer. His shock melted in an instant when he saw his wife looking at her phone. Her mischievous face glowed in the screen light, then she turned it toward him so he could see the map and their position indicated by a blue dot.

"Clever," he commented and nearly tripped over a pipe that ran across the walkway.

Sean steadied himself and focused on the path ahead. "There has to be a way out of here somewhere. Like a ladder or something."

"You mean like that one up ahead?" Tommy asked, pointing his light at a series of metal rungs that looked like they'd been made out of rebar. The ladder went up to the top of the corridor, where the occasional sound of a car passed somewhere nearby, perhaps overhead.

"Niki," Sean spoke into the radio. "We found a way out."

"You want me to come to you?"

"No. Stay put. We're coming to you."

"Okay, Sean. But I still see four of their men out in the plaza. They're hovering pretty close to the waterfront. All spread out like they're waiting for something."

"Yeah," Sean grunted as he reached the bottom of the ladder. "They're waiting for us."

He turned to Tommy and Adriana. "You two go first. I'll cover you if the Russians show up sooner than expected. Schultzie, you should probably lead. You're stronger than both of us and will have less trouble getting the lid off that."

"Russians?" Niki asked, still listening to the radio.

"Yeah," Sean answered. "Those guys you see in the square are Russians. Not sure what a bunch of them are doing looking for an artifact from the Ottoman Empire, but for right now I'm okay just getting away from them. They're definitely armed. And from the brief look I got of them, I'd say they're either private security for someone or former military, maybe both."

Tommy glanced questioningly at his friend. "You got all that from like a two-second look at the guy covered in shadows?"

"You can tell a lot about an enemy based purely on their weapon and how they carry it."

"That's how you determined they were Russian?" Niki asked.

"No," Sean laughed as Tommy started climbing the damp rungs of the ladder toward a manhole cover at the top. "I heard them down in the tunnel."

"Oh."

"Tommy is climbing up to street level now."

Sean and Adriana watched as Tommy ascended the ladder at a deliberate and cautious pace. The last thing they needed right now was a slip and a fractured ankle.

He made it to the top rung and leaned his shoulder into the cover. He grunted and pushed, but the thing didn't move.

The sound of a car roared by overhead.

"I think this is in the middle of a busy street," Tommy announced. "And I can't budge it."

Sean risked a glance back down the corridor. No sign of the Russians yet, but every second that passed drew the enemy closer.

Tommy grunted and leaned in harder, but he couldn't get the thing to move.

"I can't do it, Sean," he surrendered. "We'll have to find another way out. These things are meant to be removed from above anyway."

"Yeah, don't hurt yourself, buddy. Get down from there. Let's keep moving."

Sean looked back again. Still no sign of the enemy. But they'd killed a minute or so while standing here. That was a minute of catchup time.

Tommy scurried down the ladder, and the three continued on through the darkness.

The smells faded somewhat, turning less pungent than before. The sound of running water increased as they passed pipes on the other side of a wide trough.

What had been a trickle at first was now a six-inch-deep stream of runoff.

Sean pointed his light to the left across the water and noted a couple of rats hurrying around.

The arched tunnel curved around to the left and then back around to the right. Sean stayed in the lead with Adriana between him and Tommy in the back. Adriana kept her map on so she could track their location.

"This looks like we're heading toward the water," she observed. "It would be helpful if I had a map of the sewer system."

"I guess Google doesn't go underground yet," Tommy joked.

"Believe me. Somewhere, someone has probably pitched that idea," Sean commented.

Tommy laughed. "Oh, for sure."

The passage continued bending around to the right, and the sound of water grew louder as it rushed downhill. Sean noted it was deeper now, probably a few feet.

The churning sound swelled, drowning out any noise their feet might have made as they hurried along the path.

Sean knew they were getting near the end of the line for this watershed, but where would that put them? He hoped it wasn't one of those intersections where more tunnels met and dumped everything into a central pipe that led out of the city.

As he and the others rounded the bend, his hopes were confirmed.

The ditch in the center of the tunnel ended at a metal grate where the water spilled out into the harbor beyond.

Sean picked up his pace and rushed over to the metal barrier. An iron gate was attached to the grate through which the water flowed and tumbled off a short drop into the harbor.

He shook the gate, but it wouldn't budge thanks to an old padlock looped through one of the bars.

"You think you can pick this one?" Sean asked his wife.

She didn't answer. Instead she stood by him to inspect the lock. Adriana lifted it with her fingers and cocked her head to the side. "Yeah, just a minute."

Tommy watched her retrieve her toolkit again, then turned and faced the other direction, staring back into the darkness. He stuffed his phone into his pocket. The area where they stood received the full glow of moonlight from a cloudless sky above, and a little help from city lights across the harbor that twinkled under the stars.

Tommy's eyes narrowed to slits as he peered into the darkness of the passage. Hearing anything other than the rushing river was nearly impossible.

Tommy tiptoed away from his friends as Adriana continued to work with the lock. He stared into the corridor, eyes firmly focused on the path that wrapped around to the left where they'd just come from.

He raised his pistol, letting it lead him as he took another step deeper into the passage.

"Sean?" Niki said into the radio. "What is that noise? It's so loud? I can't hear anything else."

Sean cradled his head against his shoulder and cupped his hands. "I'll tell you in a second. Stand by." He nearly shouted but tried not to. No sense in confirming their location to the Russians if they'd made it this far.

"Understood."

Sean watched Adriana work her tools in the old lock, surprised it was taking her this long. He'd figured the aged padlock would be simple for her.

"It's so corroded," she complained, reading his thoughts. "I'll get it, but just give me a second."

Sean turned his attention back to his friend, who'd moved eight or nine steps back into the tunnel. He joined Tommy and peered into the darkness.

"You don't see anything, do you?" Sean asked.

"No. Not yet."

"I like your optimism."

Tommy snorted. "They're coming. We know that much."

"Hey, maybe they gave up and went back up through the tomb the way they came in."

"Fat chance," Tommy argued.

"Yeah, I know. But wouldn't it be nice?"

Dim reflections of artificial light danced on the wall on the right side of the drain.

"It would. But it seems we're not that lucky"

Sean looked back over his shoulder at his wife. Her hands turned and twisted, and he recognized the look of frustration on her face.

"Looks like we might have to buy her some time," Sean said to his friend.

Tommy didn't take his eyes off the curving path. "What's taking her so long?"

"Lock is corroded. Said she'll have it in a sec."

"How many of those secs does she need? Because I don't think we can buy her many."

"Yeah, you're probably right."

He rounded and stalked back to the gate where Adriana continued to manipulate the padlock's innards.

"I can't get it to budge," she confessed, exasperated.

"Step back," Sean said. He waited for his wife to pull her tools out of the lock and take a few steps back. Then he raised his pistol and aimed.

He fired, and the lock blew off with a clank.

"Subtle," Adriana chirped. She stuffed her tools back in the bag and looked back at Tommy, who remained fixed on the tunnel. She ran over to where he crouched, grabbed him by the shoulder, and said, "Come on. Let's get out of here."

He nodded and followed her to the grate, leaving the bobbing flashlight beams behind.

Sean slipped through the gate first and held it open for the other two. When they were through, he closed it shut.

The group found themselves on a walkway that ran along the water. The only thing Sean could figure was that it existed for maintenance crews to check the drains.

The water blocked any route to his right as he faced the gate, leaving only one option—to head back toward the waterfront.

Just beyond the end of the concrete landing, steps led down to docks where several pleasure boats were docked. A few were tied to the main dock that ran flush with the shore.

The vessels bobbed ceaselessly in the churning sea. Ropes clanked against masts of the sailing vessels, the sound ringing through the air.

"Hey, Niki," Sean said into the radio as he ushered the other two ahead.

"Yes?"

"We're down the waterfront from you."

Adriana checked the map again. "Less than a kilometer," she said.

"You get that, Niki?" Sean asked.

"Yeah."

"There are a bunch of boats tied up to docks down here. But there are several open spots."

"Understood. I'll swing in and get you out of there."

"Thanks," Sean said and looked back at the gate. He felt like any second the Russians would burst through.

Tommy reached the stairs and went left to go down to the waterfront docks. Adriana hurried after him while Sean covered the rear. They were sixty yards from the water spill now, and his weapon would effectively be useless at that range, but he kept his sights on the grate until he reached the top of the stairs.

Then, as he was about to turn and descend, the iron gate swung open and a black-clad gunman emerged.

Sean ducked out of sight and skipped down the steps two at a time, hoping he hadn't been spotted. Even if the gunman hadn't seen him, with only one way to go they'd figure it out within seconds.

"They're here," Sean announced as he caught up to the others on the docks.

The main dock stretched the length of four football fields along the shoreline, with boat slips attached to it like branches of a tree sticking out on one side into the harbor.

"Niki, I need you to find an empty spot at the head of one of these piers."

"Already on it, boss," he said to the tune of a throaty boat motor.

Tommy and Adriana sprinted hard in front of Sean, who looked back over his shoulder after they'd put fifty yards between themselves and the steps down to the docks.

He hoped none of their pursuers had high-powered rifles. Those could make the range problem with sidearms irrelevant.

Ahead on the water, the sound of Niki's getaway boat roared toward them.

"There he is," Tommy blurted, pointing toward the oncoming boat.

Sean glanced back over his shoulder. They were a hundred yards from the stairs now. But would that be enough?

"I found an empty one at the end of dock thirteen," Niki announced. "Pulling in now. I'll try to keep it as close as possible. Unless you want me to tie up."

"No!" Sean answered. "Don't tie it up. Just keep it as close as you can. We'll jump on."

As they passed dock seven at a dead sprint, Sean heard the first sounds of trouble behind him as the Russians appeared on the docks and started firing.

Their weapons were out of range, but if Sean and the others couldn't reach the boat in time, they would run out of real estate fast, and dock thirteen was still another hundred yards away.

Tommy instinctively looked back over his shoulder when he heard the gunfire and stumbled over an uneven board. He fell forward as Adriana reached out to grab him, but he tumbled over.

Fortunately, Tommy had the awareness to tuck and roll, and was back on his feet within a second.

"I see you up ahead," Sean said, looking through the many boats moored to their slips. The twenty-two-foot black bow rider dipped in and out of view as it sped closer.

A lucky shot cracked the air to Sean's left. The round burrowed into the bow of a shiny new, thirty-foot cabin cruiser.

Sean clenched his teeth between taking in gulps of air. *The owner is not going to be happy about that,* he thought.

Up ahead, fewer boats occupied the docks, and between the bigger openings Sean spotted Niki as the bow rider charged through the choppy waves, bouncing up and down as the driver slowed the boat and cut the wheel.

"Almost... there," Sean muttered between labored breaths.

Even in peak physical condition, a dead sprint this far would be difficult for even elite-level athletes.

And then things got worse.

At the other end of the pier, four more men with guns appeared at the base of the steps below the plaza, all running toward them.

"Sean?" Tommy gasped between breaths. His pace had already slowed. While Tommy was in great shape, his physical gifts were made for lifting—not endurance sports.

"I see them," Sean clarified. "Get to the dock. Nearly there."

While it would have taken an act of untimely, and rare, clumsiness for Russians to head them off before they could reach the dock, their weapons could make things difficult. It was a matter of seconds until they opened fire, if for no other reason than to suppress the three Americans until reinforcements from the rear could catch up.

"I'm here," Niki said through the radio.

Gunshots popped from flashing muzzles at the end of the pier, cutting him off.

"I don't think we can make it to thirteen," Sean said. "Tommy, turn here."

Tommy didn't have to be told twice. He cut to the left and charged ahead down dock eleven, which was crowded with boats on both sides.

The vessels provided temporary shielding from the gunfire, but Sean didn't know how fast Niki could get over there.

"Change of plans, Niki. You think you can get to dock eleven? Just two down."

"Yeah, but there's a center console blocking the way."

"Doesn't matter," Sean said. He looked ahead and saw the white boat Niki described. "Pull up next to it and be ready to go."

"Okay, Sean."

The sound of the boat motor roared again. Sean saw the lights on the vessel bouncing in the swells.

"What's the plan here?" Tommy asked, panting for air.

"Niki is going to pull up next to that center console at the end of the pier. Climb through that boat to get to him."

Bullets whizzed by, splintering fiberglass hulls and pinging off of outboard motors.

Sean looked back to the end of the row and saw the Russians from the tunnel nearly to dock eleven. They were firing wildly as they ran, but despite their movements were surprisingly accurate from that distance, especially with sidearms.

For a second, Sean considered stopping to provide cover fire, but he doubted anything he could offer the converging foes would cause them to worry, and probably only give them time to catch up.

Fifty meters ahead, Niki slowed the black boat as he approached the center console vessel moored to the dock.

"I see you," Niki said. "Water is pretty choppy. But I can keep it here."

Tommy pumped his legs, doing everything he could to keep up the pace even though it had fallen off considerably since the run began.

Bullets continued to zip all around them, but none came close enough to cause any real concern. It would be a lucky shot to hit a target from so far back and on the move.

Still, better not to chance it.

Tommy reached the port side of the center console and climbed into it. Adriana followed as Tommy crawled through the bouncing boat and then stood up on the ledge as Niki did his best to hold onto the center console's starboard cleat to keep the two vessels together.

"Come on," Niki urged, seeing the gunmen round the turn and run onto the dock.

Adriana skipped across the idle boat, planted her hand on the gunwale, and vaulted herself over into the speedboat.

Sean reached the center console and jumped over the port side, landing hard on the floor as rounds began peppering the side of the ship.

He rolled back to the gunwale and drew his weapon, took aim at the charging enemies, and fired. His finger twitched rapidly until the pistol clicked.

The Russians on the pier dove for cover, though none were struck by Sean's desperate volley.

It was enough, though.

He turned and leaped over the starboard side of the vessel and onto the boat with his team.

Tommy stood at the controls, and the second Sean was aboard, he shoved the lever to his right all the way forward.

Niki let go of the cleat as the motor roared, churning the blackish water behind them into a murky, foamy white.

The Russians continued their pursuit, running all the way to the end of the dock as the boat sped away. With every second, the enemy grew smaller in the distance until Tommy steered the boat beyond view around a breakwater wall and into the open sea.

17

Konstantin watched the boat vanish into the distance. His right eye twitched the only sign of his irritation. But his frustration only lasted a few seconds as another boat appeared to their right, speeding toward them.

"He's late," the major complained to no one in particular.

The boat slowed as it neared the dock where one of the other men waved the driver to pull up next to the center console just as the other boat had done.

"Find the closest boat charters online," Konstantin ordered Boris and two others. "I would prefer to know where they're going in case we don't catch them." He climbed over the gunwale of the first boat and then onto the red vessel he'd chartered earlier. "Who knows, maybe it's from the same place we got this one."

The rest of the men poured into the boat, a twenty-six-foot-long cruiser with four outboard motors on the back.

It was larger than the boat Wyatt and his team had used to get away but also faster, with twice the horsepower and only slightly heavier.

The second the entire group was on board, the man at the

controls accelerated away from the docks and guided the vessel toward the breakwater point.

Konstantin moved up to the console and held on to the roof over his head as the sea sprayed around them on both sides with every dip and rise in the swells.

"They went around that point," Konstantin said, indicating the direction with his finger.

"Yes, sir," the soldier said, and steered in the prescribed direction.

The cool evening air blew through the major's hair as their boat charged ahead. When they reached the bend in the wall, the man behind the wheel cut it to the left and steered out into open water.

"Kill the lights," Konstantin ordered.

"Sir," the driver confirmed and flipped a switch on the panel. He eased back on the throttle, too, as every man in the boat peered out across the sea.

"There they are," Boris exclaimed, pointing toward a couple of lights bouncing up and down in the water. The Americans' boat was difficult to see due to the black upper hull, but the lights were unmistakable.

"They're heading to another pier," Konstantin realized.

Their quarry barreled toward another marina with a similar array of boats moored to the docks as the one they'd just left.

"There is a place that rents boats at that marina, sir," one of the soldiers to Konstantin's left said.

"That must be where they got it from," Konstantin said. "The question is, where are they going next?"

He ordered the man at the controls to slow down a little more. "Let them dock. When they do, head over there to that empty slip between the two yachts." Konstantin pointed to a dock where a gap separated two luxury boats—each forty feet in length.

"They have something Barbarossa left behind," he continued, speaking to the rest of the men, "something that is of vital importance not only to our mission but to our way of life. We must get it back at all costs. Is that clear?"

"Yes, sir," the men barked in unison.

"Forget the empty spot over there," Konstantin ordered the man behind the controls. "No time. Pull up behind their boat. "Once we dock, everyone spread out and find them."

The soldier behind the wheel acknowledged with a bob of his head and a quick, "Sir."

He guided the boat toward the enemy vessel. Lights hanging from tall wooden posts illuminated the pier, making it easy to see the Americans park their boat next to a building. There were a couple of refueling stations set out away from the structure. This only confirmed what the major suspected; that the shack was where the Americans had rented their boat.

If they were unable to catch up, Konstantin knew at the very least his men could search the rental building and find the Americans' information. From there, they could hunt them down.

He hoped it didn't come to that.

Ocean spray misted across his face as Konstantin stood stout in the boat. His body rocked with the motion of the swells, but he took the movement like a seasoned seaman. The smell of the salty air filled his nose, heightening his senses.

The Americans scrambled off their boat and ran up to a concrete staircase that led to the street.

Once they were out of sight, the major ordered the driver to speed up. The man increased the throttle slightly but not enough to rev the engine and draw attention from the fleeing targets.

The boat cruised into the marina, and when they reached the tip of the pier, the driver eased back on the throttle and steered it in close to the dock.

One of the men in the back on the port side hopped out and grabbed a thick rope from one of the cleats on the walkway. He tossed it to another soldier, who looped it around the cleat on the boat as the driver nudged the vessel into the port.

"Go!" Konstantin shouted the second the boat was secure.

His men spilled out onto the dock and sprinted toward the stairs. Even in his fifties, he'd maintained exemplary physical condition and had no trouble keeping up with the men as they charged forward.

The sound of an occasional car passing echoed down the steps. "Keep your weapons hidden, men," Konstantin warned as they hurriedly climbed the stairs. "Don't want any attention from the locals, or the police."

The first men reached the top and spread out in both directions. The rest followed until they were all out on the sidewalk.

The street in front of them ran left to right, with another street extending straight ahead between businesses and apartments. Lights dotted the sidewalks every so often.

"Where did they go?" Boris asked. The question was half rhetorical.

"Radios on. Spread out and find them," Konstantin ordered. "They couldn't have gone far."

A third of the men took off to the left. Another third ran across the street against the signal. And the remaining group sprinted to the right.

Konstantin remained in place. Boris stayed by his side.

"What are we doing, sir?" Boris asked.

"Waiting. Just in case they try to double back."

"A good plan, sir."

They watched their men get smaller in the distance as they checked in darkened storefront windows in the shops and cafés across the street.

Konstantin was willing to be patient, but if the Americans had been able to get a cab, they were already too far gone to chase on foot. And with every passing second, they were putting more and more distance between themselves and the Russians.

The major's thoughts were abruptly interrupted by a familiar rumbling sound from behind.

He and Boris spun around.

Konstantin couldn't hide the look of surprise and disgust on his face as he watched the boat they'd chased accelerating out of the marina. One of the men on board—a blond—taunted the two Russians with a wave.

The major gritted his teeth, then barked into the radio. "Everyone back to the boat. Now."

He and Boris hurried down the stairs as the rest of the men scrambled to catch up.

The Americans' boat bobbed up and down as it continued to gain separation from the hunters.

"How could I have been so foolish?" Konstantin sneered quietly. He almost never questioned himself, never allowed regrets or doubts to creep into his mind. Yet here he was, outmaneuvered by a couple of American archaeologists.

"None of us thought of that, sir," Boris confided. He decided not to say anything else since the first comment seemed to do little to comfort his commander.

The men hit the bottom of the stairs in stride and sprinted toward their boat.

"Untie the mooring," Konstantin ordered. "I'll turn it around. Hopefully, at least some of our men will be able to jump on board."

"Yes, sir," Boris answered.

Konstantin reached the boat and vaulted over the gunwale, bracing himself with his hand on the rail. He landed, stepped over to the console, and reached for the key in the ignition, then paused.

He looked around the floor, on the captain's chair, and in the cupholders on the right side of the console, but couldn't find what he was looking for.

"Captain?" he said, the dreadful epiphany drawing lines across his forehead. "Where are the keys?"

The first of his other men appeared at the top of the stairs. The others followed in short order, all scurrying down the steps and over to the boat.

"Where are the keys?" Konstantin shouted.

The men slowed down and looked around at each other as they stood on the dock next to the boat. The blank looks in their eyes and on their faces were all Konstantin needed.

The major turned back to the sea and watched as the smaller boat cruised away, vanishing from sight around the point to the left.

He sucked in a deep breath of air and then turned to his men. "It would seem we have been outplayed."

"What are your orders, sir?" Boris asked, doing his best to sound upbeat.

"Return to the tomb," the major said. "If we don't know where they are going, we might be able to find something they missed that will give us a clue." He looked to two other men. "You two, stay behind and search that rental building. Find out if they left a real name for that boat. I want to know everything I can about them."

18

Niki shifted the motor into idle as they approached the docks. He'd taken over for Tommy behind the wheel as soon as they'd lost visual contact with the Russians.

No one had said much during the short voyage to the next marina. Between the sound of the motor and the sea flapping against the hull, they'd have had to shout, anyway.

Besides, Sean and company had their attention firmly locked on the water behind them in case the Russians somehow procured another boat.

But none ever appeared on the rippling, dark horizon.

Sean cautiously allowed relief to trickle back into his body, though his mind remained on moderate alert.

This marina looked like the other two they'd visited before, though there were more boats here, and hiding theirs would prove much easier in case they were followed.

Niki eased the boat into an empty spot while Sean hopped up onto the dock and picked up a moor. After looping the rope around the boat's cleat, Niki cut the engine. Sean hooked another rope around a second cleat on the stern's port, and extended his hand to his wife as she stepped up and out onto the dock.

"Still such a Southern gentleman," she commented with a pleased smile.

"Always."

Tommy stuck his hand up, but Sean had already turned away. "Don't make it awkward, Schultzie," he said and stepped clear of the boat.

Tommy rolled his eyes and climbed ashore with Niki right behind him.

Sean looked out toward the sea, expecting the Russians to appear any second.

"You think they'll figure out where we went?" Niki asked.

"Maybe," Sean answered. "I hope not. Better to assume they will."

"Which means we need to keep moving," Adriana said. "Find a place to hole up for a bit."

Sean half laughed. "Did you just say hole up for a bit?"

"Yeah." She looked at him. "Why?"

He snorted. "That's not a very Spanish thing to say, is it?"

"Maybe you're rubbing off on me."

"I would hope so. We've been together awhile now."

"Would you two lovebirds knock it off," Tommy whined. "She's right. We do need to get out of here and find a place to lie low. I suggest our hotel."

"We might as well assume that's not an option," Sean countered. "These guys may have figured out where we're staying. Right now, I'm just going to figure they know everything about us."

Niki looked around for a minute. "I know where we are," he said. "There's a hookah bar not far from here. It's open until three in the morning."

Everyone looked at him, surprised.

"What?" he said, sticking his hands out to the side. "I like this town."

"Okay," Sean said with an easy smile. "Lead us to it."

The four made their way along the sidewalks for five blocks until they arrived at the hookah bar. As Niki had said, it was still open for business, with several patrons still hanging out inside the lounge and on the street-side patio.

People smoked lavish hookahs with long tubes of varying colors. The aromatic scents of the specialty tobaccos drifted down the walkway in both directions—a siren song to smokers interested in a late-night fix.

Niki found the hostess of the bar at a stand next to the door and requested a seat inside.

"Back corner if possible," Sean added.

The girl nodded and looked through the open door. A curved bench with black upholstery sat in the back-left corner of the room. "I have that one available," she said, indicating it with a finger point.

"Perfect," Sean said. He slapped Niki on the back and motioned for the others to follow the hostess to the proffered table.

The group settled into their seats while the hostess distributed menus.

"Ahmed will be your server," she said in perfect English. "And just be aware we will be closing at three."

Everyone nodded. Sean and Tommy thanked her.

"I guess we'd better order something while we're here," Tommy said, looking over the menu of flavored tobaccos.

"Get whatever," Sean said. "I don't smoke."

"Yeah, but have you ever had this kind of tobacco before?"

"Sure."

"And you didn't like it?"

"Like I said, not much of a smoker. But I'll give it a pull if it will make you feel better."

Niki beamed with delight. "I'll order if it's okay with the rest of you."

Adriana chuckled at the young man's enthusiasm. "By all means. We should get what the expert is getting."

The server arrived a moment later, wearing a black tunic and gray pants. "Hello. My name is Ahmed," he said. "Is this your first time here?"

"No," Niki answered for the group.

"Oh, excellent. Welcome back. Do you know what you would like to order? I can recommend some specials we have going on."

"That won't be necessary," Niki replied. He proceeded to order a strawberry-flavored tobacco, which Ahmed noted on a pad.

"Anything else?"

"No, thank you. Just some glasses of water."

"Very good."

Ahmed disappeared behind a counter and into a back room.

"Thanks, Niki," Sean said.

"Happy to."

"So," Tommy interrupted, "not to be a buzzkill, but we need to get back to business. After all, there's a Russian death squad after us."

"Death squad?" Niki asked, looking concerned.

"Don't get him all riled up, Schultzie," Sean warned. Then he turned to Niki. "Although they could be that."

"We need to solve the second part of the riddle left by Sinan Reis," Adriana cut in, trying to get the boys back on track. "It says that only he can guide us. And like I said before, the best place to start is his tomb. That or perhaps wherever he may have lived. I suggest we search for both."

"Should I call Tara and Alex?" Tommy wondered.

Sean checked his watch. "It's still early back home. They should answer."

Tommy huffed. "Knowing those two, they're probably still at the lab."

"I'll send them a text," Sean said. "Always the better option anyway. Nine times out of ten, a text is all you need."

"Good idea."

Sean took out his phone and sent the message while the other three began searching for answers on their own devices. After he'd sent the message, Sean joined them in the online hunt.

Ahmed returned a few minutes later with a tall hookah. The frosted glass vase portion was adorned with swirling blue clouds painted on it.

"Here you go, my friends," the server said. He set the hookah down in the center of the table, then placed a tin of tobacco next to it along with two spare unlit coals. Then he gently laid the coal onto a metal plate atop the hookah and lit it with a black wand lighter. The yellow flame flickered for a few heartbeats as it lapped the side of the coal until orange sparks began to dance around the edge and up over the top of the domed chunk.

He placed the tobacco in a bowl and capped the top of the device before stepping back. "Enjoy," he said and walked over to one of the other tables.

"Friendly guy," Tommy remarked as he took the nearest hose and put the mouthpiece between his lips.

"Find anything?" Sean asked Adriana, noting her focus on the phone cradled in her hands.

"Yes. Interesting information. Apparently, there were two people of that name. And he was called the Great Jew even though he was really Muslim."

"Because he was born to a Sephardic Jewish family," Tommy said after taking a puff from the hookah. The strawberry-scented smoke plumed around his face and hung there for a few seconds before it dissipated into the air. "Seems that title hung with him despite his clear religious allegiances. It says his family fled either Spain or Portugal and went to Smyrna, then ruled by the Ottoman Empire. Interesting they were taken in by the Ottomans."

"Makes you wonder how bad the persecution must have been in the old countries, huh," Sean commented.

Sean took a puff of the hookah and continued tapping on his phone with his thumbs. "I don't see anything about where he may have lived after that, though."

"Says he became a Barbary Corsair. That was in the heyday of the Barbary Coast pirates."

"Pirates?" Niki asked. "I've studied a little about all that, but not much."

"The Barbary Corsairs were privateers operating out of North Africa," Adriana explained. "Algiers, Tunis, Salé, Rabat, and Tripoli mostly. They were a scourge to the Spanish and the Holy Roman Empire."

"Does that still bother you?" Tommy asked of her Spanish origins.

She shook her head at him like he'd asked if a spoon was for eating. "No, Tommy. That was a long time ago. And I'm not so sure we were the good guys in all that. History has a funny way of polarizing things."

"Indeed." Tommy pointed at the article on his phone. "It says here, later in his career he was based out of Santorini. There are certainly worse spots to have your home base." He chuckled at his own comment.

Sean's phone buzzed, and the preview of a message from Tara popped up on the screen.

He tapped it, and the message opened. "On it, Sean. We're on the way to the lab, but we can have the system start looking into it for us."

"The kids are on it, too," Sean announced as he answered her text with a quick "Thanks."

Tommy thumbed through a series of results in his search query and landed on the fourth one. He began reading silently. Niki did the same, and the table grew oddly silent.

Adriana took a few draws from the hookah while keeping her gaze fixed on the phone in her right hand. She scrolled through the information on one page and then skipped to another.

"Fascinating career," Sean commented as he read details about the life of Sinan Reis.

That quiet only lasted a minute before Adriana cut it. "You're not going to believe this," she said to the others, her eyes still fixed on her device. "Ugh, how did we not see this before?"

"See what before?" Tommy pressed. "Believe what?"

She turned her phone around so the others could see it.

"What is that?" Niki asked.

"It's a grave," Sean answered. "And it seems oddly familiar."

"That's because we saw it earlier tonight when we were going into the mausoleum."

"Wait. What?" Tommy blurted. He took the hose and inhaled

another puff of smoke. "Crap. That thing does look familiar. Are you saying—"

"It's the grave of Sinan Reis," Adriana she said, cutting him off. "And it's in the cemetery outside of Barbarossa's tomb."

Sean closed his eyes slowly and inhaled. Then he reached down and picked up the nearest hose and took a drag from the hookah. He inhaled deeply for a second, savoring the strawberry and tobacco. Then he set the hose down and pulled out a fistful of euros, laid them on the table, and stood up.

"I guess we're going back to the square," he said.

Niki's face donned a look of disappointment. "Oh well. So much for a relaxing smoke." He took the hose close to him and pulled a few puffs from it, then stood with the others.

"I hope Ahmed doesn't mind us doing a hit and run," Tommy said.

"Easy money," Sean replied after placing an additional euro on the table. "Let's just hope the cemetery hasn't attracted more attention by the time we get back there."

19

"I'd say it's definitely attracted some attention," Tommy noticed as he and the others stared across the square at the cemetery that housed the Barbarossa mausoleum.

They stood on the corner of the street along the edge of the plaza. The group had felt fortunate to get a ride at that time of night, although there seemed to be several rideshare drivers hovering around the hookah bar as it was one of the few places still open at that hour.

The driver dropped them off and drove away, leaving them to face what looked very much like a crime scene.

Several police cars were parked along the street with lights flashing. Some of the cops stood outside the cemetery gate, while others searched the area, talked to a few of the witnesses that had hung around, or scoured the waterfront with flashlights—perhaps hoping to find the perpetrators hiding conveniently within reach.

"Soooo, now what's the plan?" Adriana asked.

For a few seconds, no one said a thing.

Sean merely stood there gazing at the spectacle with his lips pinched together, helpless.

"I guess someone called the cops," Niki observed.

"You think?" Tommy retorted with a laugh.

"What should we do? There's no way to get to the grave now. They've blocked off the cemetery. Who knows when they'll let people back in again."

Sean saw flashlights twisting and turning inside the mausoleum. "They found the secret passage," he said, resignation in his voice. He tightened the backpack against his shoulders. He'd placed the golden key inside it to keep it safe. Now, he half wondered if he should have put it somewhere else.

"I don't suppose you can call one of your connections, Sean," Tommy suggested.

Sean looked at his watch. "Emily is still awake, unless she went to bed early. Not too late back home yet."

"You think she could help us?"

A shrug from his friend was the first answer. But the response lacked conviction.

"Not an option?" Tommy prodded. "Everything between you and Em okay?"

Sean snapped out of his daze. "Yeah. We're good. All good. I just don't like pushing that button too often. She's become a good friend. Last thing I want to do is be a bad one by asking for bailouts all the time. I prefer to save those get-out-of-jail calls for when I'm actually in a jail, or worse."

"Understood," Tommy said, though his voice betrayed how he wished they could pull that string.

"There is another possibility, though," Sean added, noting a tall Turkish man in a white button-up shirt and black slacks. The guy looked like he'd just come from a gala but ditched the tie and jacket somewhere between there and here. He spoke to a couple of investigators in suits. Both of those men looked extremely tired, and Sean couldn't blame them. They were either at the end of a long shift or at the beginning of one. Either way, the last thing they needed was to cap or start their day with a bizarre grave robbery that turned into a historical mystery. Sean knew who the two suits were, but the guy in the white shirt was the one that drew his attention.

"Who's that guy?" Adriana asked, as if reading his mind.

"I was wondering the same thing."

"He looks important," Niki said. "And tired."

The tall, slender man looked like he stood a few inches taller than Sean, who was a shade over six feet.

"Yeah, he does look tired," Sean agreed. "And he doesn't look like a cop either."

Tommy had been silent for a minute while the others contemplated who the guy might be.

He finally had the answer. "He's a historian," Tommy said. The definitive tone to his answer surprised Sean.

"You think so?"

"No doubt about it. Who else would they call in the middle of the night if an important historic place had been vandalized?"

Sean blushed and became defensive. "We didn't vandalize it. That's a bit harsh, don't you think?"

"Not in his eyes." Tommy shrugged indifferently. "I would be less than happy if someone broke into, say, the Margaret Mitchell house and uncovered a secret passage into the bowels of Atlanta."

"No you wouldn't. You'd be excited about it."

Tommy snorted. "Yeah, I guess a part of me would. If I knew it wasn't criminals that did it. But there'd be no way to know that. So, I'd probably be concerned. Especially if I thought they found something important."

"If that's a historian the detectives are talking to," Adriana said, "do you think he might know who you are? Or at least the agency?"

Tommy's eyes opened wide. "Of course. That's it. If that guy really is a historian, he's probably heard of the IAA."

"What are you waiting for, then?" Sean coaxed. "Go over there and talk to him. Just be careful with the cops. No sudden moves."

Tommy cast him a glance that suggested he knew better.

"Just follow along," he said. "I'm going in."

Sean rolled his eyes as his friend stepped into the plaza and walked with a confident stride bordering on way too cocky.

Two cops standing on the perimeter held up their hands and ordered him to stop before he'd taken ten steps.

They spoke to him in Turkish, to which he replied in English, "I'm a historian and an archaeologist," he explained. "I'm with the International Archaeological Agency." He started to produce his passport, which caused the cops to tense and reach for their weapons.

Sean shook his head. "Smooth, Schultzie."

Niki stepped in. "Sorry for the confusion," he said in Turkish. "Perhaps you have never heard of the IAA. We work to secure historical artifacts around the world. We heard there was something going on here and came to check it out."

The two cops looked at each other, dubious.

One on the right with a thick mustache that matched his black hair spoke first. "It's two in the morning. How could you possibly have heard about this?"

Niki shrugged and blushed a little. "We were at the hookah bar," he said, going with the truth since it put way less strain on his nerves. "Heard something happened at the tomb of Admiral Barbarossa and thought we should check it out. You know, see if we could help. Historical stuff is what we do, after all."

Mustache Cop narrowed his eyelids as he considered the young Greek's statement.

Then he touched the radio on his left shoulder and spoke into it.

Sean and Tommy didn't understand what he said. Neither did Adriana, but they had a feeling the cop was either asking his superior what he should do, or requesting a few more of their ranks to come and assist in kicking the Americans and their Greek friend to the curb.

Niki didn't seem concerned, which told the others the cop was asking what he should do.

Across the plaza, the investigators looked over at the group of unexpected visitors, then spoke to the supposed historian. He, then, turned his head and inspected the four, nodded, and started walking toward them.

The cop with the broom under his nose said in English, "He is coming over to speak with you."

"Look at you, Nick," Sean said. "Well done."

Niki beamed back at him. "Let's see what he has to say first."

The man marched across the square, stopping when he reached the perimeter where Sean and the others stood with the two cops.

"Hello," the man said in a weary voice. "My name is Timran Orut. They tell me you are with the International Archaeological Agency."

"They told you right," Tommy said, taking the lead. He extended his hand, and the man gripped it, shaking it for a few seconds. "I'm Tommy Schultz, and this is Sean, Adriana, and Niki."

"I'm familiar with your agency," Timran said. "You've done so much for the historical community through the years."

"We do our best," Tommy offered. "What happened here?"

"Oh, initially we thought some vandals broke into the mausoleum. But upon entering, we discovered the sarcophagus had been moved to reveal a passageway underneath it."

"Wow," Sean said, giving his best Academy Award effort. "Someone broke into it and found a secret passage?"

"Yes," Timran said. Excitement rippled across the weariness on his face. "As far as we can tell, the tomb wasn't damaged. The police are down in the tunnel right now to see if they can find the people who did this. Once they have cleared it, my team and I will go in. Probably sometime tomorrow."

"Is there any chance we could get in there and look around?" Tommy ventured.

"Oh, I'm sorry," Timran said. "Right now the entire cemetery is locked down until the police clear the area. It's possible I can allow you to go in with my group tomorrow if you like."

Tommy knew better than to press his luck on the issue. He could tell from the man's tone that he was going to play this entirely by the book with the local cops, and wasn't going to bend an inch.

"Do you have a business card or a number you don't mind me using to contact you in the morning?" Tommy asked. "It's late, and I'm sure you want to get home. We're all pretty tired ourselves."

"Yes, of course." Timran exchanged information with Tommy. "Now, if you'll excuse me, I need to get back to the investigators over there. Hopefully, they won't need me much longer."

"Thanks so much, Timran," Adriana said. "We appreciate your taking the time to speak to us."

The man nodded and turned his back to them, then walked through the plaza once more to the two investigators by the cemetery entrance.

"Thank you," Niki said to the two cops who remained next to them.

The men merely nodded.

"Come on," Sean said, twisting away from the two men. "Nothing else we can do here tonight."

Niki looked surprised, but Adriana and Tommy followed him away from the scene.

When they were out of earshot, Niki caught up to Sean as he walked toward the car they'd left there earlier in the evening.

"Wait," he insisted. "Where are we going? Are we really going to wait until morning to come back out here?"

Sean thought of his old friend Jack. He hoped Jack hadn't suffered before the Russians killed him. Assuming that was what happened. Either way, Sean had no intention of letting that happen to anyone else he knew.

Out here, even with all the cops around, he felt exposed, as though unseen eyes watched him from the shadows. His head twitched one way then the other as he checked every possible part of the area. There were dark corners, though. Windows, eaves, and other such spots could provide sanctuary for an enemy trying to stay out of sight.

"We don't have much choice right now," Sean said, deciding not to convey his concern to his Greek friend. "The cops aren't going to let us near the place, no matter who we work for."

"He's right," Tommy agreed, resigned to waiting. "Barbarossa was a national hero. Last thing we need to do is press our luck and then they find out that we were the ones who desecrated the monument to their beloved admiral."

"Fine. So, we just come back in the morning?"

"Maybe," Sean answered. "I recall passing a few of those graves outside the mausoleum. Looked like some of them had inscriptions carved into every inch of the headstones."

"I noticed that as well," Adriana said. "You don't think—"

"That the clue may be written on Sinan Reis's grave? I think it's possible."

"Definitely worth having a look."

They reached the car Niki had rented and climbed in.

"Let's head toward the hotel," Sean said as he looked out through the rear window, then the one to his left. He swept the street corner with his gaze. Adriana did the same. "We all need a good night's rest anyway. Meanwhile, let's see what we can find out about this grave."

He and the other two passengers took out their phones and started searching. Tommy sent a quick message to Tara and Alex, who both replied they were surprised he'd needed them more than once in such a short span.

As Sean and Adriana pored through the search results, Tommy's phone vibrated just as he began his query.

"Alex said one second," Tommy announced.

Niki drove the car through the quiet city streets. Few cars were out, other than the ones parked idly along the curbs. At this late hour, even the night owls were turning in.

As Niki turned the sedan to the right at an intersection, Tommy's phone started vibrating.

"Hello again," he said as he switched the device to speaker mode.

"You guys really are busy," Alex answered.

"Yeah, and it's extremely late. We're heading back to the hotel now. What did you find on the grave?"

"There are a lot of symbols on there, and a couple of interesting verses."

"Verses?" Adriana asked.

"Yeah. So, the headstone of Sinan Pasha, or Sinan Reis, has a few different verses written on it, but the one that is most interesting is a paraphrase of a text from the Suara Sura. It says, "Wealth nor hunting will benefit, but those who come to my throne with a free heart will."

Tommy's expression changed to one of confusion as he tried to process the information.

"The original text says those who come to Allah," Alex added. "I guess it's implied that's what it means on the headstone."

"Unless it's what we were hoping for," Sean argued. "What if the throne it mentions was a place where Sinan Reis ruled?"

"Or Barbarossa," Adriana ventured.

"Correct. If Barbarossa's right-hand man was talking about thrones, and he never had one, it's easy to think he was referring to his admiral."

"I can do another search for that if you like," Alex offered.

The IAA's computers were not only extremely fast; they were integrated with an AI unit that could extrapolate and fragment search quarries into thousands of new possibilities a simple search engine query could not. Tommy made sure to upgrade the systems every year, always staying ahead of everyone else, except for the government.

"Sure," Tommy said. "We still have a few minutes till we get to the hotel."

He looked over at Niki for confirmation. The driver merely nodded.

"Give me a second," Alex said. Then he went silent.

Sean looked over his shoulder, checking the road behind them to make sure they weren't being followed. A few cars lagged behind, spaced randomly apart, but one had just pulled in behind them, and the other hadn't been there long.

In the background, Sean heard Alex talking to someone. He couldn't tell if it was the AI or his wife.

"Are you sure? That sounds too easy," he said.

"What's too easy?" Sean interrupted.

"Sorry, Sean. The search pinpoints a place called Castello Barbarossa. It's on the island of Capri."

"Capri?"

Everyone else in the car looked at him.

"That's what it says. The castle is mostly ruins now. Barbarossa stormed it in 1535 and then destroyed it in 1544. He must have used it as his base of operations for a while. Now it's used by ornithologists to track migratory birds. This says some live there."

"The birds or the ornithologists?"

Alex blurted a laugh. "The ornithologists."

"That means people could be there," Sean muttered. His mind immediately went to the issue and started devising solutions to deal with the people at the old castle.

It was a tendency he'd tried to mute for years. His mind often wandered to problems that weren't there, filling his entire body with anxiety as he tried to figure out problems he'd not yet encountered.

"Shouldn't be an issue," Alex said. "This time of year there shouldn't be many people there. And besides, you guys are IAA. It's not like anyone is going to tell you that you can't be on the premises. Just tell them you're there to conduct an investigation."

Already got turned away once tonight, Sean thought. He figured it was better not to elaborate on that.

"Capri, huh," Sean said loud enough for the others in the car to hear.

"Barbarossa and his brother, Oruc, established a regional kingdom in Algiers, but I can't find anything that suggests Barbarossa himself actually used it as the seat of power."

Sean considered the answer as the car sped along the street. He needed a shower and a soft bed. Even though he was only in his late thirties, Sean felt a lack of energy he'd not detected often in his life. He blew it off as simply due to the late hour, jet lag, and lack of sleep. But he'd done this before. And it never hurt this way.

His eyelids dragged toward the earth as if attached to heavy kettlebells.

Adriana looked over at him when he mentioned Capri. The fatigue torturing his nerves didn't seem to have the same impact on her, though she was a few years younger and always had energy in spades.

"Okay," Tommy said. "Thanks, Alex. We'll look into it."

"Happy to help. Let me know if you need anything else."

"I will. Tell Tara thanks as well."

He ended the call and stared at the screen for several long breaths.

"So, Capri then?" Tommy asked.

"There's a castle there that Barbarossa took over. Alex said he destroyed it, too, which seems weird."

"Unless he didn't want anyone else to use it for military advantage," Adriana countered.

"True. Definitely possible."

"First thing in the morning I'll have the jet prepped and ready to head to Italy," Tommy said. "Niki, you want to come along, or are you ready to bail?"

"I would love to, but I have a meeting the day after tomorrow with an official from the French Archaeological Institute."

"Look at you," Tommy said with pride.

"We appreciate all your help, Niki," Adriana said.

The younger man beamed despite the utter exhaustion raking his body. "Happy to."

The car continued along the quiet early morning street, heading toward the hotel where warm beds awaited.

20

Konstantin couldn't believe his luck.
He and his group had returned to the square in hopes of finding something, anything that could give them direction with their next move.

The major hadn't given up hope, but what little he had left hung on by a rapidly fraying thread.

Frustrations over their failure to corral the Americans had nearly overtaken him, but he remained resolute. After all, Konstantin had faced greater challenges in the past, especially in the field of war, but this was different than trying to outwit a heavily armed foe with maneuvers.

When he and the rest of his team arrived back on site at the square, they'd been unpleasantly surprised by several police cars on the scene. Soon, more cops arrived, along with two men dressed in plain clothes Konstantin assumed to be detectives.

Another man showed up half an hour later wearing a white button-up shirt, though he looked less professional than the investigators. Konstantin couldn't figure the man's role among all the authorities, but one thing he noticed stood out: The cops spent a lot of time talking to that guy.

He wasn't a suspect, at least not that the major could tell from his point of view in a car parked along the street.

Watching through a pair of binoculars, Konstantin observed the police guiding the man into the cemetery, then eventually the mausoleum. He wished he could hear the exchange between the cops and the newcomer, but there was little that could be done about that. Even with the field mics he and his men had in their gear, none of them spoke enough Turkish to pick up any important details in the conversation.

Konstantin and his men had prepared themselves mentally for a long wait in the cars, potentially until morning.

Boris had protested the notion, noting that the Americans were putting more and more distance between them with every passing second.

"It doesn't matter how far away they get," Konstantin reminded, "if we don't know where they're going. Could be anywhere in the world by now. Our only chance is to figure out their destination on our own, and perhaps hope they are still here in the city somewhere by the time we do."

That had been the end of the conversation, and what Konstantin thought was the issue, until the man in the white shirt reemerged in the plaza.

He continued talking to the cops, which only heightened the major's interest in the man. Perhaps he was the police commissioner, or the mayor. Konstantin had done significant research regarding the tomb of Barbarossa and the supposed treasure the great admiral had secreted away, but little regarding the city of Istanbul, much less its police hierarchy and procedures.

None of that mattered when a familiar sedan pulled into a parking space just outside the plaza and Sean Wyatt stepped out onto the sidewalk.

The men in Konstantin's vehicle remained perfectly still, as did the other two teams waiting across the street and at the corner.

He quietly issued the order to remain in place through the radio in his ear and watched as Wyatt and his companions approached two police officers guarding the perimeter of the square.

The conversation with the two cops didn't last long. Then one of them spoke into the radio on his vest, and a minute later the man in the white shirt journeyed across the plaza and stopped where Wyatt waited.

Boris had stirred, as if he might climb out of the car, but he settled in again and watched quietly as the American spoke with the mysterious man.

"Who is that man?" Konstantin wondered to the others. "Do we have any idea?"

"No, sir," Boris answered first. The others in the car said nothing. And no one spoke through the radio. "Though he does seem important. You think he's one of the higher-ups with the police?"

"Possibly," Konstantin allowed. But this guy didn't look like a cop, or like someone who ordered other police around.

After a few minutes, the man shook his head as if denying Wyatt something. A minute later, the American and his companions turned away and returned to their car parked thirty yards away from where Konstantin sat in the shadows.

Wyatt scanned the area before getting in the car but never saw the Russians hiding in the dark. If he did, he didn't let on.

Konstantin watched as the sedan drove away. When the car disappeared around the corner, he ordered his men to follow. Boris started the engine and was about to pull out of the parking spot and fall in line behind the other two when the major saw the man in the white shirt leaving the square on foot.

The black BMW 4 series parked nearby blinked its headlights when the man pressed the button on the fob.

"Hold on," Konstantin said, putting his hand up to halt Boris. "We need to find out who this man is. Teams Two and Three, stay with the targets. You know what to do."

His men's expertise in surveillance was unmatched, and the major knew they would fold in and out of traffic enough to throw off even the most astute quarry.

"Sir?" was the only protest Boris offered.

The question didn't seem to bother the major. In fact, he responded as though he'd expected it.

"Think about it, Boris. Why would they come back here? Very risky, no?"

He watched the realization light up the captain's eyes. "Very," Boris agreed.

"That must mean there is something here they missed. Why else would they return here?"

"Maybe they dropped something."

Konstantin resisted the urge to roll his eyes. "I don't think so. What would be so important that they would risk returning here, knowing that we were so close behind them?"

"Unless they believed doubling back was the safest move. It is unlikely they would think we'd return here."

"A fair assessment, but I am hedging my bets the other direction."

"Do you think the man they were talking to knows what they wanted?"

"That's exactly what I aim to find out."

Konstantin slid out of the car and walked behind the man in the white shirt, following him quietly until the guy reached the car and opened the door.

The BMW was parked under an overhanging tree branch and was blocked off from view of the cops by a portion of the wall surrounding the cemetery.

"Excuse me," the major said, startling the man only slightly.

The guy turned around, surprised at first that someone was speaking to him, but then more so at the pistol held close to the stranger's body, shielding its view from the police.

"What is this?" the man demanded in English.

"Quiet," Konstantin replied, tapping the suppressor on the end of his pistol. "I can kill you right now and slump your body in your car, and no one would know. Even with the police so close by."

The man looked down at the weapon, then over toward the

square. He couldn't quite see the two cops guarding the perimeter but knew they had to be close.

"What do you want?" he spat.

"Just some information. What did those men want who came up to you a few minutes ago?"

The man's brow furrowed. "They are with the IAA. Thought they could use their clout to get into the tomb, but it was vandalized earlier this evening. So, no one is getting in until we find out exactly what happened and who is responsible."

"And who are you?"

The guy snorted in derision. "I'm an historian."

"You must be an important one for the police to call you at such a late hour."

The man sighed. "I'm nobody."

"Careful," Konstantin warned. "It's easy to kill a nobody. They have little usefulness."

The historian tensed at the casual threat.

Then he noticed another man, this one a burly, muscular guy approach from the same direction.

"Who are you?" the historian demanded. "If I yell for the police, you're both going to be in a lot of trouble."

"Do we look like the kinds of men who fear the police?" Konstantin asked. "We've killed men with five times the training of those officers. So, please, don't make us do that. Their blood will be on you. And all I'm asking for is information."

"What do you want?"

"Now we're getting somewhere. You said Wyatt wanted to go in and have a look around." It wasn't a question.

"Yes, that's right. I told him not until—"

"You mentioned that part. Did he say anything else?"

"No." The man shook his head, jiggling his thick, dark hair. "He didn't put up a fight."

"Strange," Konstantin said.

The historian looked puzzled at the response. "Why would that be strange?"

Konstantin permitted a sinister grin to part his lips. The breeze flapped his jacket and filled his nostrils with the smell of salty air. "Because Sean Wyatt and his friends are the ones who vandalized your tomb."

For several heartbeats, the historian contemplated the statement, mostly in disbelief. "You can't be serious. The IAA has a reputation that—"

"I'm well aware of their reputations. They seem to find their way into trouble quite often."

Having spent a considerable amount of time in the history field, it was inevitable to read articles about the famed IAA agents who made incredible discoveries. But along with their reputation for uncovering lost history, there was a side to their stories that got swept under the rug, buried from public view. While people lauded these so-called agents as heroes, Konstantin looked beyond the headlines.

He discovered a darker side of the IAA, instances where collateral damage occurred. Finding the incidents where buildings or other structures were damaged was simple enough—after all, explosions were difficult to hide from the public eye.

Blood, on the other hand, had been well hidden. But not well enough. Konstantin knew secrets the IAA kept out of the media outlets. He knew Sean Wyatt and Tommy Schultz had killed people, though proving it was both futile and nearly impossible.

Not that any of that mattered. They were the enemy, and enemies didn't get the luxury of being categorized as dangerous or not. They simply were. The major treated all enemies the same—with abject ruthlessness.

"Who are you? And what do you want?" the historian demanded.

"What did the Americans want?" Konstantin asked, deciding the direct route was best.

The man puzzled over the question for a second before answering. "They wanted to get into the cemetery."

"Why?"

"They didn't say," the historian answered. "Just that they wanted to go in and have a look around. I told them to come back in the morning."

Konstantin brandished the pistol. "You're certain they didn't say what it was they were looking for?"

"I swear," the man replied, fear trembling his voice.

The major lifted his chin and peered at the man.

"What do you want? Please. I am only a historian."

"You are going to take us into the cemetery to have a look around," Konstantin answered.

The man scoffed at the idea, twisting his head away for a second. Then he remembered there was a gun pointed at his chest, and his face returned to its fear-filled expression once more.

"You're mad," he said. "Do you think you can walk me in there at gunpoint without the police noticing?"

"That's exactly what is going to happen. Tell the police that we are your assistants here to help with the investigation."

For a moment, it seemed the man considered the possibility. Then he shook his head. "They will see through it. I already told them I was leaving."

"Then tell them you changed your mind. I don't care what you tell them. One of my men will have a rifle on you at all times. He's over there in the shadows." Konstantin pointed to a tree near the mosque off to the right. He was lying, of course, but the historian had no way of knowing that. And standing there facing a very real pistol, who was to say the Russian didn't have reinforcements placed all around the square?

The man twitched his head around to check, but it didn't matter what he saw or didn't see. The planted seed in his mind had already grown into full-blown paranoia.

"Fine," he said. "But you will let me go once I've shown you the cemetery."

"Yes," the major said.

With a sigh, the man closed his car door and stuffed the key fob back into his pocket. "What is it you're hoping to find?"

"We will know when we find it."

The historian searched Konstantin's face for more information but got none. The Russian did, however, put the gun away. The man believed he was in a sniper's sights now. Konstantin could see it in the whites of his eyes.

"That isn't much help. Is there something specific you would like to see?" Derision hung on his words like venom from a viper's fangs.

As the three men walked together toward the square, the other two guards hung back, following a few paces behind.

Konstantin played the part perfectly, pretending they had no idea what had happened earlier.

"What happened here earlier?"

The historian relaxed a touch. "Someone broke into the mausoleum."

"Why would someone break into a tomb? Was the admiral buried with some kind of treasure?"

"We don't know why. The sarcophagus was intact. Except it had been moved."

"Moved?" Konstantin embellished his disbelief.

"Yes. Apparently, there was a mechanism built into it to roll out of its position when activated." He cut himself off as they approached the two cops.

The police visibly wondered why the historian had returned, and who his new companions were.

"We thought you were leaving, Timran," one of the cops said with a tired laugh.

"Yes," Timran affirmed nervously. He glanced to the Russian to his right, the man he assumed to be the one in charge. At least he'd gleaned that much. With the pistol put away, Timran felt the urge to warn the police, but the fear of the hidden shooter kept him silent. "These men are from the university. They've worked with me before, and I thought they might be able to help solve this bizarre mystery."

"You woke them up for this?" the other cop asked.

Timran coughed another feeble attempt at laughter. "A mystery like this has to be solved, no?"

"You're the expert."

"We shouldn't be long. And it's late. We will probably come back in the morning to get a better look around in the daylight—see if there's anything we missed."

Timran made his way past the cops, half hoping they bought the story—half dreaming they could free him from the secret hostage situation.

But they went back to whatever idle conversation they'd been attempting to enjoy at this ridiculous hour.

The Russians followed Timran over to the cemetery gate, where another cop stepped aside to allow them through.

"As you can see," Timran said, motioning around to the different graves, "it is a cemetery." He did his best to make it sound like there was nothing interesting to see, a ploy Konstantin knew.

"Who are the people buried here?" the major asked. "I assume they are important historical figures."

"You assume correctly. Graves such as these, placed in a square like this, isn't a common occurrence. These men are honored, though not as greatly as the admiral. To this day, he is still a national hero of Turkey."

"As he should be," Konstantin said. "He was a grand leader, and perhaps the greatest naval commander in the world at the time. I imagine in all of history there were few as skilled as he."

The statements confused the historian. One minute, the Russian was pointing a gun at him, the next he was revering a figure from Turkish history like a fangirl.

"You have studied Barbarossa?"

Konstantin looked over at the man with an expression that said, *Isn't it obvious?*

"Why such interest?" Timran had to know. These men who came out of the blue, brandishing firearms and threats, must have had a reason for being there—especially at this hour. They were more than just fans of history or Barbarossa. And he wanted to know what they were up to.

"We are trying to locate an artifact we believe Barbarossa left behind," Konstantin admitted. He said it as if it were of no consequence.

Timran frowned at the confession. "And you believe this artifact is in his tomb?" His eyes widened. "You were the ones who moved the sarcophagus."

"No," the major shook his head. "I believe you already spoke to the people who did that."

The historian's bewilderment deepened like a puddle in a thunderstorm. That confusion only lasted for a few seconds as the epiphany streaked across his unbelieving face.

"The Americans?"

Konstantin knew he had the man now.

"They certainly seem to find themselves in secret passages quite often, don't they?" He prodded the historian with the teasing statement.

"But if they were the ones who broke into the tomb..." His voice trailed off as he looked back over his shoulder at the open mausoleum. He rounded on Konstantin again. "Why would they return?"

"Perhaps they were looking for something, something they missed on their initial visit. You said they wanted to get into the cemetery, yes?"

Timran bobbed his head once.

"Then tell me more about the men buried here." He spied a grave to his right, closer to the mausoleum. The headstone featured a vertically sliced turban atop a pillar rising up over the open stone container. "Who is buried in that one?" he asked.

"That one?" Timran clarified. "He was one of the most important men in the empire during the time of Suleiman the Magnificent, perhaps second only to Barbarossa. He was Pasha Sinan Reis. A great naval commander in his own right, and friend of Admiral Barbarossa."

That information piqued Konstantin's interest, and he felt his feet pulling him toward the grave almost on their own. He stopped when he was a few feet away from the headstone. His guards ushered Timran over to where the major stood.

"These markings," Konstantin said, wagging a finger at the stone, "what do they mean?"

"The verses?" Timran rolled his shoulders. "This one here says that wealth nor hunting will benefit, but those who come to my throne with a free heart will. It's from the Suara Sura."

Silence fell over the cemetery, only interrupted by the breeze blowing in off the water, the rustle of the trees and shrubs, and the occasional laughter of one of the cops by the street.

"Throne?" Konstantin wondered. "What throne?"

"The throne of Allah, of course."

The major wasn't sold on the notion. "Strange that this verse would be on this man's grave."

"Why do you say that?"

"I have heard of this man," Konstantin explained. "He was a corsair with Barbarossa. A pirate. Based on what I know of pirates, they weren't always the most religious sorts. Paranoid? Sure. Superstitious? Definitely. But religious? Rarely."

"Then what are you suggesting?" Timran asked.

Konstantin set his jaw. "Nothing. Just that it is a curious thing to have on this man's grave. Thank you for allowing us in, Timran. When we are gone, I will call off my sniper."

A cocktail of confusion and surprise swept the historian's face.

"That's all? You just wanted to see the cemetery?"

Konstantin half turned away from him. "Yes. Thank you for cooperating."

He finished his turn and put his back to the man. As he walked away, leaving Timran standing there still in disbelief, Boris caught up to his commander.

"What's going on, boss?" he asked. "I thought we were going to check around for a clue."

"We already found it," the major replied.

"What do you mean?" Boris's face reflected his lack of understanding.

The men passed through the cemetery gate and picked up the pace. The sooner they could get back on the trail, the better. Konstantin could only hope that the historian still believed there was a shooter hidden somewhere, keeping a watchful eye on the man.

When they were halfway across the plaza, Konstantin answered the question.

"The throne," he said. "The throne is the key to the riddle. That's why the Americans came back here. Whatever they found must have only been a piece of the puzzle, and they needed to know where to go next. Sinan Reis was not only a pirate and a commander; he was the man who wrote Barbarossa's memoirs. He would have intimate knowledge, secret information, that no one else had access to. He must have been the one to lay out the trail leading to the trident."

"Are you certain?"

"Yes," Konstantin said, masking any doubt with a confident snap of his voice. "It is the only answer."

"What do we do next?"

"We need to find out where Barbarossa set up some kind of a government, a small kingdom perhaps. Once we know that, we can get there before the Americans. If they even figure it out. The good news is, since they are coming back here in the morning, we will have a head start."

21

The early morning sun stabbed through the hotel room's window curtains without consideration of the sleepy occupants within. Not that they were still asleep.

Sean and Adriana had already been up for an hour, getting little more than a four- to five-hour nap before rousing at the break of day. Both wondered if Tommy and Niki were awake in the other room.

The answer came in the form of three firm knocks at the door.

"Housekeeping," Tommy said in the most high-pitched, feminine voice he could muster.

Sean rolled his eyes and shook his head at Adriana.

"What is he doing?" she asked.

Sean chuckled as he walked over to the door and unlocked it. "Did you ever see *Tommy Boy*?" he asked over his shoulder as he unclipped the latch.

He turned the doorknob and opened it.

"No," she said. "I think I've heard of it, though."

"Wow," Sean said in amazement as Tommy and Niki appeared in the hall just outside the doorway. "I know what our in-flight movie is going to be on the way to Rome."

"What's that?" Tommy asked, stepping past his friend to enter the room.

Niki offered a quick "Good morning, Sean."

"Morning, Niki." Then he answered Tommy's question. "She hasn't seen *Tommy Boy*."

"What? Seriously?"

Adriana looked unimpressed. "You do realize I'm not from your country. And while we get most of the American movies over in Spain, there are some we don't see. Part B: I don't make time to watch many movies anyway."

"She's right about that," Sean confirmed. "I think in all the years we've been together, we may have watched a grand total of maybe a few dozen films. Lot of shows."

"A lot of sports," she semi-corrected with a dry tone.

"Hey, I don't hear you complaining when we watch Real Madrid play."

"Because they're the best." There was no arguing with a woman who was right. Especially one with the unquestionable confidence in her eyes that Adriana carried.

"Fair."

"Okay, but he's right," Tommy said. "We definitely have to watch that on the plane ride."

"Or," Adriana suggested, "we do our jobs and actually try to figure out what is going on with these Russians, and why they are hunting for the trident."

"Okay, okay," Tommy relented. "You're right. But when we get home, the four of us are going to get together and watch that movie."

"Niki is coming to the States?" Sean asked with a mischievous glint in his eyes.

The young Greek looked confused and shook his head. "No. I'm not."

"I was talking about June and the three of us," Tommy explained.

"I know, Schultzie," Sean said and hefted his rucksack over his right shoulder. "Have you heard from the pilot?"

"Yeah. Jim said the plane is fueled up and ready to go. He and Erik the co-pilot are finishing their routine check."

"Does that guy ever sleep?"

"Probably more than we do. He just sits around and waits to fly. Plenty of time to rest while doing that."

"I guess so."

After leaving the hotel, the group stopped in a breakfast place Niki recommended a few blocks away. They enjoyed baklava and coffee, as well as an assortment of cheeses, fresh tomatoes, cucumber, eggs, and dates. The quick meal also came with fresh baked bread, which Sean regarded as some of the best he'd ever had.

He chewed the bread slowly in the back of the sedan while Niki drove them toward the airport.

"You know, there are a lot of countries that make great bread," Sean said. "But no one ever mentions Turkey."

"Oh, it's excellent here," Niki said. "And you're right. Definitely underrated."

The rest of the drive to the airport was consumed by silent eating and sipping of coffee.

The control tower appeared on the horizon after fifteen minutes of navigating the busy streets of Istanbul.

"Nearly there," Niki announced.

Sean peered out the car window at the planes taking off and landing in perfect rhythm, mesmerizing to behold.

Tommy finished his food in the front seat and stuffed the trash into one of the paper bags they'd received with the meal, then checked his phone.

He had a message from the pilot. "Oh, another message from Jim," Tommy said, realizing he'd missed the message ten minutes ago. "Must have left my phone on do not disturb."

"Problem?" Adriana asked. She sounded unconcerned.

"Huh," Tommy huffed. "Um, Niki, don't go to the private hangars."

"What?" the driver asked. "Why not?"

He'd already turned the blinker on to go left toward the private gate into the airport.

"Jim said there is a technical problem with the plane."

Tommy all but reached over and jerked the wheel the other direction for Niki.

"Do not go that way, Niki," Tommy urged.

"Okay. Take it easy. Although I don't know what you want me to do. How long will it take for the plane to get fixed?"

"There's nothing wrong with the plane," Tommy said, peering out the window across the driver. He stared down the road that ran along the outer fence of the airfield, trying to see beyond where the IAA plane was parked, he believed, in front of the hangar where they'd left it.

"What do you mean? You said—"

"That's code," Sean answered for his friend. "Our pilot has a code for us if there is some kind of holdup with any public officials."

"You mean the cops?"

"Could be. There's no way of knowing without seeing them firsthand."

"And," Tommy added, "the fact Jim hasn't sent anything else tells me he's gone radio silent. Which means he's probably being watched."

"This is crazy. What do you mean he's being watched?" Niki sounded like he was about to have a full-on panic attack.

"Relax," Sean chirped. "Better we got the memo now instead of five minutes from now."

"I'm just glad I checked my phone," Tommy said.

"Or that we stopped to get breakfast," Adriana reminded.

"Right. But now what? And why would the police be keeping us from taking off?"

Sean had a feeling he knew.

"Timran."

"What?"

"The historian from last night," Sean said. "If he thinks we had something to do with the tomb 'vandalism,'" he used air quotes with the last word, "then he'll want to bring us in for questioning."

"He can't do that," Tommy countered. "There's no evidence we were even there."

"True," Sean agreed. "But that doesn't mean he won't slow us down by a day or two. Even if we lost the Russians, I don't think it's wise to sit around and give them a bunch of time to catch up. Just in case they figure something out."

"So... what's your plan? We take a train? That'll take too long."

"No," Sean said, remembering something he'd heard basketball coach Bruce Pearl say when he was at the University of Tennessee. "We always fly."

"Okay... but the plane?"

"I didn't say we were going to fly private. Or even first class for that matter." He directed his next words to the driver. "Niki, take us to the terminal."

Fifteen minutes later, Sean stood next to his wife in front of Tommy in the ticketing line for flights to Rome

"You realize this isn't going to work, right?" Tommy whined. "They'll be watching for us."

Sean shook his head and looked down at the ground. He looked like an NFL head coach who'd just seen their kicker miss an extra point.

"They'll be watching for us at our plane, buddy. I don't think our friend Timran has the authority, or the credibility, to pull that many resources. We're not a national security threat."

"He's right," Adriana said, though she still scanned the faces in the airport just in case. "People are one-track-minded by nature. They're linear. Timran believes the only way we're leaving is on our company jet."

"Okay, fine. But when is the next flight to Rome?" Tommy questioned. He crossed his arms as if he'd just made the checkmate play.

"The next one leaves in forty-seven minutes." She showed him the phone she'd been holding in her hand. And the tickets she'd already purchased.

"Wait. You already bought tickets?"

"There were five left," Adriana explained. "One in first class. I took that one. You two boys can fly coach."

Sean blurted out a laugh.

"Then what are we doing in this line?" Tommy asked.

"I don't know. I figured maybe you wanted to check a bag." She added a mischievous wink.

"I don't need to check my stuff. If we're flying out in forty-seven minutes, we need to move."

The three left the ticketing and bag check line and hurried toward their gate. Even though Sean knew they'd left their weapons with Niki, he still felt paranoid about it. Had he checked every pouch, every part of his baggage?

He shook off the concerns. Of course he had. He'd been thorough, as had the other two.

After taking a series of walkways and corridors, they arrived at their gate as the first-class passengers were called to begin boarding.

Adriana immediately headed for the line, looking back at the two men for a moment to say, "You two have fun in coach."

Sean snorted his laughter, while Tommy painted a beleaguered expression across his face.

"So funny," he said.

The men watched as she disappeared into the bridge connecting the aircraft and the terminal.

Then they waited another ten minutes before their section was called to begin boarding.

The entire duration of their wait was spent scanning the terminal for any signs of trouble—security or police hurrying toward them, or even one of the Russians. Since neither Tommy nor Sean knew what the latter looked like, they would have had to go with their gut to identify the men. As it was, they marched onto the bridge and boarded the plane without incident.

The two passed Adriana sitting in a comfortable, plush seat near the middle of first class. She merely waved at them like a royal as they passed, dismissing them as though they were mere peasants.

"I'll remember this," Tommy warned.

"I'm sorry. Do I know you?"

Sean just laughed and kept walking.

Once their bags were stowed, the two sat down—Tommy taking the window seat and Sean on the aisle.

While his fear of heights was well documented, Sean didn't have an issue with flying. He simply preferred the aisle seat in case someone caused a problem.

Even on the plane, Sean's nerves remained tight. He wouldn't relax until they were safely in the air. And even then, he might hold back that feeling of relief until they touched down in Italy.

"Here we go," Sean said, looking across his friend and out the window.

The captain went through his routine, and then the flight attendants conducted their spiel regarding seatbelt rules, moving around in the cabin, and what to do in case of an emergency.

The aircraft started rolling during the flight attendants' info session, which extracted a relived sigh from Sean.

As the plane taxied across the tarmac, Sean repeatedly looked out the window—just trying to get a glimpse of where the IAA plane was parked, but he could never spot it.

When the jet accelerated forward, and the wheels lifted off the ground, Sean turned to his friend. "Niki is going to be fine, right?"

Tommy nodded. "Oh, sure."

"I just feel like we kind of sacrificed him on this one."

Tommy shook his head. "You worry too much. They have no evidence Niki had anything to do with what happened at the tomb."

"Yeah, I guess you're right. We just look guilty doing this."

"It was this or get taken in for questioning. And we're against the clock if those Russians figure anything out."

Sean knew it was true. But that didn't mean he had to like it. Throwing their young friend onto the sacrificial altar didn't feel right. He just hoped that Niki could handle it.

Niki drove the sedan through the security gate and guided it down the road that wrapped around the tarmac and the runways. Ahead to his left, he spotted the IAA private jet, where several police cars sat parked next to it.

He felt a twinge of nerves tickle his gut, but he kept going.

"Just relax," he said. "You've broken no laws. Except for trespassing." Then it hit him. He hadn't trespassed. He'd been in the boat. "What am I so worried about? I was just out driving a boat."

A story formed in his mind, and a cryptic smile spread across his lips.

When he pulled up to the plane, police that had been standing around talking to each other surrounded the vehicle.

The police readied weapons, aiming them into the car—straight at the driver. Despite the obvious threat, Niki felt much calmer than he had expected. He immediately recognized the historian, Timran, standing among the ten cops that waited for Niki to get out of the car.

Niki swallowed hard as one of the cops pulled on the door handle, opening the driver's side.

The cop barked at him in English, ordering him to get out.

The officer wore a bulletproof vest and a SWAT helmet, still pointing his submachine gun at Niki.

The young Greek raised his hands slowly and slid his legs out of the car, planting both feet on the ground. He stood gradually, aware that a single sudden move could startle the cop into blasting several holes through him.

The historian stepped toward the car while three other cops circled around it and aimed their weapons at the windows.

Timran scowled as he peered through the glass and saw no other occupants.

"Where are they?" the historian demanded.

"What do you mean?" Niki asked. "Where are who?"

"You know exactly who. Sean Wyatt and Tommy Schultz. And the woman. Where are they? We have some questions for them."

"Questions?" Niki wondered. Genuine curiosity streaked across his face. He could have won an Academy Award. He noticed the pilot in a black suit and tie standing next to the stairs leading up to the plane's open door. He didn't look like he'd been worked over, and seemed as if he wasn't in any distress. The tall, slender man with a shaved head and aviator sunglasses on simply stood with his hands folded across his belt as if nothing was wrong.

Niki admired the man's cool since he felt like he was struggling on the inside just to keep it together.

"Yes," Timran said, cutting through Niki's thoughts like a saber. "We have reason to believe that you and your IAA companions were the ones responsible for the damage done at the tomb of Barbarossa last night."

Behind him, the cops opened the doors to the sedan but found it empty. One of the men looked to Timran with an obvious question on his face.

"Check the trunk," Timran ordered the cops.

The historian, it seemed, held more sway with local officials than Niki would have first suspected.

The officer who extracted Niki from the vehicle shoved him aside and reached into the car. After a few seconds of searching, he found the latch to open the trunk and pulled it.

The sun burned bright overhead, warming the tarmac under Niki's feet. The roars of jets taking off and landing filled the air in a steady, rhythmic swell and lull, then up again as the next plane took its turn.

One of the men near the back of the car opened the trunk while another pointed his weapon into the cargo hold.

"Nothing," the first guy snapped. "It's empty."

Timran couldn't believe it. He walked around to the back of the car and looked into the empty trunk. His eyes flamed as he redirected them to Niki, who stood there as stoic as his nerves would allow.

"Where are they?" the historian roared.

"I honestly don't know," Niki said, telling what he figured to be the truth.

Timran stepped close enough that his toes nearly touched Niki's.

The man's aftershave wafted into Niki's nostrils, and he twitched his nose at the pungent odor.

"What are you doing here?" Timran demanded.

"I came to tell my friends goodbye. I thought they would be here by now. I had some other things I had to take care of for the agency this morning. So they were going to catch a cab or a rideshare to the airport." Niki embellished it now and looked over the historian's shoulder to the pilot. "Jim, have they not shown up yet?"

Jim kept his ice-cold stare plastered on his face as he shook his head. "Not yet, sir."

Niki shrugged. "That's strange. They said they would be here." He checked his watch to add to the show. "I suppose they'll be here any minute."

Timran's right eye twitched. He obviously didn't believe Niki, or the pilot, but what could he do?

"What are you doing here, anyway?" Niki asked, going on the offensive. "You said you think we damaged the tomb? I hadn't heard it was damaged other than what you mentioned last night. Vandalism was the word I think you used. Which makes me think of spray paint and graffiti. Or maybe broken windows. Is that what happened?"

"You know it isn't. We discussed this last night."

"Oh right. We did, didn't we? Well, all I know is I was showing the others Istanbul's nightlife. We hit my favorite hookah bar while we were out. In fact," he dug into his back pocket, which caused the cops around him to tense for a second. Niki held up his other hand. "I'm just getting a receipt, guys. I'm unarmed."

He wasn't lying. He didn't have a weapon on him, and there were none in the car. He'd been smart enough to ditch the guns the others left before returning to the airport, dropping them in a trash bin on the side of the road. He doubted any of the trash collectors would notice. *Who actually looked in trash bags while they were loading them onto a truck?*

Niki pulled the folded white paper from his back pocket and extended it toward Timran. "Here it is. Receipt from the hookah bar. I always keep receipts just in case. Tommy is pretty big on saving taxes. Can't say that I blame him. I've learned a lot about that in recent—"

"Shut up," Timran snapped, snatching the receipt from the younger man. He unfolded it and pored over the numbers, then the time of day and the date. It was from earlier that morning. Much earlier. Just before they'd arrived at the square.

His chest swelled and shrank in an elevated rhythm as anger fueled his breath.

"See?" Niki offered. "They were with me."

Timran folded the receipt and inclined his head, pinching the paper between his index finger and thumb. "You think this proves anything?"

"Would be stranger if it didn't," Niki fired back. Frustration with the historian's unwillingness to believe the half-lie started to burn in the young Greek's gut.

The historian considered the words for a moment. And Niki decided to press him further.

"Tommy and Sean's sole purpose with the agency is to preserve history, Timran. Not damage it or disturb its integrity. Seems odd you'd suspect them of that."

Timran inhaled slowly, regulating his breath. He swallowed hard and looked around at the men in uniform. "Perhaps I was mistaken."

He handed the receipt back to Niki. "My apologies."

"No problem," Niki said as relief spilled into his chest. "I am curious, though. What happened at the tomb? Did you find anything unusual during the investigation?"

Timran sized him up before speaking. "Just tunnels under the plaza. We have a team mapping it now. But it seems to reach a dead end."

"Oh. Well, I wish you luck. Are you going to stay here and wait for Tommy and the others?"

The historian thought better of it. He'd already embarrassed himself enough in front of the police surrounding him, and any further embarrassment might cost him their assistance down the road.

"No. We should be going. I need to check on the tunnel investigation. Carry on about your business. It's probably best that I'm not here when your friends arrive."

He twitched his head back toward his vehicle and the squad cars near the plane, signaling it was time to go.

The cops looked annoyed, but that was Timran's problem now.

Niki watched as the men returned to their vehicles and drove away. When they were all the way to the gate, Niki turned around and looked at the pilot, who remained at his station with the same pose he'd held the entire time.

"Good job," Jim said. "You kept your cool."

"Thanks." Niki breathed a long sigh of relief. "What happens next?"

The pilot shrugged. "Next I wait for them to tell me where to go next."

Niki watched a plane taking off in the distance. "Hopefully they're on a plane to Italy right now. So, maybe that's where you're heading next."

Jim nodded. "Thanks for the tip, kid."

He turned and ascended the stairs before disappearing into the plane. Niki nodded, suddenly alone on the tarmac.

"Yeah." He couldn't believe he'd pulled it off. "I guess I did do a good job."

22

"This is your captain speaking," the man's voice said through the overhead cabin speakers. His accent was English, somewhere in the area of Northamptonshire if Sean didn't miss his guess. "You are free to use your laptops and other electronic devices at this time."

Sean immediately flipped down the seat tray and tugged his backpack out from under the seat ahead of him. He almost always chose to fly with two carry-on bags instead of checking a bag, and in this instance that decision had been clutch.

Tommy went for his bag, too, both of the same mind.

Sean removed the laptop from his backpack and set it on the tray.

The flight attendants were down the aisle, serving the first-class passengers. Leaning around to get a better view, Sean noticed Adriana ordering something—probably a glass of complimentary wine.

Sean shook his head in good-natured humor at the woman and then returned his focus to the computer screen as it blinked to life.

He entered the password and then stared at the screen for thirty seconds.

"You okay?' Tommy asked.

Sean leaned back and pulled his fingers away from the keyboard. "Yeah," he said. "I just... I was thinking about Jack. How he found out about all this, why he got involved, and what happened to him."

"You and he were never close, right?"

"Not really," Sean admitted. "But he was one of those guys I wanted to root for. You know? Seemed like he had a couple of strikes against him early on in life. I always hope those kinds of people turn it around—make something of themselves."

"For one of the toughest guys I know, you really do have a soft heart, Sean. You know that?"

Sean's shoulders raised then slumped. "I guess. I just know that some people aren't born into circumstances as good as the ones we had when we were kids." He stopped for a second. "Then I think about what happened to you. For all those years you thought your parents were dead. You could have turned to drugs, a life of crime, desperation, depression. It would have been easy for you to fall by the wayside, to give up. Even with the money that was left for you, things could have fallen apart quickly."

"Especially with the money that was left to me. You see those stories all the time about people who get a bunch of cash and then go broke a year or two later. Sometimes sooner."

"Yeah. But you didn't. You built something that has continued to grow, and make a difference in the world, and in history itself. The IAA rewrites history the way it should have been recorded. We reveal truths through discovery and recovery—truths that no one would have known about otherwise."

Tommy blinked a few times as he stared at his friend. "You can't beat yourself up for the decisions other people make, buddy. That's how you get drawn down into the darkness and never come up."

"So, have no sympathy?" Sean half joked with a laugh.

"No. Not at all. The IAA contributes millions to charity every year. We spend a lot of our free time volunteering, too."

"True."

"But we can't feel guilty about our circumstances, either the ones in the past or the current ones. All we can do is help show people how to crawl out."

Sean nodded. "That's a good way of putting it."

Tommy inhaled deeply through his nose. "And hey, if your friend Jack is still out there, we'll find him. He reached out to you. Who knows? Maybe he's turning a corner."

"Maybe. But the fact that the Russians are involved makes me wonder who he pissed off."

Tommy chuckled. "You mean like the Russian president?"

"Who knows?"

"Seriously? You think that's possible?"

Sean shrugged again and looked across the aisle at a young couple staring out the window at the ancient city landscape dropping away from them.

He brought his focus back to the laptop in front of him and the browser he'd left open. "I've seen a lot of things since I started working with you, Schultzie. Stuff I never would have believed possible before. I've witnessed occurrences that defy explanation, and outrun every discipline of science known to man."

"Not every discipline," Tommy hedged.

"Fair enough. But most of them."

"Heck, we still get criticized as being pseudoscientists and pseudoarchaeologists. To be completely honest, I never claimed to be a scientist."

The two friends shared a laugh at that one.

"Some people are stuck in the past they've created and don't want that changed," Sean said. "They fear change."

"That and they're unbreakably cynical. When you reach the point where you ignore scientific methods and truths because the old models that were once substantiated by those things have now been proven false, you're the one who's a pseudoscientist."

"Wow. Did you stay up all night thinking about that?"

Tommy rolled his eyes. "Enough chatter about philosophy. We need to figure out why the Russians want this thing so bad."

"Yeah," Sean agreed. "I just don't get it. I've never come across anything or anyone who actually believed the trident of Poseidon was real."

"Did you ever come across anyone who believed Excalibur was real? Or the Spear of Destiny? Or Shangri-La?"

Sean pressed his lips together. "No. I suppose not."

"So, who cares what anyone believes?"

"You're right," Sean said.

His fingers started flying across the keyboard as he entered his first search. He waited for several seconds as the slow airplane Wi-Fi kicked into first gear. He half expected to hear the static, electric gurgling sounds of a dial-up modem.

Finally, the first results appeared. He saw Tommy was doing something similar on his computer.

Sean peered at the images of Barbarossa on his screen and clicked one that looked familiar.

"Whoa," he said, pointing at the monitor. "Check it out."

Tommy took his eyes off his own screen and looked to Sean's.

An image of the famed Ottoman admiral with a trident laid across his shoulder stared back at Tommy.

"That looks eerily similar to the one we saw down in the tunnel."

"Most people would blow this off as just a work of art, a depiction of the commander—perhaps symbolic of his command of the sea."

"But there's something more to it, isn't there?" Tommy breathed. "But what?"

Sean began typing again and waited another twenty seconds for the next set of results to pop up.

He raised his fist to his lips and thumbed his chin while he waited impatiently for the next links to appear.

"Looking for information on the trident itself?" Tommy asked.

"Yeah," Sean said with a head bob. "For a group of Russians to be looking for the thing, you have to wonder: Is it just something they can sell for a fortune? Or is there more to it?"

Tommy thought about the question for a few seconds before responding. "That's the thing. We don't know much about these guys other than where they came from."

Sean let out a hum then returned his gaze to the computer. He clicked on a link and read the lines on the page. The article was about Poseidon and his magical signature weapon.

"This says that Poseidon could raise the seas," Sean said, noting an image of the god extending the trident out over raging ocean waves. "I can't help but think that image looks sort of familiar."

"What do you mean?" Tommy shifted to get a little more comfortable, as he would were he about to hunker down for a long night of cramming before an exam in college.

"Moses and the staff. He did the same thing to part the sea."

"You're not suggesting the trident is the staff of Aaron and Moses, are you? Because last I checked, that was in the Ark of the Covenant. And we already solved that one. Plus, I highly doubt we'll be allowed to take a look."

"No," Sean snickered. "I'm just saying, what if the trident was a weapon of power? Like Excalibur or Thor's hammer? This wouldn't be the first time we've looked into something like this."

"Okay," Tommy said, playing along. "So, we're dealing with something that, according to the legend, could raise the seas."

"The myth also says that Poseidon created horses with it. And used it to bring forth a spring from the rock where the Acropolis was built."

"Wait. That *does* sound similar to the rod of Moses and Aaron."

"I know, right?" Sean scrolled down a little and then stopped when he'd read everything.

His eyes darted left to right as he thought, his mind racing with ideas. He mentally scratched off ones that didn't make sense and held onto the ones that showed promise.

"An instrument that can control and form matter," Sean muttered.

"What?" Tommy cast a sidelong glance at his friend, his eyes boring into Sean's temple as if drilling for the answer.

"We're talking about the transmutation of matter here. I've studied it a little here and there in my spare time."

"What spare time?"

The flight attendant in a dark blue dress approached, asking the people two rows ahead what they wanted to drink.

Sean refocused. "Funny," he said. "And so true. But with travel, we do have quite a bit of time to read, and watch YouTube videos."

"True."

"I've been interested in quantum mechanics and physics for a while now, the study of the unseen. How energy makes up everything, including matter. How a number of scientists are debating whether there even is such a thing as 'solid' matter... whether everything is a wave, or a vibration of a wave."

"Ah," Tommy realized with a long nod. "The double-slit experiment and all that."

"Yes. Matter becomes energy and vice versa. The observer is what changes it. And in between the two is information."

"Like the space between electrons and the neutrons of an atom."

"Exactly." Sean's mind quickened now. "Information passes through that space. People who can control the information have been called miracle workers. They were the ones who could transmute reality into something else."

"Like Jesus."

"And others. These masters had a level of understanding when it came to the physical plane that no one else did. It's why the disciples kept asking over and over again how it was done."

"My pastor always just thought they were dim."

Sean cracked a smile. "Quite the contrary. They were being taught something that is extremely difficult to master. Think about it. Moses spent forty years in the wilderness before he became a miracle worker. Elijah spent time in the wilderness, and in a cave. Buddha spent time under a tree. John the apostle was exiled on the island of Patmos before he began having visions of the future, essentially bridging the timelines between humanity's decisions to see the possible future outcomes."

"Okay... but what does any of this have to do with Poseidon? Are you saying he was some kind of miracle worker? Because most historians and people in our line of work—me included—don't believe he was a real being."

"What if he was?" Sean asked. He waited for Tommy's cynical scowl before continuing. "What if he was real and not a god? Just a man who did miraculous things?"

Tommy's eyes lit up. "This is a theory I've heard before about others."

"Exactly. But follow me on this one. What if there was a tool, a staff of power, or in this case—"

"A trident."

"An object or relic that could help the user shortcut the mental and spiritual power necessary to perform the unbelievable."

Tommy turned his head as he sucked in a huge gulp of air then blew it out through his lips as he gazed through the window at the passing clouds. "That's heavy," he commented, then looked back to his friend.

The flight attendant stopped the cart next to Sean. "What would you like to drink?" she asked.

"I'll have a cranberry juice," Tommy said. "With ice."

Sean looked at him with a puzzled glimmer in his eyes then said, "I'll have one, too."

The flight attendant didn't seem to care what they ordered. The young woman with dark brown hair braided over her right shoulder went to work, scooping ice into a couple of clear plastic cups before cracking open a can of cranberry juice and splitting it between the two containers.

When she was done, she handed the drinks to them. "You don't want anything else? I have beer. Vodka. Whiskey."

"No thanks," Sean said. "Gotta keep a clear head while I'm working."

The woman glanced down at his laptop, then shrugged and moved on. "Snack cart will come through shortly," she said in a pleasant tone.

"Thanks," the two replied in tandem.

"Where were we?" Sean asked, taking a sip of the dark juice.

"You were suggesting that the trident was a shortcut to doing miraculous or magical things," Tommy reminded. "Like a magic wand."

"Yes!" Sean said, a touch louder than he wanted.

The people across the aisle looked over, and he mouthed. "Sorry." Then he went back to the conversation with Tommy.

"Magic wands are the perfect example. Same principle applies to those. In the stories, magicians used them as a sort of crutch to help them connect to the ethereal power around them. But I've never seen a magic wand or anything like it that could do anything unusual."

"No, but we have seen some unusual things. India. England. Argentina. The list goes on. Why rule this one out?" He let his words hang for a moment. "What if this was one of the first wands, the first tool that could enable a human being to do miraculous things—things that would get them deified in the annals of history and culture?"

"It's a fascinating hypothesis," Tommy hedged and took a sip.

Sean nodded and sighed. He knew it was far-fetched. Then again, he and Tommy lived a far-fetched, unbelievable life. Their experiences had taught them not to discount anything.

A spark flickered in the back of Sean's mind. "Hmm. That's interesting."

Tommy was finishing another sip of cranberry juice. He swallowed then asked, "What is?"

Sean frowned as he pondered the possibility. He started typing again, entering a new search, then waited once more for the dragging internet to pull up his results. He found what he was looking for in a link to a YouTube video.

"Have you ever heard of cymatics?" Sean asked.

Tommy furrowed his brow for a second and then shook his head. "No. Should I have?"

"Only if you're into cutting-edge stuff like me," Sean teased to another eye roll from his friend. "Cymatics is the study of vibrational frequencies and how they affect matter. Research shows that frequencies, when applied to, say, a membrane with sand on top of it, will produce geometric shapes out of the sand."

"Oh, yes," Tommy realized. "I *have* heard of this. Something to do with sacred geometry, right?"

"Precisely. This video shows how frequencies can create shapes with sand or change the form of flowing water, even cause oils to take on certain forms. These guys even altered the flow of fire with frequencies."

He hit the Play button and turned the screen so Tommy could watch. The two sat there, staring at the monitor in rapt fascination until the video ended.

"That's unreal," Tommy said. "Makes you wonder what applying multiple frequencies could do."

"Yeah," Sean said. "One video I came across recently featured a guy talking about this very thing. He cited that verse from John in the Bible that said in the beginning was the word, and the word was with God, and the word was God. What is a word if not a vibration? When any of us speak, the sound is created through frequencies of vibration."

"Whoa. Wait a second." Tommy scratched the side of his head. "So, all of creation, every bit of it, exists due to frequencies of vibration?"

"You knew that. I mean, it's common knowledge that everything vibrates at certain levels. Stones have the lowest frequencies, while things like people emit higher frequencies. This also means there must be a framework, a membrane that contains it all."

"Like the fabric of space-time?"

"Yep. Now, what if there was a tool that could help a person alter frequencies to the point they could change shapes of existing matter, or form new matter altogether?"

"Like raising the seas," Tommy said as the epiphany set in. "Or creating new creatures."

Sean nodded. "What if the trident was a cymatic tool?"

Tommy leaned back in his seat and looked up at the ceiling overhead, then back down to the laptop. "In the wrong hands, something that powerful—a weapon that can control the seas, and all the other stuff—"

"Would be devastating."

23

Down the aisle, Adriana stood up from her seat and started toward the rear of the plane.

Sean watched her approach as she walked carefully so the jostling turbulence didn't send her sprawling into the lap of an unsuspecting traveler.

She smiled down at him when she stopped next to his seat. Then her face twisted with curiosity as she spied the two drinks. "Vodka cranberry?" she asked. "That doesn't seem like you."

"No, it's just cranberry juice," Sean explained.

"Oh. You don't have, like, an infection or something, do you?"

Sean immediately felt glad he hadn't been taking a sip when she asked the question. "No. He ordered one, and it sounded good so I got one, too."

"Ah." Adriana shifted gears, focusing on the computers resting on the trays next to the drinks. "Whatcha working on?" She tilted her head to the right to get a better view of his screen.

"We think we may have figured out what the trident is," Tommy answered.

"Oh, really? So, you two thought you could have all the fun without me?"

"Hey, you're the one who booked yourself first class," Sean fired back. "And don't think I didn't notice the wine you ordered." He winked at her.

She crossed her arms. "Okay, smart boys. What have you learned?"

Sean turned his computer around so she could see the video. "Remember how I was telling you about this?"

"The cymatics thing? Yes. But what does that have to do with the trident?"

"We think it might be an ancient device that can manipulate frequencies. So, it could move matter or even change the state of it completely."

Adriana crouched down next to him. She checked both directions in the aisle to make sure she wasn't in anyone's way. "You mean... like alchemy?"

"Yeah, maybe," Sean said. "Based on what we know about cymatics and vibrations, it's certainly possible."

"This changes everything," Tommy inserted. "If we're talking about tools that can use frequencies to do that stuff, you have to wonder if there are others, and if there are more legends that correspond to this theory."

Sean considered his statement. It reminded him of something else he'd seen in the last few months regarding the use of cymatics. "That isn't the only example of this kind of technology, either. Years ago, footage was released that showed monks in the Himalayas using special horns to levitate heavy stones. They moved these big slabs with no physical or mechanical tools, or manual labor. The vibrations from the horns lifted the stones into place, and once the slabs were in the desired location, the monks could maneuver them into place."

"Seriously?" Tommy blurted.

"Yeah," Sean huffed. "From what I understand, there was other footage that was confiscated by the CIA. It disappeared when they deemed it *classified*."

"That's strange," Adriana remarked. "Why would they make it classified?"

"That question ties directly into the next one we were trying to understand."

"Which is?"

"Why the Russians would want it."

"Oh," she mouthed, then stood up so a man in a red polo shirt and white pants could pass on his way to the bathroom.

"If all of this really does tie into the trident," Tommy said, "then we're talking about an extremely powerful weapon." He briefly highlighted the mythical powers Poseidon supposedly wielded and how they related—in theory—to the trident as an instrument that enabled those powers.

When he was done, she said nothing for a few seconds. "I can see how something like that would be dangerous in the wrong hands. Maybe that's why the CIA covered it up."

"They cover up a lot of things," Sean commented. "Always have. And they don't have to justify anything. Of course, after the fact they can claim that something was too dangerous for public knowledge, or that they were doing it to protect the people. But I've always been suspicious of those explanations. Then again, artifacts like this one probably would create more trouble than good if everyone had access to them. Or even a small percentage of the population."

"It's why we were never given jet packs or flying cars," Tommy suggested. "Could you imagine the chaos and death that would occur if billions of people were flying around with those things? I mean, I guess it could be solved with a self-driving element like they're putting in cars now, but they didn't have that tech thirty years ago. At least, I don't think they did."

"Right," Adriana agreed.

"See, this is why I think mystical or miraculous things are so difficult. They're designed to be. Because if everyone could use them freely and without thought or mindfulness, the world would be a terrifying place. Imagine the average, bitter, angry person able to flip over the car in front of him or her because the other driver cut them off."

The man in the red polo approached again. Adriana stood up and let him pass before crouching back down.

"All of which points to ancient instruments that were created by or for certain individuals to make it easier. With a tool like the trident, Poseidon or someone like him could have wielded the powers of the universe, and certainly appeared to be godlike to anyone who didn't understand it."

"That would have been most," Adriana groused.

Another epiphany hit Sean. "I just realized, this stuff is probably how the Israelites knocked down the walls of Jericho. Remember the story? They were instructed to march around the city seven times for seven days. Then, on the last day, they all faced the walls, the entire army encircling the city. At the directed time, they shouted and blew horns. The walls crumbled, and the army invaded."

"Whoa," Tommy exhaled. "That's crazy. I would have never thought."

"It's easy to see why someone would want this thing," Sean said. "And it makes me wonder...."

He stopped and bit his bottom lip as he pondered the idea rattling around in his head.

"Wonder what?" Adriana pressed.

Sean took a few breaths as he considered his words. When he spoke, he lowered his voice to just above the steady hum of the jet engines that filled the cabin.

"Near the end of World War Two, Hitler got desperate. We know he sent a special archaeological unit around the world in the early days of his campaigns to find proof regarding the Aryan nation being superior to everyone else."

"And everything they found was manipulated to point to that notion," Tommy injected.

"Right. But toward the end of the war, his mission for that unit changed. While their research and development programs pushed harder and harder toward nuclear weapons, jet engines, rockets, a slew of stuff the public still doesn't know about—"

"Sort of like die glöcke," Tommy interrupted, referring to a mission Sean had taken on several years before.

"Yes. Like that. But their archaeology teams began looking for ancient technologies, weapons they could use to win the war in a few swift strokes. I've even heard stories about how Hitler had his teams search for the lost city of Atlantis."

"What are you saying?" Adriana wondered. "What do the Nazis have to do with the Russians who were chasing us last night?"

"The two don't have anything to do with one another except that I'm starting to wonder if that group chasing us was military. And if they are, could it be that they've been sent out by the Russian president to search for ancient relics that could turn the tide, not only of their war in Ukraine, but for the entire planet?"

"Wow," Tommy breathed. "Did you just come up with that?"

Sean nodded slowly. "I don't know if it's right. I mean, we don't know anything about the group that was after us. But we do know they're after the same thing. Which means we can't let them get to the trident. With something that powerful, they could take over the world. Whole nations would have to bend their knees to avoid total annihilation. We've seen this Russian leader do some pretty crazy things. I mean, the invasion of Ukraine looked unprovoked and whimsical."

"Except that it cut off most of Europe from their fuel and energy supply. Not to mention the potash farmers need to grow food for everyone."

"Correct. Honestly, I wouldn't put it past him to do something like this, something that at first blush seems harebrained."

"But is rooted in a piece of history that has been hidden for thousands of years," Adriana finished.

For nearly a minute, no one said anything else as they pondered the idea.

"The problem is," Sean spoke again, "that while we figure Castello Barbarossa is the right place, we don't know for sure. And we have no idea what we're looking for once we get there."

"Well," Tommy mused, "we know the verse from Sinan Reis's grave suggested it had something to do with the throne." He entered a quick query in his search browser and waited until the results populated. He twisted his computer around and clicked on one of the images. "But the castle is in ruins now, for starters. So there may not be a throne room left. I'm just going to go ahead and assume that the throne is long gone. On top of that, it's an ornithology station now."

"As in bird watchers?" Adriana asked.

"Yep."

She scowled as she pulled her head back an inch. "Really? A historical castle has been taken over by bird watchers?"

"Seems there are migrations of a certain species that happen there. But I'm with you. It's a little weird. Although, before the ornithologists were there, the castle had fallen into disrepair and basically left to rot. So, maybe them being there has kept it in a semi-decent state."

"I guess."

"This could be a good thing," Sean offered, opting for optimism. "Maybe the people there could help us find the throne room. Or give us some ideas as to where we could look."

Tommy let out a hum of doubt then clicked his tongue. "I don't know, man. They might get suspicious of strangers coming around to snoop through the castle. Plus, it won't be easy to keep what we're looking for a secret."

Sean grinned at his friend and clapped his shoulder, shaking it for a second. "Always so pessimistic, Schultzie. Have a little faith. It's going to be fine. I just hope you've brushed up on your Italian."

Tommy stared blankly back at his friend. "Seriously?"

"No. But I speak a little."

Adriana sighed at the two men. "I speak the language." She stood up, still shaking her head at them. "I'm going back to my seat. You two have fun here in coach."

Sean smiled as he watched her walk back down the aisle toward her seat.

"Ornithologists," Tommy said next to him, as Sean tore his eyes away from his wife. "I just hope they're friendly. We'll probably have to come up with a story so they won't be suspicious."

Sean looked over at his friend with derision in his eyes. "We're with the IAA, going to a historical castle. I'm sure they'll be cool."

24

ANACAPRI, ITALY

A strong gust of wind rushed over Konstantin as he stepped out of the rental car, a red four-door sedan. The rest of his men exited their vehicles at the same time and surveyed the small parking area.

Four other cars sat parked in the spaces closest to the path leading up to the castle. He assumed they belonged to the ornithologists he'd read about online during the flight to Rome.

The ferry had taken less than an hour from Naples, and his men had been on one of the earlier ones of the morning, which Konstantin hoped would put them there ahead of the Americans—if this was where they were headed. The major assumed this to be the case, and so he would take no chances with anyone who was already in the castle.

He turned to four of his men. "Sweep the area," he ordered. "And keep your weapons out of sight unless absolutely necessary. The last thing we need is for one of the researchers here to see a bunch of men walking around with guns out in the open and call the local authorities. The rest of you, come with me."

The first four split up and fanned out to reconnoiter the exterior of the castle.

Konstantin stared up the only path leading to the castle. The five-hundred-year-old stone structure showed its age in some places—dilapidated and crumbling along the wall to the right. Some of it, however, remained in good condition. A few of the parapets still stood, along with a turret at the nearest corner of the wall. The trail disappeared into the brush and trees surrounding the overgrown mountain pinnacle.

Beyond the wall, the main structure of the castle towered above everything else, resting on the precipice of a cliff that overlooked the city and harbor far below.

"How do you want to do this with the scientists?" Boris asked, his eyes firmly locked on the hilly trail ahead.

"They will not want us here. This place has been closed to the public for a while now."

Boris waited for him to say more.

Konstantin looked over at his second. "I guess we will have to persuade them to let us stay, no?"

Boris chuckled. "I suppose so, sir."

The men left the parking area and began the trek up the winding trail. It was little more than a goat path, worn down through the years by foot traffic. A few stones marked the way, but many had been covered by erosion or an overgrowth of grass. Yellow flowers mingled with the brown and green grasses in between olive trees and other trees Konstantin couldn't identify. Dendrology hadn't been necessary in his climb up the ranks of the Russian military.

He and his team kept their eyes open for trouble, peering through the overgrowth as they hiked up the hill. There were a hundred places someone could ambush them, and he wasn't entirely sold on the notion that the Americans weren't already here.

The steep climb sucked the air out of Konstantin's lungs, despite his conditioning. He doubted it was the altitude. Even though the castle was located on the top of a mountain, it wasn't as high up as some places he'd been during combat missions.

His men didn't seem to be affected, though a few breathed heavily as they marched upward.

The castle wall loomed above them through the trees and shrubs. After several sharp turns in the trail, they reached the final curve along the path. Konstantin checked his watch, noting how long it had taken them to make the journey to the top of the mountain.

It took another minute or two before they arrived at the stone archway leading into the castle.

"Usual operating procedure," Konstantin said to his men.

They didn't need to hear anything else.

The men spilled into the open area beyond the walls and systematically checked every inch as they continued forward.

Much like the exterior of the castle, the space within the walls overflowed with grass, trees, and flowers—centuries of nature's rule in the absence of man.

The main structure of the castle lay dead ahead at the far end of the fortress. Konstantin immediately noticed a few people standing on top of a platform. Whether they could see him and his team was as uncertain as it was irrelevant. The Swedes who ran the research station wouldn't think the Russians a threat, unless the Americans had already arrived.

At this point, Konstantin was going to have to take the gamble on that and hope his instincts proved true as they so often did.

He and his men moved along the trail that cut through the center of the castle until they arrived at a pair of wooden doors at the base of the keep. The two people at the top of the building had either not noticed them, or didn't care, but the major had the feeling if they'd been spotted the ornithologists would have either waved at them or shouted.

Three windows occupied the round parapet—two higher than the one in the center. The structure jutted out to both sides from the cylindrical tower. A power line or phone line—Konstantin wasn't sure which—ran along a makeshift collection of poles and into the stonework.

Since neither happened, Konstantin figured it was the former.

"Open it," he said to the soldier in the lead.

The young man with short black hair gave a curt nod and pushed through the old door.

The Russians poured into the stone building. Boris closed the door behind as he was the last one through.

They found themselves in a room that looked like a basement with a fireplace off to the right, along with a wooden table and several chairs. The smells of breakfast filled the air, though Konstantin figured that was from earlier that morning based on the current time.

He motioned to one of the men to check the room through an open doorway to the right. Just from the limited glimpse he could get, he assumed it was the kitchen.

Then he pointed at the spiral stairs leading up to the next level, and three of his men immediately began their ascent. Boris remained with the major until the other guy returned.

The soldier merely shook his head, indicating the kitchen was empty.

Konstantin accepted the silent information and motioned for the man to head up the stairs. He and Boris took up the rear.

The men climbed up to the next level, where they found the second floor split out in two directions. The first three stood there awaiting their next orders.

Konstantin held up two fingers and pointed them at the two men to his right, then indicated they go through the archway in that direction.

He repeated the gesture with the other two.

Voices drifted into the landing from the right, though the words were indiscernible.

"You and I will go to the top," Konstantin whispered to his captain.

Boris acknowledged with a single nod.

"Weapons free," the major breathed to all of them.

The men drew their pistols and moved while Konstantin and Boris continued to climb the stairs.

Boris took point, stalking methodically up the steps until they reached the top floor and a closed wooden door.

Konstantin waited while Boris grabbed the handle. The captain looked back for confirmation, which he received from a nod, and then he pushed the door open.

He stepped through with his pistol raised. Konstantin immediately followed, pointing his weapon at a man in a green windbreaker and khakis with gray hair to his right, closest to the wall. Boris aimed at the other, a guy probably in his mid-thirties with blond hair pulled back in a ponytail. He wore a blue pullover with blue jeans.

The older man said something in Italian that Konstantin didn't understand. Not that it mattered. He was the one holding a gun.

"I don't speak that language," he replied in cold English.

"What is the meaning of this?" the blond guy asked.

"Downstairs. Now," was the only reply he'd get for the moment.

The men looked at each other, bewildered. Clearly, they hadn't expected to be held at gunpoint when they woke up and had their espresso that morning.

"I said move," Konstantin snapped.

On that cue, Boris moved around behind the men and shoved the blond toward the door.

The guy stumbled but caught his balance and kept walking, albeit hesitantly. The very real threat of death seemed to settle in with him quicker than the older man, who slowly put up his hands in surrender.

"Why are you doing this? This is a research station," he complained.

Boris answered him by pushing him toward the door to catch up with his partner.

The two Russians ushered the men down the stairs all the way to the ground floor, where they found the other four soldiers standing at the four corners around the table where four other people sat with terrified faces.

Three of the hostages were women, one who looked to be in her early sixties wearing a navy-blue jacket and jeans. The other two appeared to be younger, somewhere in their mid-thirties unless Konstantin missed his guess. The other man—the third in the group

—sat at the far corner of the table with his hands folded. His thick brown hair matched his full beard. And the flannel jacket he wore completed the lumberjack look.

Boris nudged the older guy from the terrace toward the table while the blond guy kept moving at the behest of one of the other soldiers by the door.

When the two newcomers were positioned standing at the head of the table, Konstantin spoke.

"You are probably wondering what this is all about."

"You're right about—" the lumberjack started to say.

"Do not speak unless requested," Konstantin shouted, cutting him off. His booming order startled two of the women at the table, and one of the men—the blond guy from the terrace. "We are here to find something. If you want to get out of here alive, you will assist us. We find what we're looking for, we will not harm you. Is that clear?"

The hostages exchanged confused looks, but all relented with bobbing heads.

"Good. Now, this castle was once a fortress used by the great Ottoman Admiral, Hayreddin Barbarossa, as I'm sure you know. But what I want to know is, where was his throne?"

Everyone looked around at each other again, uncertain about both the question and the answer to it.

"The throne?" the brunette woman at the table answered. "There hasn't been a throne here in centuries, I would say. But we aren't historians or archaeologists. We study birds and their migration—"

"I'm well aware of what you study," Konstantin sneered. "But you all spend a good amount of time here. Do you know where the throne was?"

The skinny blond guy tilted his head upward. "You mean the throne room?"

"Yes. The throne room."

The guy swallowed back his fear before he responded again. "It's on the next floor up. Go left at the landing."

"Is there anyone else up here?"

The man shook his head. The motion whipped his ponytail around.

"You're certain?" Konstantin asked in a threatening tone.

"Yes. I swear."

"He's not lying," the lumberjack answered. His voice was gruff and irritated. "There is no one else here."

Konstantin considered shooting him just to make an example, but he resisted.

"Very well. You two, show me to the throne room. The rest of you stay here. If you try to escape, you will die. If you try anything stupid, you will die. Do I make myself clear?"

Everyone nodded.

"Good." Konstantin ordered three of his men to stay there with the hostages, and Boris to come with him and their two tour guides.

Then he looked to the last soldier by the door. "Check in on the others. Make sure the perimeter is clear, and then have them come here. Use your radio. Theirs should already be on."

"Yes, sir," the young man said, snapping to attention. He stepped out the door.

"Now," Konstantin said, spinning back to the group, "shall we begin?"

25

The ferry horn echoed through the harbor where Grande Marina sat at the bottom of jagged, majestic mountains.

Sean and the others had traveled all over the world, explored incredible places, and seen views that pictures could never do justice. This vista easily fit into the top ten of his mental picture book of memories. Maybe the top five.

Crystal-clear green-blue water lapped against the shore as boats bobbed in neat rows, some tied to each other or hitched to posts in the water. Within the breakwater walls of the harbor, more pleasure boats were moored to docks.

Behind the marina, a narrow street ran along the water's edge. Rows of two-, three-, and four-story shops, cafés, and apartments hugged the sidewalk—their distinct colors of white, pink, yellow, and blue reminding Sean of several other coastal towns he'd visited in Europe. As he swept his gaze from left to right, the first one that came to mind was the neighborhood of Nyhavn in Copenhagen. A place he'd visited years ago while on a vacation.

He recalled seeing the home of Hans Christian Andersen and the place where the famous author sat near the water, writing his stories with pen and quill.

The similarities between the two locations, however, ended with the colorful façades of the buildings.

On the slopes behind the street-side business of Grande Marina, homes dotted vibrant green hillsides, tracing all the way up to the ridge overlooking the bay. There at the top of the hill, several more homes towered over the marina, offering sweeping views of the sea.

Behind the ridge, the majesty of Capri kept inspiring awe. A towering mountainside of jagged rock climbed into the sky. More sheer cliffs to the left dropped off into the sea, and gave way farther in that direction to slopes of trees reaching down to the water.

Standing next to the shore, the three visitors took in the splendorous view where natural beauty met man-made culture in a spectacular amalgamation to the senses.

The smell of fresh baked bread drifted through the salty sea air and mingled as one in their nostrils. The scent of coffee, too, tickled their noses, and beckoned them to grab a cup to go with a piece of ciabatta, or perhaps something sweeter.

"Pretty amazing, isn't it?" Tommy said after what seemed like an hour of standing there doing nothing but staring.

"Sure is, Schultzie," Sean agreed. "You ever been here?"

"No."

"Because you said it like you've been here before."

"No I didn't."

"Okay."

"I didn't," Tommy insisted.

"Honey, you've been here, though, right?" Sean looked at his wife.

The wind blew her dark brown hair toward the sea like a wild horse's mane. The black turtleneck zip-up and black leggings made the comparison even more fitting, as some of the most beautiful horses Sean had seen displayed that color combination.

Of course, he could never make that comparison verbally. "You think I look like a horse?" would be the first response, a hole he had no intention of digging or climbing out of.

"Yes," she answered. "I've been here twice."

"Oh, yeah?" Tommy said. "What were you doing here?"

"Once with a guy I was dating. The other to look at real estate."

"Did you buy anything?"

"No."

"And no need to hear about the other trip," Sean said awkwardly. He cleared his throat and pointed across the street to a white building. "That's the car rental place. Let's go get our vehicle and get a move on."

Sean started to walk across the street.

"Oh, I'm sorry," Tommy teased. "Does that topic make you uncomfortable?"

"Which one?"

"You know which one," Tommy said as he caught up. Adriana walked alongside Sean, shaking her head at the two of them.

"We're adults," Sean said. "She wasn't the first woman I dated. And I wasn't the first she went out with. With all the travel we do, it's inevitable that we'll visit some places where we have a past with someone else."

"Oh?" She looked at him with eyebrows raised in suspicion. "Such as?"

Sean cleared his throat again. He stepped up onto the sidewalk and sighed. "What? I mean, you know what I mean."

"Yeah," Tommy prodded. "Such as? Are there some special places you took a lady or two?"

"Come on. This wasn't even about me. How did this get twisted my direction?"

He opened the door to the rental place and held it so the other two could enter. Exasperated, he followed them inside.

A man with a thick black beard and a shaved head sat behind a desk that looked like something that belonged to a teacher in a 1950s classroom. He took his eyes off the computer monitor sitting atop the desk and stood up to greet the customers.

Sean immediately noted the man's faded, torn blue jeans and black T-shirt with an image of Mona Lisa holding an AK-47 that bulged around his midsection.

"Hello, my friends," he said in an Italian accent. "What can I do for you today? You need a car?"

Tommy answered. "Yes, sir. My name is Tommy Schultz. I made a reservation on your website."

"Oh sure. Excellent." The man beamed. "American, yeah?"

"Yes, sir."

"We love America. You like guns, yeah?"

It was all Sean could do to keep from bursting out laughing. He fought off about thirty different smart-aleck remarks. Adriana merely stared at him in astounded fascination, as she would watching a bunch of circus animals driving a truck off a cliff and into the sea.

Tommy just tried to read the room and go with it. "Yeah, sure. We have guns. Not with us," he added quickly. "Obviously, since that would be illegal." The guy didn't need to know more.

It wasn't that they liked firearms or not. They used them when needed, and in their line of work—over the years—that had been more often than they would have preferred. Going to the range now and then was fun, a good way to blow off steam or take their minds off things, but they got the sense that this guy wanted them to be modern-day cowboys with a stockpile of weapons and munitions.

The man smiled, full of mischief, and pointed at Tommy. "That's right. Illegal here, my friend." He winked dramatically. "Hey, if you do, I won't tell anyone."

Tommy raised his right hand to try to settle the guy down. "No, seriously. We don't." He wasn't lying. They'd been forced to leave everything with Niki back in Turkey, a thought that rekindled a spark of concern in Tommy's gut for the young Greek.

"I got you," the business owner said. He sat back into his seat. The chair squeaked under his weight before he pulled closer to the keyboard. He clicked the mouse and then typed in Tommy's name. "Yes, I see I have you down for a car. Let me just get the keys, and I'll show you to it."

He clicked the mouse again, and a printer on a wooden shelf with iron pipes for legs buzzed to life. The machine whirred and hummed and then spit out a piece of paper that the owner removed from the tray and handed to Tommy.

"Here is your receipt," the man said.

Tommy hesitated. "Don't you need me to sign something?"

The man shook his head, sticking out his lower lip. "No. We have your payment processed. And we don't really do things like that here."

"Okay then." Tommy felt a refreshing sense of relief fill him. "The old-school ways are the best ways."

"Yes. That's right! Now," the man stood, "come with me. I take you to your car."

The owner turned and started toward a door in the rear of the building. The three followed him out through the door and into a crumbling asphalt parking lot in the back where a collection of a dozen vehicles waited. All of the cars were small, compact or subcompact.

The owner pointed to a gray five-door hatchback straight ahead. "I gave you the nicest one we have," he said proudly.

A wry expression draped across Sean's face as he stared at the unimpressive vehicle. The thing looked like it had seen more miles than a mosquito on a windshield. He partly wondered if the thing would even run. If this was the nicest one the rental place had, he didn't want to think about some of the other options. A quick look around the parking lot told him the difference between the car they were getting and all the others was negligible.

It was all Sean could do to keep from laughing as he saw Tommy's reaction to the selection of vehicles. Adriana managed to remain stoic on the subject and merely smiled at the Italian, who clearly seemed proud of the stable of cars on offer.

"You like, yes? This one is a good car."

"For sure," Tommy replied in a pretty unbelievable tone. He obviously hoped the guy didn't suspect his disappointment. "It's great. Thank you so much."

The Italian beamed with pride. And he handed the key over to Tommy. "It has a full tank of gas. Just fill it up before you return it."

"Will do."

"Enjoy your visit to Capri," he said. Then he walked back to the rear door and disappeared inside the building again.

Tommy, Sean, and Adriana exchanged dubious looks but held back their comments until they were next to the car, opening the doors.

"I'm glad I'm only six feet tall," Sean commented, squeezing into the back.

"You don't have to sit back there," Adriana said. "You can ride shotgun."

"Know what? Let's both sit in the back and let Tommy chauffeur us around the island."

"Oh, I like that idea. You don't mind driving us about, do you, Schultzie?"

Tommy answered with an eyeball as he slid into the front seat. "Oh, and it's a stick shift. Nice."

"You sure you know how to handle one of those?" Sean teased. He slammed the door shut and put on his seatbelt.

"You're not funny. You know that, right?"

Adriana got in next to Sean and fastened her seatbelt while Tommy started the engine.

The thing rumbled to life. It wasn't a smooth sound by any means —more like a lawn mower with several loose parts in the motor grinding on each other.

Sean winced at the noise. "Sounds like it could use a little oil."

"Yeah," Tommy agreed. "Or a lot."

He stepped on the clutch and shifted the stick into reverse, then backed the car out, looping around to the left. Just as smoothly as he'd done before, he shifted into first gear and accelerated toward the street.

"You guys mind guiding me?" Tommy asked.

"On it," Adriana answered. She'd anticipated him needing directions and had already pulled out her phone. "Turn left out of the parking lot. Then you are going to make a right at the next stop sign."

"Got it."

He drove the car to the street, paused to make sure there were no other vehicles approaching, then turned left. A hundred feet up the street, he stopped at a sign and turned right.

"Take your next left onto Via Marina Grande. Then stay on that up to the top of that mountain over there."

She pointed at the rocky cliff to the right where the ruins of Castello Barbarossa jutted from a patch of green shrubs and trees that abruptly turned to a gray stone precipice.

"Ugh," Sean moaned. "I should have known."

"Known what?" Tommy asked, a flicker of mischief in his voice.

"You know what."

"Oh. You talking about how high up the ruins are?"

Irritated, Sean exhaled through his nose.

"You saw the pictures of the place, man. You didn't think it was down by the sea, did you?"

"No. I just didn't realize how high it really was."

"I guess you didn't check the topographical data in the search engine."

"No, I didn't. But I will next time."

"Can you two shut it?" Adriana interrupted. "I'm trying to make sure we don't take a wrong turn."

The way she took over the conversation put a smile on Sean's face. The two of them stopped their bickering and instead focused their attention out the windows as they drove down the winding street of the Via Marina Grande.

The road twisted and turned up the hill, offering some of the sharpest switchback curves Tommy had ever experienced in his life. When he turned the car left through one of them, Sean forced himself to close his eyes as the sweeping view of the harbor below fell away before him.

Adriana saw the reaction and put her hand on his shoulder. "You okay?" she asked.

"I'll be fine. Let's just get up to the castle."

She nodded and looked at her phone again. "In a few minutes we'll come to an intersection that goes left and right. You're going to go right on Via Provinciale Anacapri. That takes us around the top of the ridge, past the Villa San Michelle Museum."

"Museum?" Tommy's ears perked up.

"Seriously?" Sean spat. "You must be joking."

"I never joke about museums. Just a shame we don't have time to check it out," Adriana said. "You might like it if you ever get a chance to come back here. It's the former home of a famous author. Beautiful mansion with some of the most incredible views on Earth. Pretty spectacular."

Sean furrowed his brow, curiosity getting the better of him.

She noticed the expression. "What?"

He offered a shrug. "Nothing."

"You're wondering what I was doing there, aren't you?"

"No."

"Yes, you are," Tommy argued with a laugh.

Adriana sighed. "Yes, I was there with the guy I was dating at the time. It was a fundraiser. He knew some of the people involved with the foundation. Good wine, by the way."

"Cool," Sean said sardonically.

She leaned close and kissed him on the cheek—more condescension than tenderness filling the gesture. "Oh, you boys and your jealousy. Just remember, you're the one I married. And I haven't thought about him since."

"Since we got married?"

She shook her head and looked back to the phone. "Since we broke up."

"Just out of curiosity," Tommy kept on, "why did you break up?"

"Because I wasn't in love with him. I liked the idea of him, but there was little substance to it."

"Okay," Sean stepped back in. "I'm sorry I asked."

Adriana looked at him with genuine concern. "I wasn't aware you had that insecurity in you."

"I don't. Not usually. I guess it's places that bring it out of me."

"Like I said before, I'm sure there are places you've been with others that are special."

Sean met her chocolate gaze. "It's hard to remember any of them, and I don't want to. The only memories that matter are the ones with you."

Tommy's mouth gaped, and for ten seconds, no one said a thing. Until he ruined it.

"That's disgusting," he blurted. "Where in the world did you get that?"

"June," Sean fired back without thinking.

Adriana burst out laughing.

"Hilarious," Tommy said and immediately retreated from the battle of wits he knew he couldn't win.

Sean thanked his wife with a wink.

Several minutes and sharp turns later, Tommy reached the top of the mountain where the Via Provinciale Anacapri bent hard to the right. He waited as a blue compact car drove by and then spun the wheel, merging onto the road behind it.

Sean turned his head to look the other direction out his window again, keeping the mountainside squarely in his view so he didn't have to see how high up they really were.

The road undulated, dipping toward every curve in the mountain, and then back out again with every swell.

"Tell me about San Michelle," Sean said, trying anything to take his mind off the precipitous height just behind his wife's right shoulder.

"What?"

"You said an author lived there. Who was it"

"Oh. Alex Munthe, a Swedish author."

"I guess the Swedes like this place," Tommy said. "The ornithology researchers are from Sweden."

"Many people love this island," she went on. "Munthe was a fascinating character in history. He was a doctor, earning his medical standing by the age of twenty-two, which I believe was the youngest to attain such in France, where he attended medical school. Many believed him to be a miracle worker, especially from his work during an outbreak of cholera in the late nineteenth century.

"He loved architecture, and the villa he designed has been admired for decades by people all over the world."

"Sounds like this guy was much more than just a writer," Sean noticed.

"Indeed. He wrote *The Story of San Michele* and published it in the late 1920s. I think 1929. It became an international bestseller overnight."

"Huh," Sean mused. "Now I want to read it."

"I'm not sure it's to your tastes, but it's excellent."

The road ahead bent out of view to the left and gave a view of the spectacular white villa on the lip of the mountainside above.

"Wow," Tommy said, amazement in his tone. "He really could pick the spots. I'll give him that."

"It's even more impressive from the terrace."

"Maybe we'll go there sometime," Sean said. "But on another trip."

Adriana looked over at him with a flirty fire in her eyes. "You sure you want to do that?"

"Why not? Because you went there with some old boyfriend? I'm not threatened by many people. Much less ex-boyfriends."

Her lips parted in a grin. "I'll hold your hand on the terrace. It's pretty high."

He swallowed a wad of fear at the thought. "Okay."

The rest of the drive was spent in silence with the exception of Adriana giving a few more directions. When they arrived at the parking area for Castello Barbarossa, they found more cars there than they'd anticipated. Tommy had to settle for a parking spot at the end of a row, close to the road, and shifted the stick into first gear before shutting off the engine.

"How many bird watchers are at this place?" he wondered.

"I wouldn't think this many," Sean said, concern swelling in his gut. "We should be careful."

"Are we ever not careful?"

"Not usually."

They stepped out of the car and onto the crumbling asphalt

parking lot—a similar state of disrepair as they'd found at the car rental. Sean felt relief at stretching his legs, happy to get out of the cramped confines of the compact vehicle. He stretched his arms and back briefly, but also surveyed the area.

He didn't notice anyone in any of the other cars, and no one approached from the trailhead leading up to the castle wall.

They closed the doors to the rental, making sure to do so quietly, and began walking toward the path.

Off to the right, a cloud approached the mountain peak, with more trailing behind it.

He'd experienced something similar on the top of a mountain where he and friends camped when they were in high school and college. The place known as Whig's Meadow sat on the edge of the Tennessee–North Carolina border, around 4,500 feet above sea level.

The meadow offered spectacular views of the valley below, and the town of Tellico Plains, Tennessee. Those mountains were different than these. The foothills of Tennessee gradually rolled and fell until they gradually climbed into the high peaks of the Smoky Mountains of Appalachia. These peaks spiked up dramatically from sea level, with no subtlety to the climb whatsoever.

Sean enjoyed the view from Whig's Meadow much more than this. Up there, no threat of falling existed. There were no sharp cliffs with drops hundreds of feet down. He sighed, hoping he wouldn't have to get close to the edge of one of those, and continued walking.

He stopped near one of the cars—a black car that looked like most of the others on the island he'd seen. He looked at a similar one next it, and another, and stopped walking between the three. He narrowed his eyelids, and stepped toward the one in the middle—curiosity pushing him.

"What is it?" Tommy asked.

"Look at all the other cars," Sean said. "Most of them are different. I mean, they're all compact except for those two sedans over there. But these three all look like they came from the same place."

"So?"

"They're rentals."

"What's that supped to mean? And how do you know that?"

Sean spotted the sticker he was looking for on the bottom front left of the windshield in the center car. "Because they have the rental car company plastered on the windshield," Sean answered. "And it means we aren't the only visitors here."

26

The approaching clouds blew in and wrapped around Sean like a cool, moist blanket. Moist wasn't really what he was looking for, and the chill surprised him. Fortunately, he'd looked into the weather on the mountain top and prepared by bringing his gray Marmot windbreaker.

He zipped up the jacket against the cold, damp air and turned to the others, who were likewise adjusting their outerwear.

Visibility had gone from maximum distance to almost zero. Sean could see his friends in the thick, gray soup, but beyond twenty feet started to get hazy.

"You think it's the Russians?" Tommy asked. "How would they have been able to beat us here? They didn't know where we were going. Did they?"

"That's a lot of questions," Sean stated. "And no clear answer to any of them. Unfortunately, the safest thing to assume is that it is them. We can't worry about the how."

"If it is them," Adriana said, "that could be a problem. We don't have any weapons."

"No. We don't. But we have this fog for the moment. May as well use it to our advantage."

"Wait," Tommy protested, sticking out his hand to stop Sean as his friend started toward the trail—or where it had been a minute before. "We can't just go in there without any weapons and hope to take down a Russian military unit."

"Maybe you can't," Sean said matter-of-factly. "I intend to arm myself."

"And how are you going to do that?"

"Well, first of all, we don't know if it's the Russians. Could just be some friends who came to visit."

"And if it isn't?"

"Then we will just have to figure that out."

"You can't be serious."

Sean clapped his friend on the shoulder. "Always the pessimist." With that, he started marching up the hill toward the trailhead with Adriana in tow.

She glanced back at Tommy and gave him a wink. "You coming?"

He let out a sigh and looked around the murky parking lot. "Fine," he muttered to himself. "But I have a bad feeling about this."

Sean paused at the beginning of the trail and looked both directions to either side. He knew there was a drop-off somewhere to his left, and he didn't want to get anywhere close to it.

"It's okay," Adriana soothed. "Just follow the trail. Don't worry about the edge. I'm sure it doesn't get close to it."

"I hope so," Sean said.

She'd sensed his apprehension, the way she sensed so many things with him. But she couldn't see the inner turmoil, the turning stomach, the lump in his throat, the abject fear pulsing through his veins causing his palms to sweat.

He trudged onward, his eyes constantly darting left to right, always watching for movement, listening for anything out of the ordinary.

The trail was little more than a dirt-and-rock path leading up to the corner of the wall, which he still couldn't see through the fog. Sean followed the way to the right, and for a minute he felt relieved until it bent back to the left and led in the direction he'd rather have not gone.

He considered cutting through the brush, grass, and flowers to head directly to the wall, or where he remembered it being. He thought better of it. Getting off the path could have disastrous consequences. After all, there was no chance it simply dropped over the cliff's edge. *Was there?*

As the trail continued closer to the drop-off he was certain loomed beyond the next few steps, a gap in the clouds opened, and the bright sun glowed down onto the peak.

Straight ahead, a fence stood just beyond a curve in the path. Sean shuddered as he thought of what was past the fence, and quickly turned around the bend and kept walking.

Huge nettings draped over poles hung near the fence, and ran along the mountain top meadow's edge all the way up to the castle wall.

As Sean turned away from the precipice, he caught sight of something moving along the wall and immediately dropped down to his knees.

He stuck out his right hand behind him to signal the other two to do the same. They knew better than to question him, and instantly mimicked Sean's crouching stance.

The vegetation along the slope shielded them from view until another cloud blew across the mountain and once more submerged them into the fog.

Sean looked back at the others and mouthed, "Russian. Armed."

Concern streaked across Tommy's face. Ever stoic, Adriana took the information without affect.

There was no good solution as far as how to handle this. If there was one gunman walking around the perimeter, there could be two—or more. Without a weapon, Sean would have to use stealth, but the lack of visibility both helped and hindered that. Sure, he could sneak up on the guy, but he could also bump right into him, or at least come close.

"Stay down," Sean breathed and then swiveled around and started moving again.

He stayed low, keeping his knees bent, careful not to step on any loose rocks or twigs on the trail. They reached another bend where the path straightened for a few feet then overlapped back to the left and the dangerous cliff lurking beyond the fence.

Sean took a deep breath and kept moving, doing his best to keep his heart calm as it pounded in his chest. He looked to his right, up the hill, and saw the wall emerge from the mist. It towered over the slope about forty feet away. There was no sign of the gunman, though, and knowing the guy was somewhere out there, but not visible, didn't fill Sean with a ton of confidence.

It was like playing hide and seek with the Invisible Man.

The three reached the next switchback on the trail and carefully continued. Based on the distance to the wall, Sean figured this was the last turn near the edge he'd have to endure. A not-insignificant part of him felt grateful for the fog. It meant he didn't have to see the ledge or anywhere close to it. Despite the dense mist making the current task inescapably more difficult.

He passed a thicket of trees, each standing fifteen to twenty feet tall, when he heard the sound of two men's voices.

Sean froze and stuck out his palm to the other two behind him. Adriana nearly ran face-first into his hand but stopped herself a few inches away.

She and Tommy had heard the voices, too, and each of the three looked toward the wall where they believed the sounds had come from.

A figure moved slightly, then the other came into view.

Two gunmen.

The armed men stood next to the wall at the corner where a round turret towered over the hill. An arched gate just beyond them opened into the fortress courtyard, though seeing into it remained impossible at the moment.

Sean thought fast. He knew that approaching the two men

standing guard, or whatever they were doing at the gate, would be impossible now with one facing each direction.

Without a weapon to take the two down, he was left with whatever resources he could muster. It just so happened he found what he needed a foot away from his left boot.

Sean reached down and picked up a rock—about the size of a walnut shell—and held it in his palm.

Tommy and Adriana watched, both fully aware of what he was about to attempt.

Sean reared back and flung the rock over the head of the farthest gunman. The stone sailed beyond him and landed in the brush twenty feet away.

The guy to the right snapped his head around, immediately raising a submachine gun. The man behind him did the same, and the two skulked into the tall grass in the direction they were sure they'd heard something.

Sean moved, quicker than before. He only had a short window of opportunity to get to the two men, and he couldn't waste it on indecision.

Like a tiger stalking its prey in the jungle, he stalked up the trail—keeping low as he moved to use as much of the natural terrain as camouflage as possible.

His eyes never left the two gunmen. They swung their guns around from one side to the other, checking the area for what they probably thought was either an intruder or a squirrel. If it was the latter, they weren't taking any chances. One way or the other, whatever had made the noise was going to die. Or at least have the crap scared out of it.

Sean slipped around the last bend and tiptoed to the gate. It would have been easy to sneak inside and leave the two gunmen to their fruitless hunt, but if there were two out here, there'd be more inside the fortress. Their weapons would make things a lot more straightforward.

Adriana stayed close behind him, just off his right hip. She'd picked up a larger rock, roughly double the size of her fist. Sean noticed the big stone when he glanced back at her as they passed base of the turret.

He bobbed his head at her, a silent compliment to her selection of weapon, and continued toward the two men.

Twenty feet separated them. Sean scooped up another small stone and heaved it over the men's heads again, just to their right. Instantly, they snapped toward the sound, leveling their weapons in that direction.

One of them barked orders in Russian, telling whoever was out there to come out with their hands up.

But they didn't see anyone—because there was no one there to see.

If they'd had the presence of mind to look back, they might have seen the three Americans moving up from behind them and taken them down with a few point-blank shots.

Instead, the gunmen kept creeping toward the source of the sound.

Ten feet away, Sean could smell their fear, and their cheap aftershave. He closed the gap to only a few strides and was about to wrap his arm around the nearest one's neck when a twig snapped behind him.

Sean felt a weight of anxiety drop through his entire body from his head down to his toes, then back up again into his gut. All within a half second.

Tommy had stepped on a stick. Sean didn't need to turn around to confirm it. The jig was up now, and there was only one way to handle it—full offensive.

He jolted forward as the closest gunman spun around, abruptly aware of the threat behind him.

Sean sidestepped to the left and swung his arm hard at the guy's neck. He felt the hinge on the inside of his elbow sink into the man's throat as he clotheslined him. The blow had immense force behind it and knocked the man off balance, lifting his feet from the ground. Sean followed through, driving the man's skull into the rocky ground.

The second gunman whirled around to help his comrade, but

instead he saw a huge rock flying at his face. The heavy stone smashed into his nose, instantly caving it in. He screamed a short, pitiful sound, then fell to the ground writhing in agony. Blood seeped through his fingers as he felt for the demolished appendage between his eyes.

Adriana pounced immediately, picking up the man's abandoned weapon at his feet, then pointed it down at his bloody face.

Two yards away, Sean pummeled the dazed gunman two times, striking his jaw to reinforce the concussion he more than likely just received upon hitting the ground.

Then Sean pulled the guy's head up, gripping him by the collar. "How many are there?" Sean demanded.

The Russian's gray-blue eyes wandered, barely hanging on to consciousness. For a second, Sean thought maybe he'd hit the guy too hard, so he tried a different approach.

He smacked him in the cheek rapidly, as someone would if they were trying to rouse a person who'd fainted.

The eyes rolled back to center for a moment, and in that span of a few heartbeats, the Russian realized he was now a prisoner.

He frowned, then clenched his jaw.

"Answer me," Sean growled. "How many of you are there?"

The man's head began gyrating, shaking violently back and forth. His eyes climbed up behind the upper eyelids. Then his entire body convulsed, twitching and snapping.

He didn't hit the ground that hard, Sean thought. *Or did he?*

Sean got his answer within seconds. A bubbly white foam oozed between the man's lips.

"How many?" Sean pressed, knowing he had seconds before the poison capsule finished the job.

The twitching slowed, and he slumped back against Sean's grip.

With a sigh, Sean let the man drop to the ground, then looked to the other.

The same thing was happening to him. Both men had bitten down on a capsule in their mouths—an old-school way of not being taken alive.

Tommy stood several feet away, watching in mesmerized horror. "Did they just—"

"Yeah," Sean said. "This group isn't messing around." He picked up his victim's weapon and then took the radio earpiece out of the guy's right ear. He wiped it with his shirt before putting it in his corresponding ear, then found the receiver/transmitter on the dead man's belt.

"And you thought they were messing around based on what happened in Istanbul?"

Sean turned around and checked the weapon. Adriana did the same. "Come on," Sean said to his friend. "If the Russians are here, they must have done something to the ornithologists. I just hope we're not too late."

"Hold on," Tommy insisted.

Sean and Adriana stopped amid the tall grass and short shrubs.

"Don't I get a weapon?"

"Sure," Sean said. "Check them. We'll cover you."

Tommy responded with an unpleasant scowl but walked over to the dead men anyway. He quickly searched the first—the one Sean had taken down—and found a long knife. Then he rifled through the other's belongings and found a sidearm.

"A-ha," he said.

"Shh," Sean cautioned. "There could be more of them out here."

Tommy gave the pistol a once-over, then joined the other two. "Either one of you want to trade your H&K for this?" He showed off the Glock 9mm.

"No, we're good," Adriana said and turned her back to him to follow Sean, who'd given his answer by walking away toward the tower gate.

"Alrighty then."

When the three got back to the gate, Sean stopped near the edge of the opening and waited until the other two were with him. He held up two fingers, then motioned toward the courtyard within, then scurried across the face of the gate and beyond the threshold.

Sean checked the left side of the enclosure while Adriana took the center position, surveying the space directly ahead. Tommy pushed to the right close to the wall.

The fog made it nearly impossible to see much, if anything.

Not liking the situation, Sean moved over to where Adriana stood and motioned for her to join Tommy on the right side.

"Anything?" Tommy whispered.

Sean shook his head. "Can't see anything out here. Let's press up along the wall here."

"Not the path?"

"At least here we can't be ambushed from the right," Sean explained.

"Ah. Gotcha."

Sean took the lead once more and stalked along the base of the wall, moving deliberately up the slope toward the main castle. Several bushes blocked his way every so often, and he was forced to maneuver around them before getting back to the stone wall.

As he moved upward, his mind wandered to the past. He imagined what it might have been like here five hundred years ago or more, when this fortress was active. His research had been limited, but now he found himself wondering if there was only a garrison of soldiers here or if this place had been a village unto itself.

He'd visited such places before, of both kinds. This one struck him as the type that could house a blacksmith, perhaps a small market, even some homes. No matter what the past held, now it was nothing more than a giant, overgrown raised bed of trees, grass, flowers, and shrubs.

Part of him hated that the place had fallen into such disrepair through the centuries, but he'd seen it more often than not. The other part of him appreciated that no renovations had been done, like so many other historical landmarks he'd visited over the years.

While rebuilds gave modern day people a chance to see what something might have looked like hundreds or thousands of years ago, they also took away from the authenticity, the reality of what a place had become.

Sean let the thoughts enter his mind and leave just as quickly, replaced by the focus on the mission at hand.

There were several Russians still here. That much he knew. How many was another issue, but he excelled at improvisation, and this was another instance where that skill would probably be called into service.

He kept creeping up the hill, and suddenly the wall stopped in a corner and turned sharply to the left. Sean extended his left hand to the two behind him and looked along the structure. He could see the vague outline of the central parapet, and the lip of the terrace railing on the nearside of it.

He peered through the mist, squinting his eyes as if that would help give him better vision. It did nothing.

Sean took a step forward and froze.

The shadowy silhouette of a gunman on the terrace emerged from the fog. The big man paced several steps toward the near corner, stopped to look around, then went back the same direction he'd come.

Sean pointed up at the terrace so the others would know to look, but they'd already seen the guard with the high vantage point.

When the man had vanished back into the mist, Sean moved quickly along the base of the wall, picking his way through the grass and shrubs until he reached the edge of a window. He paused there, and waited for the other two to catch up.

Sean crouched low and then got on his hands and knees. He crawled under the windowsill and then stopped on the other side to stand again.

He heard someone inside the building barking orders in Russian. A woman sobbed.

Great, Sean thought.

His fear had proved correct. There were hostages inside the castle. How many, he couldn't know.

He thought fast, trying to figure out the best course of action, and how to deal with the situation just inside the wall.

Storm through the door; he and his team could get killed. On top of that, the Russians could overreact and start shooting hostages. Sean had heard of that happening in situations like this before. Thankfully, he'd never been involved in one of those. He didn't want to start today.

He looked over at Tommy and Adriana, trying to think of the best way to handle this.

Suddenly, the radio crackled, and a voice came through the earpiece.

It was in Russian, which he understood well enough from his time with Axis.

"All clear?" the voice said.

Sean found himself paralyzed for the moment. He didn't know if he was team one, or how many teams of Russian patrols there were outside, but he knew silence would only be an option for so long.

And that realization gave him an idea.

27

Sean crawled back to Tommy and Adriana, who both looked at him with unspoken questions written all over their faces. He motioned for them to retreat away from the window so they couldn't be heard or seen.

When they were back in the corner, he looked to Tommy. "Schultzie," Sean said, his voice decisive and silent. "I need you to go back down that way. Hide behind one of the trees we passed. When you're in position, fire your weapon."

"What?"

"I don't have time to explain. Just go."

"Fire it at what?"

"Doesn't matter. The sky. The ground. Just don't shoot yourself."

"Okay, but—"

"They're doing a patrol check," Sean explained hurriedly. "I have to answer them on the radio. Fire your gun. I'll tell them we need backup. That will draw at least a few of them out of the building. Make it sound like a gunfight. Here," he handed the submachine gun to Tommy. "Give me the knife. You take this. I'll get another one."

"Got it," Tommy said, exchanging the blade he'd found before for the Heckler & Koch. With both firearms in his hands, he immediately took off down the slope, disappearing into the mist.

Sean turned to his wife. "When they come out of the door, we take them down. I'll take the far side of the door."

She merely nodded her assent.

"Check in," the Russian voice in Sean's ear grew louder, sounding much more impatient than his previous casual tone.

Tommy was out of sight, and Sean didn't have a way to know how much farther his friend had to go to reach the outcropping of trees they'd passed before, so he decided to buy some time.

"We have a problem," Sean said in Russian.

"Problem?" the man asked.

Sean sensed the skepticism through the radio. Whether it was his accent, his tone, or a misused word, Sean didn't know, but he had to press on. "Three people just arrived. They're—"

A gun report echoed from somewhere down the hillside.

Sean looked up toward the terrace and saw the gunman pacing back and forth stop abruptly and lean over the rail with his weapon raised. Of course, he couldn't see more than twenty feet ahead of him, and Tommy was much farther away than that, on top of being hidden in a thicket of small trees and bushes.

"They're armed," Sean said into the radio, adding a splinter of panic to his tone. "Weapons free!"

He did his best to sound urgent, while not giving away his position with the volume of his voice.

"Team One, report in."

Tommy fired again, this time three shots.

Sean didn't say anything back through the radio this time. Instead, he and Adriana crept along the base of the wall, hurrying back toward the window.

As they passed under the windowsill, they heard the man with the radio getting louder. Sean heard him both ways, through the earpiece and through the window.

"I said report in, Team One."

Beyond the window, Sean scurried over to the other side of the door and waited. Adriana took up her position at the nearside, weapon raised.

Sean stood with his left shoulder against the wall. He gripped the combat knife in his right hand, focusing on keeping his breathing steady, his heart rate calm.

Next, he heard a commotion inside the building, and then the same voice barked orders, urging reinforcements to go help with the matter.

Sean passed one last glance over to his wife on the other side of the threshold. *Beautiful yet deadly,* he thought. Like one of those exotic plants in the rain forest that appeared so lovely on the outside, but contained toxic chemicals that could kill any predator that touched it.

The door burst open, and two men in plain clothes rushed out with their weapons held at the ready.

Sean reacted instantly, stepping out from his hiding place and wrapping his forearm around the man's neck. The soldier's legs kicked out from under him, and he tried to wriggle free—obviously caught completely off guard by the attack from behind.

He only resisted for a few seconds. When Sean slid the tip of the blade into the back of the man's skull through the base of his neck, the movement stopped almost instantly, and the heavy body slumped to the ground.

Adriana tripped her opponent and watched the man spill over, tumbling to a stop.

"Team One," the Russian giving the orders shouted. "Report!"

Sean gave him the cold, chilling gift of silence as Adriana raised her weapon and fired a single shot through her enemy's head.

With the two reinforcements dead, Sean scooped up the pistol of the man he'd eliminated and held it high as he whirled around and stepped into the building.

Inside, he found three men standing with guns pointed at six other people—three women and three men.

Sean immediately trained his weapon on the man in back of the room who didn't have his gun aimed at the hostages. The guy was in the middle of what shaped up to be an odd kill triangle, isosceles if Sean remembered his high school geometry correctly. Sean assumed this one to be the leader and the one giving orders, and therefore threatening his life would draw focus away from the researchers at the table.

The goon in the near corner fell under Adriana's aim before he could react in kind and put Sean and her in his crosshairs, scanning back and forth with his weapon.

The third gunman started to adjust his weapon toward the threat a moment after they entered, but Sean stopped him before he could. It only took a single word to stop the man in place.

"Don't."

The gunman, probably in his late twenties with pale skin and short blond hair, froze. It took him a fraction of a second to consider the command and the consequences of disregarding it.

Just to make sure there was no confusion, Sean added, "Or I will blow his head off." Cliché? Sure. But the gruesome threat painted a vivid picture in the minds of those being threatened that could not be ignored. "Understand? Comrades?"

The blond gunman's lack of movement and total silence told Sean he understood well enough.

"Now," Sean said, "these six people are going to get up and leave, and you are going to let them. If you so much as twitch the wrong way, we will take you three down before you can blink."

The leader wore an angry expression, obviously frustrated that the Americans had gotten past the perimeter patrol beyond the walls and had so easily taken out the other two he just sent out moments before. The story was written on his face. *It shouldn't have happened like this. How did it happen like this?* It was a look of disbelief in the leader's eyes, but it was also draped with incredulity.

His head tilted up slightly as he responded. "You will not get out of here alive," he threatened. "You are outnumbered by one of the most elite units in the Russian military."

Sean's lips curled to the right side of his face in a cynical smirk. "First of all, if I had a ruble for every time someone told me I wasn't going to get out of somewhere alive, I would own half of Moscow by now. Second, I don't know how to tell you this, but your patrol and the two reinforcements you sent out are all dead." He lifted his right shoulder in a half shrug, as if what he was saying didn't matter. "So, you might want to rethink that statement, Boris."

The leader's face twitched at the sound of the name. Sean noticed the reaction and huffed. "That's your name, isn't it?" he asked with a laugh. "I was just using a common Russian name. Lucky guess, I suppose."

Sean scanned the faces at the table then refocused on the man in charge. "Now, like I said, you are going to let these six folks walk out the door, and then you are going to call the rest of your team into this room. And then we're going to have ourselves a little chat."

If the leader could have consumed Sean with fireballs from his eyes, he would have. Instead, he was left to smolder in irritation.

Sean directed his next words at the other gunmen. "Put the weapons down," he ordered. "Nice and slow. Or I swear, I will paint the wall with the back of your boss's skull."

The two soldiers glanced at each other with uncertainty, then at their boss. The commanding officer met their questioning looks, first the one to his left, then the one to his right. It was easy to see the man didn't want them to drop their weapons. But there was nothing else they could do. It was obey or watch their leader gunned down, which would follow with each of them being shot.

The one on the left acted first, slowly raising his left hand and gradually lowering his gun to the floor.

"That's good," Sean said with mock encouragement. "Now you," he directed the other.

The second hesitated a few seconds more than the first before acquiescing and lowering his gun to the floor. Then he stood up straight with both hands raised.

Disappointment streaked across the commander's face, even though he knew there was nothing else he, or they, could do. The two men were acting in a way that protected their leader, potentially sacrificing themselves in the process. The one Sean assumed was called Boris probably would have preferred them to start taking out hostages, or engaging in a quick firefight. Or so Sean figured.

"Thank you very much," Sean said. "Now, kick them toward me, please."

Both of the men obeyed. With a kick, they slid the weapons across the hard floor toward the American. The guns skittered along the stone surface and stopped within a few feet of Sean's toes.

"Looks like we're making great progress, boys," Sean teased, nodding his head to the side at the soldier on his left. "If you wouldn't mind joining your comrades over there, I'd be much obliged." Then he spoke to the other goon. "Go ahead and get cozy with Boris over there."

The soldier to the left obeyed immediately, moving slowly along the back wall until he reached the corner. There, he stepped over to within arm's length of his commander. The one to the right hesitated again, just as he'd done before lowering his weapon, but after two seconds of deliberation decided to do as he'd been told.

Once the three Russian soldiers were bunched together near the far wall, Sean looked across the faces at the table. He locked eyes with what he perceived to be the oldest man at the table, and most likely the one in charge of the research group.

"How many more of them are there?" Sean asked.

The man shook his head. The gray hair atop it shimmied with the movement. "I don't know for certain. I know there are others. Unclear how many."

"Are there any more of your team in the building?"

"No," the Swede answered. "This is all of us."

Sean lifted his eyebrows as he gazed at the Russian commander at the back of the room. "Somehow, I doubt that. So, when these people are out the door, you're going to call the rest of your boys back in here. If you do anything funny, and I'm not talking about Dave Chappelle funny, I start shooting kneecaps. Maybe that bone on the top of your foot. That's a painful one from what I hear. I speak fluent Russian, so if you try anything, I'll know. Any secret code words, anything unusual, and bullets start cracking bone. Ponyatna? Davai!"

Fluent was subjective, Sean knew. But the Russians didn't know that. After all, he'd been responding to them in Russian through their own radios. He knew more than enough to put a legitimate scare in them.

"You people get out of here," Sean commanded the Swedish ornithologists. "Get back to the town, and call the police."

Reluctance filled the eyes of everyone at the table. They were scared, and Sean could see it plainly. Anyone could have. He didn't blame them. If he was an ordinary civilian being held at gunpoint, even with the gunmen lowering their weapons, there was a residual effect. It would be a terrifying proposition to move a muscle. The mind is a funny thing that way. It could fill a hostage's mind with thoughts of a hidden pistol or knife being used to take out one or two innocent victims before being gunned down by the American interlopers.

"It's okay," Sean encouraged. "If they try anything, you won't get hurt. But they will."

The old man stood first. He panned the eyes of his fellow researchers and then nodded. One by one, the rest stood, scooting their wooden chairs back away from the table with a piercing, scraping sound not dissimilar to the irritating noise one might hear with fingernails on a chalkboard. Only much louder and more abrasive.

The Swedish research team walked single file out through the front door of the castle and into the foggy courtyard.

When they were gone, Sean looked to the Russian in charge, and nodded at him. "Okay, it's just us now. So, before I have you call the rest of your pals, I want some information."

The leader puzzled over the statement but said nothing.

"I don't think you'll tell me how many more men you have here. You'll just make up some random, inflated number. There's no way you will tell me the truth." He rolled his head to the right in a gesture that conveyed he didn't care one way or the other. "What I do want to know is what you are doing here."

The officer's confusion deepened. He blinked several times in rapid succession before answering in a matter-of-fact way. "You really don't know, do you?"

"Uh, no? That's why I asked," Sean said, laying on the sarcasm as thick as the paddle hanging over his elementary school principal's desk.

"Surely, you must be joking," the leader fired back.

"I don't joke," Sean lied. "Well, I do, but only with people I know and trust. Only occasionally with psychopaths like you." Sean tightened his grip on the gun, keeping gentle pressure on the trigger with the sights aimed at the leader's chest.

"Why are you looking for the trident?" he asked, opting for the most direct-route question.

The man's mouth gaped open with an *ah*. "So, you know about the trident. Very good. The major was right not to underestimate you."

Sean abandoned the surprise that these guys somehow knew who he was. "Who's the major?"

"You will know soon enough, American dog."

Sean inched his head back, lifting his chin, pretending to be offended. "American dog? How old is that insult? Maybe you didn't hear, but the Cold War ended like three decades ago. And yes, we know about the trident. The question is, how do you know about it? I'm just not sure how you guys know about it."

Adriana had been listening quietly to the entire conversation, never taking her sights away from the goon on the right. Like a snake lurking, coiled in a patch of leaves, she could have shifted her aim to any of the three men in a split second. The men probably didn't realize that she had the capability to eliminate all of them in less time than it took to swallow.

"I told them about it," a new man said from the doorway, startling Adriana and Sean. The voice was familiar, ghostly, and beyond unexpected.

Sean and Adriana both began to turn to face the new voice, but it stopped them cold.

"I wouldn't do that," the American warned.

Sean gulped a combination of regret, anger, and bewildered betrayal. He looked back slightly over his shoulder at a man standing in the doorway holding a pistol, pressing the muzzle against Tommy's right temple.

An exhale escaped Sean's lips, blowing every ounce of energy out of his body as the realization hit him.

He'd been played. Not an easy thing for anyone to pull off. And yet here he was. A range of emotions surged through him. There was nothing he could do. He'd walked right into the ambush.

"Well," Sean said, "I guess you're still alive after all, Jack."

28

Footsteps tapped in a quick staccato on the staircase in what passed as a foyer.

Sean figured it was the sound of more Russians approaching, probably the guy he'd seen on the terrace, and maybe one or two more.

"Aww," Jack mocked his old friend while keeping the pistol pushed firmly into Tommy's temple. "You thought I was dead?"

"I'd hoped you were alive," Sean replied. "I'm starting to think that hope was misplaced."

"That isn't very nice, Sean."

"It isn't nice to play your friends to help a bunch of Russian soldiers track down a mythical weapon."

The footfalls on the steps grew louder until a man appeared, then another, and a third.

One of the newcomers looked a few years older than the one Sean resigned to call Boris, even if that wasn't the man's real name. He carried himself like a person who was accustomed to giving orders. This guy had to be the mysterious major that Boris had mentioned.

"I see you caught a rat, Jack," the man said.

Sean and Adriana didn't flinch. They still held their weapons, though they both knew surrendering those would be demanded of them soon.

"I caught three," Jack said.

"The only rat in this room is you," Tommy sneered. "I can't believe we were actually worried about you."

"That makes two of us. But I have to say, you three played the part to perfection." He laughed. "Seriously, the whole text message and all that. I bet not one second did you stop to consider that I was using you all."

"No, Jack. You're right about that," Sean answered. "But that's on me. They were just following my lead."

"And now is when you try to tell me to let them go and you'll help me find the trident. Sound about right, Sean?"

"No. I was actually going to tell you that this is your chance to put down the gun... so I don't have to kill you."

"Always so funny, Sean. Ever the comedian."

"Actually, I just got done telling this guy I don't joke that—"

"Shut up," Jack cautioned. "Now, Konstantin." He turned to the officer who'd come down the stairs. "What do you want to do with them?"

The man stood back, watching Sean as he might a crouching predator. "Put down the guns," Konstantin ordered. "Slowly."

"And here I thought you were going to let us keep them."

"Do it, or your friend dies first. Then the woman. Then the hostages outside."

Sean puzzled over the last one.

Konstantin noticed the visible reaction. "Oh, you didn't think they escaped, did you? You killed two of my men outside. There was a third patrolling the perimeter."

"Killed four of your men," Sean corrected. "Not to get into semantics. Although two of them kind of charged blindly out the door. They basically left me no choice."

"He never shuts up," Jack informed the Russian commander. "He was like that in high school, too."

"And you were always getting into trouble," Sean said. "Seems like some things never change, huh?"

"Put the guns down now," Konstantin demanded, raising his voice. "Or I start killing people."

"Okay. Okay. Take it easy." Sean glanced over at his wife and nodded. Her nostrils flared, but she knew it was pointless to resist.

The two slowly bent down and set the weapons on the floor, then stood upright again with their hands raised over their shoulders.

"That's better," Jack teased. Then he shoved Tommy into Sean and immediately pointed the gun in their direction.

"So," Sean said after he turned around to face his old acquaintance. "Let me see here. You couldn't figure out the mystery behind Barbarossa's chest, so you had to conjure a way to get us to lead you to the treasure? Sound about right?"

"Figured that one out by yourself, Sean? Of course that's what I did. And it worked." He flicked his head in the direction of the one called Konstantin. "The Russians approached me about it. I told them I could help them figure it out, for a price, obviously."

"I hope it's a boatload," Tommy scalded. "You're trying to lead them to an extremely rare artifact, if it's in fact real."

"Oh, the trident is real. And it's so much more than an artifact."

Sean and the others played dumb.

"You really don't know, do you?" Jack wondered. He looked around the room as if the cameras from *Punk'd* or one of those prank shows would appear any second. "The trident is an ancient weapon of incredible power."

"You don't believe that, do you?" Sean asked. "It's a legend. Folklore. Mythology. Nothing more. If the thing is even real."

Jack merely stared back at Sean for several seconds before he took a step toward him. "And yet you flew halfway across the world to find it."

"We flew halfway around the world in hopes of finding you, Jack. But you're the same as you always were."

"If it ain't broke. I digress. The fact is, you found something in Istanbul, and I want to know what it is."

Sean clenched his jaw. "I don't know what you're talking about."

Jack's head rolled to the left as he looked at the three as if at a butcher shop, trying to decide if he was going to buy the whole cow.

"Sean. Sean. Sean," he derided. "Am I supposed to believe you came here, to the island of Capri, the same place we came—ahead of you, I might add—and it's just one big, happy coincidence?"

Sean and Tommy had the same thought, but Sean responded first. "What are you doing here, Jack? What led you to this place? I didn't take you for an avid bird watcher."

"We found the clue on the grave of Sinan Reis," Jack said. "Actually, my Russian friends here found that. I, for obvious reasons, had to remain in the shadows during much of this. The clue led us here. I can only assume you discovered the same thing, only I'm not sure why it took you longer to get here."

"Some people like to get a good night's rest," Tommy snarled with derision.

"Adorable." He sucked in a deep breath. "I'm getting tired of this conversation. What else did you find at the mausoleum, guys? Don't make me kill Adriana. That's your name, right? Adriana?"

"You don't want to mess with that one," Sean cautioned. "Besides, I thought you were more into blondes."

Jack's gaze lingered a little too long on her for Sean's tastes, but he was in no position to do anything—yet.

"Search them," Jack said to Konstantin.

The major nodded. He barked the order to his men, who stepped close to the IAA agents and began rifling through their outerwear.

It didn't take long for the blond soldier to find the double sword in Sean's inner pocket.

As the man pulled the artifact out, it gleamed in the dim light from a yellowish light in the ceiling.

Jack's eyes widened with approval. "I guess you just carry this around for good luck."

"That thing?" Sean downplayed it. "I got that in one of those claw games at an arcade near Orange Beach, Alabama. Place called the

Wharf. A few good restaurants there. Fun for the kids on Fourth of—"

"Shut up."

The soldier brought the golden relic over to his commanding officer, who accepted it with care. He admired it and nodded.

"The sword of Barbarossa," Konstantin said. "But what does it mean?"

"That, my Russian friend, is what we have them for." Jack held Konstantin's gaze for only a second before looking back to Sean and the others. "I want to know what you three know about this. It's more than just a pretty piece of gold. Where did you find it?"

"Can't do your own work," Adriana asked.

"Why do my own when I can make someone else do it for me? Now, here is what's going to happen. These guys"—he jerked his thumb toward Konstantin—"are going to start killing the hostages out there if you don't tell me what I want to know. If we burn through all of them, then I start on your wife and friend here. You're the last one to go, Sean. Of course, if I kill you, you won't be of any use to me, so I'll be forced to keep you alive—in a permanent state of misery, of course."

Sean met Jack's cold stare with one of his own. He didn't understand where this was coming from. "What happened to you, Jack?" Sean asked, detouring the subject for as long as he could.

"Spare me the sentimental BS, Sean. We were never close friends. You had your little circle. And I wasn't in it."

"Is that what this is about? Not being a better friend to you? I'll be honest, I didn't—"

"You are joking, right?" Jack scoffed. "This isn't some daytime television movie, Sean. I'm doing this for the money. That's it. You just so happen to be the perfect tool for the job, and as fate would have it… we go back a long time."

"So, you're just evil," Sean said.

"Once a bad egg, always a bad egg. But at least I'll be a rich egg. With the money they're paying me, I'll be able to buy any island I want."

"Sipping margaritas on the beach for the rest of your days, Jack? Is that it?"

"Pretty much."

"Sounds like it would get boring," Tommy spoke up. "After a while, the drinks all taste the same. The sand is the same. Same waves crashing on the—"

"Shut up," Jack threatened, wagging the gun in his hand. "Especially you, Tommy. You had everything growing up. Everything. I had nothing. No parents around. No one to—" He stopped himself abruptly and grinned fiendishly. "It's easy to think you don't need to be rich when you already are. Well, it's my turn to give it a try. And there is nothing anyone can do to stop me."

"I was always kind to you, Jack," Sean reasoned. "I tried to help you. To be your friend."

"I didn't need your pity, Sean. And I don't need it now. Some kids get a bad hand dealt to them. Now, I'm the dealer."

"You don't know what you're getting into," Tommy cautioned. "Mixing up with the Russians? Do you really think you can trust them?"

"You think I should trust you three? Or our government? At least the Russians paid me half of what they promised up front. Now, it's going to be time to collect the rest. Just as soon as you show me the way to the trident."

"We don't even know if it's real," Sean insisted.

"And yet here we stand. Full circle, by the way, to this little conversation. Barbarossa wouldn't have left a clue like this for no reason. The trident is real. Now, I want to know where it is. So," Jack turned to Konstantin, "bring in the first hostage. Perhaps a few dead bodies will change their minds."

One of the soldiers started for the door, but Sean stopped him. "Wait," he said. The gunman halted, although the perplexed expression on his face told he wasn't sure if he should keep going.

Sean didn't want any of the ornithologists to endure the mental anguish of having a gun put to their head. Something like that was hard enough even for a well-trained operative. For ordinary citizens, it would be a horror that lasted a lifetime. And he certainly had no intention of anyone dying—except maybe Jack and the Russians.

"Sean, don't," Tommy pleaded.

"We don't have a choice," Sean said without turning his attention away from Jack. "We can't let him hurt those people."

"That's right, Tommy," Jack taunted. "Can't let the innocent people die." He cast Tommy a derisive glare, then said, "So, tell me what you know about this artifact. Or should I have Konstantin's men start bringing in the victims?"

29

Sean's teeth ground together like millstones. His nostrils flared open as he breathed, still contemplating the best course of action. He knew there were no options right now, save one.

As much as it gnawed at him, he had to give Jack what he wanted.

"It's a key," Sean said. He felt Tommy's head and shoulders slump next to him.

"A key?" Jack clarified. "What does it open?"

"We don't know. That's why we came here. As I'm sure you figured out, based on the fact you're here and because of what you said, the riddle we discovered has something to do with the throne of Barbarossa. At least, that's what we're going with."

"Yes. We figured as much. So, the question is, what are we missing?"

"The journal contained the clues," Tommy surrendered. "You know, the clue you sent us?"

Jack laughed. It was a snappy, chiding sound. "Yes. I'm aware. Thanks for assuming I'm a total idiot."

"If the shoe fits," Adriana chirped.

Another snort escaped Jack's lips. "You better put a leash on that one, Sean."

"Put your gun down and do it yourself," Sean snapped back. "I would honestly love to see you try."

Jack exhaled and blinked slowly. "You were saying that this is a key," he continued, pointing at the artifact. "Where do we use it?"

"We don't know," Tommy answered.

"Then I don't have any further use for you three, or the hostages outside." He started to turn to the gunman by the door and tell him to continue bringing in the first victim.

"But if it's here, we can find it."

"And what makes you think we couldn't?"

"If you could, you would have already," Tommy countered. "And the reality is that there will probably be another clue you need our help to solve. You don't strike me as the type to figure things out on your own."

Jack sucked in air through pursed lips. "Ouch, Tommy. Your words hurt, man." He mocked him by putting his palm over his heart. "But fair enough. You three do have a knack for figuring things out that other people can't. So, you're going to work for me now. Understood?"

"You mean the Russians," Sean corrected.

"Potato, potahto. What difference does it make? You can be a king. Or you can be a pawn. But if you're a smart pawn, you can make a boatload of money."

"At what risk?"

"Look, we've already been down this road, so spare me. The Russian president wants the trident. I intend to bring it to him." He brushed the trigger of the pistol in his hand with his finger. "Now, where is the throne?"

"I'm sure you've already looked around the premises," Sean said.

"We have."

"Did you find the throne room?"

"We believe so."

"You believe?" Tommy chuckled.

"Come with us," Jack said, ignoring Tommy's derision. "We'll show you." He turned to Konstantin. "Major, would you mind escorting our tour guides up the stairs and show them what we found?"

The Russian commander replied with a curt nod, then motioned for the two men behind the three captives. The guards stepped forward and pushed their gun muzzles into the backs of Tommy and Adriana.

"One wrong move, and they get a bullet through their backs," Jack warned. "So be good."

Sean passed him a scathing glare as he walked by and began trudging up the steps. Konstantin fell in behind him along with one of the other gunmen.

The spiral staircase led up to a second level, where the major urged Sean to the left with a not-so-subtle shove.

Sean stumbled forward on the cracked tile floor.

The arched corridor was made from the same stone as the exterior wall but with heavy beams supporting the ceiling overhead in load-bearing places. Sean wondered if that was purely for looks or if the beams had become a necessity over the years.

The guard accompanying the major and Sean stepped out in front and led the way down the short corridor, through an archway, and into a chamber. Windows allowed dim gray sunlight to fill the circular room. To the left, another archway opened into another corridor, but that hall was blocked off by a wall of stone that looked much newer than the rest of the construction materials.

"This is it?" Sean asked. Tommy and Adriana joined them in the room, both looking around at their surroundings, their investigative minds already clicking into gear.

"This makes sense for a throne room," Jack said. "It isn't upstairs, because up there is a lookout area. Down that corridor would have been residences, similar to the ones back the other direction. The rest of the barracks and dwelling spaces have been destroyed by time and weather."

"Your logic isn't misplaced," Tommy said. "I'll give you that. Often, throughout history, leaders put their throne rooms in a place of power. This would have seated Barbarossa with a spectacular view of any approaching threat."

Tommy wandered over to one of the few windows and looked out. He peered through the glass at the harbor far below and the sea with its islands rising in the distance.

Sean had no interest in going over to the window. He was perfectly content examining the floor at his feet. The floor tiles, made of what appeared to be limestone, were cut in symmetrical geometric shapes that joined in the center around a circular stone tile.

He let his eyes wander the room for a moment, taking in the now-bland decor. No tapestries adorned the walls. Any furniture that may have been in the space before was long since looted, salvaged, or sold. Or perhaps destroyed.

Now there was nothing left but a barren stone room with an incomparable view.

Sean imagined what it must have been like in here during its heyday. Visions of the powerful Barbarossa sitting atop a gilded throne, receiving patrons and vessels, or military advisers, filled his imagination. He could almost feel the ghosts of those people throughout history who'd occupied this room at one point or another in their lives. The conversations that were had, the orders issued, the decisions made, or perhaps the victories celebrated, still reverberated from the walls, floor, and ceiling.

Sean had seen grander throne rooms during his travels throughout Europe and other parts of the world. He'd seen places like this as well, ruins that had fallen into ill repair throughout the centuries, left to rot and decay and give way to the relentless ravaging of Mother Nature and Father Time.

One thing he noticed as he pulled his attention back to the floor at his feet was the stark difference between the coloring of the circular stone in the center compared to all the other stones that merged with it. Darker tiles occupied the majority of the floor, wrapping around pale ones in the middle.

The clue they'd discovered at the grave of Sinan Reis had left them wanting for more of a hint, but this was it. Sean doubted there was another room that would have operated as the seat of power for the grand admiral. If there had been, it was unlikely there was much left to investigate.

The mere fact that this structure still stood after five hundred years was a testament to its importance, and instilled both a sliver of hope and a hammer of fear in Sean's heart.

The hope was that they could take the next step in finding the trident, a lost relic of an ancient mythology long thought to be nothing more than a legend. Perhaps it was even buried here, in this place.

But the fear that seeped into Sean's chest went hand in hand with the hope. If they did indeed find the trident here, or somewhere else, and Sean's theory about it being a cymatic weapon proved true, then the Russians would now have an unstoppable weapon, making them the greatest superpower humanity had ever known.

"What do you think?" Adriana asked her husband. "I can tell when your mind is churning. You have that look."

"What look?" Sean asked.

"Your face sets in this sort of permanent frown. You look pensive and unhappy whenever you're trying to figure something difficult out, and you have too many ideas rushing through that brain of yours."

"I was just thinking about the history here in this place."

"You can think about history some other time," Jack snarled. "I want to know what this key opens. And standing here in this empty room isn't getting us anywhere fast."

He brandished the pistol again, a crutch he kept leaning on since they'd become reacquainted downstairs.

"Where is it?" he demanded.

Tommy turned away from the window. The gunman standing close behind him didn't let him drift beyond an arm's reach.

"Maybe the first thing we need to figure out is what we're looking for, not where it is?"

"I'm sure you'd love to sit around trying to conjure up some hypothesis about what is here, or what was here. But we both know you're stalling."

Sean carefully gauged each one of their armed captors. They were well trained; that much he could tell. And it was unlikely they would slip up. Unlikely, but not impossible. They were human, and humans made mistakes.

Jack grew impatient. "The clue at the grave of Sinan Reis mentioned a throne. Since there is no throne, then what are we meant to do?"

"It's possible," Adriana said, "that whatever we were meant to find was in the throne itself."

Jack scoffed at the notion. "Come on. How convenient. You're saying they hid it in a fancy chair. A chair that is no longer here. That makes no sense."

Sean went with it even though he thought it improbable; he pushed the idea forward hoping it might buy them a little time.

"I don't know. Perhaps whatever we were meant to find here was in the throne and it was relocated when Barbarossa left the fortress."

He watched Jack's eyes as he listened to the theory. Jack wasn't buying it.

"No. I don't think so," Jack argued. "It's here. I want to know where. So, you figure it out, or we go back to—"

"Back to shooting kneecaps and feet," Sean interrupted. "Yeah, yeah. We got it."

He knelt down at a seam where the circular tile met one of the other tiles. The center stone was several shades darker gray than the others. Sean ran his index finger along the smooth surface, scraping the seam. The circular tile's diameter spanned four feet, just large enough to fit someone through if there was an opening beneath it.

Sean looked up at Jack. "I think it's under the floor."

"Under the floor?"

Standing again, Sean nearly bumped into the gun Konstantin held a little too close to him. He scanned the walls again, this time more intently than before.

"What?" Tommy asked, noting Sean's interest in the blank stone wall.

"Look around the walls, near the floor. Heck, check the floor, too. See if there are any markings that might identify this as the spot."

Sean walked over to the wall and bent down, then slowly moved along the wall until he found something unusual carved into the tile.

"There," he said. "The image of a horse's head."

Tommy took the cue and began searching another portion of the floor while Adriana went the opposite way. The gunmen kept close watch over their prisoners, while Jack merely observed with curious interest.

"Trident," Adriana said, pointing to the seam between tile and wall.

Tommy kept going, creeping along until he, too, found an image in stone. "Dolphin," he proclaimed.

"What does any of that mean?" Jack asked.

Sean looked at his old friend with disdain. "Three of the primary symbols of Poseidon," he said. "Not that you'd know. You're just using us to cheat your way through it."

"Yes, I am."

"This reinforces the idea that either something was hidden here in the throne itself or it's in the floor. Since we don't have access to the former, seems like there is one way to find out about the latter."

"Notice how this center tile is different than the others?" Sean said.

"Maybe they were just trying to get some decorative contrast in the room," Jack suggested with a half laugh.

"The only option is to try to pull up this tile, or blast it away. I would recommend the first option for obvious reasons. Unless, of course, you have some kind of ground penetrating radar device that we can use to run over the floor and see what's underneath it."

Sean looked around at the Russians guarding them. "Doesn't seem like you have anything like that on hand, so I guess we try to pry it up."

The young blond Russian guard chimed in. "We found some tools in a shed outside in the courtyard. There are some things we could use to try to bust through this stone, or leverage it up."

His English was choppy and heavily accented, but he spoke it well enough that everyone understood.

Jack looked to Konstantin and issued a curt nod. "Do it," he said.

The major spoke the order in Russian, and the young soldier hurried away and back down the stairs.

His footfalls echoed down the spiral staircase, down the passage, and into the supposed throne room where the group waited for his return.

"So," Sean said, directing his words at Jack, "do you really think they're going to deliver on their promise?"

Jack snickered at the question. "Do you really think I'm going to let you manipulate me? They'll deliver."

Konstantin eyelids narrowed in suspicion, and perhaps a touch of concern. But he didn't say anything, instead choosing to listen to his ally's response.

"How can you be sure?" Sean flashed a glare at the major. "Their military invaded a sovereign nation unprovoked, and seemingly without reason. Their president is an egomaniac and probably on the verge of insanity. Thousands of people have died, and this guy," he pointed his thumb at Konstantin, "is one of them."

"And yet I remain unconcerned," Jack insisted.

Sean studied his face for a heartbeat then inhaled sharply. "Oh, I see. You have a little failsafe built in, don't you, Jack?"

The suggestion caused Jack's right eye to twitch ever so slightly. It might as well have been a billboard-size neon sign—a dead-giveaway tell if Sean had ever seen one.

As a good poker player, Sean knew how to spot a liar soon after a new player sat down at the table. He'd applied those same skills in many parts of his life, including his time with Axis, the IAA, and in standoffs just like this one.

"Good for you, Jack. Always have a backup plan." Sean knew the needling would only heighten the Russian's suspicions. "Smart. Let the Russians think they're in control of the situation, and then wham-o. You stab them in the back."

Sean kept his eyes focused on Jack until a flicker of nerves sent

Jack's eyes darting toward Konstantin. The major merely clenched his jaw, saying nothing. Either he wasn't going to be manipulated by Sean's play, or the gears of mistrust were turning in his mind and he was already trying to figure out what Jack's supposed backup plan was.

Assuming, of course, Sean thought, *the guy understood enough English to comprehend what we were saying.*

"Then again," Tommy continued, "maybe Konstantin here has a backup plan of his own."

Sean and Tommy had employed the good cop, bad cop routine more times than they could remember. In a situation like this, it was simply a matter of inverting the emotions and projecting them onto those they intended to manipulate.

"Don't listen to him," Jack said, directing his warning to the major. "I know your president will pay. He's given me no reason to think otherwise. I have no grand plans for this artifact. A few billion dollars in my various accounts is all I need. The president can do whatever he wants to the rest of the world. As long as he leaves me alone."

Sean snorted. "Billions? With a B? You must be joking. You *do* realize that their president has cut off significant fuel and agricultural supplies to the rest of Europe. The play is pretty obvious. He's going to attempt to starve and stall the entire continent, weakening every nation to the point where they will all cave to any demands he makes. If you think his plan is to stop with Ukraine, you couldn't be more wrong."

Konstantin glowered at Sean, a look of warning and anger. But Sean could tell the words had struck a nerve in Jack's mind. If Jack hadn't considered this before, he certainly was now. Even if only for a moment.

"We'll see," Jack said, blowing off concerns that began bubbling in his head. "But first things first. We need to find out if there really is something under the floor as you suggest. And if there isn't, well, I guess there's really no need to keep you three around any longer."

30

The group stood in awkward silence for several minutes, waiting for the soldier to return with the tools.

There were many things Sean wanted to say to Jack, but he kept his lips sealed tight, instead choosing to observe silently—waiting for an opportune moment to present itself.

After the seventh minute passed, the soldier's footsteps tapped on the stairs, signaling his return.

When he appeared at the intersection of the corridor, he carried a collection of items bundled in his arms—a sledgehammer, a wedge, a crowbar, and two mattocks.

Jack saw the assortment of tools and laughed. "You just brought everything but the kitchen sink, didn't you?"

The young soldier puzzled over the English idiom, clearly not catching its meaning. So, he kept walking until he reached the middle of the room and laid the tools down with a bunch of clanks. He exhaled heavily from the effort of bringing all the items up the stairs.

"Well," Jack said, shaking the gun in his hand in a circular motion as if to get things moving. "What are you waiting for, boys? Let's do this."

Sean and Tommy exchanged a concerned glance. They knew what each other was thinking. Worries about this not being the right place, or that there was nothing underneath the floor, filled their heads, and they shared that concern with one glance.

The two reluctantly moved over to the pile of tools. Sean picked up the crowbar and inspected the flat blade on one end. Tommy took one of the mattocks and hefted it up, letting the upper portion of it fall into his right palm. Both men had quick visions of using the tools as weapons to take down their captors in an old-school, medieval farmer rebellion-type way. But they both knew by the time they were able to even begin swinging the tools, the gunmen would mow them down. Or worse, kill Adriana. Instead, Sean got down on one knee and again ran his finger along the seam between the circular tile and an adjoining one.

He inspected the edge of the crowbar once more and then inserted it into the crack. It barely fit, and he knew that prying it up straightaway wasn't going to work.

Tommy slid the flat end of the mattock into another part of the seam, but due to the curvature of the tile he couldn't get enough of the blade worked into the thin gap. And just as with the crowbar, the blade was too thick.

"They really fit these in here tight," Tommy noted.

"At least there's no grout," Sean replied. "Looks like we're going to have to bust this up a little with that hammer and wedge."

"Yep. Looks that way." Tommy looked over at the leaders of the enemy. "Just a heads-up: It's going to be loud in here. You might want to cover your ears."

Jack didn't seem to care about the noise factor. "I'm sure you'd like that, wouldn't you? We cover our ears, and then you attack while we let down our guard."

"Sounds like a good plan to me," Sean chirped.

"Just pull up the tile. Do whatever you have to do. Just stop stalling."

"I'll do it," Sean volunteered, seeing their banter was getting them nowhere.

He set down the crowbar with a gentle clank and then shifted his weight to the right to pick up the heavy sledgehammer and wedge.

He'd used tools like these before, long ago when he worked as a landscaper, but much time had passed, and he hadn't been working at gunpoint in those days. Part of him missed that simpler life where the typical day's challenges involved mowing grass, blowing leaves, or pulling weeds.

Letting thoughts of those bygone days drift away, he refocused on the current problem. He worried that the sudden sounds from the hammer blows might cause one of the gunmen to accidentally discharge their weapon, but Sean didn't have a choice. There was only one way to get enough of a gap in the seam between tiles, and that was to break it away.

He fit the wedge into the crack—the thick blade too wide to slide very far into the narrow space. That wouldn't matter in a few seconds, unless the stone proved to be harder than expected.

Holding the wedge with his left hand, Sean raised the sledgehammer, gripping it high near the head. He passed a warning glance to Adriana and Tommy, who both covered their ears. Then he brought the hammer down.

The head struck the wedge with a loud bang that reverberated painfully off the walls. Everyone flinched, even Tommy and Adriana. No guns fired, but Sean's ears rang. He grimaced, and focused on the tickle of relief that the enemies hadn't mistakenly shot him or anyone else.

He inspected the damage to the tiles and was pleased to see a chunk had already broken away from only one blow. So, he repeated the process, fitting the wedge back into the crack where the piece had busted off, and then swung the hammer again.

This time, an even larger piece of the tile broke away, along with several smaller fragments that hit Sean in the face. Fortunately, he closed his eyes right at impact to shield them from such debris.

Now, he could see an opening between the tiles that went beyond the adjoining seam. It was pitch dark beneath him. He shifted around to get his weight centered again and then positioned the wedge a third time, hoping this blow would be the last. His ears rang from the blows, and he feared if he did this much longer he'd end up with a hearing problem.

He lifted the weighty hammer again and struck true on the wedge head.

This time, the wedge blasted through the gap in the tiles and fell into the darkness below leaving a fist-sized hole where it had been positioned a second before.

Sean heard the tool clanking something metal below, then against stone as it fell, just before a distant thud echoed through the tiny opening.

He looked back at Tommy with an *oops* on his face and said, "I hope we don't need that."

"No, I think it served its purpose." Tommy took one step closer and got down on all fours. He peered into the new hole in the floor. "We can work with that."

Sean set down the sledgehammer and picked up the crowbar. He slid the flat end of it into the cavity and pushed down. It was heavier than expected, although he wasn't really sure what he should have expected. In hindsight, he realized this thing was a massive piece of rock and should have anticipated it being extremely heavy.

He grunted as he forced the high end of the crowbar down, prying the tile up and away from the floor.

The second Tommy saw a half inch of space between the bottom of the center tile and the one next to it, he slipped the flat end of the mattock into the opening. "Okay, let her down."

Sean eased the tile down and slid the crowbar out of the hole. Then he stepped around Tommy and fit the black metal rod's blade into the cap held up by the mattock.

While he did that, Tommy scooped up the second mattock and overlapped back around to Sean's right as Sean levered the stone up. More space opened to the right, and Tommy inserted the second mattock's edge into the dark crack.

"Okay," Tommy announced, "it's good."

Sean looked to Jack. "You mind giving us a hand here or are you just going to stand there and supervise?"

Jack didn't even consider the suggestion for a second. Instead, he rounded to the left and motioned for Adriana to move. "Give them a hand."

She looked as though she'd expected that and didn't hesitate to step over and take hold of the first mattock at the end of the handle.

The three gripped their tools at the same time.

"Okay," Sean said. "On three, lift and slide it to the left."

The other two acknowledged with simultaneous bobs of their heads as they readied themselves.

"One. Two." Sean double-checked with both of them. "Three."

They pushed down on their makeshift levers, and the tile lifted free. They quickly twisted the tools to the right to get the heavy stone positioned over the floor to the left.

Once a third of the tile was overlapping, Sean said, "All right. That's good. Let her down."

The three exhaled from the effort and then took a few deep breaths. The tile teetered on the edge of the floor. Where it had been, a round hole opened into the floor.

"Step back," Jack commanded.

Sean and the others did as told and retreated from the opening. Jack moved close, taking their place at the lip of the cavity. He pulled a flashlight out of his jacket and pressed the button. The beam switched on and shone brightly on the floor. He pointed it into the shaft and revealed an iron ladder descending into the darkness.

He turned to Sean and bared his teeth like a predator that had just found a meal. "I guess it's not in the throne after all."

31

"In we go," Jack announced. He sounded proud. "We need to send in one of your men first, Major," he said to Konstantin.

The major considered the request. "Yes. If you believe it's safe."

"It wouldn't be prudent if we sent them down alone. They could run off. Do you want them to escape?"

"No. But I also don't want to lose one of my men. I've already lost too many as it is."

"Oh," Sean realized. "I guess he does speak good English."

"Shut up," Jack sneered.

"Fine. Just saying, I didn't think he knew much."

Jack ignored his comment. "Tommy, you go first. Do anything stupid—and I think you know what I mean by stupid—and I kill your friends."

As if Tommy needed the reminder. They'd only been threatened that way half a dozen times already.

Tommy's eyes shifted to Adriana, then to Sean, and back to Jack. "Okay. I'll go first. But I'm going to need one of those flashlights."

Jack shook his head, rejecting the idea. "We'll be right behind you and keep a light aimed down so you can see well enough. We wouldn't want you falling. Not yet anyway. And from the looks of it, I'd say that's a pretty long drop. Then again, it's a lovely day for a neck injury."

Sean's facial muscles bent into a scowl. "That's *Home Alone 2*," he pointed an accusatory finger. "He's quoting *Home Alone 2*." He looked to Tommy for confirmation.

"What? No, I'm not," Jack protested.

Tommy's head bobbed. "Yeah. You are. That's *Home Alone 2*—the last scene in the aunt and uncle's place just before he lights the—"

"When are you two going to learn to shut up?" Jack roared, his face flushing red with irritation. He brandished the pistol again, which Sean had noted several times before.

"You should be more careful with that thing," Sean cautioned. "Safety first. Especially with firearms."

"You know, Sean, you sure do have a mouth on you."

"I get that a lot. Some things never change. It got me in a lot of trouble back in elementary school. And high school. And college. And—"

"Tommy, if you don't get going, then I'm going to have to push you into that hole myself," Jack threatened, doing all he could to cut Sean off and forget the pointless direction his counterpart was trying to lead.

Tommy thought about continuing the antagonism and saying something along the lines of "I'd like to see you try," but there was no point in extending that invitation, and they'd pushed him far enough.

So, he shuffled his feet toward the opening in the floor and got down on his hands and knees. He lowered his feet over the lip and into the darkness until his shoes found purchase on one of the rungs below. Gradually, he allowed more weight to rest on the bar until it bore his entire mass. Then, he slowly lowered himself down to the next, letting his elbows drag until they were at the edge, where he put one hand down and grasped the top rung.

"I'm going to have to do this slow," he stated. "Those rungs are iron. I'm not sure how they haven't rusted away by now."

"Do you have somewhere else to be?" Jack asked.

"I guess not."

Tommy lowered his right foot down to the next rung and tested it the same way he had the first two, and then continued descending into the shaft, out of the sight of Sean and Adriana a few paces away.

Konstantin nodded at the blond soldier who'd brought the tools. The man immediately moved over to the opening and pointed his light down into the darkness.

"I was going to ask if I could get a little light down here!" Tommy shouted up. His voice echoed both down the tunnel and up into the throne room.

The soldier replicated Tommy's entry movement, getting down on his hands and knees before lowering his feet over the edge and climbing down into the shaft. He moved faster than Tommy now that he knew the rungs would hold, but their progress would bottleneck once he caught up.

Once securely on the third rung, he clipped his flashlight onto his belt so it would dangle freely and illuminate the way.

"Thanks. That's much better."

In the throne room, Jack faced Adriana and Sean. "You go next," he said to Adriana. "Then you." He pointed at another soldier. "Then the rest of us will follow," he announced to Konstantin and Boris.

Konstantin motioned for the next soldier to follow her.

The guard followed her over to the lip, keeping an arm's length away with his gun pointed at the small of her back.

She proceeded down the same as the other two. Adriana displayed no fear at the idea of climbing down into the hole and quickly disappeared from view, with the soldier left struggling to keep up.

Now Sean was alone with Jack, Boris, and Konstantin.

"You sure you don't mind if I just stay here?" Sean asked. "I'm really scared of heights. And I don't know how deep down this thing goes."

"Wow. You are joking, right? You're just ribbing me, stalling."

"I wish that were the case, Jack. I really do. But it's not. I'm terrified of heights. Really, it's the falling I'm most afraid of, I think."

"The great Sean Wyatt has a weakness after all."

Sean's head swiveled one way then the other, his eyes looking at no one, but pretending there was an audience watching. "Seriously? I didn't realize that was a secret. Then again, we haven't talked in a long time, so—"

"You can take your chances on the ladder. Or you can take them with my gun," Jack snapped. "Of course, if I shoot you, it won't be fatal. I may still need you to solve another riddle for me."

"You're like that bully in high school that made everyone do their math homework for them."

Jack beamed with a sinister sort of pride. "I did that, too. Now, get moving."

Sean obeyed this time, albeit with great reluctance, and proceeded over to the hole in the floor. He felt a familiar, uneasy feeling in his gut. That uncomfortable sensation traveled up into his chest and tightened in his throat. He tried to swallow back the swelling fear he'd become so familiar with through his life, but it merely caught in his neck like one of those oversize supplement capsules that looked like they were too big for a horse to choke down.

He told himself not to look into the darkness where the others were, but he accidentally caught a glimpse of the flashlight beams dancing around on the walls of the shaft below.

The others were down at least twenty feet already, and still going. Sean immediately wished he hadn't seen that, but there was nothing he could do about it now.

Sean had tried for years to work through his fear of heights, but nothing had done the trick. He'd faced it many times, and yet whenever he came toe-to-toe with it again, he felt the same wave of terror wash over him.

His palms perspired. Not an optimal physical reaction for someone who needed to have a death grip on the antiquated ladder below. At least he knew the rungs would support his weight. Tommy was heavier than him and everyone else in the ruins. So, Sean held on to that fact as he lowered his feet into the opening.

He slid his elbows along the tile carefully, making sure his weight was equally distributed on the balls of his feet as they touched the first rung. He inched his way down, letting his right foot go lower until it found the next hold. With half of his body into the hole, Jack stepped closer, shining the light down into the shaft while pointing his pistol at the top of Sean's head.

"That's it. You can do it," Jack taunted. He mocked Sean as though he were a ten-year-old who had just learned to tie their shoes. "Attaboy."

"Not helping," Sean bit back as he shoved his left hand down to grab the top rung.

It felt cold against this damp skin, and he squeezed it with every ounce of strength he could muster. If not for the terrifying drop beneath him, he might have wondered who had put the ladder there, securing it to the rock. Those would have been the last hands to feel this metal in five centuries.

One grip at a time, Sean descended deeper into the shaft, carefully overlapping his hands and feet in deliberate succession. He didn't dare look down again, even as Konstantin's and Jack's flashlights beamed down over his head and illuminated the rungs below and in front of him.

Sean kept his eyes focused firmly straight ahead, cautiously working his way down. He had no way of knowing how much time had passed, how long he'd been in the dark shaft, but it seemed like hours.

As he neared the bottom of the ladder, though, Tommy offered some encouragement at the first sight of Sean's feet and legs emerging from the opening in the circular room.

"Almost there, buddy," Tommy said. "Fall from here, and you won't even get a bruise."

Sean finally got up the nerve to look down and realized he was safe. He made quick work of the last several rungs and dropped down to the smooth-hewn rock floor where the other four stood waiting a few big steps away.

The round room was twelve feet wide, allowing space between the first arrivals and those still coming down.

"Move," Jack ordered from above.

Sean still stood at the base of the ladder, now looking up to see just how far he'd come—a decision that didn't make him feel any better about the encounter. He shifted out of the way, stepping toward the others who were still being held at gunpoint.

So far, the soldiers hadn't slipped up. So far.

Sean took the chance to look into an arched corridor that extended away from the shaft. Pillars braced the sides every six feet along the wall. The decorative columns didn't appear to be load bearing. They'd been carved with swirling lines and undulations that Sean had seen in Ottoman architecture from the period of Suleiman the Magnificent. As he stared into the corridor, he couldn't help but think this looked like looked like an entrance to an underground temple, carved right out of the mountain.

Despite the dire situation, Sean marveled at the impeccable craftsmanship, as if he hadn't seen anything like it before. He, Tommy, and Adriana had been in more secret passages than probably anyone, and in more hidden caves than most amateur spelunkers, but it never ceased to amaze him to discover something that hadn't been seen by human eyes for such a long time.

He couldn't see more than thirty or so feet beyond the collective glow of the flashlights, and he wondered how far all this extended into the darkness. He tried to calibrate the direction of the path based on the position of the ladder in relation to the throne room. Sean knew right away the corridor didn't go toward the cliff or the outer wall. Rather, it appeared to run perpendicular or parallel along the wall and the cliff's edge.

He and the others waited until Jack and his Russian comrades arrived at the bottom. When Jack set foot on the floor, his eyes lit up in wonder as he shined his light into the passage. It wasn't the kind of wonder Sean felt when he found something like this. The look Jack wore was one Sean had seen in many people's eyes when they spoke about the winning jackpot amount for the lottery, or believed they were about to receive a huge influx of cash, or even a few circumstances where an enemy first laid eyes on an ancient treasure worth several lifetimes' fortunes.

This same look of greed opened Jack's eyes, filling him with fantastical visions and the hope that his plans were about to reach fruition.

Jack stepped past the prisoners, continuing to shine his light into the tunnel as Konstantin and Boris stepped off the ladder and joined the group on the floor.

The flashlight beams illuminated the eight-foot-wide passage away from the circular landing where everyone stood. Jack looked back at Sean and motioned for him to take the lead.

"Okay," Jack said. "Let's see where this thing goes. I hope there aren't any booby traps down here." He let the last comment hang in the cool, musty air as a sort of cynical threat to Sean.

"Well, if there are, here's hoping it takes all of us down," Sean replied. He trudged past Jack, who motioned for Tommy and Adriana to follow.

"You, too," Jack encouraged.

They followed Sean, each smacking Jack with death glares.

Sean scanned the floor, walls, and ceiling as he moved with Jack's booby trap comment in mind. Their captor had sounded like he was joking, but Sean knew better than to underestimate a place like this. He'd seen enough crazy contraptions designed to test would-be treasure hunters, and even eliminate them if they weren't cautious enough.

The darkness continued to retreat ahead of the group as the flashlight beams lit the way, while to their rear the black enveloped the corridor where they'd been.

They'd only been walking for a minute when they found a set of four steps descending down. The ceiling mirrored the short descent at a sharp angle. A pair of torches rested in sconces designed to look like human fists.

Tommy paused as he passed the one on the left and inspected the stonework. "Incredible attention to detail," he commented just before getting a pistol muzzle shoved in his back.

"Keep moving," Jack ordered.

The jab sent a dead pain through the small of Tommy's back, and he winced as he shuffled ahead and down the steps.

The group's light penetrated ahead, revealing more of the tunnel and the same columns that adorned the walls and... something else.

Sean slowed down slightly, dragging his feet, which caused the guard behind him to nearly run into him, pistol first.

"What are you doing?" Konstantin demanded a few steps back.

"There's something there," Sean answered, pointing to the spot in the passage where the light and darkness merged.

Jack inched forward, craning his neck to the right as though that would reveal what the dimly illuminated object ahead might be.

"I guess you should check it out," he said to Sean.

"I knew you were going to say that."

"Not afraid of the dark, too, are you?"

"No," Sean answered. "Dark I can deal with. It's just the heights thing. And also snakes now." He passed an irritated, inside joke glance at Tommy.

Before Jack could prod him forward, Sean pushed ahead, descending the last three steps onto the main path.

The light continued to encroach deeper into the tunnel as the men behind him followed, but Sean could already see what lay ahead by the time his feet touched the floor.

"Is that... a skeleton?" Adriana asked, breaking her long silence.

"Not just one," Sean corrected, indicating another figure on the left side of the tunnel opposite the first, and slightly beyond it.

The group approached the figure on the right and stopped a few feet short of it.

Konstantin and Boris wrapped around the U-shaped formation to get a better look.

Chain mail covered the bones from the shoulders down to the shins, where it disappeared behind metal kneepads, reappeared for a moment, and then packed the tattered remains of dark leather boots. A wide leather belt encompassed the waist and held a dagger in a slot in the front over the abdomen. The weapon's red-and-black-striped handle jutted up awkwardly from the pouch and reached to a solid metal plate that wrapped around the sternum.

A sword sheath rested on the right side of the dead man's belt, while the bony right fingers clenched the handle of his curved kilij—a thin scimitar-style blade commonly used by Ottoman soldiers in the sixteenth century.

The skull leaned against the wall, and was propped up by one of the pillars sticking out from the rock. The conical bronze helmet tilted at a slight angle.

Sean looked away to the other soldier, whose remains were clad in nearly the exact same armor. This one lay sprawled out on the floor on its side, jaw agape as if in an eternal, haunting last scream.

"What do you think happened?" Tommy asked.

Sean shifted closer to the skeleton sitting upright against the wall. He bent down on one knee, tilting his head as he examined the chain mail. "No sign of damage to the armor," he said. Then he inspected the helmet, leaning closer to get a better look. "No blunt force to the head, and the skull looks intact."

"So?" Jack blurted. "Who cares how they died?"

Sean looked up at his old classmate. "Because every piece of the puzzle matters. It tells a story. The reason these men died gives us a clue as to what happened here."

"Okay. So, what story are these skeletons telling us?"

"No damage to the armor means they weren't run through by a sword or spear. At least not that I can tell. The fact that they're here in this tunnel suggests they were guarding it, but from who? But I doubt Barbarossa would have stationed his men here simply to die protecting something."

"So, how did they die?" Tommy asked.

Adriana knelt opposite Sean and checked the skeleton. "Assuming the other has the same absence of armor damage, I would say they were either poisoned or had their throats slit. It's the only weak spot on their protective gear, although there could have been an opening in the rear as well. So, being stabbed in the back is also a possibility."

"All right. But who killed them?" Jack wondered, curiosity finally getting the better of him.

Sean and his wife shared a knowing glance, the same thought transferring between their eyes.

"Barbarossa," Sean answered.

32

"What are you saying?" Jack clarified. "That the admiral killed his own men?"

Sean and Adriana stood, but he kept his gaze fixed on the fallen warrior. "That's exactly what I'm saying."

"Why would he do that?"

Tommy caught up to the conspiracy theory. "Because there can be no loose ends. I imagine only a select group of people knew about this place—those who built it and those who helped Barbarossa hide whatever is down here."

"So, you're telling me the admiral executed his men so they wouldn't loot the place?"

"He was a pirate," Tommy explained. "That sort of thing was pretty common for their lot. Captains lived paranoid lives, always wary of a mutiny or that their treasure would be stolen by the very men who helped them attain it."

"Mutineers," Sean said in a snide tone. "Reminds me of someone."

"Is that supposed to hurt my feelings?" Jack asked. "Because I don't have any. A lifetime of disappointment cures you of that problem."

"Disappointment?"

"Get moving," Jack commanded, shoving his pistol at the air between him and Sean. "Our employer is eager to get his hands on the trident."

"I'm sure he is."

Sean snaked his way past the second skeleton, only looking down at the armored bones for a second before turning his eyes ahead. The theory about Barbarossa executing his men made sense, but that didn't mean it was gospel. Something else down here may have killed the men, and Sean didn't want to trigger it if that were the case.

The tunnel continued another sixty feet to another set of stairs. Two more sconces exactly like the previous ones, held torches. Jack reached into his right pocket and pulled out a matte black Zippo lighter with a white spade on the side. He flicked the lid open, then struck the flint wheel with his thumb. The flame instantly burst to life, and he held up the lighter until the fire touched the tip of the black torch.

To his surprise, it sparked a few times before the fire caught. The flames danced on the walls, casting eerie shadows on the surface.

"I always wanted to do that," Jack said with a wry smirk. "Keep moving."

He and the Russian contingent waited for the three hostages to continue down the stairs, then followed them to the next level.

Sean tried to figure how far they'd come from the base of the ladder and guessed they were getting fairly close to the middle of the wall that ran along the cliffside. He also realized he could have miscalculated the distance, putting them farther down the wall and closer to the crumbled remains of the turret that once stood there.

He and the others carefully moved deeper into the tunnel. Sean remained on full alert, wary that one wrong step might trip a string stretched across the floor and set into motion some ancient, hidden countermeasures that would leave them all dead.

He saw no such thread, but just ahead, as the darkness peeled away along the walls, the lights sparkled off of something shiny. Several more twinkling yellow points appeared with each step.

Then the tunnel ended abruptly.

Sean found himself facing a curved wall before him. The solid stone floor gave way to three rectangular stones that stretched from one side to the other, each separated by a thin seam. A curved, rectangular stone panel stood flush with the wall to the left.

"What is all this?" Jack asked as the group huddled into the ten-foot-wide space.

He and the Russians shined their lights on the curved wall ahead where dozens of golden beads glimmered. The marble-size metallic dots hung in tracks that curved, bent, and angled in different directions.

Sean stepped close to the wall, mesmerized by the design. It only took him a few seconds to recognize a pattern in one set of the beads.

"That looks an awful lot like Orion's belt," Sean said, pointing at the constellation set in the center of the wall about five feet above the floor. He noted two holes cut into a stone circle embedded in the wall four feet to the left of the stars.

He scanned the rest of the panel, poring over it with tempered excitement. Even with a gun pointed at both him and the two people he cared about most in the world, Sean couldn't help sensing something sacred about a discovery such as this.

"Okay," Jack blathered. "What are we supposed to do?"

"Give me the key," Sean answered. He turned and extended his hand toward Jack.

"What? I'm not giving you the key."

"Fine," Sean said. "You can stick it in those two holes right there." He pointed at the wheel in the wall.

Jack hesitated. He clearly didn't like the idea, perhaps because his own words about booby traps had suddenly caught up to him.

"No," he said, handing the golden double sword over to Sean. "You do it."

"It looks like the constellation is out of sorts," Tommy realized. "And that's the only constellation that's improperly aligned."

"Agreed," Adriana said. "It looks like the beads move along the tracks. I wonder if we're meant to move them around to line up in the correct patterns. At least you have the rest of the formations to act as a guide."

"It's the only explanation I can come up with," Sean confessed. "Unless you guys think there's something else I'm missing."

Both shook their heads.

"Then what are you waiting for?" Jack insisted. "I hope you remember your astronomy."

Sean had taken astronomy in college, along with a philosophical physics class, both as electives. Some of his buddies had made fun of him for taking rigorous courses as electives instead of racquetball or music appreciation, but he'd always been fascinated by the stars. As his learning of ancient history had expanded through the years, he realized that so many civilizations throughout the past had an advanced level of understanding when it came to the stars.

Cultures dating back twelve thousand years, and perhaps more, constructed megaliths that tracked the stars and aligned with significant events such as the solstices and the equinoxes. He also learned that places such as Göbekli Tepe were built to line up with the binary star Sirius.

At first, he'd felt resistance to the deeper time model of human history. Growing up, he'd been taught the world was only so many years old. But that pushback only lasted a short time when he realized that both this new information and his old beliefs didn't have to be mutually exclusive.

Now, as Sean stared at the strange wall before him, all that study of charts and archaeoastronomy flooded his mind.

He stepped to the wall and inserted the key into the two holes until the hilt stopped it. Then he pinched the first golden bead to the right of Orion's belt. "This," he muttered, "should be Bellatrix." He moved the bead up a diagonal track until he felt it catch on something, exactly where the right shoulder of Orion should be.

A click echoed from somewhere inside the wall.

Everyone in the room looked around at the sudden sound, but there was nothing to show for Sean's effort.

"What was that?" Jack asked.

"Maybe it's one of your booby traps you were talking about," Sean replied in a tone as cold as an iceberg.

"Very funny. I don't remember telling you to stop, wise guy." Jack motioned with the gun for Sean to keep going.

"This should be Rigel," he said and lowered another bead into position to the southeast of the belt.

Another click.

"I really hope you're two for two," Tommy said.

The uneasy look on the Russians' faces betrayed their uncertainty. The blond soldier took a wary step back toward the corridor and stopped just on the inner side of the threshold. He kept his gun leveled at the prisoners, but the flashlight in his hand shook.

He'd probably seen and done horrific things in his young life as a warrior, but deep down in the bowels of this castle, surrounded by darkness and mystery, his nerves split in two. The flashlight shook in his hand, and were it not for all the other lights, his beam would have vibrated wildly on the wall.

"This one should go right here," Sean said and slid one of the beads up to the right. He received another click for his effort. The sound continued with every placement of a star in the formation of Orion's bow.

He studied the chart for a few breaths before moving another piece into place at the constellation's head. "And this one"—he said, pinching a bead—"should be Betelgeuse." He shifted the golden piece down from where it rested and fit it into place.

Click.

Sean turned his head up and around. He'd thought that would be the last piece, but nothing changed.

"What is the problem?" Konstantin asked, growing impatient.

"I'm not sure," Sean answered. "That should be it. Everything else lines up perfectly." He rubbed his forehead and analyzed the stone chart again. "Oh, this one is out of place."

He slid another dot from below and to the left of Orion until it was positioned diagonally from the wall. He stepped back for a second and judged his handiwork, then moved to the key and grabbed the hilt.

"Moment of truth," he announced.

Everyone in the room held their breath as Sean twisted the hilt to the right. Moving the key took effort. The stone wheel ground against the rock around it, then stopped halfway through the turn.

A loud clap thundered through the room.

The blond soldier at the opening shrieked. Everyone else spun around at the sound. They saw his upper body and face drop through a hole in the floor where one of the tiles had been. His hands smacked against the next stone, and his gun skittered across the floor. Then he disappeared through the opening, his screams fading as he fell into the abyss.

Konstantin and Boris immediately stepped over to the opening. Sean started to make a move, but Jack reminded him to stay right where he was with a warning glare and the words, "I don't think so."

"What did you do?" Konstantin shouted, looking back over his shoulder at Sean. He aimed the gun in his hand at Sean's face.

"I... don't know," Sean admitted.

"It looks like it was on a couple of slats," Tommy suggested, leaning toward the opening where the three remaining Russians aimed their flashlights. Then he faced Jack. "You did warn us about booby traps."

Konstantin grabbed Tommy by the collar and spun him around. Tommy was stronger than the major and could hold his own in a fight, but it was hard to throw a punch when you had a gun pointed at your chest.

"You think is funny I lose one of my men?" Konstantin growled. "I throw you in next."

"Hey now!" Jack snapped. He stepped toward the Russian commander with his gun now pointed at Konstantin. This resulted in Boris and the last of their guard aiming weapons at Jack.

Sean and Adriana both saw the opening, but if they tried anything, Tommy would die. Being forced into inaction made Sean feel like a wild animal stuck in a tiny cage.

"Let him go, Konstantin," Jack insisted. "This is not what we agreed to. Remember? We get the trident for your boss. I get paid. And I get to kill these three. Not you."

The major considered the words, but from the looks of it they were bouncing off him like rain on a windshield.

"He mocked the death of one of my men. And how do you know that one didn't do it on purpose?" He indicated Sean by tilting up his chin.

"That's a fair question, Major. And I understand you've lost a lot of men."

"You understand nothing. You are a civilian. You have no one. No attachments. Nothing but yourself. That is all you know. My men are my brothers. How could you understand that?"

"You're right," Jack agreed.

But Sean sensed a punchline coming.

"I don't know what that's like," Jack continued. "I've never had anyone. I looked up to this guy, and he alienated me. He got me in trouble in school, always telling the teacher about things I did. I got kicked out of school, then another one, and another. I went from foster home to foster home. No one cared about me. At least you have your brothers. I never had anything!"

His shouts echoed down the corridor.

Sean blinked hard, trying to process everything. "Jack..." He stumbled over the words. "I never—"

"Save it, Sean. Your time is coming. But if you screw up the next piece to your little star puzzle there, then Tommy dies. Understand? He goes in. So, do us all a favor, and don't mess this one up. Okay?"

Jack turned his attention back to Konstantin. "We're on the same team here, Major. And we're at the finish line. Just keep them alive a little while longer. Then I'll dust every one of them for you."

Konstantin breathed heavily. A raging fire burned in his eyes, full of righteous indignation. "Fine," he said, shoving Tommy back away from the hole. "But I kill this one. No compromises, American pig."

"Yeah, well you're a big man with a gun, aren't you?"

"I kill you with my bare hands," he said in his thick accent. "I need no weapon to eliminate you."

"Then drop it."

"Everyone just shut up!" Jack yelled. When the scene settled down, he rounded on Sean. "Now, if you would be so kind, please put that little dot where it's supposed to go."

He aimed his pistol at Sean's head again.

Sean sighed. His heart felt heavy. Was that really how all this had gone down? Had he been mean to Jack as a child, and that was the cause of Jack's downfall? It sounded thin. Sean had heard all manner of backstories, or close to it. Seemed like Jack was reaching.

Then again, he'd seen many children who were bullied end up in bad ways later on in life. They became vindictive, or abusive, or addicted, or criminals, or politicians. His instinct was to question the difference between the last two, but he was facing a serious moment, and one that had him questioning his life.

He didn't recall being a bully to Jack, but maybe that's how Jack saw it. And perception was reality.

"Okay, Jack," Sean resigned. "Just... take it easy. I know where this is supposed to go now. It's Sirius. The brightest star in the heavens. And it goes here."

He slid the golden bead down to a position southwest of Orion's belt. It clicked into place, then Sean turned the golden key again.

Several sequential clicks resounded in the room, and then the panel to the left of the wheel slid down, slamming into a lower floor beneath it so that the top was flush with the threshold.

Jack grinned at the result. "Good job," he said through his teeth.

Then more clicks started, and the group felt the vibrations through the floor.

"Quick!" Tommy shouted. "The floor is about to drop!"

Sean grabbed Adriana and shoved her through the new doorway, then grabbed Tommy and pulled him past before diving behind them.

Jack and the three Russians scrambled.

The second piece of stone in the floor dropped away just as Jack dove into the open door. Konstantin hurried after him, followed by Boris.

The last of their soldiers planted his foot to leap, but the final stone tile fell away, completing the ten-foot gap in the floor.

His elbows hit the threshold. The jarring blow ripped the gun from his hand, and he clawed at the edge to keep from falling.

Gravity pulled at him, tugging him toward the abyss. He kicked his feet, trying to find a foothold, but found nothing but cold, deathly air.

"Hold on!" Konstantin shouted in Russian and dove toward the young soldier.

The last guard's fingers slipped. Konstantin reached out his right hand and grabbed the falling man's wrist and locked on tight.

"I have you," the major said. "Just hang on."

The guard continued to claw at the floor, desperately trying to pull himself up. Fear screeched across the whites of his eyes. "Don't let me go!" he cried in Russian. "Don't let me go!"

Konstantin's grip began to fail. He thought of grabbing on with both hands, but he was using his right to brace himself against the corner of the door; otherwise, he too would fall into the darkness.

"Don't let me go, Major," the younger man pleaded.

He slipped away, but at the last second another hand shot into view and grabbed the soldier's other wrist.

Boris clamped down hard and pulled upward. The assistance gave Konstantin a second to tighten his own grip, and together the two officers pulled the soldier up.

The Russians gasped for air and slowly stood up. Jack was on all fours, breathing heavily, mostly out of relief.

He stood up, grinning at his fortune. That grin flipped upside down when he turned and saw Sean standing ten feet away holding the Russian soldier's pistol, the sights aimed squarely at his head.

"Drop it, Jack," Sean ordered. "All of you. Drop your weapons. Now, please."

Jack froze. The Russians merely hesitated. Their allegiance was proved in the moment Boris and Konstantin disobeyed by lifting their guns, each taking aim at Adriana and Tommy respectively.

"You drop it," Konstantin barked back. "Or they die."

Sean felt the sliver of hope he'd seen through the crack in the walls of their prison disappear, as if a new dark cloud blew in over it.

With a sigh, Sean lowered the gun and let it fall to the floor.

"Good boy, Sean," Jack taunted. "Now, move back."

Sean took two steps away from the firearm. The golden key still dangled in his other hand. He'd had the presence of mind to snag it out of the wall just before making his escape, thinking it might still be needed at some point.

The Russian soldier, still shaking from the near-death experience, hurried forward to retrieve his weapon. Once it was in his hand, he pointed it at Sean as he retreated back to his commanding officers.

"I know that hurt," Jack said. Then his eyes wandered away from Sean and searched the new room in complete wonder. "This... is absolutely incredible."

33

The colossal chamber reached thirty feet high at its domed peak above a floor that took up what Sean estimated to be at least two thousand square feet. Each of the four corners housed gigantic pillars similar to the ones they'd seen in the tunnel, only much larger.

Golden oars lined the walls to the left; they were held in gilded racks beneath images of a muscular, shirtless man with a long beard and flowing locks of hair. He stood amid a raging sea, a trident in his hand extended out over the waters.

More frescoes adorned the walls all around the room. The wall to the right featured ships from the Ottoman Empire fighting an epic sea battle. Based on the symbols and flags on the enemy ships, Sean discerned them to be the Spanish.

Straight ahead, that wall displayed the constellations they'd seen in the previous room—stars hanging in a black backdrop over a peaceful sea with ancient ships sailing along the glassy surface. Those vessels were of Greek design from thousands of years before.

An open door at the base of that wall offered a way out, or possibly a way to death.

Behind them, the sun beamed on the wall above a moderately

calm sea. The water broke with white caps. Birds flew in the sky over a series of ships that neither Sean, Tommy, nor Adriana could identify. They were constructed with fluid, curving lines from every angle and looked like they could have originated in an Elvish kingdom in one of Tolkien's fables.

"Spectacular," Tommy blurted.

"Yeah," Adriana agreed. "Pretty amazing. And we're the first ones—"

"To see it in five hundred years. Yaddah, yaddah," Jack interrupted. "What I want to know is what's in those three chests over there."

Everyone followed Jack's gaze to the center of the room, where three eight-foot-long alabaster chests sat in a neat row, separated by a few feet each. An image carved within a disc adorned the end of each container.

For several seconds, no one moved.

"Well?" Jack asked, seemingly to no one in particular at first. "What are you doing? Get over there and open those chests. The trident must be in one of them."

Sean looked over at him, questioning the order. "There's only one trident. And three boxes."

"Your point is?"

"Well, this one over here is an owl, a symbol of Athena. The one in the middle is the trident. And the one to the right is a lightning bolt. Doesn't take a history major to know who that one represents."

"Three symbols of three great Greek deities," Adriana realized. "Zeus, God of the sky. Poseidon, God of water. And Athena, Goddess of wisdom and war. One of the boxes could be a trap," she said, turning to see Sean's reaction.

"Which is precisely why I want *you* to open them and not me," Jack explained. "The good news is if the first one kills you, there are two more for your wife and best friend to open."

"So generous of you," Tommy drawled.

Sean didn't wait to be told again. He knew there was no point in going around and around with Jack. Instead, he walked over to the center of the room, where the three chests rested. Stopping at the base of the center one, he looked down at the floor and noticed for the first time a design embedded in the tile. The sequence of oddly shaped pieces formed a giant symbol—a trident.

Could this really be the location of Poseidon's mystical weapon?

The thought shook Sean to his core. A week ago, he'd have largely dismissed the notion that the artifact was even real. Despite all the crazy things he'd seen, the unbelievable experiences and the incredible discoveries he, Tommy, and Adriana had made, he still approached things like this with a healthy dose of skepticism.

And yet here he was, standing over a mosaic that displayed the symbol of the fabled Greek god of water, and over three chests—perhaps one of them holding the trident itself.

He stepped to the side and studied an inscription carved into the top of the first chest to his left—the one with the owl on the end of it. He recognized the writing as Ancient Greek and immediately knew he needed backup.

"There's something written on the top of these chests," Sean said over his shoulder.

Jack and his Russian buddies remained a safe distance away, probably out of fear of what could happen if the wrong chest was opened. Sean was certain they had Hollywood visions of acid bursting out of the lid, consuming their flesh, or of a nest of venomous serpents that sprang forth, somehow surviving for centuries in the sealed box.

While those two threats were irrational, there was no denying the probability that if he opened the wrong one, something bad would happen.

"I need Tommy and Adriana for this, Jack. They know that language better than I."

"Help him," Jack surrendered, motioning with his gun for the two to join Sean by the chests. "I suppose it's fine if you all die should you open the wrong one."

Sean ignored him, and indicated the message on the chest with his index finger. "I just want to make sure I'm seeing this correctly," he said. "What do you guys think?"

"It says that appearances are deceptions," Tommy answered. "The clear path is not always the right one. Be wise in all things. From that wisdom shall many branches bloom."

"He's correct," Adriana confirmed. "Although I'm not sure what it means. Unless"—she stepped back and looked at the images on the ends of the chests—"it's a reference to these three symbols."

"Appearances are deceptions," Sean said thoughtfully. He scratched his nose and put his hands on his hips while he pondered the riddle. The first thing that came to mind was that the chest with the trident on it was the obvious one to check, for someone who wasn't interested in reading the fine print. A potential looter would pry it open and receive whatever punishment Barbarossa had designed for them. "I think that means we should rule out the one with the trident on it."

"What?" Boris protested. The man had remained steadily silent for the entire journey through the passage. "He's lying, sir," he said to Konstantin.

The major took a bold step toward the chests. "Yes, I believe he is." He turned to the last of their soldiers in the room. "Open the one with the trident on it," he ordered. "You three, step away from the chests. Now. I don't want any of you thinking you can take this away from me."

Jack looked suddenly torn. "You mean us," he said.

Konstantin didn't turn to face him. "Yes. Of course. Us."

Jack's cheek muscles flinched, and for a second, Sean noticed a flash of indignation.

Sean, Tommy, and Adriana stepped away from the chests as they were told and watched the young soldier approach. He ran his fingers along the edge of the lid and then proceeded to push it. The object was heavier than he first assumed, and he had to lean into it to get it to budge.

The grinding sound of stone on stone vibrated through the chamber as he pushed the lid all the way off the chest. It landed with a heavy thud and a thunderous aftershock through the floor, chipping away one of the corners of the lid.

Tommy winced at the damage to such an amazing piece of history, now no longer in mint condition.

The soldier leaned over the box, peering into it with curiosity for a second. Then he turned to his superiors, bracing himself with his hands on either side of the container's top edge.

"There's nothing in here," he announced. "It's just sand."

He turned his head back to the inside of the chest. It was nearly filled to the brim with the stuff, a pristine white sand as if straight from the beaches of 30A. He stuck his hand into the softness and started pulling it away. He did the same with the other hand, drawing the sand away from the center to see what contents may have been hidden within.

Unexpectedly, a loud flick echoed through the huge room.

The soldier gurgled, and slumped into the chest, his hands no longer able to support his weight.

"What happened?" Jack asked, suddenly worried.

The two Russian officers rushed over to the container but stopped six feet short when they thought better of it.

Konstantin rounded to Sean. "Look at him. Get him out of there."

The soldier's legs and torso twitched, but his head barely moved. Konstantin and Boris saw dark crimson spilling into the white sand.

"He's bleeding," Boris said, panic filling his voice.

Sean moved over to the soldier, unafraid of the box's contents.

He'd seen the quick-burst spikes that shot up from the bottom of the chest and punctured several places in the soldier's body—chest, neck, and left eye. The guy was dead before his body hit the sand. Figuring it had to be some kind of weighted trap within the container, Sean felt it safe enough to get close since he had no intention of prying through the sand.

He bent down and pulled the soldier over by his left shoulder and let the bloody body hit the floor.

For a couple of hardened warriors, both Konstantin and Boris looked as if they might empty their stomachs right there on the floor.

Apparently, the grisly sight of the dead man—the man just a few moments before they'd saved from a horrific fall—was almost too much for them to bear.

It wasn't lost on Sean that the soldier's own choices—serving under a butcher like Konstantin, helping him desecrate humanity's shared sacred heritage—had helped seal what now seemed like his predetermined fate.

Konstantin whipped his pistol around at Sean and aimed it at his head. "You tricked us."

"We told you not to open that one," Sean reminded him in a cold, deep voice. "You didn't listen. That one is on you, comrade."

The officer's trigger finger caressed the trigger. Sean could see in the man's eyes that he was debating pulling it just to make a statement. It was a position Sean had found himself in more times than he would have liked. Staring down the barrel of a gun with a psycho on the other end of it was never an easy thing.

Tommy had asked him once how he handled it so coolly, to which Sean replied, "I just tell myself that you gotta go sometime. Today's as good a day as any."

Tommy had balked at the response, but Sean never flinched, just as he didn't here in the chamber of Hayreddin Barbarossa's hidden vault.

"We still may need him," Jack said, cutting through the tension. "We kill them after we have the trident. Got it?"

After another ten seconds of deliberation, Konstantin took a step back and leveled his pistol at Sean's waist.

"Now, Sean, if you don't mind, open the chest you think is the right one. Although, now that we know what will happen, I'm going to be watching you very closely. So, which one is it?"

Sean shrugged, then swallowed. "The inscription says to be wise," he said as he moved deliberately over to the chest with the owl on the end. "What is wiser than an owl? It's also the symbol of Athena, who defeated Poseidon in a contest of wonders for rule over the city of Athens. The contest happened at the Acropolis. Poseidon brought forth water from the rock. Athena touched her spear to the ground, and an olive tree grew out of it. She was awarded the city. I think that last part has to do with the part of the riddle about many branches blooming."

Jack's head bobbed with eager agreement. "Yes. Yes, that makes sense." He shuffled close, hemming Sean toward the chest. "Open it."

The gun's muzzle was less than a foot from the side of Sean's head. He wished he could have ripped the weapon away in one quick, unexpected move. He'd done so before, but not at this angle. Jack's reaction time would be too quick.

Instead, Sean leaned over the chest and put his hands on the lid, one on either side, and shoved.

The grinding sound from the stone filled the air again until the lid teetered on the far edge. Unlike the soldier with the first box, Sean lowered the top down slowly so it wouldn't be damaged. Then he stood upright and waited for further instructions.

Jack passed him an annoyed look that wondered what he was doing. "Well? I see sand in there just like the first one."

"I guess it's not the right one after all," Sean said.

Jack didn't buy it. "I don't think so. Dig it out."

"Dig what out?"

"Don't play dumb, Sean. Odds are, every one of those chests has sand in them. But one has the trident. We both know that. So, put your hands in there, and see if this is the one."

Sean sniffled, then nodded as he stuck out his bottom lip. "Okay, Jack."

He turned to the open box and leaned over it.

Tommy and Adriana watched helplessly from the side, both under the watch of Boris.

Sean bent down so that his torso was hovering over the smooth sandy surface, then pulled back a layer.

Fear filled him, even though he believed his reasoning to be correct. Just because it made sense didn't mean it was right, and that splinter of doubt needled at his gut as he pulled back a second, third, and fourth layer of sand.

The stuff spilled over the side of the chest, piling up around his feet as he continued to dig for another two minutes. Then, he suddenly stopped when his fingers touched something cool and metallic.

The others in the room couldn't see what he'd found, and neither could he yet, but he felt it. The object was a shaft, and as his fingers brushed against the side, he felt a warm vibration rush through the tips.

His eyes widened at the sensation—a display Jack didn't miss hovering right next to him.

"That's enough," Jack said. "Step away from it."

Sean clenched his jaw. "It's just an empty—"

"Save it, Sean. I saw that look in your eye. You found something in there."

Sean put on his best poker face—emotionless, uninterested, vague.

"I don't know what you're—" Jack swung the pistol around and aimed it at Adriana. "Move. Or she dies now."

"Okay," Sean said, pulling his hands out of the chest. Sand dripped from his sleeves and hands like a white, grainy liquid.

"Over there, please," Jack ordered, motioning for Sean to step to the side next to Konstantin's right.

He did as told and moved cautiously away from the chest.

"Watch him," Jack said to the two Russians.

Konstantin obeyed, something he was accustomed to doing in his line of work. He pointed his weapon at Sean, leaving Boris to cover the other two.

Jack stuck his left hand into the sand and scraped away a layer of it. He gasped, then started laughing. He bent deeper down and then straightened up holding a seven-foot-long golden trident.

He breathed heavily, energy filling his face as if drawing it from the relic. "It's mine," he said, drunk on power.

"And now we take it to Russia," Konstantin reminded.

A serpent's grin creased Jack's face, and he turned his pistol at the major. "I don't think so."

Konstantin frowned, immediately incensed at the sudden threat. "What are you doing, Jack?"

"Sorry about this, Sean," Jack said. "I had to make it look like I was helping them."

Sean looked just as confused as the Russians. Tommy and Adriana were equally lost.

Boris instinctively aimed his gun at Jack in an effort to defend his commander.

"Put it down," Boris demanded.

"Put what down?" Jack asked. "The gun or the trident?"

The question caught Boris off guard, but he quickly gathered his thoughts. "Both. You will give the trident to us."

Jack shook his head. "I don't think so. You see, Sean, I had to make them think I was bringing them something that could end the war in Ukraine quickly and easily, that could give the Russians the ultimate weapon on Earth. Their president was so desperate, he didn't even think twice about the operation. Seems history repeats itself in that way. Losing a hundred thousand soldiers in a war no one wants will do that to a leader."

"I don't understand," Sean admitted.

"I work for the Ukrainians," Jack confessed. "I bring them the trident. We drive the Russians back, never to return, and we stop any other egomaniacs like him from ever doing this again. I hold the ultimate power on Earth in my hand."

Sean rapidly put the pieces together in his head. They were jagged, mismatched, and still seemed off. "So, all that stuff about how we treated you as kids?"

"A thin backstory, just as you suspected. It was the best I could come up with on such short notice, but it worked. Gotta love the language barrier, right?"

"Put it down!" Boris shouted. "Or I shoot!"

"You shoot me; I kill him," Jack said, indicating Konstantin with a casual nod.

"You work for the Ukrainians?" Konstantin asked. Disbelief

streaked across his face. "Pathetic. Just like them. I knew you were not to be trusted."

"Maybe. But like I said, I hold the ultimate power in my hand. The power to raise the oceans." He paused. "The power to create from all the material around me." He stopped again, this time flicking a message to Sean with his eyes. "And the power to move the Earth itself."

Jack closed his eyes and exhaled, squeezing the trident shaft tight. Motes of blue and white light blinked in the air around the three prongs of the trident. Then they began to swirl, flowing in and around the tips of the ancient weapon.

The second the breath left Jack's lungs, the Earth trembled.

34

Konstantin and Boris looked at each other, and in that split second of uncertainty, Sean pounced.

He'd noticed the look Jack gave him. It was a way of telling Sean to be ready, though Sean wasn't sure why.

When the floor of the vault began to shake, Sean lunged into Konstantin, delivering a shoulder to the man's tricep. As momentum carried them to the floor, Sean wrapped his arms around him and drove the major into the hard tile with a crunch.

The impact with the floor should have knocked the gun from Konstantin's hand, but the man somehow held on tight as the two rolled to a stop with Sean straddling the man's torso.

Boris swung his weapon around at the first sight of trouble. Tommy reacted in an instant, barreling forward into Konstantin's would-be savior, and tackled the Russian captain to the ground with a heavy thud.

The impact from Tommy's bulk jarred the gun from Boris's hand, and it fell to the floor with a clatter.

Adriana dove toward the firearm, grasped it, and in a single fluid movement rolled up to one knee and aimed the gun at Jack, who she thought had his eyes closed.

Instead, he was already pointing his pistol at her with his eyes wide open, placing them both in the sights of each other's weapons.

Fifteen feet away, Sean grappled with Konstantin, trying to wrest the pistol from the man's left hand. The major attempted to raise the weapon and end the fight with a pull of the trigger, but Sean drove his hand back down into the floor, again and again until he saw the pistol loosen in the Russian's grip.

Konstantin swung his right fist at Sean's face. Sean was so focused on freeing the firearm, that he only managed to deflect the blow. The Russian's fist slammed into Sean's jaw, and snapped his head to the side.

For a few seconds, Sean felt disoriented, and a harsh pain bloomed in the left side of his face. The amount of force he applied to Konstantin's wrist weakened slightly.

The Russian punched again, this time into Sean's ribs. The sharp pain that followed sent Sean sprawling to his right side where the pistol lay in Konstantin's hand.

The major attempted to lift the weapon again, but Sean kicked out his legs and rolled away while jerking the gun barrel backward. Konstantin howled as the tendons in his forearm and fingers stretched to their tearing point. He had no choice but to release the gun as Sean pried it away.

As Sean started to aim down at the Russian officer, Konstantin raised his hips and kicked the heel of his right boot into Sean's abdomen, doubling him over before he could fire.

Just a few paces away, Tommy wrestled with Boris, both men now unarmed.

Boris managed to slip to the side and elude Tommy's grasp for a moment, then swung his right elbow back at Tommy's head as the American bent forward to keep his enemy from escaping.

The elbow struck a glancing blow against Tommy's jaw, dangerously close to knocking him out.

Tommy slumped over to the left and wriggled forward like a worm, clenching and unclenching his jowls to make sure he wouldn't be eating breakfast through a straw for the foreseeable future. The room blurred in his vision, and he looked back, dazed, and saw the stocky captain stand up.

Boris went on the offensive and kicked his right leg into Tommy's chest just as he managed to clamber up onto all fours. The impact crumpled Tommy's arms and legs, and he fell to the floor again. Boris didn't wait to have another go. He wound up and drove the tip of his boot into Tommy's gut, twisting him around it like a human pretzel.

The Russian captain sucked in a deep breath and kicked again, this time at Tommy's face. Tommy fought through the multiple points of screaming pain enough to raise his forearms just in time to block the kick, but the impact still hurt, and the force was enough that Tommy effectively punched himself.

Behind Boris, Adriana kept her new pistol trained at Jack, who replied in kind.

"I am not your enemy, Adriana," Jack said. He lowered the pistol in a show of good faith. He nodded his head once toward Boris several paces behind her. "Tommy needs help."

Doubt filled her eyes.

Jack saw it and dropped the pistol down to the floor. "Help him."

Adriana had the perfect chance to kill him right then, but other than the trident, he was unarmed—and she still wasn't sure if that counted. Killing an unarmed person wasn't her thing. But his surrender of the firearm signaled that there was at least an element of truth to his gesture.

She whipped her head around and saw Boris rear back to kick Tommy again.

Adriana took aim at the center of the man's back and squeezed the trigger.

Tommy hadn't noticed her coming to his aide, and in a last desperate attempt to save his neck, twisted his body around and slung his right leg backward. The leg sweep struck the Russian's heel as he planted to kick again, and tripped him just enough that he lost his balance and fell over.

Adriana's pistol popped from nearby. The round missed the target as he tumbled over. The projectile ricocheted off the mural near the entrance to the vault, and bounced one more time before dying somewhere on the floor.

She fixed her aim again and tried to lock on to the stumbling man, but Tommy kicked up his legs, driving his left heel into the man's groin.

The enemy bent over at the waist with a loud grunt. Tommy grabbed him by the collar and rolled back, using leverage to throw the man toward the nearby open door.

Boris rolled to his feet, breathing heavily and doing everything he could to work through the throbbing pain in his perineum.

Tommy stood up crooked, like a prize fighter who'd gone too many rounds and taken the brunt of the punishment. But he wasn't going to surrender. He staggered toward Boris, who stood near the threshold of the entrance.

The Russian almost seemed to be waiting for something, something Tommy didn't expect.

Adriana couldn't get off a clear shot with Tommy in the way. "Tommy, move!" she shouted.

Tommy heard the order, but instead turned around to see why it had been given.

In that instant, Boris drew a knife from a sheath at his side, and lunged toward Tommy with the black Cerakote blade's tip aimed at the unsuspecting American's neck.

Adriana dipped a few inches to the side. She twitched her trigger finger, and the muzzle erupted with a pop.

The bullet cracked the air as it zipped by Tommy's face, tickling his skin with its wake as it passed, missing him by less than five inches.

The round found its mark, burrowing into the Russian captain's chest and driving him backward.

Tommy dropped to the floor out of sheer instinct, and Adriana loosed another three shots, each one pushing the man farther back with the force. The last one went through the bridge of his nose, and for a second, Boris teetered on the lip of the abyss. Then gravity tugged him down into the darkness, and out of sight.

While Adriana and Tommy battled Boris, Sean had his own problems.

His abdomen radiated pain from the kick Konstantin delivered. The Russian wasted no time going on the attack again, even though he was on his back. He swung his right leg around, pounding the side of Sean's face with his shin.

The devastating kick spun Sean around 180 degrees before he fell in a heap to the floor, twisting and writhing.

Konstantin stood up and heard a gunshot from somewhere behind.

Adriana had one of their firearms but was aiming it at Boris. She'd missed, but the major couldn't worry about that just yet. He had his own problem, but that would be dealt with soon.

Sean pushed himself up onto his hands and knees and tried to raise the pistol again, but the Russian kicked it out of his hand with one strike. The pistol clattered on the ground and slid to a stop against the wall. Then Konstantin punched Sean in the face just between the left cheek and the nose.

The hit rocked Sean's head back, and he nearly toppled over onto the floor. But he narrowly managed to retain his balance long enough to raise his left hand and catch Konstantin's fist as the man tried to deliver the knockout punch.

The Russian pulled back with his arm, but Sean didn't let go and allowed the momentum to drag him up from the floor, sending him crashing into the major.

The two men tripped as they embraced in battle and fell to the floor again. On the way down, however, Sean made sure he was on top and pushed his elbow up and into the Russian's throat so that when they hit the hard surface, the back of Konstantin's skull hit first with a devastating, sickening crack.

The enemy's head rolled to the side, eyes half-open and brimming with a glaze. His arms moved slightly but without the motor control he'd exhibited seconds before.

Sean stood up, gasping for air and grabbing his stomach. He winced at the pain, and then again when he heard a gunshot from nearby. For an instant, he felt worry snake through his body. Then he heard more reports and looked to the doorway in time to see Boris tip over and disappear into the hole in the tunnel floor.

"You okay?" Sean asked Tommy, who hunched over clutching his ribs.

Tommy's head bobbed absently. "I'll be fine," he said, his eyes locked on the floor.

Sean sensed movement back to his left, and turned back to where he thought Konstantin was lying unconscious.

The Russian leader was back on his feet, albeit unsteadily. He took a step toward Sean, a combat knife in his right hand.

Sean twisted his upper body and raised his left arm to try to knock the attacker's forearm away.

Instead, a flash of gold-and-blue light touched Sean's periphery just before he saw the trident prongs thrust into the Russian's side.

Sean looked farther to his left and saw Jack holding the ancient weapon with both hands, fingers wrapped tight around the shaft as he lifted Konstantin up, skewering him with the center blade.

The major grunted, then yelled as the sharp point punctured, then ran through, his vital organs.

Sean couldn't believe what he saw. There was no way Jack was strong enough to lift the man in such a way, and yet there he was, holding up the enemy at the end of the trident.

Jack shook the weapon twice as he might with a stick that was roasting a marshmallow, then spun around and flung the man's body against the wall. It hit with a thump then fell to the floor, where Konstantin remained perfectly still.

Sean faced Jack and noticed the peculiar lack of blood on the trident's fork.

Jack wasn't even out of breath. He set the base of the shaft down onto the floor and held the weapon upright.

"Good work," Jack said with a nod. "I was afraid he might get the better of you for a second."

"You and me both," Sean admitted as he caught his breath.

"Thanks for the assist." He double-checked the body. "You just killed a guy with a trident."

"You're welcome." Jack beamed proudly.

"Now, we need to get that thing as far away from here as possible."

"What?" Confusion painted Jack's face.

"Barbarossa's last message mentioned returning the trident, but I don't think that meant any person. He understood this thing is too powerful for any one person to wield. I believe he meant return it to where it belongs, with the god of the sea."

Jack twisted his facial muscles into a bewildered scowl. "You mean throw it in the ocean?"

"Yes," Sean affirmed. "We take it to the deepest place we can find in the Mediterranean, and we drop it in so no one will ever be able to use that thing again."

Jack's head twisted back and forth in disbelief, as if on its own accord. "What are you talking about, Sean? This gives us the power to stop wars like the one in Ukraine from ever happening again. Don't you see? No more bloodshed from tyrants. The innocent will be able to live in peace."

"But whose peace?" Sean asked. "Yours? No one should have this much power, Jack. No one." He extended his hand out, as if to accept the trident in good faith.

But Jack retreated a step. "No. I can't let you do that, Sean. You would throw away a generation's chance at safety, and for what? I can't even wrap my head around that."

"Oppenheimer wasn't sure any human should have the power of the atom bomb either, Jack. This thing is too much responsibility. If it ever fell into the wrong hands—"

"It won't. I'll make sure of it."

"And what if your hands are the wrong hands, Jack? What if mine are? None of us knows what that thing is capable of doing. I wouldn't trust myself with it. And neither should you."

Jack took another step away from him, moving toward the door opposite the entrance.

"That's where you and I differ, then, Sean. See, I know I can make the world a safer place. And I can get paid to do it. No one will think of invading another country ever again, without thinking of me first."

"Put it down," Adriana commanded from Sean's left.

He looked over his shoulder and saw Tommy and Adriana both holding pistols aimed at Jack's head.

Betrayal washed through Jack's eyes. He almost looked hurt, like some wannabe messiah who'd just discovered they'd been sold out for thirty pieces of Bitcoin.

"What are you doing?" Jack demanded. "Put those down before someone gets hurt."

"Jack," Sean interrupted. "Give me the trident. And we'll put all this behind us. Okay? Maybe you come work with us. We could use a—"

"A what? A thief? Like me? Is that what you were going to say?"

"No. I was about to say—"

"Save it."

The blue-and-white motes of light began swirling around the trident once more. The floor shook, sending the other three off balance, each sticking out their hands to keep from falling.

"I have the ultimate power on Earth," Jack repeated his statement from before. "And I will not let you or anyone else take that away from me."

A loud crack thundered from the ceiling overhead. Sean looked up and saw a huge chunk of the ceiling break away.

He dove toward Adriana and Tommy, hitting her first with his right arm, and Tommy with his left. His momentum was just enough to carry them both to the floor as the chunk of stone crashed into the surface where they'd been standing a second before.

Dust billowed through the chamber, forcing Sean, Adriana, and Tommy to cover their faces with their sleeves.

They couldn't see anything, and the swirling light that had been there before abruptly disappeared, leaving nothing but the glow of a few flashlights lying on the floor around them.

Sean picked one of them up and pointed the beam around in

every direction, but with the dust still looming in the air, he couldn't see anything.

The vault had ceased trembling, and as he took a wary step toward the mangled pile of debris on the floor, a terrifying realization hit him.

Jack had escaped. And he still had the trident.

35

"He's gone," Sean said, dejected. "We have to catch up to him."

Tommy grimaced behind his forearm, still holding the fabric against his face to filter out the dust from entering his lungs. "You're on your own on this one, buddy. I think I have a couple of cracked ribs." He handed his newfound pistol to Sean. "I think the mag is full."

Sean accepted the weapon but wore concern for his friend on his face.

Adriana braced the muscular Tommy with her arm under his left armpit and looped over his shoulders.

She approved with a curt nod. "Go. I'll take care of him. Get Jack."

"You sure?"

"Go," she repeated.

Sean knew better than to ask twice. He turned away from them and plunged into the clouds of dust muddying the air.

He shielded his mouth and nose to keep from breathing the stuff in and slowly picked his way over and around the debris until he found a clear patch of floor again. Then he picked up his pace until he reached the wall. From there, he moved toward the place he remembered seeing the opening and discovered it still intact.

Once he was through the doorway, the air cleared and visibility returned.

But there was no sign of Jack.

Sean didn't have time to be careful. He couldn't let Jack get away.

As he sprinted forward into the dark with the flashlight, terrible thoughts rushed into Sean's head like a tidal wave crashing onto the rocks.

If Jack made it to the water... there was no telling what havoc he could wreak. And there was no way to know whether he even needed to be close to it to command the seas.

Sean left those worries in the corridor behind him as it bent to the left and then back to the right. The slight uphill grade of the path suggested he was ascending, perhaps back up to the castle courtyard grounds, or maybe just outside the wall.

He continued running through the loop, certain he was overlapping his previous steps somewhere in the mountain below.

The thick muscles in his legs began to burn after only a few minutes of running at 90 percent, and he felt his pace beginning to slow.

Sean could run all day if he had to. He trained five to six days a week, and at least two of those were long-distance running days. Endurance wasn't a problem, as long as he stayed within his optimal range. This speed was more akin to high-intensity interval training, and he wondered when his quarry would have to slow down to the resting pace—at least for a minute.

Before he received that answer, Sean saw a dim light illuminating the bending tunnel ahead.

The sight signaled him to ease his pace to a trot, and then to a stealthy but quick walk, keeping his right shoulder near the inner, curved wall and the pistol extended ahead of him.

He leaned out to the left, expecting to find the source of light with the next step but found only more of the passage turning in front of him.

As he continued, though, he realized that the light wasn't coming from an artificial source. It was daylight. *A literal light at the end of the tunnel,* he thought.

Not that it made him feel all that much better. There was still no sign of Jack, and he wondered if his old acquaintance had somehow figured out a way to teleport with the mysterious trident.

He dismissed the idea, for the most part, as he kept moving ahead, allowing the pistol in his hands to lead.

The light grew brighter seemingly with every step. And soon, a new sense tingled with it—the sound of wind. That, too, was joined with the smell of fresh air, and Sean knew he was getting close to the tunnel's end.

The wind howled and whistled, louder and louder until he finally saw the source of the noise, light, and smell.

Sean had hoped he was nearing a staircase leading up to an open trap door somewhere on the castle's premises. But that hope faded like the setting sun on time-lapse.

His heart sank, and he involuntarily let go of the pistol grip with his right hand to place his palm against the smooth wall.

The tunnel straightened and stopped abruptly twenty feet away where door-shaped space led into the open air. Sean didn't have to get close to know where the door was positioned, but he knew he couldn't turn back.

He shuffled forward, dragging his feet a few times until he reached the end of the line, and looked out through the opening. He dared to stick his head just over the edge at the abrupt drop-off and the rocky ground far below.

Sean swallowed and retreated back a step, gripping the corner of the opening with his right hand and lowering the pistol with his left.

He shook his head, the air unwilling to fill his lungs despite every attempt to breathe.

The escape from the vault was built into the side of the cliff overlooking the harbor.

Sean didn't want to calculate how far the drop was, but his mind did it for him. Numbers in the hundreds filled his head, no matter how much he tried to swat them away like flies, but they kept coming, kept biting at him, warning him of imminent and terrifying death.

"Get a hold of yourself, Sean," he breathed and forced himself to step to the ledge once more. "Jack found a way out of here."

Then it hit him. *Jack wasn't in here. He must have climbed up.*

Sean switched the pistol to his right hand and held the left corner of the door, carefully leaning out while doing everything he could to keep his weight inside.

He looked up and found his quarry, carefully scaling the cliffside about thirty feet above. The trident was wedged into Jack's daypack strapped to his back—somewhat carelessly in Sean's opinion.

With his left hand still gripping the stone corner like a vise, Sean raised the weapon and fired.

The round sparked off the rock above. Jack cringed, leaning in closer to the mountain as if that would shield him from the onslaught below.

He looked down at Sean and shook his head. "Shoulda sent your wife," Jack teased and reached up to another handhold. "Or is she afraid of heights, too?"

Sean couldn't get the right angle to hit the target with half of his body still inside the tunnel. That didn't stop him from firing again two more times in the hope that he'd get lucky and hit the mark.

"Go back, Sean!" Jack shouted over the chilly wind. "You're going to hurt yourself. But don't worry, the war in Ukraine will be over soon. You can thank me later!"

He raised his right foot and planted it on a ledge above the previous, then pushed himself up. He was only fifteen feet away from the top, and once there, catching him would be even harder.

He's right, Sean admitted to himself. *I should have sent Adriana. She could have handled this.*

But a voice deep inside him disagreed. It was the voice of something ancient, primal, angry. "Yes, you can," it told him. "What you can't do is let him go."

Sean knew it was his imagination, some kind of internal monologue that pushed him out of his comfort zone when absolutely necessary.

He blinked rapidly. His breath quickened.

"Just like pulling a Band-Aid," he said. "Rip it."

He exhaled one deep time, then shifted his weight out onto a ledge perpendicular to the opening and slid his feet onto it.

Bracing himself with one hand on a ledge above, Sean aimed the pistol at Jack.

"Stop right there, Jack!" he yelled. "I don't want to kill you."

Jack looked down again. He still wore an amused grin, but now it weakened with a stream of concern. "Look at you, Sean. Out here on a cliff. Good for you. But you can't climb with one hand holding that gun. So, you're going to have to choose. Shoot me or chase me. I don't think you want to do either."

"You're right," Sean agreed. "I don't want to do either one of those things." His knuckles paled from clenching the rock so hard.

"Why don't you just come back down and—"

"I'm sure you'd like that, Sean." He reached up and picked another ledge for his left hand and ran his fingers along it until they found purchase. Then Jack pulled himself up another level, bringing his left foot along and planting it on the previous spot where the hand had been. "But I got no problem free climbing five hundred feet above the ground. Oh, sorry. That probably didn't help you, did it?"

Sean ground his teeth together. It *didn't* help. It was just the sort of thing he was trying *not* to think about.

"It's okay, Sean. Just don't look down. That would scare the crap out of you, for sure."

Sean swallowed back the irritation and the fear. Not that it did much good. His gut still wrenched and churned. And it wasn't the cold that caused his body to shake.

He fired another shot, this time deliberately missing Jack.

"Whoa! Are you crazy?" Jack blared. "You almost hit me with that one. Jeez, man! You're not seriously trying to shoot me, are you?"

Sean didn't want to, and he found himself in the unusual position of being unsure of what to do.

"Don't make me kill you," Sean answered back. Another gust of wind blasted into the mountainside. "Like you said, Jack. You're not the enemy."

Above, ten feet from the lip of the cliff top, Jack tried to find another grip for his right hand. "You know, Sean, your problem is you think too small." He grabbed a piece of rock shaped like the top of a milk jug. It jutted out two inches from the main wall. It was the kind of hold climbers loved to find after a long, arduous ascent. "I'm going to make world peace, brother. Don't you understand that? No more war. No more unnecessary death. Why do you not want that? Or are you the bad guy here?"

He grabbed the jughead-shaped hold with his right hand and pulled, testing its strength. The rock held firm.

The question took Sean by surprise, which was no easy feat. But his mind was clear. "No one person or government should have that much power, Jack. It's too much for anyone. And not only that, do you really want that big target on your back? Every terrorist group and tyrannical government in the world will be coming after you. What kind of life is that?"

"I'm sure I'll manage, Sean. But I appreciate your conc—"

As Jack put more weight onto the jughead, gripping it hard, he felt a sudden and sickening snap, then nothing.

"Jack!" Sean yelled.

Jack's left hand held on by a thread, and he tried to keep his toes pressed against their respective edges, but the abrupt shift in weight threw him off balance, sending his right side swinging out away from the rock.

"Hold on, Jack!"

Sean stuffed the pistol into the back of his belt and eased himself out onto the ledge, putting both hands above his head until he found the first seam he could grip.

He kept his eyes squarely locked on the stone in front of him as he raised his right foot and felt around for a place to stick it. A lip about two feet up caught the tip of his boot, and he wedged it into place.

Jack managed to fling his body back around and into the rock wall, where he scrambled to find another hold. But the only one he saw was the previous one just below.

He could descend a little, reset, and continue upward. There was always another grip.

Sean saw the risky move from below. "What are you doing, Jack?"

"Just let me go, Sean. I'm going to make the world a better place. Isn't that what everyone says they want to do? Well, I'm going to be the one to—"

His right foot slipped off the ledge, cutting off his speech in midsentence. This time, there was no possible way for Jack to regain traction, and he fell downward toward Sean, half sliding along the rock face.

Sean reacted without thinking and shifted his right foot back down, then his left foot over into the doorway. Jack continued the slide down the slightly angled cliff, and when he was only eight feet away, Sean grabbed the inner corner of the door, wedging his hand into a seam.

As Jack slid by, Sean reached out with his right hand to grab him, but instead his fingers found something cold and metallic. He squeezed the trident before his hand reached the head.

"Grab on!" he commanded as the weapon slid out of the makeshift rigging Jack had created with his daypack.

Desperately clawing at the rock, Jack somehow grabbed on to the trident shaft with both hands.

Sean's left hand strained from the sudden weight. His right shoulder screamed, and he felt the joint shift just slightly. His muscles stretched to their limit as he held up Jack. And he felt his left hand's knuckles scraping hard against stone inside the seam.

"Find a foothold!" Sean barked over the howling wind. "I can't hold you much longer."

Jack kicked his feet around, panic making his movements erratic and quick.

"Just find a foothold, Jack! Calm down."

"Easy for you to say," Jack answered back.

"Hey! I'm the one who's scared of heights. Remember? So, pretty please, find something to hold your weight, or we're both gonna die."

Jack inched his left foot toward a narrow ledge and pressed his toe down onto it.

Sean felt some of the weight ease on the rod.

"Good," he encouraged.

Jack found another edge for his right foot and pressed his body into the rock face.

Sean was only holding up a quarter of the man's weight now, and a surge of relief filled him.

"Can you pull me up?" Jack asked. "If I climb with my feet on the way?"

"Yeah. Sure. You ready?"

"I think so."

Sean wanted to vomit, but now wasn't the time. There would be later, probably in this tunnel.

"Okay," Jack said. "Do it."

Sean braced his right foot against the lip of the threshold and pulled with his right hand. He felt his weight shift deeper into the tunnel. Whatever Jack found below worked because within two seconds, both men spilled into the corridor, with Jack landing to Sean's side.

They breathed hard for a few seconds, both staring out the opening at the same time. Neither said a thing for nearly a minute.

Then Sean shook his head and started to get up. "I don't ever want to do that again. Ever."

Jack laughed. "You didn't find it exhilarating?"

"No," Sean said, feeling bile creep up in his throat.

He stood, still holding the trident, and took a step deeper into the tunnel to get away from the edge. The more distance he could put between himself and that drop, the better.

"Where are you going?" Jack asked from behind.

Sean mustered a snort. He turned as he said, "As far from that—"

His voice faltered. Standing between him and the door was Jack holding a pistol, his heels a mere foot from the opening.

"I'm sorry, Sean. I mean, for doing this to you. Not for the rest of it. This has to happen. It's my destiny. I'm sure if you don't understand now, someday you will. But you have to give me back the trident now. I truly don't want to kill you."

Sean huffed thoughtfully. "You know... you talk about saving lives, but to do that, I imagine you're going to kill a whole lot of people."

"Bad people, sure," Jack said matter-of-factly. "Someone has to."

"And I suppose you're the one with the authority to make that judgment call?"

"Someone has to do it. Now, please, Sean. The trident." He flicked his fingers, begging it be handed over. "Don't make me kill you. But I will not let anyone stand in my way. Nice and slow. And I'll let you walk back to your friends. I'm sure someone can fly a helicopter in here and get you three out. You'll live a long, happy life. And in a much safer world."

Sean exhaled through his nose and lowered his head in resignation. "Okay, Jack. You win." He twisted the trident around in a fluid motion so the butt of the thing faced Jack.

"Mighty kind of you to do that for me, turning it around so I don't feel threatened by the pointy ends."

"Yeah." Sean felt a warm tingle trickling through his fingers, then his palm, then his forearm. The energy radiated from the staff, coursing through his entire body.

Blue-and-white motes swirled around the trident's prongs. Droplets of water formed in the air around him.

"What are you doing, Sean?" Jack asked, fear littering his words.

The water droplets quickly formed huge drops, then spheres, until a sheet of water hovered in the air between the two men.

"What the—" Jack cut himself off and raised the weapon. "Give me the trident, Sean. You don't know what you're doing."

"And you do?" Sean retorted.

Jack fired the gun at the fluid, shimmering image behind the bizarre water shield. The bullet splashed into it, but the figure behind remained upright.

He was about to shoot again when the golden base of the trident pierced the water and struck him in the chest with immense force.

The blow sent Jack backward four feet, and down five hundred.

Sean released the trident and let it fall to the floor. Instantly, the wall of water vanished, and the droplets fizzled into nothing more than the clouds whence they came.

He stood there for a minute, staring through the opening. His instincts told him to look down and make sure Jack was dead, but Sean couldn't make himself do it. He'd get confirmation later from recovery crews.

With a sigh, he looked down at the golden weapon on the floor. He'd never felt anything like that before, or seen anything like the wall of water that had formed, almost by the command of his imagination.

Not almost. It had been. He'd thought of a shield, and that was what happened, at least partially on its own.

"I'm sorry, Jack," Sean said, his voice faintly echoing down the passage. "But no one should have this thing."

Sean slowly shifted his feet and turned around. To his surprise, he found Tommy and Adriana standing in the corridor at the edge of the bend.

"Hey," Sean gulped. "How long have you two been standing there?"

Both of their jaws hung low, but it was Tommy who answered first. He was slightly hunched to the right, a hand over his ribcage. "Long enough to see what that thing can do." His eyes remained fixed on the trident.

"You saw that?" Sean asked, as if it was no big deal.

Tommy and Adriana both nodded.

"Incredible," she murmured, just loud enough for her voice to reach him over the sound of the wind.

"Yeah," Sean agreed. "And we need to get this thing out of here before someone else finds out about it. We have to return it to the sea."

"That's not far from here," Adriana said.

"No. I mean the deepest part. The riddle mentioned a return. We thought it had something to do with returning this thing to mankind. But that's not it. We're meant to take it back to the sea, to where it came from. At least according to the legend, where it came from. It's the only way to keep it out of the wrong hands. Or even the right ones."

36

CALYPSO DEEP, IONIAN SEA

Sean felt his weight shift and toss as choppy swells rocked the forty-foot yacht. He sucked in a deep breath of salty air, letting it cleanse his nostrils and his mind. The motors trolled from his left at the back of the vessel, humming an almost soothing baritone.

He stood on the port side, looking out across the waters of the Ionian Sea. The fact they were at Calypso Deep, the deepest part of the Mediterranean, didn't exactly make him feel comfortable.

Rather, it felt like he was in an extremely high place.

Calypso Deep's most recent measurements put its bottom at over five thousand meters below sea level, or a little more than three miles down from the surface.

Sean had seen video footage of exploration of the bottom, but mostly all that had been found was a flat seabed covered in sand and a few pieces of litter.

"Trash finds its way everywhere," he'd said when he noticed a wadded-up plastic bag drifting along the sandy floor.

He, Tommy, and Adriana discussed taking the trident to another part of the ocean, to the deepest known point on the planet—the

Mariana Trench in the Pacific. At more than thirty-six thousand feet deep, no one would likely ever find the ancient weapon down there, but this place, this water, was where the trident belonged. It was born here, at least according to the legends, and the man who wielded it, whether real or imagined, was just as much a part of this region as the sea itself.

"What are you thinking about?" Adriana asked, standing by his side.

"Oh, nothing," Sean answered. "Just wondering if we made the right decision to bring it here instead of the Pacific."

"This is where it was meant to be. Barbarossa would have wanted it to stay here."

Tommy ambled around the corner of the cabin and stopped next to her. "Niki said this spot is as good as any." He looked out over the white crests of five-foot swells and bobbed his head. "Amazing the history these waters hold, isn't it?"

The other two merely nodded.

Niki walked around the corner and joined the other three. "Clear sailing for days," he announced with a smile. He looked out over the waters, taking a cue from the others.

"It's a shame we can't study this thing," Tommy said after a minute of silence. "If I could just keep it for a month, we could learn so much."

Sean half twisted his head around, casting a wary glance at his friend. "You're sounding a little like Frodo right now. You know that, right?"

Tommy chuckled, then winced as the laughter sent a sharp pain through his ribcage. The fight with Boris had resulted in two cracked ribs. He'd be okay, but it felt like someone stabbed him with a knife whenever he made a sudden movement or laughed.

"I'm not saying I want to keep it," he explained. "I just wish we could understand the technology better."

"I know. But there's no way we can guarantee someone won't try to take it and use it for their own designs. Imagine if word got out about it, say if we had it in the lab back in Atlanta. We'd have the biggest target on our backs known to man. Including from our own government."

His mind drifted for a second to President McCarthy, and to Emily Starks—his old boss with the Axis agency.

Those two he trusted, but beyond that there were few who operated under the government umbrella he believed he could count on.

"It's true," Adriana added. "Wars would be fought just to get control of this thing. We must get rid of it."

Many people had already died as a result. Fortunately, the hostages at Castello Barbarossa weren't part of that statistic.

Instead of trying to scale the rock face, something Sean swore he would never come close to doing again, the three backtracked through the hidden passages until they arrived at the vault again. There, they used the long golden oars along the wall to construct a rudimentary bridge across the gap where Boris and two of the other soldiers had fallen.

The oars were barely long enough to overlap the edge on both sides, and when pushed together created a sturdy enough walkway for the Americans to escape—though none of them were jazzed about it until they'd safely reached the other side.

When they arrived back in the castle, they found that the last Russian soldier had fled, though none of the Swedish ornithologists seemed to understand why.

They claimed when the earthquake happened, he took off and never looked back.

Too afraid to run themselves, the bird watchers had remained at the castle until Sean and the others reappeared.

The long object covered with three jackets drew many a curious eye, but Sean quickly expedited the conversation and hurried back to the vehicle, which presented its own challenge.

Driving down the winding road with the trident sticking out of the back window at a sharp angle was hardly his idea of discreet, but they'd had no choice.

Now, a day later, they found themselves here at Calypso Deep, about to dump one more piece of litter into the water.

Sean looked over at Tommy and nodded. "You ready?"

"No," Tommy answered with regret. He met Sean's gray eyes with a hint of sadness. "But now's as good a time as any."

The two bent their knees and picked up the trident, its gleaming gold surface out of view, wrapped in a beige, fabric tarp with a thirty-pound dumbbell attached to either end with chains.

The two men grunted as they lifted the object, then shifted their weight to swing it over the gunwale.

The trident and dumbbells hit the water with a huge splash. Bubbles and foam swirled around it. And then it was gone, vanishing into the deep within seconds, never to be seen again—Sean hoped.

He nodded as he stared into the water where it had landed, no trace that it was ever there.

"So," Tommy said, dusting off his hands of the deed. "What plans do you have for the weekend?"

Sean chuckled at the casual question. "No plans. Which sounds pretty good after all this."

"Yeah. Nice to kick back and relax every now and then. Seems the older I get the more I feel that need tugging at me."

"Old? We're not old yet, Schultzie."

"Yet being the operative word. We will be someday, buddy. Can't keep running like this forever."

Sean absently bobbed his head as he pondered the statement. It was one he'd considered before, and more frequently as of late. In his early forties, he wasn't ready to hang up his IAA boots just yet, but just like the sun burning bright in the sky, it inevitably began its slow descent to the west where it would fade from view.

Sean inhaled the salty sea air deeply again and raised his gaze to the horizon to the west, wondering where his next discovery might lead them, and if it would be the next in a seeming never-ending series of adventures, or their last.

THANK YOU

I just wanted to say thank you for reading this story. I truly appreciate it and hope you enjoyed this story as much as I did creating it.

If you loved this mystery and others like it, subscribe to my YouTube channel to see more fascinating mysteries from history: https://www.youtube.com/ErnestDempsey

Come have some fun with like minded readers, get access to exclusive contests and giveaways, and more, join the Ernest Dempsey's Hunters and Runners Facebook group: https://www.facebook.com/groups/dempseyshuntersandrunners

Be sure to swing by https://www.ernestdempsey.net to grab free stories, and dive deeper into the universe I've created for you.

Come on over to YouTube where I do weekly shows to chat with readers just like you. Drinks With Dempsey is on Friday afternoons at 4:30 pm EST, and Coffee Nation is Sunday morning at 9:00 am EST. Bring your questions, or just hang out and enjoy the conversation. You can find my channel here: https://yhttps://www.youtube.com/@ErnestDempsey

I'll see you in the next story.

Your friendly neighborhood author,

Ernest

FACTS AND FICTION: AUTHOR'S NOTES

Welcome, friend. It's time for that special part of the story where we dive a little deeper into what's real and what isn't.

As with any work of fiction, the author takes certain liberties, applying their own spin of possibilities into how things unfold. With my Sean Wyatt books, I try to weave in as many facts as possible, both from history and geography, to blur the lines between true events and what could happen, or could have happened.

So, I'll do my best to break down what's real and what isn't so you can get a look behind the scenes.

The Prologue:

The characters hunting for the trident in 1547 were figments of my imagination, though the events surrounding the creation of Barbarossa's memoirs were based on real events with some creative liberties taken on my part. We don't know how it all actually unfolded, but it's fun to consider the possibility that the Spanish, in their desperation to grab power, could have sent agents out on a mission as described in the story.

This is, as you know, a recurring theme both in this story, in real history, and in potentially real events playing out in the world at the time of writing this novel.

Kilwa Kisiwani, Tanzania:

This is a real place where many ruins of a long lost culture still litter the landscape. The secret chamber within the temple in this scene is a figment of my imagining, as far as I know, but one never knows....

The artifact Sean discovers in the chamber is also one of my invention as I am unaware of such an object being lost to antiquity. But, as with every artifact I invent, there is always the possibility of it truly existing.

Besiktas, Istanbul:

This affluent neighborhood in Istanbul is home to a wide array of cultural delights. From food to coffee, shopping, art, and history, there are so many cool things about this place, the most fascinating of which is the tomb of Admiral Hayreddin Barbarossa.

The mausoleum is real, and can be visited, as can be the cemetery that surrounds it. But the tomb interior is only open one day out of the year. That doesn't mean you can't enjoy it from the outside.

The flag draped over the sarcophagus is also real, as were most of the details I included in the description of this location.

The monument outside the mausoleum, in the plaza, is also real, as is the historical ceremony the Turkish navy goes through to pay tribute to one of their most revered military heroes.

The secret passage beneath the tomb was my invention, but one never knows....

The grave of Sinan Reis is also located just outside the tomb, just as depicted in the story.

Castello Barbarossa:

Perched high atop the cliffs on the Island of Capri, Castello Barbarossa is mere ruins now compared to its former glory. The history of this place spans centuries prior to its eventual destruction.

Funnily enough, it really is an Ornithology station now, and is closed to the public. That last part is unfortunate, but I'm certain the bird watchers are doing a good job maintaining the historical integrity of the old castle.

The throne room was designed from my imagination, as were the secret passages beneath.

The mansion of the late author, Axel Munthe, is a real place too, and the museum can be visited by those who wish to learn more about the man's life, art, and contributions to the world.

Calypso Deep:

This is the deepest place in the Mediterranean, and while perhaps the trident of Poseidon might better be hidden in the Mariana Trench—the deepest known place on Earth—it felt unjust to put it there since this powerful artifact was birthed from the Mediterranean and the ancient god of the sea the Greeks revered. To put it anywhere else seems wrong. So, Calypso it had to be.

Cymatics:

This is a real and fascinating subject I stumbled upon during my research into sacred geometry and the frequencies that constantly surround us, and bind us.

Who knows what the ancients were able to use with this sort of technology? Were they able to create weapons to harness it? Or did they make tools that could build incredible structures purely through the use of vibration. Is it possible this is how the Pyramids and other megalithic structures were built?

I don't know. But I would certainly like to find out.

Until next time, my adventurous friend, I hope you have had a wonderful journey.

We're only just getting started.

Your friendly neighborhood adventurer,

Ernest

OTHER BOOKS BY ERNEST DEMPSEY

Sean Wyatt Adventures:
The Secret of the Stones
The Cleric's Vault
The Last Chamber
The Grecian Manifesto
The Norse Directive
Game of Shadows
The Jerusalem Creed
The Samurai Cipher
The Cairo Vendetta
The Uluru Code
The Excalibur Key
The Denali Deception
The Sahara Legacy
The Fourth Prophecy
The Templar Curse
The Forbidden Temple
The Omega Project
The Napoleon Affair
The Second Sign
The Milestone Protocol
Where Horizons End
Adriana Villa Adventures:
War of Thieves Box Set

When Shadows Call

Shadows Rising

Shadow Hour

The Relic Runner - A Dak Harper Series:

The Relic Runner Origin Story

The Courier

Two Nights In Mumbai

Country Roads

Heavy Lies the Crown

Moscow Sky

The Adventure Guild (ALL AGES):

The Caesar Secret: Books 1-3

The Carolina Caper

Beta Force:

Operation Zulu

London Calling

Paranormal Archaeology Division:

Hell's Gate

Guardians of Earth:

Emergence: Gideon Wolf Book 1

Righteous Dawn: Gideon Wolf Book 2

Crimson Winter: Gideon Wolf Book 3

ACKNOWLEDGMENTS

As always, I would like to thank my terrific editors, Anne and Jason, for their hard work. What they do makes my stories so much better for readers all over the world. Anne Storer and Jason Whited are the best editorial team a writer could hope for and I appreciate everything they do.

I also want to thank Elena at L1 Graphics for her tremendous work on my book covers and for always overdelivering. Elena definitely rocks.

A big thank you has to go out to my friend James Slater for his proofing work. James has added another layer of quality control to these stories, and I can't thank him enough.

Last but not least, I need to thank all my wonderful fans and especially the advance reader team. Their feedback and reviews are always so helpful and I can't say enough good things about all of them.

Printed in Great Britain
by Amazon